The Conquering Dark

By Clay Griffith and Susan Griffith

CROWN & KEY TRILOGY
The Shadow Revolution
The Undying Legion
The Conquering Dark

VAMPIRE EMPIRE TRILOGY
The Greyfriar
The Rift Walker
The Kingmakers

The Conquering Dark

Crown & Key

BOOK 3

Clay Griffith

and Susan Griffith

DEL REY * NEW YORK

The Conquering Dark is a work of fiction. Names, characters, places, and incidents either are the product of imagination or are used fictitiously. Any resemblance to actual persons, living or dead, events, or locales is entirely coincidental.

A Del Rey Mass Market Original

Published in the United States by Del Rey, an imprint of Random House, a division of Penguin Random House LLC, New York.

Del Rey and the House colophon are registered trademarks of Penguin Random House LLC.

ISBN 978-0-345-54050-8
eBook ISBN 978-0-345-54051-5

Printed in the United States of America

www.delreybooks.com

9 8 7 6 5 4 3 2 1

Del Rey mass market edition: August 2015

All of our books seem to come back to parents.
We can't express the gratitude we hold for our parents,
except by creating characters
who are forever seeking to know the same warmth
that we enjoyed our entire lives.

The Conquering Dark

Chapter 1

THE MADMAN'S BOOTS RANG HEAVILY AS HE strode up the nave of Westminster Abbey. His embroidered attire was old-fashioned and unkempt, including ridiculously tasseled boots and lace cuffs. The fires of hell and damnation drenched his hands in a shimmering hot blaze, causing dignitaries on the aisle to stand and rear back while those farther away stared. Passing tomb by tomb, the red-haired man marched down the stream of time. Statues of marble men stood stoic while stone angels mourned the intrusion. An overdressed guard rushed forward. The intruder set him ablaze with a wave of his hand, then pitilessly sidestepped the flailing soldier.

The stunned throngs began to move in a panic toward the doors. The man with the burning hands swept under the arch of the choir screen and looked on the theater of coronation. His feet muddied the black-and-white-diamond floor as a squad of guardsmen formed a solid line between the intruder and the royal family, who sat facing forward on a raised dais in the spiritual center of the church.

King William IV rose from his chair, resplendent in an admiral's uniform, and turned with annoyance to view the disturbance. Beside him, the queen gained her feet as well, nervous and pale, contrasting against the white satin of her gown overlaid with a fine gold gauze. Her purple velvet train lined with white satin and a rich border of gold and ermine bunched around her legs as she twisted toward the line of soldiers standing with their backs to them.

King William motioned for the queen and the other grandees nearby to be removed from harm's way. More scarlet-breasted soldiers moved quickly to rush the dignitaries toward the north transept, where they found their way blocked by a woman.

She had shocking short white hair and wore trousers with high boots and a metallic corset over her midsection. Even more shocking than her mannish attire and hair was the fact that she had four arms made of strong rods and struts of brass and steel. Two of her hands held pistols like some mechanical horror of a highwayman. In a third, she brandished a thin walking stick like a country squire. Her free hand gestured threateningly at the approaching crowd. "I suggest you all remain in your places."

"What is the meaning of this?" King William's voice echoed through the hallowed halls of the Abbey, even above the sounds of fear and shuffling feet. "You want to stop my coronation? So be it! But spare the lives of my subjects."

The redheaded man in the nave laughed, eyes crazed and hair wild. The heat radiating from his hands could be felt as he sneered, showing he was missing a few teeth. "You're all guilty of the same sins as the rest of us. Why should we let anyone go?"

"Enough ranting, O'Malley." The white-haired woman pointed at the king with her walking stick. "You have something we want, Your Majesty. We intend to take it."

From the shrine of Edward the Confessor located behind the altar emerged a tall, languid gentleman dressed in the finest black silks, a fashionable top hat gracing his head. His sophisticated attire was hardly complemented by the strange bulky steel gauntlets that covered his hands and forearms. In his steel-sheathed right hand he worked a thin-bladed sword that gleamed wickedly in the candlelight. Where all others fell back, only Simon Archer came forward.

"I think not," was his calm reply.

One of the woman's pistols swung with the clicking sound of a geared arm to cover the newcomer. The other gun lifted directly at the king. Simon Archer leapt onto the dais, seizing the sovereign and pushing him down behind the throne. Two lead balls slammed into the chair, splintering it across Simon's back as he huddled over the king.

The sound of shots unleashed the panic anew. Hordes of people made for the closest doors, some shoving and pushing to save themselves, others shouting to allow the women to go first, struggling to assert a hint of civilization in the madness. Terrified crowds roared from the makeshift galleries in the north transept, swarming around the woman with the mechanical arms but fighting to keep their distance. She tossed her empty pistols aside and began to muscle her way through the panicked herd toward the dais.

"Baroness!" shouted the fiery lunatic, but he turned as he heard the sound of weapons cocking behind him.

"That's right, lad. Face yer better," scolded a new voice, one laced with a thick brogue.

The wild eyes of the madman turned gleefully, pleased that someone had dared challenge him. His desire for violence was not going to be soothed quickly. "Who are you to say such? A pompous duke or lazy English lord?"

"A Scotsman!"

Laughter roared as loud as the flames around him as

Ferghus O'Malley pointed a hand at the challenger dressed in a long frock coat striding up the nave toward him. "You're a dead man."

The Scotsman's black hair was pulled back from his widow's peak into a tight tail behind him. He sported a brace of four-barreled Lancaster pistols. Malcolm MacFarlane fired off two shots before he ducked below a bolt of fire that flared over his head. From his crouched position Malcolm shot again, and the shells shattered near the cackling Irishman's head before the flaming target leapt into the surging mob that was only trying to escape him. Malcolm cursed and fought into the crowd to close on the Irishman.

Assured that the gun-wielding Scotsman protected his flank, Simon Archer drew the confused King William onto his feet. "Apologies for manhandling you, Your Majesty, but please follow the lovely lady behind you. She will lead you and the queen to safety." Though it was phrased as a polite request, the timbre of his voice brooked no argument. These two attackers—Ferghus O'Malley and Baroness Conrad—were terrible threats with a legendary history of carnage and horror.

Simon didn't check to see if, in fact, the *lovely lady* was present; he knew she would be in the proper place. A tall regal woman with auburn hair was already busy herding bishops and earls and countesses under the shadows of the poet Chaucer in the south transept. She wore a full-length velvet cloak of royal blue trimmed with gold. Despite hurried gestures, her stature and grace depicted breeding and manners.

The king hesitated with fear in his expression. "My niece. I can't leave—"

Simon turned to the north transept where the king stared. Amidst the frantic mob being shoved aside by the annoyed Baroness, he noted the small shape of a desperate child nearly lost in the melee. No one paid the young girl any mind. Simon nodded sharply to the worried old man. "I'll see to her, on my word. You must go quickly, sir, before the Baroness can reach you." Simon signaled toward the woman behind them. "Kate, take His Majesty, would you?"

The auburn-haired woman finished giving an archbishop a shove through the door, sending his high mitre flying, then she put two fingers to her lips and let loose a sharp whistle at the king. She jerked her head at the exit behind her and tossed back her elegant cloak to reveal a calf-length wool skirt and a linen blouse across which was draped a soldier's bandolier. In place of ammunition, the leather slots held numerous glass vials. From her belt, she pulled a length of metal some two feet long with a curved grip at one end. With a flick of a finger on an unseen switch, two prongs unfolded from its front. It was a strange crossbow. She came toward the king, impatient that he was barely shuffling in her direction.

King William regarded her suspiciously until his eyes widened in recognition. "My word. Katherine Anstruther." Then he started to turn away. "But I can't leave that poor girl."

Kate grabbed the king by the arm and yanked him to the exit. She spared only a brief glance at Simon before giving the king another more gentle shove out. "Simon Archer will fetch your niece. Now come on, a little faster would be better."

With the king safe, Simon spun to the Baroness, watching the stark white of her hair as she came closer through the mob. Finally the last of the stumbling nobility cleared and the strange woman with four arms stood facing Simon twenty yards away. Something moved beside her. One of her metal hands was clamped around the lacy wrist of the small girl Simon had been after.

Princess Victoria, the niece of the king and queen and the heir to the realm.

The Baroness lifted the girl, who was barely eleven years old, off the ground like a fresh-bagged quail. "The king left something important behind. Now stand aside or I'll kill her."

Simon kept his sword raised but froze in his tracks.

"Run her through!" the young princess shouted, grasping the Baroness's goggles and wrenching them aside.

Simon gave only the barest thought to the bold attack of the little girl before he was on the Baroness, the point of his sharp blade aimed at her heart. The half-mechanical woman flinched aside, sweeping up an arm to block the thrust. Gears and pistons clicked and a series of spinning blades ratcheted out along her forearm. Sparks flew and Simon leaned forward, forcing the deadly appendage back. Princess Victoria yelped in alarm and kicked at her captor, who finally tossed the troublesome princess aside.

Simon fell back now, ducking under the arm with the whirring blades. He instantly returned to the attack, weaving his sword with masterful precision. His skill allowed him to counter and riposte the swipes from the woman without fear if she had just the one weapon. However, all four of her arms struck at him. Simon almost smiled at the challenge as the steel fists came at him with incredible speed. He parried and ducked and whirled across the floor, trying to draw the Baroness away from the winnowing crowd and the small girl, who came forward rather than retreating with the mob. The ring of steel meeting steel echoed through the church.

As he deflected one mechanical arm her bladed limb drove at him from the other side. Simon grabbed it and instinctively whispered a word of power. Her incredible strength smashed through his feeble defense and the lethal blades whirred inches from his cheek before he realized his idiocy. Only months ago he would have been able to fight back by summoning magic from the aether. No more.

He flexed his fingers wide, as Penny has shown him, to activate the small power source inside his gauntlet, and electrical current rippled over his knuckles. A shower of sparks brought the spinning blades to a whining halt. The Baroness screamed as the current coursed along the length of her metal arm and surged into her body. That shock should have dropped a draft horse, but she still moved forward with a face contorted by pain and bloody fury. Her mechanical body was clearly insulated.

One steel arm clamped around Simon's lower back and locked into place. Then he felt her walking stick pressed against his throat. She pushed down into him. The merciless strength of the Baroness bent him over backward until he feared his spine would snap.

"Surrender!" Simon croaked with a ludicrous confidence he didn't feel.

The Baroness smiled at him, enjoying the pain she brought and the flash of worry that crossed his features. She licked her lips with pleasure.

Simon reached up and clutched the walking stick with his metal gauntlet. He stared directly into her goggle eyes as he twisted his arm and snapped the stick. He was a bit surprised it was just a simple walking stick, a mere affectation. But the action caused the Baroness to look at her shattered accouterment with both rage and confusion. The pressure against his backbone slackened slightly.

Simon took advantage of the brief delay in her murderous attack and immediately fell back, bringing her down with him. His legs jammed into her stomach and leveraged her into the air; he was surprised at the difficulty of such a feat without magic to fuel his strength. With a shriek of alarm, she made to grasp at him, but he gave her no opportunity, slamming her into the high altar. The impact rang throughout the church.

She took a deep breath, seemingly stunned by the unexpected resistance, and eyed Simon warily as she pressed a small device on her belt. There was an inhuman roar from the north transept. When it was echoed by a child's scream, Simon smashed his steel fist into the Baroness's face. Her head slammed into marble and she slumped against the altar. He left her there and ran toward the scream.

Princess Victoria stood facing a massive manlike shape crowding the doorway of the north transept. The hulking thing dwarfed the girl like an Alp towering over a tiny chalet. The brute was huge and muscular, hunching forward and pounding the floor with bulging arms. Its head turned and a great toothy mouth opened in a snarl. Small sharp eyes peered angrily from under a heavy brow. It was a huge ape.

The monstrous gorilla rammed its way through the small door, breaking the frame with sheer will and muscle as it fought to answer its mistress's call. Once inside, it rested its bulk on steel knuckles. Its spine was exposed and bristled with wires and metal rods like a horrific streak of silver running along its back.

"Run, Your Highness!" Simon shouted as he raced toward her and the monster. The child backed away.

The great ape came at Simon like an avalanche, scattering chairs in its wake. The man leapt to the side and, as the beast's momentum took it past him, his arm fell like a piston on the back of its wired skull. The gauntlet crackled and arcs of electricity scurried like spiders from his hand to its metallic silver back. The ape crashed heavily to the stone floor in a heap, sparking and twitching.

Victoria stopped at the edge of the choir to watch Simon's confrontation with the gorilla. She instinctively reached up to Simon, who gathered the young child into his arms on the run. He sprinted past the dais, sparing a glance at the Baroness, who was beginning to struggle to her feet. Simon wanted to get the girl into trustworthy hands.

A column of blistering flame rose before them. Simon covered Victoria. The copper-headed Ferghus glared at them from the nave, his fiery hand feeding the flames that blocked their way.

"This line ends here!" Ferghus laughed. "If I can't have the king, I'll take the wee one."

"We're not done!" came Malcolm's ragged voice as he kicked his way free of a barricade of smoldering chairs beneath the burning choir screen. He fired his heavy pistols.

Flame shot out of Ferghus's gesturing hand to form a barrier between him and the Scotsman. The bullets never reached him but melted into slag and went astray.

"Bloody hell!" Malcolm cursed.

"Malcolm, get out of the way!" shouted a woman's voice from the tiers of graceful arches above. A pert figure aimed a long tube at the Irishman amidst the flames.

Malcolm MacFarlane dove between the empty pews as Penny Carter fired a canister. Ferghus flared again, renewing the wall of flame around him. The canister struck the barrier and exploded. The concussion blasted Ferghus off his feet.

Young Victoria looked up at Simon. "He breathes fire like a dragon."

With the princess still in his arms, Simon ran past the guttering fire column into the south transept. "Have no fear. We've slain many."

Victoria's eyes widened farther when Simon deposited her in front of a young girl not much older than the princess herself, slender and dressed in a simple white shift. The blond-haired girl was staring angrily into the church as if straining to join the fight herself. "Mr. Simon, the lady with the arms is up. Do you want me to—"

"I'll see to it, thank you, Charlotte." Simon coolly took up his sword and started toward the Kaliesque woman whose form wavered beyond the flames. She had seized hold of the legendary chair of King Edward. "That won't do." He nodded knowingly to himself and called back to Charlotte, "Take Princess Victoria to Kate."

Charlotte gasped at the princess and attempted a panicked curtsy. "Your Majesty!"

Victoria kept her eyes locked on Simon as he charged back into the fiery maw. "Who is he? Who are you all?"

Charlotte was already pulling the princess out the door, away from the blistering heat of the flames. "His name is Simon Archer. I'm Charlotte. We fight monsters."

Chapter 2

KATE TRAILED THE NOBLES, WHO HURRIED AS best they could in their elaborate regalia. She ached to push them through the passages of Westminster, force them along so she could return to fight beside Simon. No ordinary man could stand against Baroness Conrad. She knew that Simon was extraordinary, but his reliance on aether was ingrained in him and could mean disaster. Simon had been the one who brought them all together and had sacrificed so much for her, and for all of them. Kate couldn't stand to see him lose anything more. And she couldn't stand the chilling thought of losing him. But she had a task at hand to protect these innocent people. She exhaled impatiently and continued to attend her frightened charges.

Ahead of the crowd, screams sounded as a huge shape filled an archway. Kate stared at it, barely comprehending. It was a terrible sight. It appeared to be an incredible mechanized great ape. She had never seen a gorilla before, nor most likely had anyone around her, but her father was an intrepid explorer and had numerous journals on exotic animals including gorillas. None had looked quite like this one, particularly with its inhuman silver back clicking and shifting with every movement.

Kate raised the sleek crossbow and fired a vial of amber solution over the heads of the grandees, who were surging backward. Thankfully none spoiled her aim. The glass crashed against the chest of the hairy ape, spewing forth a fine ocher mist that enveloped the creature. The gorilla flailed at the thickening cloud with a muscular arm, making its metal tubing clank together. The beast raged as the mist turned denser to become a block of solid amber.

"Move on!" Kate extended her arms to prevent the crowd from fleeing back into the sanctuary where the main battle raged. "Run past it! It can't harm you!"

They balked at the sight of the frozen monstrosity, but a woman dressed in a gown of finest satin and velvet stepped toward the fearsome creature and turned her delicate back on it. Grace North, the wife of the prime minister, regarded the horrified crowd with a strangely calm face like delicate porcelain.

With complete confidence in Kate's amber, Grace called, "The beast is secured. Move on!"

King William responded first, escorting the queen past the trapped monster. The other nobles were prodded to do likewise, although some of the women and a few of the men were close to fainting and had to be manhandled along by others. Grace North resisted the tugging grasp of her husband, Prime Minister North, and stood staring at the trapped ape.

Kate gave an impatient gesture. "On your way, Mrs. North. This isn't a salon for God's sake."

Grace gave Kate a curious, almost humorous, glance before taking her husband's hand and following the crowd out. Kate urged the elegantly bundled grandees through a courtyard of grey-and-buff stone and into another small room. She motioned them toward the door on the far side of the room that would lead them to safety outside.

Just then, that door smashed apart and a huge gruesome ape filled the exit. Its massive head almost pushed against the ceiling. It reached out with an arm twice the girth of its leg and grabbed the nearest person in a hairy fist. Screams of terror filled the halls as the group tried to shift around a long table that took up the full length of the chamber.

Kate pushed forward against the tide of terrified nobles. The tight space left little room to use her deadly arsenal of toxic dust and gas. Two andirons stood propped against the wall near an empty fireplace. She grabbed one of them, gripping a circular end as a handle. She hooked the crossbow onto her belt and drew a pistol.

Kate pushed her way in front of the fierce gorilla and screaming woman, whom she recognized as the queen's sister, the Duchess of Saxe-Weimar. She swung the andiron and slammed it into the gorilla's chest. To Kate's relief, the ape cried out in surprise and pain. It looked down with dark yellow eyes. Its thin lips curled back over buttery tusks that were five inches long. A thick-barreled arm swung down at the slender woman.

Kate braced her arm over her head with the cold cast iron set along her forearm. It absorbed the majority of the blow, protecting her bones, but the force brought her onto one knee and the hard iron bent inward. She aimed her pistol at the broad chest and fired point-blank. Blood spurted over Kate and flowed with a rhythmic flush that meant she had struck a major vein. The gorilla stayed on its feet, perhaps kept so by the attached machinery, but it dropped the unconscious duchess and turned all its attention on its attacker. The ape growled and foamed a frothy red mix.

"Run! All of you outside!" Kate tossed the spent pistol aside and pulled a short sword from the scabbard at her waist. The silverback reared up into the ceiling, beating its broad chest, baring its teeth at her in an ear-splitting challenge. It followed her a few steps from the door, giving space for the nobles to flee. Several hands grabbed the unfortunate duchess and carried her out. As the last of the grandees disappeared into the daylight, Kate snarled and shoved the sword into the ape a scant distance from the bullet wound. She tried to twist the blade but couldn't because of the solid muscle around the steel.

The ape's high-domed cranium and bulging forehead loomed over Kate. Her father would find it ironic for her to be killed in the heart of London by one of the exotic beasts he had written to her about from the wilds of Africa.

Suddenly a new roar shook the room. Even the gorilla's head jerked toward the horrific sound. Kate recognized it instantly.

"Charlotte!"

The once child stood beside a gaping Princess Victoria, now as a towering werewolf. Kate had no time to wonder how the two children had found each other.

"Get her out of here," Kate shouted.

The ape's attention returned to Kate and its large fist rose into the air. She lifted her iron-braced arm to intercept another crushing blow.

Lanky canine legs bunched and launched Charlotte across the table onto the mountainous shoulders of the silverback. Her long snout bit deep into the ape's bulging neck. The gorilla dwarfed even Charlotte's impressive werewolf form. It roared and flung itself against the wall. She clung to its back, twisting away from the ape's massive hands as it reached for her with meaty fingers.

Kate had the moment she needed. She grabbed a vial from her bandolier. Inside it, a fine grey dust swirled. Dodging the ape's desperate grappling, Kate slapped the vial inside its gaping mouth between the extended tusks.

Then before the animal could spit it out, she slammed the heavy andiron straight up under its chin. Large jaws snapped shut and the vial shattered inside its mouth.

"Charlotte! Move away!" Kate warned as she scrambled back herself.

The agile werewolf leapt aside as a cloud of toxic dust swirled out from between the gorilla's hairless lips. The beast gagged, coughing violently, its muscular chest seizing with a rigid spasm. It swayed and toppled forward, crashing through the solid wooden table.

Kate grabbed Charlotte's long-fingered hand and turned to the princess. She knelt, and Charlotte did so also but only because she followed Kate's example. Victoria couldn't draw her stunned attention away from the werewolf hunched awkwardly in front of her.

"Your Highness," Kate said, "don't be afraid. Charlotte is a friend."

"Is she afflicted? She was a little girl like me just a moment ago."

Amazed by Victoria's presence of mind, Kate replied, "She still is at heart. Charlotte can do remarkable things."

"Is she a dog?"

"No. Dogs mind."

"I'm a werewolf," Charlotte growled bluntly and with a bit of pride.

Young Victoria curiously regarded Charlotte's long-nosed countenance and smiled. "You are very brave."

Kate knew if it were possible, Charlotte would have blushed. Instead the werewolf gave a low keening whine and pressed her hairy head against Kate's forearm. Kate retrieved her empty pistol and reached out her hand to Victoria. "Come with us, Your Highness."

Victoria glanced at the dead silverback ape quivering on the shattered remains of the table. "Are there more of those?"

"Possibly. But we will deal with them."

"I'll eat them if there are!" Charlotte announced.

"You will not," scolded Kate. "No eating anyone."

Charlotte's head drooped. "I was only joking." She looked up with her expressive eyebrows shifting rapidly up and down. "I would never eat anyone! Unless they were really, really bad?"

"No. Not even then."

Charlotte sighed, but then smiled a toothy grin pointing at the dead animal. "I don't even know what that is."

"It's never wise to eat anything you don't recognize," Victoria replied.

The two girls giggled. Kate rolled her eyes at their antics. Had she ever been that young and preposterous? She held each one's hand, and moved to the door. "Come on, you two. And that creature is called a gorilla."

"What's a gorilla?" asked Charlotte.

"Like a giant monkey."

"Are they evil?"

"Only if evil is done to them."

The two girls quickly began to chatter away about the ape, but Kate's attention was already focused at what they might be facing outside. She could only hope that any danger had been dealt with.

That hope was dashed as they came out onto the Broad Sanctuary, a wide thoroughfare leading from Parliament Square to the southwest, named for a place where once the unfortunate were protected from the civil power by the sacred character of the Abbey. Sadly, that was not the case today. The area was a disaster.

The late-summer day was chilly and dreary, rain had fallen heavily through the night, and dark clouds crossed the sky. Crowds had remained undeterred by drenching showers, and vast numbers had lined the streets for the coronation. Now they found themselves in the midst of terror. A mechanized ape was crushing an overturned carriage and tossing soldiers left and right. Two other gorillas lay dead, their heads crushed.

"Imogen!" Kate shouted, looking wildly about the chaotic grounds for her sister, who had been told to hold her station here. Kate had feared Imogen wasn't ready for such a violent mission.

"Here," answered a deep masculine voice. Kate's manservant, Hogarth, stepped out of the shadows. In his hands he carried a massive iron and bloodied mace. Beside him stood a specter-thin figure draped in black silk mourning clothes with an opaque veil over her face that hid her peculiar eyes, one milky white and the other mechanical. Curiously, only her right arm was bared, revealing opal white skin.

"Imogen." Kate breathed a sigh of relief. "You're both all right?"

"Yes, Miss Kate," Hogarth replied confidently.

Charlotte bounded over, jumping about the two of them with unrestrained energy. "I bit a big monkey!"

Imogen lifted her milky right arm, which bristled with long hairlike quills, and motioned to one of the apes lying in the gutter. Its huge body was punctured with the same filaments that graced Imogen's arm.

"Marvelous," Charlotte decreed. She pointed to the girl on the other side of Kate. "I met the princess! Princess, this is Imogen. She's afflicted too."

Kate interrupted the impromptu introductions. "Hogarth, you and Imogen take Her Highness to safety."

"Of course," said the manservant. "Come with me if you please, Your Highness."

The young heir did not hesitate to go with the towering man and his mournful companion, especially since Charlotte was nodding encouragement.

Behind them, an ape barreled through a long wrought-iron fence. It scattered panicked dignitaries and gawking commoners alike across the thoroughfare. With frightening intent, the brute paused in its rampage and plunged a mighty arm into the tumbled crowd. It grabbed up Prime Minister North in a crushing grip.

Kate started at a run, fumbling for a vial to load into her crossbow. By the time she fought her way across the yard, close enough for even a desperate shot, the prime minister had stopped screaming and was dangling limp in the ape's large hand. The gorilla poised to strike at the slender figure of Mrs. North, who watched the scene of horror. The ape's loud roar fluttered Grace North's hair and satin dress. To Kate's amazement, the woman didn't flinch. She simply stood staring at her husband. She must be in shock, Kate thought, and ran all the harder, dodging people and debris. Then Grace's hands lifted from her sides, palms open in what appeared to be supplication before the great beast. Her head cocked, as if she were studying the murderous animal with scientific curiosity.

The gorilla shuddered and, before Kate's eyes, withered. It seemed to shrink in size and muscle mass, hunching to the ground as if it lacked the strength to hold itself upright. The distinctive silver tinge on its furry back spread to cover the rest of its dark hair until it looked old and feeble. The prime minister slipped from the quivering grip of the collapsed ape. He crumpled at the feet of his wife, who knelt slowly beside him. His face was still and bloodless. Her delicate hand rested on his motionless chest.

Kate ran up and fell to her knees, reaching for a vial of her *elixir vitae,* although she doubted it would be of any help now. Before she could administer it, the prime minister gasped and shot up into the embrace of his wife. Grace North looked neither distressed nor ecstatic over his abrupt recovery from what Kate had perceived as near death. Kate glanced back at the ape. It was alive, but barely. Its dark brown eyes were watching them with fear and confusion. It no longer was a terrifying monster but a sad, decrepit creature. Kate actually felt sorry for it.

Her attention returned to Grace North and her husband. The woman was cooing over him and telling him how brave he was. Then Grace flashed a radiant smile at Kate. "Thank you. He would have died without your heroic intervention. England owes you much."

Kate stared at her, not sure how to respond.

INSIDE WESTMINSTER, WOODEN PEWS BURNED like seats in Perdition. Flames flew from the bare hands of the enraged Irishman. Malcolm crouched behind a colossal column at the foot of the choir as liquid fire rushed around him, singeing his skin and hair. He took the moment to reload his weapons.

Malcolm looked above him at the stone arches coated in flame. Penny wasn't visible through the smoke and fire. He hoped she had gotten out and was angling for a better position to blow this elemental bastard to kingdom come.

The wave of fire that had swept around Malcolm ceased. All magic users, whether magicians like Simon had once been or elementals like the Irishman, used aether. Ferghus had used it wastefully, spending far too much of it in a single attack. Malcolm now had precious seconds to take him out before the aether recharged. He braved the terrible heat, feeling it soak into his face. He spun toward the choir and emptied his pistols. They roared in a rhythmic song, as the self-ratcheting gears aligned the quad barrels one after the other. The Irishman couldn't form another heat shield so he dropped to the ground as bullets peppered stone memorials behind him. Malcolm holstered his guns and rushed forward, leaping onto the Irishman. He pummeled the man's head with his fists, hoping to keep him disoriented.

"Come on, you bloody Paddy," Malcolm shouted into his opponent's face. "Or don't you have the bollocks to take me on?"

Ferghus's temper consumed him as quickly as his flames. He surged up and they fell against the ornate choir screen, rolling under the organ loft. Malcolm felt Ferghus's fingers starting to burn as they dug into his face. The fire elemental's power was coming back. Malcolm fumbled for one of his spent pistols and slammed the thick barrel against Ferghus's head. The man reeled and his grip weakened. Malcolm kicked out from under the elemental as flames started to coat the man's face and hands in a blazing drape. Malcolm's trousers caught fire, but he had no time to put them out. He ran toward a column. Heat surged at his back and he knew he wasn't going to make it in time.

A boom sounded from the top of the choir and a shell exploded where Ferghus stood. It rocked the church. The organ loft shimmied, then settled. Dust fell through the shafts of colored light. Penny lowered her smoking blunderbuss. Soot covered her triumphant face. She pushed ash-coated goggles above her eyes to see the damage she had wrought. She let out a low whistle of amazement.

"Jesus Christ, woman!" shouted Malcolm, extracting himself from beneath an iron candlestick that had shaken loose from a column.

"Would you rather be roasted, you ill-tempered Scotsman?" she shot back.

Malcolm glared at her and ran toward the collapsed archway where Ferghus had hopefully fallen, but the man was not there.

From her high perch, Penny saw the Irishman running toward King Edward's chair. "There!" She pointed and reloaded her stovepipe cannon.

Ferghus vaulted up to the ancient chair, which lay on its side. The thought of Penny's blowing to dust the ancient Scottish relic, the Stone of Scone that lay beneath the chair, propelled Malcolm toward the Irishman. They collided and tumbled over the chair to crash at the feet of Simon and the Baroness, who were still locked in struggle.

Simon was clearly weakening, his movement slowing, his sword point lower. He grew vulnerable to the Baroness's untiring machine power. A gauntleted hand grabbed the wires connecting one of the right forearms to the biceps and yanked. Her arm bent awkwardly in a shower of sparks, eliciting a scream from her. She grabbed Simon's shoulder and jerked him forward into her knee. He gasped for breath as his unprotected abdomen took the blow. He fell backward over Malcolm.

The Scotsman heard Simon say an ancient word in desperation. No aether came to bear and frustration washed over the powerless magician. Simon cursed in English and dropped his sword to the stone floor. He lunged up awkwardly at the Baroness, just ducking a blow from the mechanical arm with its spinning blades, which seemed to have repaired themselves. With one hand, Simon pulled a lever on the other gauntlet. He brought his hands close together and a fierce arc of electricity formed between them, making his hair stand on end. His hands came in contact with a mechanical arm and the Baroness's body locked in a rictus seizure as the current coursed through her. Smoke rose from her metal arms. Simon screamed in pain but was unable to let go.

Malcolm threw himself at Simon, bearing him to the ground. The connection broke, but Simon still writhed in agony. From the floor, Malcolm shouted, "Penny! Blow them to hell!"

At the same time, the sound of tramping feet came from the front of the Abbey. Soldiers approached through the smoke. Some stopped and raised muskets, loosing a thunderous volley. Ferghus ducked and cursed. More soldiers leveled their guns. The Irishman flung the senseless Baroness over his shoulder and ran for the north transept past the body of the dead gorilla.

"Stop them," Simon gasped. Malcolm rose only to hear Penny shout.

"Everybody down!"

"Bloody hell!" Malcolm threw himself over Simon as another boom sounded and the north transept exploded with a mix of fire and black smoke.

When the dust cleared, the alcove was empty. Penny had missed. The two villains had slipped out of the Abbey. Malcolm staggered toward the exit. As he came out, he dodged a huge meaty fist and ducked back inside. By the time he spun back around the corner, the mechanical ape was gone. He heard screams and saw a disruption in the crowd including a few bodies flying into the air. Malcolm fought his way into the chaos, shoving and pushing as best he could with his flagging strength. He gasped for breath as he ran, finally reaching the river where he saw the great ape leap from a jetty onto a strange steam launch with paddle wheels amidships. The boat's funnel belched greenish smoke, similar to the hue of aether that Malcolm had witnessed in the past. On the deck, he saw Ferghus kneeling next to the Baroness. The behemoth ape used its foot to cast off with enough force to put the boat a good distance from the dock. The paddle wheels roared with amazing speed and the launch churned out onto the river, throwing up an admirable wake.

Malcolm returned to Westminster through the tumultuous and bloody aftermath. Soldiers were trying to restore some order, but it was futile. Once inside the Abbey, Malcolm found Penny yanking the gauntlets from Simon's hands. The flesh underneath was burned, but he was able to move his fingers. Kate stood next to him with a small bottle ready.

Simon turned to face Malcolm for a report, but when he saw the Scotsman staring at his seared skin, he lowered his hands, hiding the pain. "What happened?"

"They got away," Malcolm said simply. "Boat waiting on the river."

Simon grimaced as Kate massaged ointment into his burnt hands. He surveyed the church. "Unfortunate, but at least they didn't get what they came for."

"Yes, King William is safe, right?" Penny asked.

"He is." Kate tried not to wince at Simon's seared flesh.

Simon smiled at her. "Thank you, Kate. But His Majesty wasn't the target."

Malcolm shook his head. "Well if they wanted to destroy the Abbey, they did a brilliant job of it." The church smoldered in many places, and other sections were a broken ruin.

"I think that was mainly me," Penny admitted sheepishly.

"Not to be helped," Simon assured her. "Churches can be rebuilt. Lives cannot. We're fortunate to be alive, but we did well against two very formidable foes. Without your gauntlets to match that woman's mechanical terrors, I would be lying dead now. Well done, everyone."

Penny puffed with satisfaction and cavalierly shouldered her stovepipe blunderbuss. However, she pointed at Simon's damaged hands. "They hurt you as much as they hurt her. I'm sorry, Simon."

"Don't be silly. They worked like a . . ." Simon winced in pain. ". . . a charm."

"What were they after then," Malcolm demanded to know, "if not the king?"

Simon's gaze swept to the overturned Seat of King Edward and the greyish lump of heavy stone resting beneath it. The rock seemed unexceptional, a few feet across and maybe a foot high. "Something a bit more mythical, I think."

Chapter 3

THE DEVIL'S LOOM WAS AN OLD HAUNT OF SImon's. It was a down-and-out public house in the St. Giles Parish of London on the edge of the disreputable area of poverty and misery known as the Rookery. Simon kept a town house not far away to the west between Crown Road and Soho Square in a little-known alley called Gaunt Lane.

Simon and Kate sat with Malcolm and Penny in a back booth. The pub was hot with summer damp and crowded with late-night gatherers. Even here among the working class, the conversation was largely the disaster at the king's coronation yesterday. The speculation about the event ranged from an attack by radicals to a battle between demons and angels. The general tone was one of support for King William, who was mostly popular with the common people.

A stout barmaid with dyed red hair shoved through the clutches of arguing drinkers and approached with three new ales and a whiskey. She spared an interested look at Malcolm and hardly contained a sour glance at Kate. Then she leaned close to Simon, noting the bandages that covered his hands.

"You don't come around no more," she said with

playful sadness. "Haven't seen you hardly half a dozen times since last autumn. And Nick not at all. Have you gone off from London?"

Simon closed his small notebook around a pencil and laid a hand on her red dry fingers. "I spend more time in the country now, Rebecca."

The barmaid reared up reproachfully. "Oh, is that it? You're a squire now." She quickly glanced at Kate again. "And Nick? Is he with you?"

Simon tried to keep the smile on his face, but failed. "No. Nick has gone off."

Now Rebecca had a truly regretful expression. "Oh dear. I'm sorry. You two were such lads."

"Good times." Simon raised the ale to her, signaling that he had to return to his companions. She patted his cheek, picked up several rounds of empty glasses, and went away.

"Seems you and Barker were popular with the locals here," Malcolm observed.

"Simon and Nick were prodigious drinkers," Kate said.

"We did our part." Simon sat back with a sad smile.

Penny raised her glass and said with a baronial huff, "That's all England can expect."

Kate caught another embittered glance directed at her from the barmaid across the room. "Your friend, Rebecca, is still glaring at me."

"Not surprising. She was very fond of me."

"You must have been more attentive in those days."

"What do you mean?"

"You virtually sent that woman away just now. She clearly has an interest and wanted a bit of fun from you. You gave her no lascivious repartee. No charming banter. Not even a hint of repressed desire. I keep hearing that you were something of a rake in your former life.

But so far it's all hearsay. I've never seen more than a glimpse of it."

Simon stared at Kate with surprise. "Do you want to see it?"

"Perhaps. Every so often." Kate grinned. "I've heard tales about that Simon Archer. He must've been quite interesting."

"If you like that sort of man." He laughed. "Battling with werewolves and demigods and fire elementals doesn't usually call for those skills."

Kate gave him a wry glance, one eyebrow lifting. "We aren't dealing with werewolves and elementals every day, are we?"

"Seems like it."

Her fingers played over his as they rested on the table. "If you don't make time, there won't be time."

Simon stared at Kate. He studied the small flecks of orange in the green of her eyes. The fire behind them made his body flare with a warmth that had little to do with the temperature in the pub or the alcohol he had consumed. The challenge in her expression didn't waver.

It took a great deal of concentration not to give her the demonstration she wanted in a public place. Though it would serve her right. With a wry smile, he opened the notebook and fumbled with the pencil in his bandaged hands. Without looking away from Kate, he began to sketch a rather bawdy picture of her. Kate's eyes finally glanced down and she gasped with shock. She shoved his hand away and flipped a page to cover it before anyone else, especially Malcolm and Penny, could see it.

Kate raised an eyebrow. "How charmingly lewd."

"I can still manage it just."

The two of them laughed. Penny guffawed also as she pulled a cigar from one of her many pockets. She offered it to Malcolm, who seemed uninterested by the banter and waved a hand in refusal. She shrugged and proceeded to light it up herself.

Simon returned to sketching, but this time he switched to runes. His little journal was filled with a variety of mystic symbols derived from many traditions. There were also countless sketches of keys with runic phrases etched along their surfaces. This was something Simon had been doing for months, often without even noticing.

He ignored the fact that writing was causing slight pain to vibrate through his burnt hands. Kate's alchemical balm would heal it soon enough, but the bandages reminded him again of his vulnerability without magic. The cuts and burns and bruises of his companions caused Simon even more distress than any pain he felt himself. A sense of dismay came over him, which he had struggled to banish over the months since his magic was ripped from him by the horrific demigod Ra. He had spent the first few months after the terrible event waiting for the spark of aether to return with that familiar surge of excitement that he relished. Every morning when he opened his eyes, his heart throbbed with the expectation that he would see the wisps of eldritch green slipping through the air around him, unseen by all except magicians such as himself who had intimate ties to the aether realm.

The air stayed empty. Morning after morning he saw nothing but the ceiling. Weeks passed. Months turned to seasons. The wonder that he had known for most of his life was gone. And he had begun to accept that it might—no, that it would—never return. All these runes he drew absently were nothing more than strange art. He could never use them to create magic again.

"You're right, of course, Kate. We'll have time enough.

I promise." Simon looked away from her because he didn't want to see her reaction when he said, "An excellent job at Westminster, all. Malcolm, your months of scouting for hints of Gaios in the fringes of the arcane world paid off handsomely. Your hunch that his agents would make an attack on the coronation was impeccable."

Malcolm barely nodded, his glance flicking to Kate, then away. He was content with the success of his efforts and quietly grateful for the praise.

Simon continued, "And thank you, Penny, for your masterful accouterment that helped balance my lack of magic."

Kate turned from Simon with pursed lips of disappointment but brightened when she looked at the young engineer. "The crossbow you designed for hurling my alchemical solutions worked like a charm and should prevent my right arm bulking up more than my left with all the throwing I was doing. Thank you. Now, if you could make it so small I could carry it on my person around town without attracting attention, that would be lovely."

"Oh, good idea, Kate." Penny nodded her thanks to both, puffing away on her cigar.

Simon continued, "We managed to accomplish our primary goals. Kate, what do you have on our fencing partners at Westminster?"

Penny leaned forward onto her elbows. "Yes, I want to hear about this Baroness woman. I looked at her gorillas and noted her engineering mark. It's been tainting most everything we've come across from the sextant at the Mansfields' house to even Dr. White's homunculi."

Kate's mouth tightened as she regarded the engineer. "Are you sure?"

"Oh yes. Her mark is pretty unmistakable." Penny

poured some salt on the table and drew the odd symbol in the grains. "That and her blatant cruelty to animals."

Simon offered a wan smile. "She did seem to enjoy pain. Mine at least."

Kate opened a book she had retrieved from her home at Hartley Hall when she accompanied Imogen and Charlotte back there after the battle at Westminster. "Our new enemies. Ferghus O'Malley and Baroness Conrad. Both of them formerly imprisoned by Byron Pendragon in the Bastille and therefore servants of Gaios now, just as Gretta Aldfather and Dr. White and Nephthys before them. My father's old journals have a bit of information." She turned the book so Simon could see it. "Baroness Conrad. Born Minerva Clark, to unexceptional parents, in the eighteenth century. She connived her way into Magdelene College Society of Supraphysical Design and Special Engineering, Cambridge. Isn't that your old outfit, Penny?"

Penny gave a yelp of surprise. "Oh my God. The Maddy Boys. Yes. I knew there had been a few other women before me, but I can't believe they'd train that monster." She stared at the passage in Kate's book, but there was nothing more about the Maddy Boys or Cambridge, where she had perfected her own engineering skills.

Kate said soothingly, "The Baroness was there nearly a century before you. Let's see. She married Baron William Conrad, who was on the court of directors of the East India Company. They went to India to his tea plantation. After Baron Conrad disappeared mysteriously, the entire operation passed to his wife. It was then that she embarked on her career of experimentation on animals and humans, creating biomechanical wonders and horrors. At some point, she turned her experiments on herself, grafting mechanical arms onto her torso. According to my father, she had a terrible fear of weakness so she re-formed her own body into a machine. There was an uprising of workers on the plantation that evoked a response from the Baroness, who slaughtered a good portion of the district. That brought her to the attention of Byron Pendragon, who traveled to India, seized her, and delivered her into bondage in the Bastille, where she remained until the Revolution. After her escape, we have no idea of her movements."

"Africa, at least, unless she had someone procure those unfortunate apes for her." Simon flipped a few more pages. "Your father spent time in India. Do you think he ever encountered her personally?"

"He traveled to India in 1815, but he left no journal of that trip. All I know is that very few survived including his old hunting companion, Emmett Walker. He never talked about that expedition; not to me, in any case."

"What do we know about the fellow who shoots fire?" Penny reached out for the book.

"We can hope he's an Oxford man." Simon laughed and handed her the journal so she could reread the passage about the Baroness. "His name is Ferghus O'Malley. Irish. Fire elemental. He didn't show up frequently in the grimoires or histories like some of the more flamboyant Bastille Bastards did. Kept to himself, apparently. It's said that he was responsible for the Great Fire of London in 1666, and that's why Pendragon clapped him in the Bastille."

Malcolm grunted with interest. "Why did he try to burn London?"

"I'm not sure. In any case, we must stop him and the Baroness now."

"Stop them so your king can put his arse on the Scottish rock again?" Malcolm retorted.

Simon grinned at the Scotsman. "He's your king too, Malcolm. And yes, I rather suspect the two villains were after the Stone of Scone. I've no idea for what purpose, but it is an immensely powerful artifact. Druids and magicians have worshipped and respected that stone for centuries. It's a lodestone, magically tied to these islands."

"Immensely powerful *Scottish* artifact." Malcolm downed his whiskey and grimaced at its mediocre quality.

"Point taken." Simon was careful not to mock Malcolm's rarely displayed but always present national pride. "Its power is the very reason we English stole the Stone from you Scots in the first place. Of course, there is that whole legend about how the loss of the Stone will result in the fall of the realm. And all legends have a grain of truth in them."

Malcolm scowled. "It would be a shame if that happened."

"We must formulate a plan to find those two creatures before they go after the Stone again. I dread to think of such an object in the hands of Gaios."

"If it's the Stone of Scone they're after," Malcolm said, "why don't we hide it? Back in Scotland, for instance."

"The Stone is as safe as can be," Simon answered. "It's kept in a vault beneath the Abbey, warded by Byron Pendragon himself ages ago, and only brought out for coronations. That's why they struck when they did. But since it won't come out again until there's a new monarch, we don't want them to do something rash to good King William. We want to keep London safe."

"Murder!" a voice shot through the hum of the crowd.

Simon and his companions were on their feet immediately. A distraught woman stood at the tavern's open door. Her eyes were wide and she turned her head, looking for immediate help.

"Murder!" she called again. "Oh Lord! They're killing some poor man. Won't someone come?"

Malcolm parted the crowd, reaching for a pistol under his coat. "It appears London remains as safe as ever."

"You lot know all the exciting spots in town." The prospect of an evening's adventure lit Penny's eyes. She hefted her massive rucksack, which might've contained anything.

They all came to the door, a few steps ahead of several men who were also responding to the woman's plea. Kate gave her a soothing touch, "Where's the trouble?"

"By the Resurrection Gate," the woman stammered. "They're going to kill him."

Simon ran down the street, Kate and Penny at his side. Malcolm followed, a massive four-barreled Lancaster already in his grip. Simon knew the area well and cut through a narrow stinking alley, crowded with onlookers leaning out of windows or standing on the curbs, wondering about the shouting mob that poured out of the Devil's Loom. Simon reached a wrought-iron fence. Through the rails, he saw a disturbance in the churchyard of St. Giles-in-the-Field. Shadowed figures surrounded someone on the ground.

Simon passed through the columns of the Resurrection Gate and pulled a sword from his walking stick. "Here! Leave off!"

A face turned from the mob. It was grey and flaking with teeth bared. More cold stares rose as the cadaverous group stopped flailing and froze.

Penny's steps faltered slightly at the sight, covering her nose at the horrific stench. Her eyes widened and her breath panted faster. No doubt she was remembering the night her undead mother paid her a visit. Kate's eyes darted to Penny, and the engineer nodded her resolve after a moment.

"Oh for God's sake," Malcolm muttered. "More undead. I thought they were all at rest."

"Careful," Kate cautioned Simon, reaching into her bag for useful alchemical vials. "You don't have Penny's gauntlets."

Penny dragged her attention back to the matter at hand. She hefted her rucksack. "I could have easily fit them in here."

Malcolm snorted.

There were nearly twenty of the dead things; several had their clawlike hands on a man lost from sight among their bony legs and ragged grave clothes. Most of the cadavers moved toward Simon and his companions while a few dragged their insensible victim toward the steps leading down to the crypt under the church.

Malcolm immediately moved in front of Simon with annoying protectiveness and opened fire with his pistol. Each careful shot smashed into a walking corpse, shattering leg bones, caving in rib cages, and splattering heads. He drew a second Lancaster. Penny pulled a pistol and fired too.

Kate put a shoulder ahead of Simon and lobbed a vial toward the undead. It shattered on the ground and a black substance began to spread around the shuffling feet. The creatures were soon held fast in the treacle.

"If you don't mind." Simon pushed past his colleagues with an exasperated sigh. He started around the trapped cadavers who grasped for him, but they fell forward, dropping awkwardly into the pool of black tar. He approached the three undead who were busy hauling the unconscious man down the worn steps into the crypt. When one looked up, it received Simon's sword through its cheek. He ripped the blade free, breaking off a good portion of the thing's head. A quick counterswipe lopped off its head completely. Simon used his foot to hold a second cadaver back. It seemed very desiccated, so he kicked hard through its face and pushed it down the steps where it lay flopping at the crypt door. The last undead seized Simon's calf and he felt sharp fingernails tearing his flesh. He fell back onto the ground. Teeth gnashed close to Simon's face.

He drew the length of the sword through the undead's mouth, slicing off the lower jaw. The thing paused in confusion, allowing Simon to slash straight down through its skull. It fell back with its arms still scrabbling for prey. Then a blast from Malcolm's Lancaster blew the body into pieces.

"Well, thank you, Malcolm." Simon reached for the battered man lying on the steps.

Kate had deterred the crowd that followed from the pub, shouting something about plague and leprosy. Even the angry drunks of the Devil's Loom paled at the mention of those dreaded maladies. Most covered their mouths and retreated.

Simon felt along the neck of the fallen man, finding a strong pulse. There was an odd familiarity to the victim. He looked up. "Malcolm, help Penny disable those last undead. I'll bring this fellow."

Simon slid his hands under the man's arms, dragging him back up the steps. Kate joined him, kicking flailing limbs out of their way. Simon heard a deep groan of returning consciousness. He knelt and tilted the fellow's face upward.

"Nick?" Simon gasped and fell back on his haunches in amazement.

Kate shouted, "Jesus Christ!"

"Not quite, but close." Nick Barker smiled up at them

with lips and teeth bloody. "It's about time you saved *me* for once."

NICK BARKER WAS ENSCONCED IN HIS OLD SPOT in the sitting room at Gaunt Lane with his head on one upholstered arm of the sofa and his feet on the other. He was cleaned up and wore fresh clothes. His face had swollen purple in the two hours since they had left the St. Giles churchyard. He clutched a glass of whiskey, his third. "You're keeping the place tidier, Simon. Must be Miss Anstruther's influence."

Simon's chair was close by Nick. Malcolm lurked in a shadowed corner.

Nick groaned. "That crypt trash took me by surprise. Hit me with a brick or something, then beat me stupid. Didn't have time to do anything."

"Lucky we were in the area," Simon said.

Kate sat at a table, pretending to study a grimoire. "Or was it luck?"

Penny walked about the outskirts of the room, fascinated by the numerous artifacts on the shelves. She stopped by a window and cooed at a large marmalade cat strolling past in the untended garden outside. The cat glared back at her.

Nick drank and held out his glass. "I wouldn't make eye contact with that cat if I was you. He's bad."

Penny scoffed but turned away from the window anyway.

Kate sounded dubious. "So you weren't in the parish to keep an eye on Simon? As you were at Warden Abbey last winter?"

Nick made a dismissive noise. "I was just having an ale in the Devil's Loom when I saw you walk in. Thought I'd take my leave, as I know I'm not your favorite fellow."

"The barmaid said you hadn't been around in ages."

Nick shifted stiffly, hissing in pain. "I used a glamour spell if you must know."

Kate continued, "And you just happened to pass St. Giles when the dead were rising? And they just happened to decide to lob a brick at you? I understand their decision, but it's awfully coincidental."

Nick glared at her.

"She makes a good point," Simon said.

"Thank you." Kate flipped a page. "I thought so."

"You're welcome. Well, Nick?"

"Why so odd? Undead were all the rage around London a few months ago."

"That outbreak is over. Once Pendragon's resurrection spell ended, the undead plague stopped. There've been no living dead for six months. Why tonight? Why you?"

"Simon," Nick wheezed, "I'm too beaten and drunk for the Star Chamber. I need a bit of sleep, old boy. Is my room still free?"

Simon stared at his old friend, not relenting.

Nick laughed, which turned into a dry cough. When he brought the hacking under control, he saw that Simon wasn't hovering with concern. Nick gave him a pleading look and held out the glass.

Simon set the bottle on the floor. He felt like a bastard. He wanted to do anything he could to make his friend welcome and comfortable, but he couldn't do it. The others weren't so enamored of Nick Barker although they didn't know him like Simon did. But their suspicions were valid.

"Oh, have a heart," Nick breathed.

"I'm trying, Nick. Give me a reason. A good reason."

Nick threw his forearm over his eyes. "I was going to tell you everything tomorrow, but if I have to talk before you'll let me sleep, fine. I have fallen afoul of a magician. Those undead were her way of saying *I'd rather have you dead, Nick Barker.*"

"So," Simon said, "you've made a powerful enemy?"

"Shocking," Kate mumbled.

Simon kept his eyes glued to Nick. "Who is this perturbed magician? Perhaps I can intercede on your behalf."

"I don't think so," Nick replied. "I just need a bit of a hiding spot for a while, until I can disappear proper-like."

Simon noted a tremor of fear in Nick's voice. "Who is it?"

"What is wrong with you, Simon?" Nick fell back against the sofa. "Why can't you accept me at my word and just move on?"

"Who is it?" Simon demanded loudly.

"Ash," Nick said with such simplicity that it seemed he hadn't said what everyone heard.

"Ash!" Simon sat up like a bolt. The necromancer's name sent a wave of hate through him so strong it made him nauseous. He immediately thought of his mother, who had not even been safe in her grave from Ash's abuse. The necromancer had tried to uncover the secret of Simon's parentage, seeking the roots of his scribing abilities. His mother, who had no reason to be attacked other than to have fallen in love with a magician and borne his son, had refused to bow to Ash's power. "What have you to do with Ash?"

"We go way back." Nick actually smiled that he had surprised his old friend and the entire group. "Bit of a misunderstanding. I just need to vanish for a few years . . . or centuries. She has a long memory and carries a grudge like a Borgia."

Simon stared at Nick. "You never told me that you knew Ash. Even when I spoke of her, my suspicions of her, and my doubts about the Order of the Oak, you never said a word. You looked me in the eye, and you never said a word. Why?"

"Right." Nick took an angry breath and nodded spitefully, as if he had been forced into a decision that everyone would regret. He swung his feet onto the floor. When he sat up, he put a hand to his head with a sick groan. He froze as if the room was spinning. His voice was weak. "Simon, old boy, I've always wanted to tell you something. And I always hoped I'd never have to."

A chill seeped into Simon. He sat forward, watching the creases of pain deepen on Nick's face. He heard the others shifting restlessly in the background.

Nick stared at the floor. "It wasn't an accident us meeting years ago. I was sent to find you. Ash had heard that there was a scribe in London, but she found it hard to credit. She had thought that Pendragon and Cavendish were the last two in the known world, and they were both dead."

"Did Ash know Edward Cavendish was my father?" Simon asked coldly.

"No. She had no idea and still doesn't, as far as I know. Hell, I didn't know until you told me last fall."

"And you never reported it back to Ash?" Kate accused.

"No," Nick snarled at her. "That's why she wants me dead. You see, I was charged with judging your skills, improving them as best I could, then delivering you to her if you were worthy. But I didn't steer you to Ash as I was supposed to, and she hasn't forgiven me."

"Why didn't you? Why would you defy Ash?" Simon was nearly incapable of speaking. He watched every small twitch that Nick made, listened to the exhaustion pouring out of the man as if he no longer had the energy to lie. The words felt like a jagged piece of glass tearing Simon's stomach open.

"I couldn't do it." Nick met Simon's gaze, but now the

scribe looked away. "She didn't deserve you. You were better than that."

The room lay silent for a moment.

"Rot," came Malcolm's measured voice. "He's a liar."

"You're right, Angus," Nick said bitterly. "The entire time we were together, Simon, I was lying to you. But once I realized you deserved the truth, I couldn't tell you."

Simon stood and walked across the room. "Why didn't you at least tell me after Bedlam? You were leaving us anyway."

"Because I wasn't really leaving. I knew the battle was coming between Ash and Gaios, and Ash wanted you as her Galahad. I was afraid you would stumble into the fight just because you're good at heart. I hoped I could protect you." Nick noted the skeptical glances that met his words. "Fine. Not the greatest strategy, but it was all I had. I couldn't tell you that I had been spying on you for years. Would that have pushed you to listen to me?"

"Simon, throw him out," Malcolm said. "Let Ash hunt him down and kill him if that part of his story is even true. And I hope it is."

Penny looked at Malcolm's ferocious glare with concern.

Simon stood behind Kate's chair, clenching and unclenching his fingers on the wood. "Ash never mentioned you to me."

Nick stopped reaching for the whiskey bottle and looked up in alarm. "What do you mean? Have you talked to Ash? Did she approach you?"

"We've spoken. I haven't heard from her in a few months. I thought perhaps she might have fled England to escape Gaios."

"She won't give up England without a fight, or rather without sending someone to fight for her. Jesus, Simon, don't go near her. She's the most twisted creature in the history of time. She will do nothing but corrupt and leave you for dead. She only wants you so you can win her war with Gaios."

Simon said, "I'm choosy about whom I play Galahad to."

"I am begging you." Nick started to stand, but fell back onto the sofa, more from the drink than from the beating. "Please. Don't have any dealings with her."

"Tell me who she really is," Simon demanded.

"I have no idea. I've never talked to the real Ash, only her corpse mouthpieces. No one knows who Ash is. She's been hundreds of people over the centuries, moving from one place to another, one name to another. I heard she's been everything from the queen of France to the pope's mistress. Some say she was Empress Josephine. No one knows. Her black arts allow her to stay young and beautiful, so she moves to a new place, manufactures a past, and lives the life of someone wealthy and powerful until she has to move on for whatever reason: revolution, invasion, or just prying questions about why she's still young and pretty while her friends are old and dead. Simon, do what you will with me. I'll leave now. But, please, don't deal with Ash."

While Nick talked, Simon strode across the sitting room, treading the worn carpet. He removed his coat and tossed it aside. He began to unfasten his cuffs out of habit. Nick watched him intently. Simon paused to open a window. The ragged orange cat strolled in past Simon, shooting him an angry glare. Penny reached out and stroked the feline, whose back arched with pleasure.

"Where are your tattoos?" Nick pointed at his former friend.

Simon looked down at his muscular forearm where

he had been rolling up the sleeve of his white shirt. He quickly slid the sleeve down and refastened it.

Nick's shock seemed to have knocked the alcohol out of his system. His voice was clear and worried. "Where are your inscriptions, Simon? What happened to you?"

"We're not discussing me." Simon turned back to the window. "You may stay, Nick."

"Simon," Malcolm began to argue.

"No," Simon said with an exhausted voice and held up his hand. "He is in danger, partly because he sought to protect me in the past."

"You don't believe any of that, do you?" Malcolm asked incredulously.

"I have to." Simon leaned against the window, silhouetted in the moonlight. "Otherwise, everything could be a lie. And I won't have that."

Chapter 4

THE NEXT MORNING, SIMON WOKE EARLY AND went out to his favorite coffee cart. He returned with a pot of coffee and a serviceable breakfast. Kate brightened as he entered the kitchen. Morning was her element. The dawn's light illuminated the cherry tones in her hair until it sparked like fire. Her smile quickly faded as she eyed the lumps of greasy paper Simon pulled from the basket.

She abandoned her search of the cabinets and the pantry for any food to prepare. "I was hoping you'd just buy a few eggs and some bread. I could have managed with those."

"No need. These are a popular favorite here."

"Did you muck those off the bank of the Thames?" she asked, her nose wrinkling. "Now I know why Penny preferred to go to her own home last night. The fear of a Gaunt Lane breakfast."

"Nonsense. She just wanted to continue her work on the key." Simon pulled a gold chain from his waistcoat pocket and twirled it. It felt particularly empty because normally there would have been a special gold key attached to the end. It was his prized possession, even though he didn't truly own it. "Ever since the key started functioning again, she works on it all the time. And why wouldn't she? It is one of the greatest magical items ever created. Such a simple object having the power of instantaneous transportation around the globe is still so incredible. Just as incredible, Penny seems close to understanding the engineering concepts your father used to design it. She is confident that she'll be able to replicate the construction and build working copies." He spun the empty chain a few more times, then watched it fall limp in his hand. "Penny is ever the optimist. She keeps forging facsimiles even though she knows I can't inscribe and empower them, as my father did to the original." Simon tucked the chain into his waistcoat with a sigh. "Well, fortunately we still have that one marvelous key, and by some miracle, it still works. It has served us in the past, and no doubt will in the future."

"If the key has reconnected to the aether, there's no reason you won't as well," Kate said with practiced sympathy. "You were both drained by Ra at the same time. Clearly, there's a limit to the persistence of the magic-eater's power."

"Clearly. Although we did destroy the mummy months ago. The key has come back admirably. Me?" Simon pantomimed removing a hat from his head and holding it out in front of him. He reached into the invisible hat, then drew out his hand with the flourish of a stage magician. He slowly uncurled his fingers to reveal that his hand was empty. "I can't even pull a hedgehog out of my hat."

"One day you will."

Simon was grateful for Kate's endless confidence whether she actually felt it or was just saying it to prevent his having a bout of self-pity. So he quickly unwrapped what appeared to be a pile of scorched crust. "These are delicious. It's a meat pie."

"I know what it is, but I don't want to know what sort of meat." Kate poised a fork over the pie before setting the utensil on the table with a sigh. "Simon, really, we're not without resources. Can't you arrange a servant to keep the house ready for occasional use?"

"No. Not with my interests. It's too dangerous." He started sketching keys and runes onto the paper bag.

"I have the same interests as you plus a preference for edible meals. I have servants at Hartley Hall, and my home is certainly as dangerous as yours."

"Agreed." Simon lifted the fork and slipped it back into her hand. "Here, you dropped this. I assume your father gave your servants to understand they were in for peculiar times. And you pay them many times the going rate."

Kate prodded the pie listlessly while Simon seized one by hand and began to devour it. Malcolm entered the kitchen and, without a word, took up one of the doughy things and started eating.

"No Barker," Malcolm said to Simon through a mouthful of meat pie. "So you came to your senses?"

Simon poured coffee for Malcolm. "No, he's still asleep. He's staying as long as he likes. We're taking him on faith."

Malcolm nodded with thanks and drank. "I know my judgment has no leverage after how I argued against Charlotte, but I'll say it anyway. Nick Barker is a bad man. To my mind, there's nothing admirable about him. There, I've said it. I'm done with the topic."

"Noted." Simon pointed questioningly at Kate's pie. She pushed it to him. He took a huge bite. "I understand your opinion, Malcolm. But I must do what I must."

The Scotsman tightened his lips and held up his hands

to show he was indeed finished. Then he glanced curiously at Kate. "Not hungry?"

Simon took his pipe from the counter and loaded it with tobacco. He rubbed his thumb over a rune incised on the bowl of the pipe. Out of habit, he waited for it to flare into life. He stared into the cold tobacco and the depressing realization dawned on him yet again that he was an exile from the aether. Simon grumbled and stood up. He went to the stove and lit his pipe with a taper, puffing heavily with effort.

"Fire," Malcolm commented. "Great invention."

When Simon returned to the table, he looked at the paper bag covered in his drawings. He snatched it up with annoyance, crumpled it into a ball, and shoved it into the burning stove.

Kate leaned her chin into her hand, watching Simon. "Aren't you the man who once told me, in this very kitchen, I believe, that using magic for everyday facilities, such as lighting a teapot or a pipe, was a criminal waste of skill?"

"That's when I had a choice." Simon then huffed with a shake of his head. "Thank you both for your outpouring of sympathy."

"If anyone deserves sympathy, it's me." Kate tapped the greasy paper that once held the food. "Next time I breakfast here, if there is a next time, this horror show can't happen."

Simon took the pipe from his mouth, admiring the even glow of the tobacco. "I'll have chickens and a pig brought in for your dining pleasure."

Kate started to retort, but a knock came from the front door. Simon stiffened with alarm. Malcolm looked confused at his overreaction.

Simon said, "This house is warded to the shadows, and it is still in effect. Only one person has ever seen through those wards." Simon went down the corridor and swung open the door. "Hogarth, come in."

The Anstruther's manservant bowed. "Mr. Archer, good morning, sir."

A small shape pushed past Hogarth. Charlotte was fashionably attired in a rather formal dress and bonnet. She grinned as she stared around the foyer.

"This is where you live in London, Mr. Simon? I couldn't even see it, but Mr. Hogarth swore it was here. And it is." She wrinkled her nose. "Do you have cats?"

"It's lovely to see you, Charlotte, even this early. And Imogen, welcome." Simon shut the door after Kate's sister glided into the hall dressed in her traditional full mourning. "To what do we owe this surprise?"

"Miss Kate!" Charlotte scampered to Kate, who was coming from the kitchen. She wrapped her arms around the smiling woman's waist. "Guess what?"

"You are now suddenly craving bananas?" Kate winked at her.

The young girl's delighted laughter filled the room. "No, silly!"

"Then wha—?"

"We're going to see the king!" Charlotte blurted over her. "He asked for me too!"

"The king?" Kate looked down at the overexcited girl. "What are you talking about, dear?"

Hogarth held up a thick gilt envelope. "This letter came from the Court of St. James to Hartley Hall last night. You are requested to attend His Majesty, King William IV, with all due haste."

THE SITTING ROOM IN CLARENCE HOUSE WAS crowded. Simon paced to work off unaccustomed nerves, struggling to appear merely energetic. Kate was truly at ease; she wasn't used to meeting kings, per se, but she had grown up in rarified air, mixing frequently with the nation's greatest. Malcolm stared out the window toward wide Pall Mall beyond the trees with its parade of carriages. Imogen stood like a statue behind Kate's chair, and Charlotte was in the process of touching every lamp, vase, and painting in the room.

"Charlotte," Kate said for the tenth time, "please sit down."

"Who is this, Mr. Malcolm?" The girl looked at Malcolm as she pointed at a portrait of a woman.

Malcolm didn't look at the picture, grumbling, "I don't know."

Simon said, "That's Princess Augusta Sophia. The king's younger sister."

"Oh." Charlotte stared at the auburn-haired woman in oil. She took a step and pointed at another. "Who's this, Mr. Malcolm?"

"I don't know," Malcolm muttered a bit louder.

"Mr. Malcolm doesn't know, dear." Kate froze Simon, who was opening his mouth preparing to answer. "And neither does Mr. Simon. Now, I must insist you sit next to me and stop pawing the king's things."

Imogen made a grunting sound like a laugh. Charlotte giggled too.

"What's so funny?" Kate asked.

Charlotte came toward Malcolm, playing hopscotch on the checkerboard-tile floor. "You said *pawing*. And I'm a werewolf."

Imogen snorted again.

Kate shared a bemused look with Simon, but then he turned quickly at the sound of a door opening. King William entered the room, dressed in a common suit, his white hair mussed. The elderly king took in the crowd and smiled.

"Ah, here you are." He closed the door behind him.

There were no secretaries, no clerks, no valets, only the king himself.

Simon inclined his head respectfully as Kate rose and curtsied. Charlotte yelped, trying to copy the curtsy. Imogen remained motionless, and Malcolm posed with an inhospitable glower.

King William went to Kate and grasped her hand. "So good to see you, Miss Anstruther. Thank you for coming so promptly."

"Of course, Your Majesty. You may recall Mr. Simon Archer."

"I do, indeed! Welcome to Clarence House, Mr. Archer. I'm glad to speak to you under less tumultuous circumstances." The king then caught sight of the focused Charlotte and smiled genuinely at her. "You may belay curtsying, my dear. One will suffice for the entire day."

"Oh." Charlotte covered her face with embarrassment.

William chuckled pleasantly at her before greeting Malcolm.

"This," Kate said, "is Malcolm MacFarlane."

"Mr. MacFarlane," the king said to Malcolm's begrudging nod, "I saw your pistols in the antechamber. Remarkable. I'd say a brace of those equal the firepower of a sloop of war."

"They serve."

"Quite, quite." William narrowed his gaze at the Scotsman and turned with a bow to Imogen without the slightest hint that he found her mourning dress unusual. Her veil barely quivered in reaction. He motioned for everyone to resume their seats as he found a plain wooden chair. "First, I want to express my thanks again for your efforts at that horrible coronation. You have my gratitude, and that of Her Majesty the Queen as well."

"We did little enough," Kate said.

"Please, let's speak plainly, Miss Anstruther. There is no one here but I. And I know what you are."

"Sir?"

"Magicians, Miss Anstruther. Conjurers. Alchemists. Sorcerers and the like. That's why I sent for you. Those creatures who attacked the coronation were obviously not normal human beings, and they represent an extreme threat to this nation."

"We are endeavoring to meet that threat, sir," Kate said.

"I'm sure you are, I'm sure you are. But I require more than that. I am the king, and I must have access to all the resources that can protect my subjects and preserve order in the land and across our empire."

"Perhaps you should speak a bit more plainly, sir," Kate said with admirable clarity.

"Quite." The king was unaffected by the straight talk. He seemed quite content and sure of himself. "I want you and your colleagues here to serve the Crown. First, to hunt down those devils that threatened so many lives so recklessly at Westminster, and beyond that, to work to protect this realm from a growing occult threat. Is that plain enough?" The king's eyes twinkled like a playful uncle, but there was a hard political mind behind them.

"It is, sir." Kate raised her hand to Simon. "I must direct you to Mr. Archer as this band is his creation, in many ways."

William looked shocked. "Indeed? I've been told of you, Mr. Archer. Nothing in your background indicated great generalship in your nature. No offense."

"None taken, sir," Simon said. "I am generally known as something of a fatuous playboy."

"Something of?" The king slapped his knee. "The very definition of, I'd say. I had occasion to hear about you once from Lady Dunston at a garden party that went rather astray."

"Ah yes." Simon struggled to stay serious as Kate playfully scowled from behind the king. "Lady Dunston is a fine woman of uncommon . . . a fine woman."

"Yes." King William chortled, one man to another. "Quite fine. So what do you all say to my proposal?"

"We are eager," Simon said, "to protect the innocent, anywhere. If you are offering the resources of the Crown to that end, I'd say we are in business, Your Majesty."

"Excellent! Well said, sir! Your sovereign and your nation thank you." The king stood. "Now that we are agreed, I'd like to bring in another conspirator." He went to the door and motioned into the anteroom.

Grace North strode in and gave a perfunctory curtsy to the king.

Simon exchanged a concerned glance with Kate, who was already on her feet.

"This," King William said calmly, "is Grace North, as I'm sure you know. She has served as coordinator of the government's magical efforts since early in my reign. Are you acquainted?"

Grace looked typically angelic in yellow satin. "I am, Your Majesty, at least with Mr. Archer and Miss Anstruther." She was calm and professional, the model of a political actor.

"So, Mrs. North"—Simon caught Grace's gaze with false simplicity—"you recommended us to His Majesty?"

"I did, Mr. Archer." Grace took a position under a portrait of George III. "I perceive you are shocked to see me here, and I believe I know why. There are no secrets in this room. You are no doubt curious about my advocacy of Rowan Barnes and the disaster that resulted in the destruction of St. Mary Woolnoth."

"As well as a series of murders. You recall the Sacred Heart Murders?"

Grace gave Simon a cold glare that swiftly vanished. "His Majesty has been fully advised of that regrettable situation. I was supportive of Mr. Barnes because my magical advisors recommended him to me as the best solution to the Gaios problem. In hindsight, it was likely a mistake."

"Likely." Simon stared at the powerful and beautiful Mrs. North. At the very least this nationally beloved woman had supported a dangerous lunatic, Rowan Barnes, who had murdered several women for ritual purposes. She had championed his cause as patriotic and threatened Simon with destruction if he moved to stop Barnes. At worst, Grace North also knew Barnes had actually been the cat's-paw of the vile necromancer, Ash. And perhaps that wasn't the worst of it at all. Kate had observed Mrs. North at Westminster doing something that seemed to be magical, withering one of the apes and restoring the prime minister to health. In Grace North's eyes there was something deep and hidden, a cold blue secret. Or perhaps Simon was imagining it.

"Those advisors have been removed from service."

Kate said, "May we ask who those advisors were?"

Grace gave her an indulgent smile. "It was Lord Argyle."

Simon laughed harshly. "Are you serious?"

"I am," Grace replied coolly.

Kate looked nonplussed. "The Archdruid of the Mercury Club? That sherry-sotted reprobate was the Crown's magical expert?"

"Yes," King William said with embarrassment. "We are aware that he is not exactly Merlin. He has been cached, and I believe has since left England."

"Yes, Your Majesty," Grace said softly.

William continued to Kate, persisting with his opinion that she was the leader of the team. "That is why you are here today. As Mrs. North said, mistakes were made with this Barnes fellow. I regret I was not as active as I should have been, but that has changed. From this point forward, the Crown's magical agents will receive their orders from the Crown. No magical decisions will be made without royal approval. The only people who know about your existence are in this room today. And that is all who will ever know." He cast an eye on Grace.

She bowed in supplication.

"And so let's move on," said the king to Kate. "What are our options for running these frightful brigands to ground?"

"Miss Anstruther." Simon raised a finger. "I have an idea, if I may."

Kate looked at him evenly, pausing as if unsure she would deign to allow him to speak. Then, fighting her amusement, she gave him an excellent imperious silent nod for him to proceed.

Simon stretched out his legs, feeling suddenly quite comfortable with the highest of the high. "We need to draw them out, force them to fight on our terms. And they want one thing."

William scowled. "That would be me, sir."

"No, Your Majesty. What they wanted, I believe, is the Stone of Scone."

"Oh." The king looked a bit disappointed.

"Your coronation was their opportunity since the true Stone is rarely removed from the vault's protection. I assume the Stone has been returned to its place of safety."

King William rubbed his hands together, staring at the floor. He seemed hesitant to reply.

Simon sat forward. "Is there some problem with the Stone of Scone, sir?"

King William leaned against a table. He took a deep, contemplative breath. "Mr. Archer, I regret to tell you that we no longer have the true Stone."

"They succeeded in stealing it!" Kate exclaimed. "We should have been watching it, no matter the vault."

"No, Miss Anstruther." William calmed her. "We haven't had the true Stone for some years now."

"What?" Simon exclaimed loudly, then cleared his throat. "I mean, what do you mean, sir?"

The king exhaled. "The last time we were sure of the true Stone was my brother's coronation ten years ago. Then it was returned to the vault. When we went to retrieve it for my coronation last year upon my brother's death, our experts proclaimed the Stone in the vault to be a fake. Despite our best efforts to track it down, it has vanished."

Malcolm grunted from the corner. "Maybe it's gone back to Scotland where it belongs."

The king laughed at the irony. "Which is why we postponed my coronation for so long. It's said that there is power in the Stone that preserves the monarchy. But political pressures were such that we had to hold the ceremony. The Stone of Scone that I sat upon in Westminster was a fake we fashioned."

Simon looked at Kate. "Clearly, wherever the true Stone may be, Gaios doesn't have it. He doesn't know the Stone in Westminster is a fake. That may work to our advantage." He turned to the king. "Sir, what I propose is that you allow us to take your makeshift Stone. We can create a false story that the vault was damaged in their attack, and the Stone is being taken to another hiding spot. This will bring our miscreants out to seize it."

"It's our best option," Kate said.

"Well and good," King William replied. "You may have our Stone as bait. And when you encounter the monsters, deal with them." He stressed the final phrase.

"We need them," Simon said pointedly. "They may

have useful information to uncover a greater threat to Britain."

William's brow knitted with concern. "I'd prefer a permanent solution, for the safety of the monarchy, you understand."

"Then you've come to the wrong people, sir." Simon rose from his seat.

"I beg your pardon?" King William's voice was cold with sudden anger.

"I can assure you, Your Majesty, we are not timid in dealing with threats. We have eliminated many in the past, as Mrs. North will vouch. But in this matter you must trust my judgment. The powers we wield are too dangerous to be driven by mere political concerns. Forgive my bluntness, but we are not a cannon that you may aim as you will. We dare not become assassins for the Crown."

"Damn you, Archer, but you forget yourself. I am your king. You presume to stroll in off the dance floor and appreciate the welfare of this land better than I who have served it my entire life? You would dare tell *me* when the danger is sufficient for you to act?"

"That is the sum of it, sir."

The king was red-faced, nearly sputtering. "Are you mad? These monsters who struck at Westminster would kill you or anyone without a pause for breath."

Imogen's strange voice seeped out from behind her veil. "But we're not like them. We're not monsters."

A silence fell on the room. Simon watched the stern face of William as the king regarded Imogen with angry curiosity. Kate took Imogen's hand and smiled. Malcolm seemed relaxed now, and he nodded at Imogen with a look of respect. Charlotte was the only one nervous.

Finally the king shook his head and cleared his throat quietly. "Well said, miss. I am content for now to leave the . . . details of the situation in your very capable hands." He indicated Grace North and Kate. "And I will leave you to it."

"Oh!" came the alarmed cry from Charlotte. "Are you leaving? Is the princess here today? Victoria? I had hoped to see her."

King William smiled and bent at the waist to be closer to Charlotte's worried face. "She is not, I fear. But I know that she would enjoy having you to tea at some point."

"Oh yes!" Charlotte cried. "Today?"

"No, dear." Kate pressed down on the hopping girl's shoulder. "Not today. We are grateful to wait on an invitation from the princess."

The king said, "Your monarch thanks you all. Even you, Mr. MacFarlane. Needless to say, once you have dealt with these troublemakers, we would very much like for you to find the true Stone and return it to us."

Malcolm crossed his arms in silence.

William laughed nervously. "Mrs. North, I'll expect a full report later today."

When the door closed, Grace showed a much colder visage, assuming control of the room. She turned to Simon. "Shall we get down to business?"

Chapter 5

"NICK BARKER!" REBECCA SHOUTED WHEN NICK entered the Devil's Loom with a strange companion. The barmaid hardly spared a glance to Nick's tall hunched friend as she bustled toward him with arms outstretched and gathered the stocky man into a sweaty embrace. "First Simon and now you. I wish you two lads would come back together."

Nick accepted her wet kiss on his cheek. "Simon is so jealous of me and how you love me."

"Oh, I've bosom enough for both of you, should you care to try."

Nick nodded approvingly in confirmation of her statement. "For now, two ales will do."

The two men found a back bench. The crowd was thin because it was early. The ambient conversation had finally turned back to parish gossip and turf racing. What happened in far-off Westminster was nearly as distant to these folk as news from India or China.

Nick studied the crowd for a familiar face as he drank. He spoke to his companion out of the corner of his mouth. "Mind you keep near me, old boy. I can't keep the glamour spell on you if you move too far away. In fact, don't move about much at all. More chance for people to see the blur in the glamour. It's hard enough casting it on someone else to begin with."

Simon sat back with the peculiar feeling of looking exactly like himself as far as he was concerned. "Would it help to drink more of that potion of yours?"

"No. The potion's only part of it."

"Good. It's terrible." Simon rose slightly and caught sight of himself in the mirror behind the bar. He was a huge man with a jowly ruddy face and a very noticeable mole square on his nose. He was peculiarly long and hunched like a gargoyle. He waved to himself, laughing at the experience of the strange arm in the glass moving with his own muscular forearm.

"Sit down," Nick hissed. "And stop waving at yourself, you great horse. Have you forgotten everything I taught you?"

"I didn't forget how to avoid getting savagely beaten by a group of undead."

Nick grunted in mild annoyance. "There was a brick involved. Let me hit you with a brick and see how it works for you."

Simon continued to look at himself in the reflection. "Could you have made me any uglier? Was a leper beyond your ability?"

"Just shut it." Nick continued to study the shifting crowd. "You get to be Satanically handsome all your days. A bit of plainness won't kill you. Lets you know how the other half lives."

"I don't see Tommy." Simon took unobtrusive glances about the room. Then he found himself staring again in the mirror. "I hear he used to have a talking monkey."

"He did. Nice enough. Utterly filthy. Just remember, keep quiet. I'll do the talking. Me and Tommy were mates once. And it's very important this be handled with subtlety and grace." Nick suddenly sprang to his feet and waved his arm. "Oy! Tommy! Over here, mate!"

A heavyset man at the far end of the bar turned to peer through the crowd. He looked to be about sixty years old and wore a very old-fashioned summer suit from a generation ago. Old magicians, among their greater failings, had difficulty keeping up with fashion. He narrowed his eyes in the dim room, then pulled back his head in surprised recognition. He grabbed his glass of beer and came over.

"Tommy!" Nick stood and shook the man's hand vigorously. "Fancy seeing you here."

"I'm always here. I used to see you here all the time."

"I know." Nick pointed at Simon. "This is my best mate, Sim . . . uh . . . Mac . . . Clydesdale."

"MacClydesdale?" Tommy repeated.

"Um. Aye." Simon pushed out a chair with his foot, trying to cover his mix of anger and amusement that they had forgotten to craft a name for his new persona. "It's Scottish."

"Sounds fake." Tommy creaked into the seat.

Simon stayed quiet and regarded Nick cheerfully for the timely clever response.

Nick leaned close to Tommy with a finger over his lips. "Shhh. You know how it is with names."

"Oh right." Tommy winked. "Where's the bloke you used to come in with? That dandy."

Nick made an annoyed growl in his throat. "You mean Archer?"

"Yes. That's the name." Tommy noted the scowl on Nick's face. "What became of him? He seemed a right poser."

Simon shifted grumpily in his chair.

"I gave him the boot," Nick snarled. "He was so full of himself. Got intolerable." He tapped his glass against Tommy's with a refreshed smile. "So what's new with you, mate?"

"Nothing much."

The table went silent. A minute passed. The fat man drank and wiped his mouth. Simon raised smug eyebrows, enjoying Nick's perturbed face as the man drummed his fingers on the table and took a long breath. Simon crossed his arms like a spectator.

"So," Nick began again, "that was some coronation the other day, eh?"

Tommy shrugged and drank his beer.

Nick rested on his elbow and exhaled. "I remember you being a bit more chatty."

Tommy gave a direct stare. "I remember you not being marked for death by Ash."

Nick tilted his head in surprise. "You know about that, do you?"

"Of course. I could make a lot of money if I let certain people know where you are."

Nick grew cold and hard. His voice was quiet. "You needing money that bad, mate?"

"No." The fat man turned, his voice quavering a bit.

"Good. Let's get to it. I'm looking for Ferghus O'Malley."

"Are you?" Tommy's eyes shot to Simon, then back to Nick. "What've I to do with that?"

"I need cover from the other side. But I haven't seen Ferghus in years. Not since the Fire. I'm not sure how he'd take to me. I'd appreciate a word to him. You two were always close."

Tommy chuckled without mirth. "Oh yes, the Fire. He went away after that. And you walked."

"I had nothing to do with it."

"Sure, Nick. You never have nothing to do with anything. Not sure he sees it that way."

"Look, I'm not coming empty-handed. I'm bearing a gift." Nick leaned close and lowered his voice. "Tell him they're moving the Stone of Scone."

Tommy paused midsip. He swallowed nervously. "What's that to me?"

"I don't care what it is to you. It's something to Ferghus. Trust me. In two days, they're taking the Stone from the vault in Westminster and hiding it in an old storage pit under one of the piers of old London Bridge."

"That's interesting."

"Yeah, it is, and it's free to Ferghus. I just hope he'll see his way clear to help out an old mate in these times of trouble."

Tommy asked quietly, "How did you come by this information?"

Nick took a breath. "Tell the truth, it was from Archer. I still see him around and he still thinks we're mates. He told me all about it. He was involved in that row at Westminster. Working for the Crown now like a proper little soldier. Makes me sick."

Tommy slugged back the last of the ale and slammed down his glass. He gave Nick a collegial nod. "Thanks for the drink, Nick, and the chat. Pleasure, Mr. MacClydesdale."

Simon sat quietly until he felt a kick in the shins. "Oh! Yes. Pleasure was mine."

The fat man shoved his bulk up with a suspicious glance at Simon. He shook Nick's hand again and waddled out.

"Right." Nick watched the door until it shut. "That's well done."

Simon leaned on the table with an exasperated glare. "*Proper little soldier,* eh? So you were mates with Ferghus O'Malley too? You were with him the night of the Great Fire? How did you neglect to mention that?"

Nick motioned for more beer. "Must you always dwell on the past, MacClydesdale? I knew a lot of people. I'm old and social." He straightened with surprise. "Oy. It's the missus."

Simon turned to see Kate weaving through the crowd

with a determined look. He shot to his feet. "What's wrong?"

"This came to Hartley Hall this morning." She held out a piece of paper to Simon.

He took the sheet. "How do you do that? How do you see through Nick's spell?"

Kate sat in the chair vacated by Tommy, looking Simon up and down curiously. "I've always been able to see through Barker's glamour; he uses cheap potions. Nice mole."

Nick sputtered angrily. "That's a load of rubbish. My magic is solid. You're the only one who ever saw through it."

Kate rolled her eyes as she intercepted Simon's fresh beer and started drinking it.

Simon's eyes scanned the paper and he let it drop to his side. "Well, that's unexpected. A note from Ash."

Nick spun in alarm. "What?"

"Easy, old man. It's not about you. Ash wants to see me." Simon pulled his half-empty glass from Kate as she wiped foam from her mouth. He picked up his hat and took her arm. "I suppose we should go. How did you know where to find me?"

Kate rolled her eyes at the question. "Since I've known you, you're only ever three places. My house. Your house. Or this pub."

Simon stared deep into her eyes. "Not exactly a man of mystery, am I?"

"No. You're like an old married man."

He moved close to her and whispered, "That won't do."

Kate gave an expectant smile and they started for the door.

THE STARS PULSED OVERHEAD. A WARM BREEZE rustled the leaves with scents of the blooms, the last thick fragrances before the sharp bite of autumn. Simon and Kate posted along a wagon trail. Kate's wolfhound, Aethelred, raced ahead of them, enjoying his freedom. Beyond a distant copse of trees, they heard muffled chatter and laughter. A small village enjoyed a soft night, delaying their bedtimes for a few moments of pleasure.

Kate's red stallion moved like a ship before the wind, tall and strong, unmindful of any around him. Simon wrestled with his fitful grey Arabian mare, which Kate delighted to saddle him with. He found the horse spirited, game to be sure, but angry and likely to bite. Kate glanced back from her perch some four hands above him. She hid a smile.

"I'm still here," Simon called cheerfully. "Don't fret. Your hellish mare hasn't eaten me yet."

"Good to see you haven't lost your touch with the ladies then."

A lascivious eyebrow rose at her. "Only one lady matters to me."

Her smile flashed brilliantly at him in the moonlight. She turned forward and her good mood faded with what lay ahead of them. "You should have worn your armor, Galahad. We don't know what we're walking into."

Simon patted the side of the saddle where his walking stick was wedged. "I didn't come unarmed. And besides, I'm not afraid of Ash. Clearly she still wants me for *her* Galahad."

"You're already taken. You'd think she'd have figured that out by now."

Kate's claiming tone started a warming heat inside Simon. He stared at her ramrod-straight back and curvaceous hips. "Yes, it seems unlike her to beat a dead horse. No pun intended. Why would she have sent a note to meet with us otherwise?"

"I don't know. I could live happily never talking to

Ash again. She makes my skin crawl. Just thinking how she groped me when she was animating Rowan Barnes." Kate shuddered.

"I understand. You need not have come. But it's important to speak to her tonight while we have a moment. Tomorrow, we should have our equipment from the Crown and we'll move."

They rounded a corner to see a figure before them twisting in the wind. The body of a man hung from a roadside gallows, hands tied behind his back. His head drooped on a broken neck. His eyes were open and staring at the dark ground below his bare feet. As he turned slowly about, a note was revealed pinned to his shirt: *Housebreaker.*

Aethelred dropped to a crouch and growled, his hackles rising along his spine. Simon rode closer and the stench of death ruined the late-summer sweetness. He could tell from the color and taut dryness of the face that the man had been hanging several days at least.

Kate reined in, listening to the sound of merriment beyond the trees. "Will they not cut him down at least?"

"Doubtful. I'm surprised resurrectionists didn't take him; we're not so far from London. But he's no good to the surgeon now."

"Barbaric." Kate scowled. "Executing men and women and leaving them hanging like worthless meat."

"I was a housebreaker," came a dry voice from the gibbet.

Kate started and her horse reacted to her, neighing and clattering his hooves on the rocky path. The dog lunged at the cadaver's dangling heels.

Simon looked up at the hanged man. "I beg your pardon?"

The dead countenance slowly revolved toward them with the creaking of the rope. As starlight hit the grey features, milky eyes moved. The lips quivered. "I said, I was a housebreaker. I struck a man with a maul, nearly killing him. And I stole silver from him." The corpse continued to rotate. "I deserve to be here."

Kate narrowed her eyes. "It isn't a matter of your character; it's a matter of ours."

"You're arguing with a dead man," Simon interrupted. "That's pointless enough, but there's even less point in arguing with Ash."

Kate grunted in annoyance at being drawn out by the reanimated presence of the vile necromancer.

The hanging cadaver seemed to chuckle though it came out more of a strangled gurgle. "I'm glad you found me, Archer."

Simon took a deep breath and clenched his teeth. He tried not to think of his poor mother. Finally, he said, "The note you sent to Hartley Hall was fairly specific, Ash. Couldn't you simply come by and speak as yourself?"

"I haven't survived for centuries by letting others know my true identity. I called you out here because London is full of spies. I trust no one."

"Even me?" Simon asked, coolly covering any reaction.

The cadaver moved quietly in the breeze. "We need to work together to bring Gaios down."

"Why?"

"You know his agents are seeking the Stone of Scone. He wants its power."

Simon feigned surprised interest. "For what purpose?"

"I don't know, but it must serve his goal to destroy me. Don't delude yourself, however. He won't be satisfied with my death. Once I'm gone, he will mow through the magicians of this world like a thresher. He'll come for you and your people eventually because he fears power. And he's quite insane. You have no idea the carnage he is capable of wreaking."

"I do actually. He's reputed to have caused the eruption of Vesuvius."

"Which is true, and he did it in a mere fit of pique. A temper tantrum that doomed thousands. His insanity is why Pendragon imprisoned him in the Bastille. Unfortunately the dim-witted mob freed him and his vile allies. That terrible moment cost Pendragon his life."

"Gaios killed Pendragon?"

"He did." The cadaver tried to nod for emphasis. "In Paris. He killed Pendragon, and tried to kill me. With one stroke he shattered the old Order of the Oak, which the three of us had founded centuries before. But it cost him. Gaios went into hiding, sending his Bastille Bastards around the world to do his bidding, waiting for the time when he would unleash his vengeance on me."

"Why you?" Kate asked sharply. "If Pendragon was his gaoler, and he had settled that debt, what's his quarrel with you?"

The hanged man was caught in the wind and began to swing faster. "I was Pendragon's lover. Our great love threatened Gaios. He always feared we would join forces against him and take the Order of the Oak as our own."

Simon spun the mare, trying to bring the restless horse under control. "Where is your Order now? Where are all the great magicians to help you?"

"Gone." The corpse's laugh was like dust from a tomb. "All of them cowards. Or dead. Gaios winnowed them in the years after Pendragon's fall and drove others into hiding. He hated many, including your father, Miss Anstruther. If Sir Roland had cooperated with me, we might have exterminated Gaios, but your father refused my proffered hand."

Kate smiled with satisfaction.

"You Anstruthers never change," the cadaver said.

"Proud and ultimately pointless. How is dear Imogen? There is an example of Gaios's handiwork that your father could have prevented."

"Shut up!" Kate twisted her riding crop in her hands. "Don't ever mention my sister's name."

"Dr. White abused her, broke her, mutilated her into an inhuman thing. The doctor was under Gaios's command. Gaios has no respect for humanity."

Kate pressured her horse with her knee and faced him away from the groaning cadaver, back toward the way they had come.

Simon said, "That's odd talk coming from the mouth of a reanimated murderer."

"Archer, you know we are different. We're magicians. We aren't truly human. Most magicians choose to hide, but some, like Gaios, prey on the weak. And some, like us, protect the weak from such predators."

"Like *us*?" Simon laughed.

"We may be allies of convenience," the dead man said, "but we are allies nonetheless. We must band together or we will be obliterated separately."

"You surely know that I have been banished from the aether. I have no power for you to exploit. Do you have a scheme to stop Gaios that doesn't require magic?"

"There are ways to make you what you were, Archer. There are ways to reconnect to the aether. I have spent these last few months since our encounter with Ra studying the possibilities. You see, when I was reanimating Rowan Barnes, I lost some of my powers when the filthy magic-eater touched him. However, I found a way back, and I can bring you along that same path too. Look closer at my condemnation."

Kate looked at Simon, confused. Then she heard the note pinned to the cadaver's chest fluttering in the breeze. *Housebreaker.* Kate nudged her horse closer to the dead man as Simon's hand slipped to his cane's handle. She took the paper carefully, pulling out the heavy needle that fastened it to the shirt. She flipped the paper over and gasped.

Simon rode closer because Kate sat in the saddle staring down with intense concentration. When he drew near, he could see the sheet wasn't simple paper. It was vellum. It had once been a scroll and appeared quite old. The vellum was crowded with handwritten words in peculiar script.

"Medieval?" he asked.

"German. Probably ninth-century." She nodded without looking up. "It's blood magic."

The cadaver said, "It is called the Womb of Schattenwald. It will restore your magic, Archer. It is my gift to you."

"I don't practice blood magic," Simon replied icily.

"I can instruct you."

"I mean I *won't* do it."

"It's your only way. Without your powers, you stand no chance against Gaios. He will kill you and everyone and everything you love. Only blood has the power to open the road to the aether. You have been changed by some of the most powerful magic in history."

"So a little blood will wipe away the magic of Ra? I find that hard to believe."

"A *little* blood? No."

Simon growled, "Do you truly believe I would lower myself to sacrifice some innocent just to regain my powers?"

"Not some innocent." The hanged man swung silently in his noose for a moment until dead eyes fell on Kate. "It must be the blood of someone who loves you."

Simon shouted in sudden rage. His hand swept up with a flash of steel and he sliced the cadaver through the neck. The dry thing's body parted just under the jaw and the torso dropped to the ground. The head tumbled through the night air to fall into the grass and roll a few feet against a rock. Aethelred pounced forward, barking loudly at it.

Simon stood in his stirrups, chest heaving, trying to determine if he would trample the body into dust. The fact that he was thinking about it meant he wouldn't do it. He reined his horse back and dropped his sword arm. His voice was ragged with anger. "Kate, destroy that damned thing and let's go."

"I think we should keep it," Kate said.

"What?" Simon turned to her in surprise.

"Spells can be refashioned." Her gaze fell on the German script again with undisguised curiosity. "We should study it."

"Kate, it's from Ash."

"We can't be afraid of her." She glanced up at Simon. "That seems like something you would have said once."

Simon said nothing now. It wasn't that he didn't trust Kate, or even himself for that matter, but magic this black had a way of tainting any who even touched it. It was why he had always cautioned Nick about using necromancy. With power that vile, control was an illusion. And now they were bringing *it* into their home, bringing *Ash* into their home. They might as well bring in Satan himself.

He kicked his mount into a gallop up the dark road. They rode the way they had come, with the diminishing sounds of late-summer frolic in the background.

Chapter 6

AN ARMORED WAGON CREAKED LABORIOUSLY down the street despite the fact that a brace of powerful steeds pulled it. The bed was tented with steel plates, hiding some sort of unseen cargo. The wagon attracted attention and, even though the moon hung high in the sky, gawking traffic was thick along Borough High Street. London never slept.

From the wagon's bench, Simon scanned the shifting masses clogging the streets around them. Beneath his dark frock coat he wore a breastplate, and he hid his hands with their steel gauntlets under a blanket. Beside him, Nick maneuvered the team around a broken-down cart and continued east. To their rear rode Malcolm on a stocky black Friesian, while Kate rode a steady bay gelding ahead on their right. She was dressed as a man, her long auburn hair braided and stuffed under a tweed cap.

A voice came from behind Simon as a head popped out of a small hatch in the top of the wagon's iron chamber. "Are we there yet? It's hot in here and I'm sticky from that stuff Miss Kate smeared on me."

"We're all sticky, Charlotte." Simon reached back and opened another plate section to allow more air inside. "Not long now. You're not standing on the Stone of Scone, are you?"

There was a lengthy pause. "No."

Simon's eyebrow rose. Behind Charlotte inside the wagon was Penny, mopping her brow. She pulled the child back inside with a halfhearted scolding. "That stone is a relic!"

"But you said it was a—"

"Hush now." Penny shook her head as Charlotte folded her arms crossly and glared at the young woman.

Imogen gave a low giggle from the shadows.

Simon turned away, smiling at their affable antics, but his expression turned serious quickly enough. His eyes scanned the dark streets around them. It was quite possible they were being watched. The enemy was likely waiting for the perfect opportunity to strike.

London Bridge appeared through the waterfront factories and warehouses. Actually, there were two London Bridges and it was the glorious new bridge with its high wide arches that came into view first. It had only been open a month and was still pristine with flags flying from its pinnacles. Wagons and pedestrians flowed over its new stonework.

Just downstream, like a forgotten less successful sibling, was Old London Bridge. The empty bridge was set to be demolished in just a few months. The roar of water rushing between its arches could already be heard. At the base of the bridge's stone piers, every piling was surrounded by a veritable wooden island, or starling, which narrowed the space for the river to flow under the bridge into cramped sluices. During low tide, as was now approaching, water upstream of the bridge was six feet higher than down, and the river became dreadful falling rapids as it thundered through the constricting arches.

There was no movement on the old bridge as Nick guided the wagon toward it, which made Simon nervous. Sweat rolled down his chest under the steel breastplate. "Are you sure Tommy got the word out?"

"You doubt my ability to spread gossip?"

"About a loose woman, no. About a rock, yes."

"Have no fear."

Simon leapt down and unlocked an iron gate that blocked access to the bridge. Kate held her nervous horse in check as it pranced past. Simon waved Nick on, and his friend expertly drove the wagon through. After Malcolm passed, Simon quickly closed and locked the gate.

The wagon rolled up to a gap cut into the balustrades, which was the entrance to the cofferdam that sat in the water between the old and new bridges. It was a circular island made of upright timbers lashed tightly together. From it rose tall poles that had once held pile-driving machines for breaking the foundation for the new bridge. A stretched canvas awning covered it and the bright colors of the flag billowed in the wind that swept boldly down the river.

Union Jacks atop the cofferdam snapped stiffly in the breeze and startled Kate's bay gelding, but she kept her seat admirably and turned the shying horse away from the noise. Malcolm's mount barely batted an eye at the commotion, large hooves clopping over the stones. The big Friesian's calm demeanor soothed the bay. Malcolm's attention, however, was on the far end of the bridge.

Simon thought at first the vibrations he felt came from Malcolm's massive horse. However, when the mounts stopped moving, he still sensed the thuds through the soles of his shoes. It felt like the rhythmic pounding of pile drivers, but Simon knew for a fact that the equipment had been dismantled.

"What in holy hell is that thing?" Simon stared off the eastern side of the bridge.

Penny poked her head out of the wagon and followed his gaze. Her jaw dropped. "It's . . . beautiful."

A dark leviathan rose from the water. Spindly legs worked like long pistons adjusting for the river's depth. At their tips were diamond-shaped daggers that drove down one after another as the strange machine approached the bridge, practically flowing in a mechanized process.

The rotund body of the machine rivaled their wagon in size. Inside a bulbous eye of convex glass could be seen intricate gears that moved and whirred like a massive brain. Tubes jutted from various spots on the body, but all gathered up behind the eye, where they vented clouds of hot vapor.

Penny gasped at the alien nature of the contraption. Where Penny's creations resembled actual life, this did not. She climbed out and stood atop the wagon. Imogen clamored up beside her.

The mecha creature drew close with a uniform clicking and huffing sound. It waded against the torrent of water pouring through the arches. A single long jointed arm extended from the body and grabbed hold of a stone pier with three tendril-like fingers. The machine began to climb out of the river. The pointed diamond legs impaled the stone, adjusting again for the new terrain. It moved like a centipede, legs rolling forward in a sequential motion as each one grabbed or pushed itself over the uneven surface until it landed atop the bridge. The machine squatted slightly as pistons relaxed and stilled. The great pipes vented a torrent of steam. The machine waited.

Kate snapped her crossbow open and slid from the saddle. Malcolm swung off his mount too and they slapped their horses' hindquarters to urge them out of harm's way. He quickly unhitched the team from the wagon and sent them clattering off.

"At least they waited until we got here, as I hoped," Simon said. "I didn't want to risk innocent lives in this mad gamble."

"What about our lives?" muttered Malcolm.

"You have never been innocent," Simon pointed out.

With a grunt Malcolm drew his weapon. "The Irishman is here."

The outline of a figure could be seen in the darkness walking toward them from Fish Street Hill on the north end of the bridge. The horses trotted past him, wandering through the demolished gate into the city. The steeple of St. Magnus the Martyr rose into the night sky behind the approaching man. There was no mistaking the glowing aura of fire surrounding Ferghus O'Malley. They were trapped between the elemental and the strange machine.

"Good evening, Mr. O'Malley," Simon greeted the Irishman pleasantly.

Ferghus leveled a hard stare through blazing red eyes. "We weren't expecting resistance at Westminster. That's not the case tonight."

"What? No pleasant chitchat before fisticuffs?" Simon sighed.

"I'm here for one thing only and since you've been so obliging as to deliver it, I'll take it and go."

Simon shook his head. "That won't be happening."

"Bloody hell," cursed an agitated Malcolm. "Let's just fight."

"I agree with Scotty," snarled Ferghus. The flame coating on his hands flared.

"With pleasure then." Simon shouted orders. "Nick! Go with Kate, Malcolm, and Imogen! Penny, Charlotte, with me on the machine."

In a billow of white vapor, the weird mechanical thing lifted a leg and slammed forward, impaling the bridge with a seismic shudder. One leg after another lifted like daggers and the behemoth came at them.

Penny raced after Simon, pulling the stovepipe cannon from her back and shouldering the long tube. "What's the plan?"

"I need you to determine that thing's weakness."

Penny gave a faint laugh. "Oh, is that all?"

"You're our best shot at bringing it down."

The machine clattered nearer, towering over them. Simon suddenly felt like David against Goliath. He had to remind himself that the young giant-killer had needed nothing but a stone.

Simon slipped a canister into Penny's blunderbuss as she dropped to one knee and took aim. She let the shell fly. It struck the glass eye true and the explosion rocked the creature back on its rear legs, pistons whining madly. When the smoke cleared, it stood upright again with nary a crack in the glass.

"Well, that ain't good." Penny bit her lip in frustration as she scrutinized the thing, seeking a chink in its complex armor.

Simon asked, "You think the glass eye is the way to go?"

"It's all I have at the moment," she admitted.

"Then we need to get you inside of it."

Penny brightened at the prospect of getting up close to such an incredible machine. "Sure, but how?"

Simon pushed the blunderbuss's muzzle down. Penny gaped at him, but then just as suddenly relished the idea. Simon loaded another shell and she fired at the spot where the monstrosity stood. Stones flew and the machine tottered, then tumbled into a cavernous crater. Penny let out a whoop of triumph until long fingers curled around the parapet, and it hauled itself back onto the bridge.

"That thing is more agile than I gave it credit for." Simon scowled.

"Now what?" Penny looked at him expectantly.

"Keep firing until something breaks."

A long steel leg lifted over them and they dove in opposite directions. It struck the spot they had just occupied in a shower of stone and rubble. Simon stretched his fingers, bringing a small charge of electricity to arc across his gauntlets. He reached out to grab the steel leg, which was the size of a tree trunk. Spiders of electricity crawled out over the metal, but they seemed to find no purchase and dissipated.

"The Baroness insulated this too!" Penny shouted. "Bloody genius! Look out!"

A shadow loomed over Simon as another leg lifted. He rolled aside again, but jammed against a pile of rubble. He tried to get to his feet, but he knew he wouldn't be fast enough. A blur of grey fur collided with him, carrying him beyond the impact. They tumbled to a stop.

"Thank you, Charlotte," he gasped as soon as he caught his breath. They were under the machine and the heat of the engine felt like the mouth of an erupting volcano. "Look for a way inside. A hatch. A seam. Anything. Make one if you have to."

Charlotte howled with far too much enthusiasm. She leapt, her powerful haunches propelling her straight up onto one of the legs swinging overhead. She crouched and another leap sent her atop the bulging head. Her claws struggled to find purchase on its smooth surface. Then Simon lost sight of her.

Another wash of flame made Simon's skin prickle. It came from behind him on the north end of the bridge.

* * *

KATE DODGED A BOLT OF FLAME. SHE WAS SWEATing in the scorching heat. The canvas over the cofferdam was ablaze and lit the entire area. She wasn't able to get close enough to Ferghus to do anything. She followed Malcolm's example and tried to shoot the fire elemental, but the man was wise to fighting such weapons. He continually erected a flash heat shield in front of him. Swift lead balls turned to slow worthless chunks of slag.

"Come on, you cowards!" Ferghus's words slurred slightly. "Or I'll burn you where you stand."

Kate's brow furrowed. "The man's bloody drunk."

"That should make things easier." Malcolm fired off another round.

"It makes him more dangerous, not less," Nick said. "He burned down London in one of his drunken rages."

"I'm not drunk enough for that, Barker, you lying sack of offal," Ferghus spat. "But I'll welcome turning your corpse to ash and raise a dram about it later." The flame from one of the flickering gas lamps jumped to his hand and a blast of fire burst from his fingertips toward Kate. She dove to the ground under the blistering stream, but it was hot enough to catch her long coat. She slapped at it frantically, but the fire would not go out. Ferghus's laughter rang in her ears. Her hands fumbled on her bandolier as the flames licked at her waist. Nick stood over her and, to her amazement, the flames fled from her clothes to his hand. He threw the ball of flame coiling across his palm into the river.

Ferghus unleashed a torrent of fire at the two of them. Kate cried out, but Nick didn't flinch. He held up both hands and the flames split around them. He swung his arms and the flames gathered on him. Kate scrambled away as Nick became wreathed in fire. He continued pulling the flames away from Ferghus, but Kate could see the ferocious strain on him. Nick had not used her fire gel because he often used flame as a weapon, but she feared he would be consumed by it. He was adept at most mystic arts, but a true master of none. Ferghus had been a fire elemental for centuries.

Kate shot a vial at the Irishman as he struggled to regain control of his flames. Black treacle splashed him in a dark sticky shroud. He shouted in surprise. Nick let loose the flames straight back at Ferghus. The man caught fire. Kate gasped. She hadn't expected that, but her treacle was a tar-based substance. However, the flames did nothing to Ferghus. He laughed, wild-eyed, his form shimmering in the heat. He leveled another ball of fire at her.

Kate ran and dove for shelter in one of the stone alcoves that lined the parapets of the bridge. She slammed her back against the wall of the domed niche as the flames curved around it. The hair on her skin seared off and the fire stole the oxygen around her.

Abruptly the vacuum was gone and Kate sucked in a deep hot breath. The retort of Malcolm's pistols sounded. She dared to peer out and saw Nick on his hands and knees, looking spent. Malcolm was covering him as best he could.

Imogen moved awkwardly toward Ferghus. The flames illuminated her black mourning clothes. She unbuttoned her right cuff and pulled the sleeve up over her elbow. From the ghastly white skin of her forearm rose a host of thin filaments, some six inches long, wavering in the firelight. The young woman halted and swept her arm in front of her, sending several of the strange quills flying toward the Irishman. The needles never reached him because Ferghus's heat shield rose again and the filaments virtually melted out of the air. The strange specter of the veiled Imogen distracted Ferghus enough, however, that he turned away from Kate.

With fingers that felt tight from the heat, Kate pulled free the canister at her hip. She ran at Ferghus, pulling the top and pointing the canister at the mad elemental. Her hat tumbled from her head and her long braid swung free. She pressed a trigger and the cylinder sprayed a wide stream of clear gelatinous goo that hit Ferghus in the back. The canister moved up and down, coating him. He turned, dripping, with burning hands and brutal eyes. She prayed there was enough left in the canister as she aimed for his chest. She pressed the lever. The substance whooshed out and splashed over him. The flames rising from his fingers smoldered out. Ferghus stared at his hands in confusion.

"Now!" she shouted.

Imogen loosed a single quill, which struck Ferghus in the neck. Malcolm tackled him, and the two men tumbled across the bridge. The Irishman grabbed Malcolm's coat with slippery hands and tried to ignite it. He yelled angrily as his powers failed him. His limbs slowed as his strength faded. He flopped to the ground weakly as Imogen's toxin hit his system. Malcolm reared back an elbow and struck Ferghus in the face. The Irishman was so drunk he didn't feel it. Blood poured from his mouth, but he just grinned through it. Ferghus crashed his fist into Malcolm's cheek.

Nick came up behind Ferghus and slammed a chunk of stone against Ferghus's head. The Irishman slumped over, unconscious.

* * *

SIMON DODGED THE MASSIVE MECHANICAL ARM as it tore off a section of the balustrade larger than their wagon and chucked it at Penny. She aimed her blunderbuss at it and fired. The flying stone shattered as she ducked under the dust and shrapnel.

Charlotte called down from somewhere atop the mechanized beast. "No way in!" Then she had to dodge aside as the arm swiped for her. It struck the top of the machine and dented it. Charlotte eagerly renewed tearing at that section of the metal.

Simon threw one of Kate's vials at the creature's legs as it swept past. Mist swirled and hardened, encasing it in a block of amber. The crawler stumbled, but steadied itself quickly. The arm reached down and the segmented fingers examined the rock-hard substance. The tentacle-like appendages then crushed it to dust. The arm slammed down onto the ground and brought everyone to their hands and knees. The bridge cracked, a line racing down its length. It groaned, shifting from side to side. The machine headed straight for the wagon. Penny started to intercept it.

"Fall back!" Simon ordered. Penny paused but then moved to his side.

Mechanical fingers seized the armored wagon in a crushing grip, lifting it as if it were but a child's toy. The steel groaned and bent inward but the three-hundred-pound stone inside didn't fall out. Then the machine's head swiveled on some sort of axis to face behind it, and it scuttled toward the western side of the bridge.

"Charlotte!" Simon shouted at the figure still attacking the machine. "Get off!"

Charlotte either didn't hear him or was too enveloped by her rage to take note of what was happening. Simon took off in the wake of the machine and saw Kate angling toward them. She was focused on Charlotte high above so he assumed that meant Ferghus was captured or dead.

With its prize in hand, the machine strode straight to the balustrade and crashed through the rail, sending massive stones into the river. Its forward legs whirred and stretched out to the new bridge upstream. People who had been crowding the rail there shouted and scattered before the steel barbs slammed down among them. Horses reared and screeched. Wagons careened into chaotic mobs. Charlotte dug in her claws to maintain her grip as the machine tilted suddenly and winched itself over the water. Its legs continued to work furiously, lumbering over the new bridge, breaking flagpoles and smashing lampposts. Then it dropped off the far side into the swirling Thames. The machine began to wade forward, lowering into the dark water.

Only when a wave suddenly splashed against her did Charlotte look up from ferociously pounding on the machine. She climbed higher atop the thing's head.

"Does she know how to swim?" Malcolm asked anxiously, rushing to the broken balustrade.

"No!" Imogen cried out. "We have to get to her!"

The machine was submerging. The werewolf looked back at their distant figures, her molten yellow eyes reflecting her sudden terror. She flinched as wave after wave crashed over her, almost dislodging her.

"She'll drown if she stays there." Malcolm's normally steady tone rose in alarm.

"Jump, Charlotte," Simon shouted, hoping her keen hearing would pick up his cry. He already had a leg over the edge when Nick grabbed him.

"What do you think you are doing? You can't swim out to her. You're wearing bloody armor."

"I don't intend to, but the current will bring her back to us. I can grab her."

"If she isn't dragged under first!"

Simon glared back at him firmly asking, "Can you swim?"

Nick shook his head. "No."

"Then we have to hope Charlotte's lycanthropy gives her the strength to stay afloat until she gets to us." Simon climbed over the rail and lowered himself down onto a stone pier.

Charlotte cried out in fear, glancing at the water that was now at her knees.

"Simon will grab you as you come past," shouted Kate, signaling the girl to come toward them.

"Kick for all you're worth," Imogen encouraged her. The young woman's veil was off, and fear drenched her white features.

Charlotte hesitated, but only for a moment as the water closed in around her waist. With her last purchase of solid ground, she jumped back toward the bridges. She landed with a great splash fifty feet upriver from the new bridge. She was now below their line of sight, so they all crowded lower to peer through its high arches.

Simon climbed down farther. He crouched on the broad top of the piling with the frothing water just a few feet below him. He watched the oddly small shape of the werewolf flailing in the water. Poor Charlotte was getting dunked over and over, her long muscular arms paddling madly. The current shoved her against the arch of the new bridge, smashing her into the slick stones. She scrabbled with her claws, gouging deep lines in the wet walls, but always bouncing back into the flow.

She emerged from beneath the far bridge. Kate gasped loudly as Charlotte went under the dark brown water. There was a deafening silence as everyone held their breath, waiting for her to surface again. Finally, her head burst into the air, her arms flailing madly.

Simon judged which side of the pier the current would take her. His steel fingers dug into the stone above him. Malcolm reached to grab his other arm. Nick was behind him, anchoring Malcolm. Should Simon catch Charlotte's heavy form, there was real danger they would all be dragged into the churning river. The turbulent water roared through the narrow arch and over a drop of at least six feet into the swirling currents on the downstream side of the bridge. Even in a sturdy craft, only the bravest and most foolhardy riverman would dare "shoot the bridge."

The young werewolf rushed toward Simon, reaching out in a panic. He leaned into the hard spray, the water pounding him. His feet slipped and he nearly took Malcolm and Nick off the bridge behind him. His fingers were battered in the rolling water just where it plunged over the churning waterfall into the whirlpools beyond.

"Reach, Charlotte!" Simon shouted. "Reach for my hand!"

A hairy arm stretched up to him. She was tiring against the power of the water and its icy chill. Charlotte's heavy hand slapped against his arm and for frantic seconds her grip slipped, but then her claws dug along his flesh and into the steel of his gauntlets. Her sudden added weight pulled him away from his hold on the piling. He heard Malcolm shouting with alarm. Water cascaded over Charlotte's face as she hung on to Simon, sputtering. The waterfall roared behind her.

Simon gasped under the strain, but he didn't have the strength to do more than just hold on. She was too heavy to lift and she was too spent and frozen to pull herself up. With Malcolm's death grip on his other arm, it felt like his limb would be torn from its socket. "Charlotte, change form!"

Her terrified expression showed she was afraid of how vulnerable she would be as a little girl. If they lost their hold on each other, she couldn't survive the drop into the vortex. Their eyes met and instead of a hulking werewolf, suddenly she was only a small child. Strength fled and her grip on Simon's arm loosened.

"No!" she screamed as her small fingers slipped.

But Simon's steel gauntleted hand held on. Inch by inch Charlotte was dragged up. Her drenched frame emerged from the torrent, so frail and battered. Simon pulled her close, fairly crushing her against his sodden coat and hard breastplate as Malcolm drew Simon back onto the ledge of the pier several feet above the water. Simon handed the girl to Malcolm. The Scotsman wiped her sodden hair from her face. He looked uncommonly distraught.

"Pass her up!" Kate shouted from the bridge.

Malcolm almost unwillingly handed her to Nick, who lifted her to the shattered railing. Kate and Penny took the limp girl and Kate threw her jacket over Charlotte's shivering body.

"We've got you, child," Kate soothed, wrapping her arms around Charlotte tightly. Her expression of gratitude warmed Simon as she looked down for him. Imogen fell to her knees beside her friend, clutching her wet form tight.

Malcolm and Nick slumped on the stones next to Simon.

"You damn fool," muttered Nick. "We could have all drowned."

"Yes." Simon climbed wearily to his feet.

Malcolm looked at him, his teeth chattering from the cold. "Thank you."

Simon laid an aching hand on his shoulder and climbed up. He went to Charlotte and tilted her chin. "Reckless. But admirable."

"I knew you wouldn't let me go." She embraced him. "Even without your magic."

Simon caught sight of Kate's grateful, expressive eyes. That look was always well worth any risk.

Chapter 7

WHEN SIMON HEARD THE FIRST EXPLOSION RUM-ble through Hartley Hall, he ran for the library. They had secured Ferghus in the cellars yesterday and he was relieved to see the door intact. Simon opened it and heard no disturbances from below.

"Nick!" he shouted. "Are you all right?"

"Yes." Nick appeared at the base of the stairs and started up. "What the hell was that noise?"

"I thought it was Ferghus."

"No. He's still down here coated in that goo. And he's still not talking."

Another boom sounded in the distance, and Kate appeared in the library door as Simon turned to the French windows. "The wards to the north. Something supernatural has entered the grounds." He reached for the door handle when a series of rolling explosions shook the room, vibrating through his chest.

Penny rushed in behind Kate, balancing her brass cannon on her shoulder. She had a collection of pistols shoved in her belt, and she carried Simon's gauntlets as well. She tossed the heavy metal gloves to him.

He shoved his hands in and flexed the fingers to test the charge. "Where are Malcolm and the girls?"

Penny stepped past him out onto the terrace. "Malcolm went for the roof with a scope. The girls went to find Hogarth and get the servants to safety."

The floor rocked and Simon only kept his feet by grabbing a chair. He staggered out beside the stumbling Penny. The stones of the terrace were quivering and cracking.

"Simon!" came a hoarse shout from above. Malcolm hung off the eaves at the northeast corner at the front of the house, clutching a stone gargoyle with one hand and a brass spyglass in the other. He gestured out beyond the front of the mansion. "Something is in the forest. Something big. I can see the trees moving!"

Simon ran to the front corner of Hartley Hall, watching flocks of birds circling overhead and others streaming away into the distance. Kate, Penny, and Nick followed him. The vast manicured lawn stretched away from the house for about two hundred yards, dotted by shrubs and ornamental trees before reaching the distant line of heavy woods. The trees shook as if in a stiff wind, but the air was still. The disturbance continued to come closer accompanied by the cracking sound of wood.

A gravel road led from the front of the house and into the forest. The ground around it shuddered and undulations surged outward. Ancient trees teetered and were torn from the earth. The noise was deafening. Branches and trunks snapped as the massive forest giants were tossed aside as if a huge child were digging sand at the beach. Trees toppled into terrifying heaps of rolling and tumbling colossi, shedding landslides of dirt from their roots and raising a cloud bank of dust and debris.

Then the ground rose into a wall. That embankment became a solid wave of dirt and stone and timber some twenty feet high roaring toward Hartley Hall. Turf and arbors and statues were all dragged into the thundering swell that smashed everything in its path into bits of flotsam.

Simon grabbed Kate and Penny. Running was the only option. There was no standing up to this. As they neared the house, stones clattered loose under their feet. The moving mountain closed in on them, filling the air with a roar that pounded through their heads.

The wave seemed to slow as it came nearer. The rippling line of rocks and brush along the crest was blasted backward like an ocean wave fighting a heavy gale. Barely twenty yards from the house, the avalanche stopped dead, crashing against an unseen barrier and smashing itself to bits. The air exploded with choking dirt. Debris rained atop the huddled figures.

Then everything went still except for the sound of stones and sticks clattering to the ground. Simon was on his knees, stunned. Kate stared with her mouth agape at the proof of destruction beginning to show through the clearing haze. The entire facing grounds of the hall were a churned field. Beyond that, the grand old forest was a jagged wasteland.

"My God," Kate breathed. "My God."

Penny felt for her cannon, which was partially covered in sand and stones, but her eyes were wide. Her lower lip clamped between her teeth.

In the distance, something moved through the dust. A man-sized shadow grew clearer. A tall man with white hair and beard emerged from the smoking hell that just had been a peaceful forest. He stopped and stared at Hartley Hall in surprise. His eyes were angry; his mouth drew tight with bitter acceptance. Brushing dirt from his fashionable suit, he started toward the house. The ruined earth seemed to flatten out before him.

"You must be Archer!" the man shouted. "A word with you if you please."

Simon actually laughed. The incredibly inappropriate statement stabbed his sense of the absurd. He stood, kicking idly at a nearby rock. "Were we expecting you, Gaios?"

The white-haired man frowned at the glib reply. His gaze shifted up, and in a sudden motion his hand swung around. A wall of rock bloomed on his left at the same instant a shot sounded from above. The rifle ball cracked harmlessly off the rock shield.

Gaios snarled and used both hands to gesture. The stone wall shifted like water, flowing into a shape some fifteen feet tall. It gathered itself into a humanlike frame and began to move. The living rock creature reached down with long jagged arms to wrench a huge stone from the ground and hurl it at Hartley Hall in a single fluid motion.

The rock flew like a cannonball for the spot where Malcolm crouched. The Scotsman scrambled back as the huge stone seemed to smash against the house and explode. Nick pulled Simon and Kate back under the feeble cover of ledges and window settings. Stones and dust rained down around them.

"Malcolm!" Penny shouted, pushing away from the house, unmindful of the detritus plummeting around her.

They saw an arm waving from above. Malcolm peered down, his face white with dust. The house was uninjured. The stone had been obliterated before impact through some unknown force. Still, Penny turned angrily toward Gaios.

"No!" Simon grabbed her arm before she could bring her cannon to bear. "You can't harm him. Stay next to the house. We're safe here. I think."

"You are partly correct. You can't harm me." Gaios strode closer so his booming voice could be heard more clearly. The stone golem moved beside him with pounding, grinding steps to stay between its master and Malcolm. "But you are not safe. Not even here in the house that Sir Roland built."

"It's still standing!" Kate proclaimed with a vial in one hand and a sword in the other.

"For now." The white-haired earth elemental shifted his glowering gaze to Kate. "When I'm done, there will be nothing left of the Anstruthers. All those years of Sir Roland's hounding me around the world, prying into my affairs. I was never able to seize him because of that key of his. Do you still have it?"

Simon pulled a gold key from his trouser pocket and held it up. "It's worthless thanks to your Egyptian magic-eater."

"Just like you, Archer." Gaios stared at the key. "If it's powerless, you won't object to giving it to me."

After a moment's hesitation, Simon threw it toward the elemental. Kate and Penny both cried out in alarm. As the golden key spiraled through the air, a column of dirt shot up from the ground, surrounded the object, and collapsed back to the earth.

"Simon!" Kate rounded on him. "What are you doing?"

"It's worthless, Kate," he replied with a subtle quirk of his lips. "And there's no way to re-create it."

A short column of dirt rose next to Gaios with the key resting on top. He reached down and took it between two fingers, lifting it close to his eyes. He considered the key for a minute, turning it around from every angle, even appearing to smell it. Then he tossed it into the air. The golem caught it and held it between his two massive hands, which transformed to red-hot magma. The hands parted and dribbles of molten gold fell between its thick fingers.

"There," Gaios said. "It's a shame to lose such a magnificent artifact. But if I can't use it, I don't want you to find a way."

"Are we done then, Gaios?" Simon asked. "That key was what you wanted from us?"

"It was once, but now you have something else I want," Gaios bellowed. "Where is Ferghus O'Malley?"

"I don't know. Did you check every pub in the British Isles before coming here?"

Gaios clenched his fists. "You are making a mistake, Archer. There are only two sides: me or Ash. You are not on mine, so you must be on hers. That means you will die. You may not know me—"

"I know you!" Simon interrupted harshly. "You are Gaios, murderer of Byron Pendragon and his followers. Destroyer of the Order of the Oak." The ground vibrated under Simon's feet.

The elemental glared from downturned eyes. "Ash told you all about me, did she?" Gaios guffawed, throwing back his head and stretching his arms out. "The day you believe anything she tells you is the day you are lost. Did she tell you that Pendragon loved her?"

"Yes. The two of them struggled to keep you in check because you were a dangerous lunatic."

"He never loved her." Gaios sneered.

"Strange then that, of the three, you were the one in prison."

"Ash lied to Pendragon to convince him to chain me. I had trusted that he was too smart for her, but I was wrong. So I sat in a tiny dark cell for centuries. Fed through a slot in an iron door. Never seeing the sky. Never feeling the pulse of the earth."

"You poor misunderstood innocent. However did that rumor get started that you caused Vesuvius to erupt, burying Pompeii with all those pesky bystanders?"

Gaios narrowed his gaze. "That was a terrible mistake, but that had nothing to do with my imprisonment. Ash hated me because she feared Pendragon and I would ally against her."

"Was she right?"

"My only mistake was waiting too long to move against her."

"Then why didn't you kill Ash when you escaped the Bastille rather than Pendragon?"

The elemental stared into empty space. The intensity drained from his eyes and he seemed a tired old man. "He was my friend and he turned his back on me. He locked me in with vile sorcerers and monsters for my only companions. Forced me to turn to that disgusting rabble for my allies. She . . . she lied to me and convinced me that he was going to execute me because he was afraid. I believed her. I wanted to believe her because I was so angry with him." Gaios held his powerful hands out in front of him. "He told me I was wrong. He told me Ash was lying, but I refused to hear him. And I killed him. My friend." He looked up with human concern. "We three were once like you, shoulder to shoulder, facing the future, fighting for what we believed in. And now because of her, we've come to this. One of us is dead. One of us will soon be. And one of us has been driven mad."

Simon stepped toward Gaios and felt Kate's hand grab his coattail. "You can end it. You can walk away."

The elemental shook his head with disappointment. "All I have is Ash. Before I kill her, I will destroy everything she loves. And I will be sure she knows I did it."

"Meaning London?"

"Meaning all of Britain. When I am done, this land will be no more."

Simon watched the white-haired man and there was a simple purity to his rage. He wasn't dreaming or bragging. He was planning and anticipating. It was terrifying, but also fascinating. Simon didn't conjure the same disgust and fury over Gaios as he did from Ash. This powerful elemental seemed more like a storm or a volcano. It was appropriate to be awestruck, but there was no purpose to being angry. Gaios was a force that couldn't be turned aside with reason or emotion. You could only strive to protect yourself.

"And that's why you need the Stone of Scone?" Simon asked.

Gaios raised an eyebrow. He reached into his coat pocket, then held out his arm, and a fine stream of sand sifted out from his fist. "Here is your Stone back. Did you think I wouldn't know it was a fake?"

Simon shrugged. "I had hoped."

"I have the power to find the true Stone." Gaios dusted his hands together. "But I would prefer not to expend the time and my energy."

"I wish you very good luck in your search."

The elemental glared again, the fury building inside him. "I dislike clowns, Archer. I thought you might have some value, but I was wrong. You are insubstantial. There is nothing in you. Even if you had your power, you would be a worthless shadow of a scribe. You are to Pendragon as a parakeet is to an eagle."

"Let's recap, shall we?" Simon replied evenly. "So far in this contest of mouse versus elephant we have defeated your toadies, Gretta Aldfather and Dr. White, and dismantled their network. We destroyed your Egyptian demigod. We have removed your fire elemental. And we have kept the Stone of Scone from you. I'm not usually one to boast, but we're winning."

The ground began to reverberate again. Dirt quivered and small stones rolled from the vibrations. The green leaves of uprooted trees shook loudly.

The voice of Gaios rumbled like the ground. "Your world is now limited to that house. If that constitutes victory to you, so be it. If you dare step against me, you will die."

The earth lifted Gaios. He disappeared from view as

the ground carried him away. The stone golem ground to a halt and seemed to lose its life spark. It froze like a statue.

Penny dropped onto the ground with a grunt and let her cannon slide to the wrecked stone terrace. She looked up, giving Malcolm a reassuring gesture.

"Simon, what about our fathers' key?" Kate asked with alarmed exasperation. "We went through hell last year! Imogen gave up her humanity to protect it! If you were so willing to give it up, why did we suffer to save it?"

Simon turned with a sympathetic smile and threw an arm over Kate. He drew the gold key from his waistcoat pocket and dangled it from the chain. "That was one of Penny's facsimiles. It was a worthless piece of gold." Simon laughed out of habit.

Kate looked at him in surprise, but she didn't see the wild glare in his eyes that used to accompany the aether intoxication. She leaned on her sword like a walking stick. "What in the hell is so funny?"

"Gaios is afraid of us."

Nick exhaled to release the tension. "I never thought I'd see the like when I was beating you at whist and billiards. By God! Simon Archer going toe-to-toe with Gaios. But is it completely necessary for you to antagonize the most powerful sorcerer on Earth?"

Simon gave Nick a collegial tap on his cheek. "Do you see how well you trained me? Gaios knows he can be defeated. Pendragon chained him for centuries, and he's petrified of its happening again."

Penny passed by. "Of course Pendragon did have his powers."

Kate stood stock-still, surveying the obliterated acreage. All the carefully tended lawns and gardens were turned into a smashed field of upturned earth. The ancient forest where she and Imogen had played as children, dutifully tended and preserved by her father, had been swept away, uprooted like unneeded annuals in a garden.

"I'm sorry, Kate." Simon kissed her on the cheek. "We'll repair it when this is over. Somehow. We will."

"It's hard to repair a forest."

He didn't reply but merely stood close beside her. She put a hand to her head with a sigh and pointed at the giant stone golem that still stood amidst the destruction. "I hate to think that's the first thing guests will see when they drive in."

"I shouldn't worry about that. I can't imagine you'll have any guests out here after all this."

Kate laughed, wiping the unaccustomed wetness from her eyes.

Chapter 8

SIMON CRAWLED ON HIS HANDS AND KNEES through the dirt. The wooden braces of Hartley Hall's main floor were just overhead. He worked his way past the outer walls and stone columns that served as part of the great house's foundation. The dim space smelled musty. He followed a bright light, which burned in the palm of Nick Barker's right hand. His old friend crawled awkwardly ahead, shuffling to keep his illuminated hand raised. Both men wore rough twill work togs, and they were caked with mud and streaming with cobwebs.

"There!" Simon called. "On your left."

Nick swung around, banging his head on a beam. He cursed and rubbed his close-cropped hair. The support structure inches from his face wasn't the typical stone column; it was forged steel with thick compressed springs and odd flanges. Entwined gears and pistons offered flexible support. Nick whistled with admiration.

"Christ," he said. "Look at this thing. This is what kept the house up when Gaios came."

Simon inched up beside Nick, studying the fantastic machinery. "There's probably at least one in every corner. And look here!" He pointed to a flat surface on the beam where several symbols were inscribed. "Runes. My father's inscriptions. They worked together on this too."

"They built it to stand against Gaios. Protects the house and a bit of ground away from the walls."

"I can appreciate that now." Simon pulled a small notebook and pencil from his pocket and began to sketch the runes in the light of Nick's hand.

Nick said, "I find it hard to believe your father's inscriptions could hold back Gaios. Cavendish was reputed to be powerful, but he was no Pendragon."

Simon detected no scorn in Nick's words, merely a statement of truth. "I agree. It is surprising. But he was working with Sir Roland. And he was Pendragon's protégé." Simon worked his way around the column, copying all the runic strings. "Remarkable. These runes are a bit different from others of his. But still, his inscriptions are so elegant, like a perfect cantata, while mine are children strumming a lute with a clamshell."

Nick shook his head. "Do you really believe all that claptrap you spew about yourself? Or do you just do it to keep people from taking you seriously?"

Simon smiled and stayed silent.

"Simon, you're not going to let her mess about with Ash's blood spell, are you?"

"Who? Kate? I trust her judgment on that."

"I know Ash better than anyone here and you should burn that spell now."

"No." Simon sighed and started through the dirt toward a small rectangle of light. They weaved between columns until they reached the open hatchway and crawled outside into the bright sun. They were at the back of the mansion.

Nick brushed dirt from his trousers. "I'm not trying to cause trouble. I just don't think you know how devious Ash can be."

Simon held up his hand. "I would just as soon see Ash dead for what she did to my mother. But if there is any way she can help defeat Gaios . . ."

Nick shook his head as the two men went to the door of the kitchen. "It's not worth it. No matter what Ash gave you, the cost would be too much."

"I don't think you understand the people I've gathered. Kate. Malcolm. Penny. They are extraordinary. As smart as any I've encountered, and good decent people. I would trust any one of them with my life."

Nick gave a cynical grin as he poured a glass of water for Simon, then drank from the pitcher under the baleful glare of Cook and one of the kitchen maids. He wiped his mouth with his sleeve. He tore a chunk of bread from a loaf, forcing Cook to remove the bread from the table. "Listen, Simon, you know all that stuff with Ash and me, it's in the past."

"In the past."

"I mean, you and I, we're mates again, right?"

"We always were." Simon looked at Nick with a smile. "You brought me back from the dead and you helped my mother. How could I repay you for that?"

Nick nodded sadly. "We're on the square then?"

Simon clinked his glass against the water pitcher Nick held. "Square."

KATE STUDIED THE VELLUM SHEET AS IF THEIR lives depended on it. Over the previous hours, she had made copious notes and occasionally consulted stacks of books at her side. Food rested on a sideboard, ignored. She muttered angrily about allowing her Old High German to become so rusty. Aethelred the wolfhound raised his head to look at his mistress, then returned to his ever-patient repose in the corner. Kate pointed at a word on the scroll. "Boargelt. Who has boargelt?" She strode to the shelves of glass jars in her laboratory. "Oh. There's some. Good."

Simon watched her rummage. He closed his finger in a massive German lexicon, in which he had been sketching Norse runes along the margins. Concerns raised by Nick's warning still swirled in his head, as well as his own natural misgivings that Ash was creeping among them. His instinct was to tear the thing away from Kate and destroy it. However, the look of intense concentration on Kate's face, the sheer joy of discovery, was too strong for him. She was in her element here, a sort of intellectual swashbuckling that Simon found intoxicating to watch. Her eyes slipped along the arcane script, fighting to understand. Seeing her take new ancient information and put it together with disparate pieces of other knowledge caused his heart to pound in his chest. Every nerve and muscle in her seemed etched against her skin.

"Holy God, Simon." Kate looked up. The intensity in her gaze was almost dangerous. "There is more magic in the Womb of Schattenwald than in half my library. There are principles here for applications far beyond the purpose of the spell. This passage is on the vital fluid of the blood. It claims to alter the blood into an entirely new substance that bonds with aether. I think this could certainly help you. But there's so much more to it. It might be similar to what Dr. White accomplished using alchemy when he created his homunculi. It might serve me to help Imogen. It could make me into an alchemist on a level with Dr. White." When Simon raised an eyebrow, Kate shook her head. "You know what I mean. White's alchemy was at the edge of miraculous. He was altering life, altering matter. This spell discusses that very thing."

He kept his voice even, fighting against his fears. "I

can't pretend to follow you, but I'd remind you that it's blood magic, Kate."

She slapped her hand against the desk in frustration. Aethelred jumped. "Repeating the same phrase isn't an argument! If you want to convince me, do better."

Simon regarded her, considering the validity of her words. "Recovering my power isn't worth it if it means accompanying Ash along her path."

"This isn't just about your power. Granted, I think the Womb definitely touches on that problem. But it has so much more. There are foundational magical principles here, Simon. This spell transcends mere *blood magic* and *necromancy.* Those are just words. When I translate it fully, you'll see."

"Kate, I appreciate your enthusiasm, but you do know that it's possible that what has been done, cannot be undone? Or should not?"

She stared at him, almost angrily. Then her gaze softened. "I've spent the last few months working to help Imogen. I've read every book and each scroll in this library, which is one of the finest occult repositories in the world. And yet, every single day I have to look at her and tell her that I haven't found the solution. But here in this scroll, I can see breakthroughs. There are real physical advancements that I can make in my approach to Imogen's condition. Do you understand that, Simon? Do you understand what that could mean to her?"

Before Simon could reply in sympathy, there was a knock at the door.

Hogarth entered and pretended not to see the emotion on their faces. "Miss Kate, there is a visitor. I have put her in the West Room."

Kate gave an exasperated sigh.

"It is Grace North."

Simon stood quickly. "Hogarth, please find Mr. Barker and tell him to stay out of sight upstairs. We'll attend Mrs. North presently."

"Why do you want Nick to stay out of sight?" Kate asked. "Aside from general good taste."

"I'll tell you later. Just an idea I've been toying with."

When they entered the dim West Room, an opulent but rarely used sitting room in the far west wing, they found Grace North pacing before the windows in the setting sun. She was staring out at the swathe of destruction across the front. Imogen stood near her, silent and still. Charlotte was across the room, spinning herself in a desk chair.

Grace turned at the sound of the door. She was pale. "What in God's name happened here? Gaios?"

As Simon went to the sideboard to pour sherry for three, Kate said, "Yes, he disagreed with my landscaping choices."

Charlotte chuckled, pushing herself faster. Kate grabbed the back of the chair and unwittingly nearly sent the girl flying.

"That's impolite, dear. We have a guest." Kate patted Charlotte's back. "And isn't it making you sick?"

"Almost." Charlotte hopped off the chair and staggered about like a drunk.

Grace demanded, "Why didn't you inform me immediately that Gaios had been here? I am your liaison." She shivered slightly, glancing at the cold hearth.

Simon stepped around the weaving Charlotte and handed a sherry to Grace. "What would you have done about it, Mrs. North?"

Grace eyed him suspiciously and downed the wine in a single unladylike gulp. "What happened? How did you survive him?"

"It was very genteel. We had a bit of a chat and he went on his way."

"A bit of a chat?" Grace looked to Kate for some sanity, but Kate nodded in agreement. "He destroyed your grounds as a precursor to a chat?"

"No, he originally wanted to kill us, but he could not." Simon held a chair for Kate and put an easy hand on her shoulder, but he stayed on his feet since Grace was still standing. He maintained a diffident manner as if he were a country squire discussing the latest garden party. "He warned us to stay out of his way or we would die. The usual blather."

"He was toying with you," Grace said firmly. "Trying to frighten you. That must be it. If he had wanted you dead, you would be. Archer, you simply cannot continue being so vulnerable. Surely there is a way for you to recover your magic. The stakes are very high. Your nation is counting on you."

Simon returned to the sideboard to pour another sherry. His voice was strained. "Everything that can be done is being done."

"That seems—" Grace North started to turn again to Kate but stopped to stare at Imogen, who stood only a few feet away. She then stepped back uncomfortably and focused her attention on Kate. "That seems unlikely. Miss Anstruther, surely there is something you can do with your great alchemy skills. You must impress upon Mr. Archer that he has a duty. You understand duty, do you not?"

"I do." Kate kept her polite demeanor. "Charlotte, you and Imogen go play in another room."

Charlotte sat on a sofa and huffed. "But I'm being quiet."

"Please, dear. Go find Mr. Malcolm. He would love your company."

Charlotte exchanged a quick gleeful grin with Imogen but then placed a frown back on her angelic face and stomped to the door. She spun and curtsied to Grace before leaving. Grace looked slowly toward Imogen, who had not yet moved. There was an awkward moment, then Imogen seemed to glide out of the sitting room. Simon closed the door behind the girls with a wry smile at their minor anarchy.

Grace continued, "Miss Anstruther, Gaios came here, with no fear of your combined strength, and wreaked havoc on your home. Imagine what he can do to those who are unprepared throughout Britain. He must be stopped. We must do all we can or who knows what innocent lives will be lost by our failures. We can't afford to ignore any possible effort."

Kate nodded with false agreement. "We are endeavoring to learn more about Gaios's plans from his confederate."

"The Irishman?" Grace grew stern. "Ah, that's why it's so cold here. No fires. Have you extracted any information from him?"

"Nothing. Yet."

"He likely doesn't know anything." The sophisticated blond woman straightened the lace on her cuff. "Gaios doesn't fall into the trap of confiding secrets in underlings, particularly if they're lunatics. Gaios might be crazy, but he's not an idiot. You must do more if you hope to stop him."

Simon gave Kate a sidelong glance to defuse some of his growing anger. But even her steady look did not settle him. "I'll certainly keep that sentiment in mind, Mrs. North. If you'll excuse me."

Anger boiled inside him as he left the room. Hogarth stood just outside in the hallway. Simon shot him a quick glance, indicating that the manservant should hold his ground and keep tabs on their guest. Then Simon moved farther down the corridor and stepped into the silence of the billiard room. The arrogant expression on Grace North's face only made matters worse. Everything about her was a lie. And he was forced to stand by and say nothing. His fists clenched as he tried to wrest back his fury.

Footsteps entered the room and Kate approached him. "That was unusual. I've never seen you unable to play the magnanimous host before." Her hand lifted to his chest.

Simon contemplated if he should voice all he had been long considering. Finally, he said, "I think Grace North is Ash."

Kate's eyes widened. "You think what?" Then she lowered her voice. "Why would you think that?"

"I've been doing a bit of research. It turns out that Grace North was supposedly away at a spa in Germany during the Sacred Heart Murders, and we know that to be false as we spoke with her in Sussex. She had a connection to Rowan Barnes. She had been playing a role in the magical affairs of the kingdom, by her own admission."

"That's thin," Kate commented.

"I know, but what isn't thin is that you saw one of those monstrous apes virtually wither on the vine when Grace North merely glanced at it. And her husband, the pointless prime minister, seemed to recover from near death at her touch. This is all consistent with the abilities of a necromancer such as Ash." Simon flexed his arms to loosen stiff muscles. "And the position of Grace North fits what Nick said about Ash."

"Then why isn't she the queen instead of the prime minister's wife?"

"Perhaps one was easier to arrange than the other."

"What does it mean to us if Mrs. North is Ash?"

Simon bounced a loose billiard ball off the bumper. "On the one hand, it's good because at least we would know where she is. On the other hand, she has distressing access to the power of the government."

Kate leaned on the green surface of the table and caught the ball he had sent spinning. She rolled it under the open palm of her hand. "How high could it go? Do you think the prime minister knows? Or the king?"

"That wouldn't be Ash's style. She prefers to manipulate mere humans, and I've no hints that either Prime Minister North or King William is a magician of any sort."

"Why did she come here?"

"Publicly, to get a report on the battle at Old London Bridge. Privately, I suspect, to ensure we received her *gift*, the blood spell. And to press home the urgency of our situation so we are more disposed to use it."

Kate glared in the direction of the West Room. "Ash is in my house."

Simon placed his hand over hers but neither of them was comforted by it.

Chapter 9

MALCOLM PLACED A NEWLY CLEANED SHOTGUN into the case and pulled out another one to inspect. It was spotless and oiled. He had heard the servants talking about the prime minister's wife being in the house and he had no interest being civil to someone so vile. Let Simon and Kate play that game; such subterfuge suited them as magicians. Instead, Malcolm decided to pay attention to maintaining the arsenal of Hartley Hall. The weapons were a beautiful collection of shotguns, muskets, and pistols. English, German, Italian, even several Persian and Arabian. Then there were some that Sir Roland had built. Malcolm hadn't the slightest idea how to care for them, and a few he frankly wasn't even sure how they operated. And knowing Sir Roland, if Malcolm tried to take the contraptions apart, he might blow up the house. Those he left for Penny.

He took a gorgeous pistol with an engraved walnut stock and a beautiful forged hammer back to the main table in the library, where he had laid down a cloth. He systemically began to break the gun down to its components, laying each piece carefully in front of him. Malcolm put the dismantled barrel to his eye. There were no fires allowed in this wing of the house. No candles or lamps. They had shut off the gas just to be safe since Ferghus was locked below, and it would have been dim in the late afternoon but for a strange lantern on the table. The glowing light buzzed and occasionally a tiny dark shape bounced against the inside of the frosted glass with a ticking noise.

Brownies, Malcolm thought with disgust. Hateful little faerie folk that Simon used as a source of light at Gaunt Lane. Kate and Penny had used the key for a quick jaunt to London and brought a few of the little creatures out to Hartley Hall to provide light in the absence of fire. He had to concede, they gave off a useful glow.

There was a commotion at the door and in ran Imogen and Charlotte. They were giggling and clutching something. To his annoyance, they plopped down in the center of the room and started setting up a wooden ark complete with a number of paired animals. He almost told the girls to go find someplace else to play, but it was actually nice to hear the sound of laughter and revelry. Too long had there been nothing but the sound of battle and war councils, and there would be more of that in the coming days also. Where once Malcolm would have balked at having these two on the front lines, he knew that they had been baptized in fire. They deserved a moment of joy. There were so few for any of them.

Charlotte let out a sharp squeal of laughter because Imogen placed her pet hedgehog in the ark. It immediately began investigating one of the wooden animals. Shaking his head, Malcolm resumed his work.

A few minutes later, Barnaby the butler came in carrying a tray with food and a glass of water. Malcolm looked up expectantly until he realized with disappointment that the meal was not for him but for the prisoner below. The butler fumbled with a set of keys to unlock the heavy door leading downstairs to the cellar. Malcolm had returned his concentration to the dismantled pistol when he caught a scent. With a clatter, he was on his feet and racing after Barnaby, grabbing one of his pistols off the table. The servant was already downstairs when Malcolm seized his arm. Barnaby looked panicked.

Malcolm pinched the flame from the candle that stood on the tray, plunging the hallway into deep, black shadows. He growled. "No fire of any sort. You were warned, weren't you? There's a lantern in the library you can use."

"I'm sorry, sir. I wasn't thinking. I didn't want to bother you. You were engaged. I'll remind the staff."

"Make sure you do." Malcolm plucked the candle off the tray and tossed it to the floor. They were close to Ferghus's cell, so Malcolm led Barnaby through the dimness. When they reached the door at the end of the hallway, Malcolm toed open a slot near the floor.

Barnaby placed the tray down and carefully slid it inside. There was a rattle of chains and the tray disappeared with a throaty, "'Bout bloody time. Starving down here. How the hell am I supposed to see what it is?"

Malcolm ignored him and went for the stairs. He paused halfway up when he realized the butler wasn't following.

"Should I wait for the tray, sir?"

Malcolm scowled with exasperation. A breeze suddenly blew in through the door above. Perhaps someone had opened a window in the library. One of the girls likely.

The wind fanned the candle's wick and an ember glowed pinpoint red in the darkness. There was a muffled laugh from the far end of the corridor.

Malcolm's shout of alarm was lost as the air caught fire. The flames engulfed the butler in a deafening roar.

Malcolm dove out of the stairwell and hurried to close the door behind him.

"Charlotte! Imogen! Get ou—!"

He never finished. The wood-and-iron door blasted off its hinges sending Malcolm flying across the room. He slammed against a bookcase and the heavy door landed on top of him. Searing heat and flame became his world.

Ferghus appeared in the cellar door and the flame in the room drew back into his left hand. He had managed to clear one hand of the flame-retardant gel. His grasp on the doorjamb set the wood on fire. He eyed Malcolm, trapped and seemingly oblivious under the heavy door, which crackled with fire. He then looked up to see the two girls standing in shock, silhouetted against the windows.

"Stand aside, girls." Ferghus grinned. Flames licked from his fingertips as he stepped into the room. "I've no desire to hurt you."

Charlotte looked at Malcolm with alarm. The sight of the Scotsman groaning and struggling to regain his senses frightened her. Then her eyes narrowed at Ferghus as she placed herself between the two men. "No. You go back downstairs where you belong."

The elemental stood straight in surprise. He laughed. "Where I come from, children are seen and not heard."

Charlotte squared off with her lips tight and her fists clenched. "I don't know where you come from, but you're not supposed to leave the house."

Imogen moved a few steps away. Ferghus stared at the tentacle fingers of her right hand with a twisted expression. He came closer and leaned on a chair, setting it alight.

"Stop that!" Charlotte screamed. "This is our home!"

Imogen flicked a button on the end of her lacy cuff and shook her sleeve loose. Long hairlike quills stood on her forearm like the bristles of an angry cat. Imogen then reached up and pulled the black veil from her pale face. Her strange inhuman eyes fixed on him.

Ferghus paused with astonishment. "What in the name of God are you?"

Imogen raised her arm toward him and quills shot across the library. A thin filament struck Ferghus in the face. He screeched in shock and anger, reaching up and grasping the dangling thread stuck in his cheek. His hand flared and the quill sizzled into nothing.

Ferghus waved his hand in front of him, creating a barrier of fire. Imogen squeezed her fist again and more quills flew. This time, they hit the fire wall and frayed in the air. The Irishmen started to laugh, but then suddenly he jerked, and his eyes went wide. He staggered and his mouth opened. He paused, as if waiting to see what would happen. He started to breathe hard.

He glared at the young woman clad in mourning. "What did you do? What in hell did you do?" He lowered his head, summoning his focus and pushed a hand toward Imogen. A column of searing flame roared out at her. She screamed and leapt to the side with her black gown catching fire. Behind her, the drapes flared into red flame and several panes of glass shattered.

"No!" Charlotte shouted. She bounded two steps and jumped onto the back of the sofa. Her frame was already beginning to grow, arms lengthening, legs turning powerful and oddly jointed. Her pretty frock ripped as muscles expanded. By the time she sprang from the back of the furniture, her furious expression hardened and exploded into dark snarling features with monstrous eyes and rows of sharp teeth.

Ferghus stumbled back, unprepared for this new horror that launched at him. He raised his arm in feeble defense as the werewolf slammed into his chest. They piled back against the bookshelves. Claws and teeth ripped into him. The room filled with the whoosh of igniting books.

Malcolm distantly heard the sound of the werewolf's snarling. The crackling roar of walls and books and furniture igniting surrounded him. Something slammed against the flaming wooden prison of the door and shifted it off his legs and hip. He pushed frantically with his bare hands. Ignoring the pain, he hauled himself out to find Imogen slumped over the end of the smoldering door. She struggled to rise. Malcolm didn't see any blood, but much of her mourning clothes were burned away. He placed a hand on her to keep her still but she struggled under it, her inhuman eyes focused on the fight behind them.

Malcolm turned and saw Charlotte with her jaws clamped down hard on Ferghus's shoulder. The elemental's hand was around her neck trying to dislodge her. It suddenly flared with an intense flame that bloomed over Charlotte, obscuring her. The smell of burning flesh reached Malcolm, cloying at his throat. Bile rose when he realized Ferghus was roasting the child alive. Charlotte's growls suddenly became a high-pitched screech of pain and distress. Her claws scrabbled across the Irishman's chest. Ferghus screamed in panic and a wave of blistering heat roared over Malcolm, forcing him to dive for cover.

Ferghus and Charlotte careened off a wall and the flames abated momentarily. Malcolm scrambled to his feet and saw Charlotte. Most of the fur of her upper torso and face was seared off, revealing burned glistening red flesh beneath that boiled into blisters. She had little control over her movements, her pathetic scorched limbs sagged. Still her jaws remained locked on Ferghus, refusing to release the elemental.

"No!" Malcolm shouted, fumbling for his pistols, but they weren't there. He didn't pause to search for them.

Instead he picked up a heavy fireplace poker from the floor. With both hands, he swung the iron pole and connected with Ferghus's back. The Irishman howled and swung his fiery left hand. The Scotsman roared in rage and slammed the hard iron against the man's hand. Bones shattered. Ferghus screamed.

"Charlotte, let go!" Malcolm hoarsely shouted into the searing air.

The young werewolf continued to clamp down on the fire elemental out of pure instinct or excruciating pain. Her sobs of agony could still be heard over the crackling of the flames. Ferghus flailed wildly in an attempt to dislodge her. Charlotte blindly bit deeper. The agony caused fire to surge like a molten fissure from Ferghus's shattered arm. Gobs of flames flew outward and slapped against Charlotte's burnt flesh, charring it black. Her skin cracked and peeled away. Fire licked at Malcolm's shirt, but it didn't stop him from swinging the iron poker against the Irishman's spine.

Charlotte could hold on no longer. Even her instinct failed. Her massive jaws tore a chunk of muscle from Ferghus as her ravaged body slumped to the floor. With a harsh rattling breath, she collapsed and didn't move. Malcolm could barely recognize her charred form and all sense of reason fled.

The iron bar crashed down into Ferghus's unprotected gut, bending him over. When the man collapsed on the burning rug, Malcolm kicked him onto his back. He sank to his knees, straddling the fire elemental. Malcolm dropped the bar and began beating Ferghus with his fists. The Irishman's head snapped back and forth with the blows, blood spurting from his mouth and nose, splattering the room and Malcolm alike. Ferghus lifted a feeble arm to fend Malcolm off, but the Scotsman shoved it aside and continued his brutal attack.

From a great distance, he recognized Imogen's cries.

Flames rolled along the ceiling like a lake of fire. Bits of hot ash floated in the air around him. All he saw was the monster trapped under his fists. Rage blinded him. Deafened him.

Ferghus had stopped moving, no longer even defending himself, limp on the bloody floor. Malcolm didn't stop.

Someone grabbed him from behind. "Malcolm! Enough!"

Malcolm struggled against the grip.

"Stop! You'll kill him!" A voice shouted and Malcolm felt himself being dragged away from the Irishman.

Malcolm tore free and turned to strike. He stared into Simon's eyes. He managed to freeze his blow in midair. Simon's gaze flicked to the bloody fist suspended a few inches from his chin. He looked back at Malcolm as if seeking a glint of reason.

Simon put out a cautious hand, his voice even. "Stop, Malcolm. Do you hear me?"

Malcolm waited for a long minute, gasping for air, tasting blood and smelling charred flesh. He looked at the figure of Ferghus, who lay helpless in a pool of red. Malcolm's arms dropped to his sides. He managed to gasp out, "Charlotte," but his voice didn't even sound like his own. It sounded older.

Beyond Simon, Penny was quickly dousing the fire in the room with a canister of Kate's oily flame retardant. Under the coating of goo, the walls and shelves and floors were charred.

Then Malcolm caught sight of Charlotte's burnt body on the floor and it wiped all the rage from him. He pulled away from Simon and ran toward her, dropping to his knees. Kate was already at the girl's side and slathering a salve on the worst of her injuries. She pushed the container into Malcolm's hands, which were wet with Ferghus's blood.

"Smear this over the burns. All of them." It was a command and he took Charlotte's scalded frame onto his lap. He dug his fingers into the cooling gel and began to wipe it on the back of the little girl. When she wasn't a beast, she was so small.

Kate left to check on Imogen, who stood helplessly nearby, shaking. Imogen stared at Charlotte with panic etched on her bloodless features. Kate approached her gently. She touched the burnt fabric of Imogen's tattered dress. "You did all you could. Are you hurt?"

Imogen shook her head.

"Let me look." To Kate's relief, Imogen didn't fight her, and she was telling the truth. Her pale skin was only slightly red, as if she had stayed too long out in the sun. Perhaps she had her own remarkable healing ability or she was just plain lucky.

"She should have let go," Imogen said, her eyes never leaving Charlotte's still form. "Why didn't she let go?"

Kate shook her head. "She was protecting us. Nothing stops her."

Malcolm rubbed salve over Charlotte's blistered raw cheek. His hands were shaking. They had never done that before. Her burns looked horrific. His breath rasped in and out as he held the panting girl.

Kate lifted his chin, forcing his face to turn to her. "All right. I'll take her now. Go and help Simon with Ferghus."

Malcolm slowly nodded, easing Charlotte down onto a pillow that Penny brought. He stood over her. He wiped his hands then along the length of his pants, but couldn't remove the blood or the gel. Finally, he went over to Simon, who was kneeling low over Ferghus. Malcolm focused on the bloody froth bubbling from the Irishman's lips and immediately started to seethe. "How is he? Dead?"

Simon looked up. The line of his jaw was set hard. "Not quite, but not far."

The Scotsman took Simon's reaction for anger, and rage burst in him. "I'm glad. You didn't see what he did to Charlotte and to Imogen. And Barnaby is downstairs, burned to death. Don't you dare say anything to me about that filth."

"Thank God you were here," was all Simon replied. He stood up and shook his head with an accepting sigh.

"Yes, well done, Mr. MacFarlane," said a delicate voice from the doorway.

Grace North.

"Put your foot on his throat," she said with a faint smile, "and I can assure you the Crown will be grateful."

Malcolm looked down at the man he had brutalized, and at his own ragged knuckles. A sickening realization hit him hard in the gut. "God. I'm my father. A mindless thug. It didn't take me long to fall into that role, did it? After years of running, I found him."

"Mrs. North, it's rather dangerous in here." Simon moved rapidly to Grace and firmly pressured her back out into the hall. "I'd hate for the ceiling to cave in on top of you. Ah, here's Hogarth. Would you escort Mrs. North back to her carriage, thank you so much. Good day to you, Mrs. North." Outrage marred her pretty face as Hogarth appeared, but he brooked no argument with nothing more than a polite nod up the hallway. Simon shut the blackened door in her face.

"Malcolm, you idiot." Simon turned to the Scotsman with a softening demeanor. "You aren't becoming *your* father. You're becoming *a* father." He pointed at the two girls.

Malcolm saw Kate cradling Charlotte. Imogen stood over them and Penny looked up at Malcolm with a reassuring smile. She nodded as if to say that everything would be fine. Charlotte's chest rose and fell. Malcolm watched the lass breathe slowly in and out. Her blistered face was relaxed.

For the first time, Malcolm truly understood what Simon was about. Simon would do anything to protect those he loved. Incredibly, so would Malcolm. These people had crawled their way into his heart and he cared about all of them. Even Simon.

The pain in Malcolm's heart changed.

Chapter 10

IT WAS THE NEXT EVENING AND KATE'S LABORAtory was in a state of organized chaos. Separate experiments bubbled furiously in different corners of the room. Wulfsyl was brewing on one table near the back. More black treacle and her special *elixir vitae* were being processed on a bench by the door. She allowed herself small burners because Ferghus was comatose, and even if he was not, they were sure to be more careful to prevent him washing off the flame-retardant gel.

Imogen sat in a chair nearby, fiddling with the wrist of her sleeve, having given yet another sample of her blood for the never-ending tests. Kate watched her curiously. Normally, Imogen would suffer through the bleeding with impatience, then depart as soon as Kate released her. This evening, she lingered, staring at bottles and vials without real interest, looking into the darkness outside. She yawned and held herself with the stiff posture of someone who was overly tired, but refusing to yield.

Imogen's odd behavior might have come from her distress over Charlotte, but the young girl was healing with remarkable facility. The burns still covered much of Charlotte's body, and she was clearly in pain, but she was already able to talk and move about. Her werewolf physiology was amazing, and Imogen knew that Charlotte would heal with time.

"You should go to bed, dear." Kate tried to sound conversational as she labeled tubes of her sister's blood.

"I'm not tired." Imogen stared at the two lanterns on Kate's table glowing with the eldritch light of brownies. She yawned again.

"You seem very tired."

"I'm fine, thank you."

Kate then realized the dilemma as she watched her sister's head droop. Imogen had taken such strides forward since Bedlam that Kate had almost forgotten. "Imogen, you may take one of the lanterns."

Imogen straightened and spun. Her nearly featureless face shone in the stark light. She protested, "I'm not afraid of the dark. Perhaps I was once, but not now."

Kate nodded. "I know you're not, dear. But the house is very dangerous. There is a great deal of wreckage. I'd feel better if you had a lantern."

The tension in Imogen's features faded. "Are you sure? Don't you need them for your work?"

"One will do nicely. Please, take it."

A pale hand lifted the lantern and she went to the door. When she stepped out into the black hallway, the light threw off a bit of comfort around her. She regarded Kate with a look of gratitude that didn't need explanation.

"Good night, Imogen."

"Good night." Imogen's voice was relieved. She shut the door behind her, leaving Kate alone in the laboratory.

Kate sighed and slipped the blood vials into a rack. She thought of Imogen, who was walking the dark house on her own. They should all be so brave. And then she turned to her desk where the current challenge to her own bravery rested.

Ash's blood scroll.

Flasks and a few dusty tomes that held the only references she could find relating to the magic within the spell held down the corners of the ancient parchment. The apparatus before her held what had been a sample of her own blood. It had been transformed by the spell into a state she no longer recognized as blood. It had turned a lighter color and thicker, like honey. It almost mimicked the current state of Imogen's blood. Kate assumed that Ash used such new blood from her victims to preserve her youth and power. She probably bathed in it and her necromancy would allow her to absorb the vitality from it. This must have been how Ash returned to power after her brush with Ra. However, Kate found that the altered blood quickly turned black, rendering it inert and useless. This was a spell that clearly required precise timing. It also needed a vast amount of fresh blood, meaning murder and exsanguination.

The dark spell both thrilled and terrified her. It held secrets she was determined to unlock, and not just for Simon's sake. Hope welled up inside Kate like a hot geyser that couldn't be capped. She hadn't told her sister about it. She couldn't bear Imogen's disappointment if she failed.

But she wouldn't fail! Not with both Simon and Imogen at stake.

Kate scrubbed at her face to push away the grit in her eyes. She had been at it all day and very deep into the night. Forcing her burning eyes to scrutinize the spell again, she looked for some element she could seize and conform to her personal use. It was a matter of separating the components of the spell into their unique forms and functions. A portion here regarding the blood of the heart. A fragment there describing the drawing of the aether. She scribbled a new base formula. Crossed it out and tried again. If only she could find a way to reduce the amount of blood needed as well as increase the life span of its transformation.

It was possible there was no way to use the spell to restore magical power without giving up her life. After all she had preached to Simon about the selfishness of sacrifice, that would be ironic to say the least. The stakes were higher though. Was self-sacrifice ever the final recourse? To save the lives of those she loved? To save countless millions?

Perhaps that was how Ash justified her actions using the blood of innocents to achieve immortality. Ash believed it was her right as an ancient guardian, or whatever the hell she believed she was. This was magic that was tainted by the very act of the user. It was a dark art when used for dark purposes.

Kate knew she could never use a blood spell in its true form. Not to save Britain, not even to save Simon or Imogen. Perhaps she might have once, she might have been enticed by the intellectual challenge, but that already felt like eons ago. However, this blood spell showed her that the impossible was possible. That was the key to magic. With an exhausted sigh, Kate returned to her books and to what seemed to be a library full of blank walls.

The next thing Kate knew, it was hours later and the door opened. In surged Penny, wearing a thick leather apron and smelling of soot and smoke. She appeared even more excited than was usual when in the process of inventing.

"I need you to look at something."

"Of course." Kate leaned back from her papers. She wasn't even surprised that Penny was still awake too. "What do you have?"

"You know, I've been trying to forge a new key. So I've been studying the original hoping to discover its creation mechanism. I found something odd in the key's makeup. Some strange substance."

Kate's curiosity rose as Penny brought the gold key to Kate's microscope on the opposite table. The young engineer adjusted the settings on the device and made room for Kate.

"Here, look. Tell me what this is."

Kate pressed her eye to the lens. She gasped. "I can't believe I missed this."

Penny blushed sheepishly. "Well, it's not really obvious until you chip away a bit of the gold. I had to in order to test the density. I had no idea the core of it was *that*."

Kate retrieved some liquid from a shelf and proceeded to test the substance under the microscope. After several minutes of painstaking work, she proved what she suspected. She sat back in astonishment.

"Well, what is it?" Penny asked, unable to stand the suspense.

"If I'm not mistaken, that substance is similar to something ancient magi called a *spirit stone*. A conglomeration that, when properly treated by an alchemist, absorbs the spirits of the dead."

"Eww," was Penny's reaction. "That doesn't sound good. Why is it in our key?"

Kate looked through the microscope again. "This conglomeration isn't a true spirit stone. It's similar but different. This harnesses another mystical substance, namely aether. Do you know what this means? An alchemist was also involved in the forging of the key!" Kate felt closer to her father than ever before. The wonder of it made her reel. "Everything makes sense suddenly. This component is what brought the key back even after Ra's power drained it. The alchemy in the key continued to work and slowly allowed the metal to be infused with aether again."

"Can you make such a thing?"

"Perhaps." Kate glanced back at the scroll and her mountain of notes. Possibilities yawned wide before her. The formula began to make more sense. She knew what she needed to do. She had the mechanism right here in her hand. Impulsively she hugged a surprised Penny.

"So this is a good thing?"

"It's a bloody fantastic thing, Penny! The conglomeration is the piece that we've been missing. With that, we can bring Simon's aether back to him."

"Are you serious?" Penny gaped.

"Very!"

"So we don't need to use that revolting blood spell then?"

"Only parts of it. I will adapt the blood spell with my alchemy. The basic transformational principle should combine with the absorption properties of the conglomeration."

"I don't understand a word of what you're saying, but if it brings Simon's aether back, I'm excited."

"It will." The confidence in Kate's voice surprised even her, but she saw it all so clearly.

There was a thump outside the door to the laboratory. Both Kate and Penny turned.

"Maybe it's Simon," the engineer remarked. "We can tell him the good news."

Then something scratched at the door. "Sounds more like Aethelred," Kate said with a grin, caught up in her elation. "He likes to lie by the grate while I work." She opened the door to let the wolfhound inside.

A tall shadow filled the doorway. A blackened cadaver lunged into the room. There was a flash of a knife. Kate grabbed the arm before it struck. Her hands wrapped around dry, leathery flesh that cracked and broke away under her pressure. She stared at the gruesome face, whose teeth were split in a rictus grin. Then she recognized it.

"Barnaby!"

Penny didn't care who it was, but rushed forward to pull the dead man off Kate. Where the living man had been weak, his dead counterpart was immensely strong.

Kate's back bent over the table behind her. She forced herself to look up at Barnaby's charred blank face as the knife hovered over her heart. His eyes were drenched in horror as if he knew what he was doing but couldn't help himself. "Barnaby! Stop!"

Penny pulled something from her pocket and swept it open with a twist of her wrist. It was a fan.

"Really?" Kate grunted as she struggled to shove an elbow in the servant's face.

Penny made a quick adjustment on the delicate accouterment and sharpened steel blades poked out. She raised the fan over her head and swept it down along the arm holding the knife. The limb separated from Barnaby's torso, and Kate let it drop to the floor.

Kate smashed her free fist into Barnaby's jaw. Flakes of desiccated flesh came off and his head wrenched to the side. He still would not relinquish his hold. He lurched forward with his deadweight, pressing Kate down so she lay under him. His teeth bared to tear at her neck.

Kate fumbled across the top of the bench until she snatched up something hard and slammed it into Barnaby's face. Glass shattered and cut into her hand, but the blow did little to her opponent. The contents of the flask filled the inside of his mouth with black treacle. It dripped onto Kate as well, serving to lock her together with Barnaby in the sticky mess. At least it covered his jaw, preventing him from closing his teeth around her throat.

Penny swung with her fan and sliced deep through his neck. The cadaver's head lolled to the side. Penny struck again, ripping through the remaining tendons. The severed head parted from the body but it remained attached to Kate's hand by the treacle.

"The white jar on that shelf." Kate kicked Barnaby's decapitated torso away. It continued to thrash without direction, slamming into tables and bookcases. It dropped to the hard floor and shook uncontrollably. "Pour it over my hand."

Penny did so and soon Barnaby's head fell to the floor. Kate poured more treacle over the corpse's limbs, pinning it to the stone floor. It squirmed, but it was rendered harmless.

"What the hell was that about?" Penny pointed at the charred body.

"Ash," Kate snarled, leaning down to stare at Barnaby's face. "Are you still in there, Ash? What did you think? Kill me and present Simon with a *fait accompli* and a vat of my blood. You disgusting creature." It took all her control not to slap Barnaby's face, but she knew Ash wouldn't feel it, and it wasn't right for Barnaby.

"Simon would never!" Penny said in outrage. "Doesn't Ash know that?"

"She thought to force his hand. I'd be dead, and in order for my death to have any meaning, Simon would be compelled to use my blood to regain his powers and defeat Gaios." Kate regarded the dead eye staring at her boldly. "No doubt you thought he'd come to you to work the spell."

"That scheming witch!" The engineer growled.

"You failed, Ash. Are you so afraid of Gaios? You think you can manipulate Simon as easily as you manipulated Pendragon? You're wrong. You don't know Simon at all."

Barnaby's lips stretched back into a gaping black grin. Then the muscles abruptly slackened and the expression stilled again in death.

"Is she gone?" Penny asked.

"I think so." Kate pulled a heavy cloth off a table and laid it over the head of the butler. "Poor Barnaby. He didn't deserve this indignity."

"I hate necromancers."

"That makes two of us."

"Are you hurt?"

"I'm fine." Kate smiled to reassure her young friend. "Unusual fan. Is it a family heirloom?"

"No, I made it."

"May I?" Kate reached toward it.

"Oh careful. You may get hurt." Penny guffawed at the ridiculousness of that given what they had just gone through. The fan appeared to be a normal bone-and-lace accessory, but Penny indicated a small panel with tiny buttons and levers. "I modified it with a few tricks. There are times when a girl must have fashionable accessories and can't carry a gun or a knife."

Kate looked at Penny's leather apron and stained face. "You're not exactly dressed for the opera."

"Well, sometimes I just get hot."

Kate laughed. "I love you, dear."

Chapter 11

SIMON STARED AT KATE.

"Did you hear me?" Kate's face beamed with excitement.

"Yes." He stifled his fury at Ash's malevolent interference. He would have loved to have seen Kate take the manipulative necromancer to task. "I'm just taken aback by it all. You've had a productive night."

"Very," she replied, and plowed ahead with her practical theorizing. "There is some risk, to be sure. No magic is foolproof, but—"

"Risk? That's an understatement. I'm sorry, Kate. It's unwise to say the least."

"I'm not using the full spell. Only a part of it."

"And the part where I drain your blood dry?" Simon crossed his arms and regarded her.

"Oh please. We just need enough of my blood to forge a connection between us." Kate turned and headed for the laboratory. "Come with me."

"You believe this conglomeration you found in the key will allow me to collect aether?" He was struggling to understand her alchemical theories and rapid thought process.

"The conglomeration makes everything possible. I'll

create a special ink using the conglomeration mixed with my blood. I'll use that ink to create your new tattoo. That tattoo should spark a reconnection to the aether. Just as it did for the key."

"Just how much blood?" His eyes narrowed.

"Barely a vial. I draw more than that from Imogen on a weekly basis."

Simon stopped in the hallway. "It's still blood magic, Kate. It's Ash's magic."

Kate grunted with frustration and turned back toward him. "Ash didn't get where she is by being an idiot. She was right that blood is the path back to aether. And the blood of someone who loves you is more powerful in its essence. However, the difference between us and Ash is that she's a glutton, wasteful. Her original spell worked by converting blood into a new substance, but it's how you use it that defines it. Ash uses necromancy to achieve her effect. I don't intend to do that. I'll be using your own scribing and my alchemy to do the deed. The blood aspect is only a small piece of a larger new spell that I've crafted."

"Then why is it dangerous?"

Kate smiled dismissively. "Because the blood will forge a bond between us. The spell will use my blood, or more accurately my essence, to reconnect you. You will actually be using me as a conduit to draw energy into you. Once you absorb enough aether, your own link to magic will be restored, and you will need to break the connection between us."

"Or?" Simon's face was stern.

"Or you could drain my life."

"If you die because of me, then I will be no better than Ash."

Kate's chin lifted. "Then don't let me die."

He drew a deep breath. "Your confidence in me is bracing."

"Simon, stop hesitating. There is no time for doubt. You know as well as I that our best hope of defeating Gaios is your inscription abilities. We know he's out there somewhere seeking the Stone. How can you even stand to wait another minute? We're running out of time. All of Britain is running out of time."

Kate had him and he knew it. If Gaios had only been stalking Ash, Simon would've been able to walk away from this proposal. With the whole nation at stake, neither of them had a choice. And as Kate so often proved there were ways to circumvent blockades. How long before Gaios found a way to his goal with or without the Stone?

Simon stared into her eyes, which were fired by determination and hope. How could one not feed off that energy and not believe in her? "No time to waste then."

Kate exhaled the breath she had been holding; her argument finally won. She took his hand and led him down the hall to her laboratory. Malcolm, Nick, and Penny stood just outside as if waiting all along.

"So you're going through with it then?" Nick asked, stifling a yawn. It was early for him.

"It's foolproof." Simon's face was set in stone.

Malcolm regarded him. "You're content using blood magic?"

"We're not going through all that again," Kate countered in exasperation.

Simon shrugged with mock helplessness. "She has gone to a great deal of trouble after all. It would be a shame to stop now."

"As always, you're too glib by half," the Scotsman muttered. "This is why I hate magic. It's too damn murky."

Kate forged on into her domain. Nick and Penny followed her into the laboratory. But Simon lingered outside near Malcolm. His voice dropped to a mere whisper.

"Malcolm, if things go awry and Kate is in danger . . .

you need to take me out of the equation. Do you understand?"

Malcolm's dark eyes lifted. "Why not ask Barker? He's your best mate."

"He might not make the right choice between me and Kate. You will."

There was a long pause, but finally the Scotsman nodded sharply. Simon breathed easier and clapped Malcolm on the arm.

Apparatus in Kate's laboratory already bubbled and toiled. Sharp morning sun sliced through the French windows. Kate turned when Simon entered, waving him to a cleared table. "Take off your shirt and lie down there."

His eyebrow rose with a bawdy grin, but she was immune to distraction now that they had begun her ritual. "Please. This is science."

Simon sighed. "Even Isaac Newton enjoyed the fruits of his labor."

"When this is all said and done, I'll be happy to drop an apple on you."

"I'll take that as a metaphor for something." Simon brightened, removing his shirt with a flourish and flinging it across the room. His body was muscular with white scars crisscrossing his flesh. Where once his arms and torso had been covered with dark runes of ink, now he was a blank canvas. He examined a tattooing kit resting on the table, a wooden box covered with intricate carvings. Old shamans of untold experience in remote villages across the globe had incised his previous tattoos. The thought of Kate inking his flesh sent an erotic shiver through his body. He lay back upon the table, his eyes never leaving her.

"Cold?" she asked, running a light hand boldly over his bare chest though she was still regarding him rather clinically.

"No," he said quietly. "Warm."

Kate finally looked at his face and smiled. "I'm not an expert at tattooing. This may come off looking like one of Charlotte's little stick figures."

"That will be fine." His voice was low, coming from deep in his chest.

She swallowed with more effort than usual. "Anyplace in particular you wish me to put it?"

He smiled darkly. "I can think of several."

Penny giggled from across the room and Kate's lips pursed. "You're such a romantic."

"That's a polite way of saying it."

She slapped his arm gently and he grabbed her hand, drawing it down to his left breast. "Here. Where it can be guided by the beating of my heart. Like blood, the heart is a powerful organ that will aid in the creation and dissemination of the aether."

Kate's fingers brushed his chest gently and then she leaned over to kiss it. Simon couldn't help but draw in a sharp breath. She moved up and kissed his lips slowly. Then she pulled away. "Excuse me, but I have important tasks to attend. The conglomeration is almost complete."

"I love it when you talk alchemy."

"If I don't finish the preparations just so, it will be worthless." She went to the opposite table. "And you will have removed your shirt for no reason but to expose your immense self-satisfaction."

"Reason enough." Simon watched Kate's sure hands manipulate tubes and flames and beakers and jars full of unknown materials. She worked as if playing a well-worn concerto. No hesitation. No doubt. And yet, despite practiced movements, he could tell from the slight wrinkles at the corners of her eyes that she was nervous and a little unsure.

Malcolm slipped inside the room and stood in the far corner. While Kate was working, Penny arranged a chair by Simon's bedside for Kate to steady herself while doing the tattoo. She opened the wooden box. Inside were long thin tubes of bamboo tipped with rows of needles laid out in a line. The interior of the box had an indentation for the ink. Soon clean cloth strips and a bowl of water were placed next to Simon.

A stone mortar and pestle sat on the table nearest Kate, along with other odd bits of cinder and ink. The conglomeration was still in a liquid form, but it would solidify soon enough so she had to move quickly. She began combining elements, adding alcohol to act as a carrier from the needle to the skin. At last, she held a vial of her blood over the conglomeration. The minute she poured the blood into the stone bowl, the black inky mixture absorbed it with an inhaling hiss.

Kate carefully brought the heated amalgam over to the table and set it beside the tattooing needles. Her eyes met Simon's. "Are you ready?"

Simon almost said no, but he knew Kate believed this was the right path. And she was a genius. He exchanged a glance with Malcolm, whose stern countenance put him at ease. Simon nodded.

Kate used one hand to steady and stretch the skin of Simon's bare chest. Making use of the spread of her fingers, she rested the base of the rod onto her thumb and began to rhythmically pierce the skin, injecting the powerful ink with each tap. Simon breathed in and out slowly despite the sharp and steady pain, so as not to disturb the area she was marking. Kate's fingers were warm against his cooling flesh. He watched as the tip of her tongue pressed against her shapely upper lip in concentration. She paused every few seconds to wipe the excess ink and blood off his skin and study her line.

Kate's tattooing method was her own. The act wasn't masterful, but the result was precise and that was all that counted. Beads of sweat marked her brow. Slowly the design of a long-dead rune took form. Compared to his old tattoos, this symbol was relatively simplistic. But she might have been weaving the Bayeux tapestry for all the concentration that Kate was forced to expend on it. It was the same symbol that had been used on the bow of the golden key, a rune created by Simon's father. He had long thought the emblem to be a stylized compass, but he wondered now if it was a rising sun. Hopefully not a setting sun.

Minute after minute crawled by. Simon's chest grew numb so he no longer felt the jabs of the needle. Kate blinked constantly, growing fatigued from the focused strain. Penny stood close to Kate, watching with great interest, studying technique more than product. Nick paced before the French windows, occasionally glancing up but preferring to stare at the floor. Malcolm stood quiet and motionless, never removing his eyes from the arcane activity.

Kate hesitated, holding the needle above Simon's skin. He looked up, but before he could ask her what was wrong, she jabbed down as if in punctuation. With a whisper that could have been a word, the arcane ink sank into Simon's skin. He gasped hard as his blood burned. The outline of the tattoo glowed a vivid green as if there were a light source behind it.

Just as abruptly, Kate's tools dropped from her fingers. Her breathing sharpened into short gulps. She leaned dizzily over him.

"Kate!" Simon half rose off the table, his hands grabbing her forearms before she tilted to the side.

"I wasn't expecting it to hit me so fast," Kate muttered, holding a hand to her head.

The house suddenly shook. Penny and Nick were thrown to the floor. Glassware rattled.

Malcolm rushed across the laboratory and took hold

of Kate. Simon leapt off the table and together they laid her there. The Scotsman looked at Simon with dread in his gaze. "Can you help her?"

Hogarth appeared in the doorway and started to speak, but the sight of Kate's supine form stopped him.

Trying to keep the dread from his face, Simon said grimly, "She is fine, Hogarth. What's the matter?"

With his gaze locked on Kate, the manservant said with unnerving calm, "We have a situation."

Simon turned to Malcolm. "Go."

"But you said—" Malcolm hesitated.

"I've my wits about me. I'll make the right decision, if need be. Go. All of you."

Malcolm nodded and ran out of the laboratory, with Penny and Nick on his heels. Hogarth paused, but then turned and headed for the front of the house.

Kate's eyes rolled up in the back of her head and she slumped, insensible. Anger surged in Simon, fearing they had fallen into Ash's trap. Even so, he would not lose Kate. He ripped open her bodice so her upper chest was bare right above her corseted breasts. He grabbed the ink bowl beside him, thrusting a finger in the mixture. He drew quick strokes on her with his dripping finger, writing the standard rune for *desist*. There was no reaction from Kate, neither did the burning of his blood abate. His inscription wasn't working. He felt no connection to the aether.

Kate moaned again and Simon brushed the hair back from her face, desperate now. She trusted him to save her. If he couldn't figure this out fast enough, he would drain Kate dry. He had to dam up the flow of energy between them.

He scribed another black rune across her pale flesh. The new word did nothing. Simon slammed a hand down onto the table. "Damn it!"

An explosion vibrated in the distance. Penny's blunderbuss from the sound of it. He had no idea what they were facing outside, but if it was Gaios, they would need help from both him and Kate.

He blackened his finger again and once more drew over Kate's flesh, this time inverting his father's rune, a mirror opposite of his own. Her breathing grew even more shallow, her lips losing color.

Maybe he didn't have enough aether yet. But there was no time. It could take hours, days even. Kate had mere minutes. They should have known better than to use blood magic. *He* should have known better. Blood spells were insidious and—

Then he knew. He rushed for another table and grabbed a scalpel. Without hesitation, he sliced into his open palm, carving an inverted version of his father's rune. Blood dripped bold red to the floor. Then he turned back to Kate and slapped his hand right above her left breast beneath her collarbone.

Kate arched off the table, crying out. Simon held her down through the spasm. She took a last deep gasp and collapsed. He desperately sought for the rise and fall of her chest under his hand. Several seconds passed with no further breaths. Simon grabbed the blade again, his thoughts plunging dark. Turning the blade inward, he looked back at Kate, memorizing her face.

Her eyelashes fluttered and at last she took a breath, normal and gentle as if she were just waking from a distant dream. The scalpel dropped to the floor with a clatter as he gathered her in his arms.

"Kate!"

She opened her eyes. "Simon. You're all right."

He clutched her tight and in her surprise she held him, her hand cupping the back of his head as it pressed against her neck.

"I knew you would save me," she whispered.

He couldn't answer her, the state of his voice was precarious. She was alive, that was all that mattered.

"Your powers? Have they returned?" Kate pushed him back, taking in his torso, blank but for the single tattoo over his heart. Frantic hope filled her. "Please tell me this wasn't all in vain."

"I don't know. I feel different. My blood feels like it's on fire, but I can't command the aether."

"Then how did you—?" It was then she noticed the state of her undress and the runic patterns of ink and blood smeared across her chest. "Oh!"

"It was my blood that halted the flow of energy passing between us."

Just over Kate's heart, like Simon's, an inverted rune was burned into her flesh. The skin was puckered and tight like a brand. It was then she noticed his hand dripping blood. She ripped what was left of her blouse and quickly tied it around his palm.

"Blood against blood," she realized.

"More specifically your blood to begin and mine to end. It took me precious minutes to figure it out. I almost lost you in my folly. I am not familiar with the illogic of blood magic."

The house shook violently again. Wide-eyed, Kate regarded him with questions.

"We have visitors," Simon said.

"Jesus. You'd think I was running a bloody public house." Her mouth quirked into a weary smile. "We need a holiday."

"I know a spot by a stream in the Scottish Highlands near Fort Augustus," Simon offered.

Kate's eyes softened as she slid off the table. "It sounds lovely. I'll meet you there when this is all over." She retrieved a bandolier of vials and slung it over her bare shoulder. She lifted her special crossbow and snapped it open, ready for battle. "Shall we go greet our guests?"

MALCOLM DODGED A SMASHING BLOW BY A MEchanical arm. He fired his massive Lancasters, but the heavy balls merely bounced off the metal beast that rose before him. Hogarth's mace slammed down against the steel limb, sending flakes of paint flying. That was the extent of the damage he did to the same mechanical monstrosity they had faced on Old London Bridge and which now crawled on its piston-driven legs over the ruined north grounds toward Hartley Hall.

"Where the hell is Penny?" Malcolm shouted. "This thing will tear us to pieces."

In answer came a thunderous boom over their heads, and the front of the mecha blossomed into smoke and fire. It fell off balance, kicking up dirt and dust.

"Keep your kilt on," the engineer yelled back, a bit out of breath and lugging her long brass blunderbuss. "I'm right here. Holy God, I need to make this gun more portable."

Malcolm helped her bring the cannon back onto her shoulder and shoved another canister in. "Keep it away from the house."

She fired the blunderbuss at the crawler's undercarriage just as it propped itself up on its long arm, trying to get its flailing legs under it again. The blast knocked it face-first onto the gravel drive.

"Find Barker!" Malcolm yelled to Hogarth. "We need him."

"Yes, sir."

"And then go to Charlotte and keep her out of the fight. She's still too weak."

"Yes, sir." Hogarth raced for the house.

"Look at you, giving orders." Penny smirked.

"Just take that bloody thing down!"

"With pleasure. I loaded more powder in these canisters. I could take down a cathedral." Penny let another canister fly. The blast sent both Malcolm and Penny to the ground as a wave of smoke and dirt rained down on them.

Nick appeared through the haze. He pulled Penny to her feet and stared at the metal monster. "Great. Just what we need. We fared so well against it last time."

"Got anything more helpful than that?" growled Malcolm just as the machine lurched back to its feet. The mecha abruptly vented steam. The pistons in the legs contracted and it crouched on the ground like a huge elephant settling. Gears ground and numerous panels lifted and shifted aside along its abdomen.

"I don't like this," muttered Nick.

Things began falling from the body of the giant machine. Each one moved on spindly legs out of the way of other objects dropping behind it. They were the size of large cats, but resembled metal spiders with bulbous translucent abdomens of different colors.

"They're heading for the house!" Penny shouted in alarm.

Nick shook his hands into flame. "Come on!"

Malcolm turned to Penny. "Keep on the machine. You're the only thing that can dent it." He then ran with Nick, barely keeping ahead of the group of wee beasties scuttling toward Hartley Hall.

Penny lifted her blunderbuss and took aim, this time firing into the bared belly from where the spiders had dropped. The explosion shook the mecha violently and flames roared out of one of the hatches.

Malcolm reached the door just before the first of the small mechanical things skittered up the portico at his heels. He opened fire. Bullets struck the metal body, and to his surprise, it stopped and raised its green abdomen. Then it slammed its body against the step, shattering the translucent bulb and spewing green fumes. Malcolm's throat closed abruptly as if the air was gone. He hacked and covered his mouth with his sleeve.

Nick pulled him back toward the door. "Deadly little buggers."

Malcolm wheezed. "Poison."

"Don't fret, Angus." Nick waved his hand and set the air in front of them on fire, burning off the noxious gas.

Another mechanical spider scurried along the wall, closing on the door where they stood. Instead of a green abdomen, this one was red. It rose up high on its legs, lifting a swollen belly. Malcolm grabbed Nick just as the creature tapped its abdomen on the bricks. The explosion blew them both back inside the foyer.

More insect-things filled the door and the broken windows. Malcolm aimed for the colorful bellies and fired again. Green spiders exploded and toxic gas billowed in the hall.

"What the hell are you doing shooting them?" Nick yelled.

"Burn off the gas. We can't let them get past us and spread into the house." Malcolm reloaded with practiced speed.

Nick's flames torched the poisonous vapors and scorched the walls. Malcolm spun and fired, hitting a red spider and detonating it in the doorway. Several nearby companions blew up around it, creating a massive fireball. Nick cursed and held out his hands, controlling the fire as it rushed toward them. He deftly swirled the flames like a tornado in the high space of the foyer, then pushed them to a fireplace. The twisting fire rushed up through the chimney and out of the house.

There was a great grinding sound. The claw from the mecha ripped off a section of the roof. Nick barely leapt aside as a huge oaken beam plummeted to the floor.

Malcolm threw himself against the wall to avoid an avalanche of wood, plaster, and marble. "I thought the bloody house could withstand an earthquake."

"This isn't Gaios. It's just a demolisher and if we can't stop it, we're in trouble."

"You worry too much, Nick," came a voice from behind.

"Simon." Malcolm spun with renewed hope. Then he noted the state of undress of both Simon and Kate. "What the hell were you two doing? Time and place, for God's sake." He also noticed that Simon was wearing the steel gauntlets.

The spell hadn't worked. And they had monsters at the door.

Chapter 12

KATE KICKED HER WAY THROUGH THE DE-stroyed foyer with barely a glance at the damage done to her childhood home. Too much had already passed to afford this anything more than a brief scowl. Simon activated his steel gauntlets with a sharp snap of electricity. Malcolm's eyes briefly registered disappointment before he ducked as a huge section of the front façade was ripped off. Kate pressed against the wall to avoid the raining thunderous wreckage. She heard shouting from above.

Hogarth appeared at the top of the staircase assisting a pale and unsteady Charlotte. Imogen waved a group of servants to follow. Most of them gaped at the open sky visible now through the wall of the house.

"Everyone move down below!" Kate yelled to Hogarth. "Hurry!"

Charlotte tried to straighten up using Hogarth's firm arm. "I can help."

"No!" Malcolm ordered before even Kate could respond. "Go with the rest."

Charlotte's lower lip immediately protruded in a defiant manner so Kate quickly interceded. "Help Imogen protect the servants."

Nodding, Charlotte looked at her friend and together she and Imogen led the parade down the stairs and to the back of the house toward hopeful safety.

More spiders appeared, scrambling over detritus. Kate responded immediately by throwing several vials of black treacle at the approaching cluster. The sticky substance held them fast, both legs and abdomens.

Malcolm raised a pistol. "Everyone stand back." He fired at a red spider. It exploded and again set off its struggling companions.

More bricks and plaster rained down. Nick scorched the rising cloud of poison and sent the flames out into the open air. Malcolm slammed new cartridges into his pistols.

Simon pointed back into the house. "Malcolm, sweep the premises for more of these insects. We must protect the others. And we don't want them to find Ferghus because we don't know if they can communicate. The rest of you come with me."

The Scotsman took off down the corridor toward the library while Simon led the way out with Kate and Nick, scrambling around mounds of brick and plaster past the shattered front wall of the once-magnificent home. The huge machine crawled toward the eastern corner, paying no attention to the humans. It stretched its long arm upward and smashed its fingers through windows. Penny knelt fifty yards away across the churned lawn with her blunderbuss ready. Simon waved her to the right, signaling her to the far side of the machine.

He motioned Nick away from the house. "Stand by to strike with fire. We're going for the brain, and hopefully we'll short it out. Kate, I want you to do what you can to immobilize the legs." Simon suddenly clutched at his tattooed breast and cried out with pain. He bent over at the waist though there was no enemy around him.

"Simon!" Kate reached for him.

"Something's wrong," Simon hissed through clenched teeth, trying to catch his breath before the next wave of pain washed over him. "My skin . . . it's burning."

Kate took Simon's arm, but the instant her bare hand touched him, flashes of color sparked in her vision and her own rune seared with pain. The world around her flared with aether. Simon arched backward. Bright green lines cut a path across his torso and arms. The tattoos were rewriting themselves. He let out a sharp cry. Beneath Kate's hands, Simon's muscles strained. Amazement and terror ripped through her. He was draped in emerald flame, the outline of a god. His features were no longer flesh and bone. He was living aether. It poured into him like a flood. His eyes flashed open and aether boiled out.

He slumped over, gasping for breath. Together they collapsed to their knees. Only Kate's hold kept him from falling flat on the ground. He slowly straightened, his lips parted in wonder and relief. Aether swirled around them like the flames of an inferno. There was no heat, but she felt it nonetheless. The world glowed. It was beautiful.

Simon stood, slipping away from her and the world abruptly reverted to its usual state so fast it made her dizzy. She put a hand down in the dirt to steady herself. Simon looked normal too, but she knew he wasn't. He would never be.

"I'm all right." He smiled calmly down at her as he removed the iron gauntlets and tossed them aside. He raised a hand to Penny and pointed at the machine, which was busy ripping heavy stones off the eastern corner of Hartley Hall. "Aim for the head!"

Nick took a step toward him in alarm, but Simon sent him at the mechanized beast with a nod. With a whispered word on his lips, a green line swiftly traced a tattoo high on his shoulder. Simon ran at the mecha. Just as he reached it, a small vial flew past him, shot out of Kate's crossbow, and a sizeable chunk of amber swallowed the machine's back legs, holding it firm. Grabbing one of its free legs, Simon lifted it easily off the ground. Gears whined and hot steam blew furiously as the machine tried to adjust. Simon bent the steel leg in half, then he grasped another beside it.

The machine seemed to recognize its predicament. The long segmented arm released the side of the house and swung at Simon. The blow would have crushed him, but he dove to the side and the steel fingers gouged a long furrow in the ground.

Nick sent a steady stream of fire at the machine's bulbous head, hopefully blinding it as well as doing damage. Penny's blunderbuss roared yet again. The canister sailed overhead and slammed into the center of Nick's fireball. The explosion that resulted pounded them all. When the smoke cleared, there was a new dent in the metallic surface.

The machine slammed its fist down again at Simon but he grabbed hold. The mecha tried to retract its arm, but Simon roared, the muscles of his back rolling like marble. With the grinding sound of twisting metal, he ripped the arm off the machine. It reared back, off balance. Penny fired another shell directly at the indentation she already made. The blast forced the machine to stumble. Nick flung two fireballs at the round eye. It erupted in a shower of sparks and ash.

"Keep it up!" Simon shouted. The central eye pivoted with difficulty to face him. Multiple piston-driven legs stabbed furiously at him, but he dodged the pounding attacks. Then he leapt straight up. "Now!"

Penny and Nick let loose with all they had left. Above the chaos, Kate heard Simon shout, and he plunged down on top of the mecha. He smashed through the softened metal into the heart of the thing. Kate cried out in alarm, but then saw Simon crash out the bottom and fall heavily beneath the monstrosity. He hit the ground like a meteor. He had cast his stone spell on the way down and had plummeted all the way through the machine like a catapult boulder.

The mecha staggered with a horrific whine building inside. The smoke blew away from the machine to reveal a large jagged hole through its crown. Fires ignited in what was left of its brain. Gears and wires were in a tangled ruin. An explosion in its belly erupted, casting debris everywhere. The great mechanical creature shuddered and froze. Then it toppled backward with a horrific creak of metal and collapsed in the dirt in a cloud of dust and smoke.

Nick hooted in triumph. Kate ran past him, diving into the smoke, coming as close as she dared to the flaming wreckage. She searched frantically for a sign of Simon. Through the haze and flying cinders, she saw him in a hollowed-out crater, still bent in a silent motionless crouch. She turned back, searching for Nick through the impenetrable choking cloud.

Malcolm sprinted into view, with Nick at his side. The Scotsman followed Kate's frantic gesture. "Barker, clear off the fire. He can only stay in stone form for a few minutes."

Nick was already waving his arms, gathering the flames. He dumped them somewhere to the north where the grounds were more dirt than forest and the fire would burn itself out quickly. Nick then made another gesture and a stiff wind drove the smoke away from the crater.

The stone spell wore off and Simon stood up in the midst of the smoldering debris. He saw the group surrounding him, staring down in concern, and he took a bow. A low formal bow. And then he raised his arms like an actor at the end of a bravura performance. "And *that* is how you destroy an infernal machine."

"Show-off," Malcolm mumbled, giving him a hand out of the crater.

Simon laughed with unrestrained glee. "It felt damn good to do that." He was breathing hard though Kate doubted it was from exertion.

"You're aether drunk." Malcolm steadied Simon as he weaved slightly.

"I am indeed." Simon grinned. "And I hope soon to be conventionally drunk!"

Penny was already scrabbling through mechanical debris. "Damn it, the brain's in pieces."

"My sincerest apologies, Miss Carter," Simon offered. "But I have no doubt you'll have it back together and thinking good thoughts in no time."

Penny pulled out a thick leather glove and began rooting through the shattered pieces. Kate swore she heard humming.

She looked at her side and saw Nick staring at Simon with his mouth agape. The older magician was in pure wonder at his former student. Kate said with a bubbling laugh, "You've never seen him like that, have you? He's amazing."

"God Almighty," Nick breathed.

Simon lurched forward, planting a kiss on Kate's forehead. Her perception of the world did not shift at his touch, but she wasn't sure if she was relieved or not. While she didn't see aether surrounding them, she did feel his muscular tattooed arms warm around her waist.

"So, it worked, did it?" she asked with mock humility.

Simon stepped back and slid his hands along her bare arms until he was clasping both of her hands. "Kate, do you know what you did? I'm sure you do"—he raised his voice—"but for everyone's benefit, you have converted blood magic into white magic. There are none in this world, the history of the world, who have ever done such a thing. None. Not Pendragon. Not Merlin. Not Hermes Trismegistus."

"It was nothing." Kate blushed in spite of herself. Seeing Simon whole and unharmed made her chest ache with joy. "If I'm such a wizard, why can't I keep my house from being destroyed?"

"A house? What's a house? Some sticks and mud? Anyone can build a house." Simon touched the tattoo above Kate's heart, the mirror image of the one above his. "Only you could make this."

"Simon, darling." Kate put her hand over his.

"Yes, my dear?"

"Might I cover my bosom? I feel a bit tawdry."

"If you must." Simon kissed her.

SIMON STOOD IN FRONT OF THE ORNATE SILVER mirror in his room. It was late and shadows crowded around him. A lantern lit by sparkling brownies stood on the night table, but the glow was feeble. The little fae inside chattered away incessantly, staring at Simon through the glass, whispering foul things, but he turned a deaf ear. He was too mesmerized by the new tattoo over his heart. The raw red lines made it stand out from the others. The rune looked remarkably different, less identifiable but more personal. It burned against his flesh, a constant reminder that it was there. The well of aether inside him bubbled like an incessant cauldron. He could call it forth and touch it with but a word if he so wanted. The temptation to do so forever on his lips.

He drew in a deep breath and exhaled slowly, remembering the feel of Kate's hands on his skin. A well of fire burned suddenly in him that had nothing to do with aether. Her light feather touch had struck cleanly and rhythmically, searing his soul as well as his flesh.

Leaning over a porcelain basin, he madly splashed the cool water over his face. It did nothing to soothe him. His hands rubbed his face hard with a towel and he turned to the bed, slipping under a single sheet. With damaged Hartley Hall open to the night airs, the house was even cooler than usual, but Simon was flushed and warm.

There would be no rest tonight. His mind and heart raced with indecent thoughts of Kate. On any other night he would have welcomed them, but there were plans to make and a war to fight. Even with his added strength, Simon wasn't sure it was enough to take Gaios down, but their fortunes did seem improved suddenly thanks to Kate.

Gaios could not remain free. Pendragon had contained him once. Simon could do no less. And he knew just where to find what he needed. Tomorrow morning, they would take the key portal to Paris. Pendragon's old prison might hold the answers.

A creak at the door made him turn. It opened and Kate stood there, draped in a light night shift. His breath caught in his chest, thoughts of business scattered like leaves on the wind. The glow of a small lantern in her hand illuminated the soft curves of her body through the delicate material. Simon's mouth went dry.

She walked softly to him, holding the light steady, padding quietly to the edge of the bed. Like a moth to a flame, she came forward slowly. With great deliberateness she placed her light on the table, then returned her attention to Simon. In her other hand she held a small vial.

"What's that?" Simon's voice was barely above a whisper.

She didn't reply, but merely uncapped the container. A thick honey liquid oozed into her palm. Her finger dipped into the liquid. Then she applied it to his bare chest, tracing the rune on his heart. Immediately the burning eased. He sucked in a deep breath.

"Is that better?" she asked.

"Much," he breathed.

Simon took her open palm and brushed his own fingers through the honeylike balm. He sat up and gently pulled the neck of her shift aside to expose the scar above her breast. Her own inhale was sharp and long. He pressed his lips lightly against it. He stroked the inverted rune, spreading the gel over her smooth skin. The burnt symbol was still inflamed. Kate sighed and closed her eyes.

"Better?" he asked her.

"Much." The word was low and full of need.

Kate slipped between the sheets, the length of her stretching out alongside him. Her chilled body against his rising heat. He gently arranged her hair on his pillow. She was quiet and there were no lines on her face as if she were in a dream world where her life was always sweet and pleasant. Her green eyes remained warm and inviting.

"I've come to enjoy the fruits of my labor," Kate told him, the edges of her lips lifting.

Everything he wanted lay before him. "Are you sure, Kate? One night with me and you can never go back."

Her mouth quirked and an eyebrow rose. "Oh? You think you're so special then?"

"I truly don't, and society even less so. Your reputation will be ruined. You know who I am. People will talk."

Kate's head moved slightly on his pillow. "They already do, since the first day you came to Hartley Hall. Whether we did or we didn't, whether we do or we don't."

Simon traced the line of her jaw, and said playfully, "Your prospects will be limited."

"*You* are my prospect."

He frowned, wondering what her life would have been like if their circles had never intertwined. "Do you regret it?"

"Hardly." She shifted closer, her lips a scant distance from his own, and murmured, "And what about your considerable reputation? Can you settle for just one?"

Blood pounded in his ears. "I have since the first time we met. You changed me. I measure myself by you now." His hand touched the brand over his heart. "We're joined, Kate. From now until our dying breath."

Her palm closed over his and he was sure she could feel the frantic hammering of his heart.

"Today I saw you wreathed in aether," she whispered. "Like a phoenix rising in flame. So much power. Am I different now too?" Her hand moved to hover over the rune on her breast.

"We'll never be like normal people. Not that we ever were. We'll be able to touch each other in ways we've yet to discover. But I can think of no one else I would rather caress, now and forever." Simon's chest shuddered as she touched him, her own inhale of breath tenuous and shaking. It nearly undid him. "You're beautiful."

"My God, you talk too much. I'm bloody well wooed."

His lips smashed into hers as she pressed just as hungrily. Her arms curled around him, light fingers tracing the emerald runes incised along his knotted muscles. Her touch burned sweetly. When his head buried in her neck licking the soft flesh there, she coughed lightly and her hands stilled.

He pulled back, fearful that she had changed her mind. "What is it?"

Her eyes were staring at the lantern by the bedside. "They're watching us."

The brownies had stopped their chattering and were pressed up against the glass curiously.

With an annoyed curse, Simon yanked off her nightgown with a firm tug. Kate gasped more out of surprise than impropriety as the cool night air hit her bare skin. An accurate toss later, and the shift landed over the lantern, draping it completely. One by one the grumpy lights went out until the lantern was silent and dark.

Then his lips were on her again, his broad hands spreading out on either side of her as he rose over her exquisite form, marred by only one small mark. His mark. He gazed down into her eyes, as fathomless as a midnight forest. But from their depths a light shone like a candle in a distant window, calling him home. Her warm breath brushed against his skin. She raised her arms and encircled his neck, drawing him down until their bodies melded. And the world shifted.

Aether filled the room, flooding it with serene light that only they could see. It coalesced around them, filling the space, filling them, blown about by the winds of possibility.

Chapter 13

SIMON WAS BRIEFLY DISORIENTED FROM PASSING through the portal, but it cleared quickly. Kate was alert, as was Penny; they had all used the portal before. Malcolm and Nick were not so fresh. Nick leaned near a shuttered window in the stifling room with an astonished grin on his face. Malcolm was squatting in a corner, groaning and sick, with a shaking hand on the back of his head.

"Steady," Simon soothed. "It can be a bit of a shock the first time through."

"Jesus," the Scotsman breathed. "That's unnatural."

"But it is a fast way to get about." Penny rubbed his back.

"No excuse." Malcolm massaged his forehead. "God created distance and time for a reason." He moaned again as the room suddenly filled with sunlight.

"We're in Paris!" Nick announced triumphantly from the open window. Distant sounds of conversation and laughter wafted in. "Good God. We just stepped from Surrey to Paris."

"Yes." Simon joined him at the window.

Penny crowded in between them and gazed out with wonder on a vast tree-filled quadrangle bordered by columned galleries with a large fountain in the center. It was crowded with strollers and sellers.

"My brother, Charles, will be so jealous!" she exclaimed, then she paused. "What am I looking at?"

Simon smiled and looked at the beautiful yellowish Baroque architecture and grey slate roof around the attic window where he stood. "It's the Palais-Royal."

"You're damn right it is!" Nick laughed and pointed out. "The Café de la Rotonde is just there. We met many a lovely lady there. Remember, Simon?"

Kate looked out on the gardens with a crooked smile. "You've never mentioned you spent time in Paris, Simon."

"I've never mentioned almost everything. And it wasn't much time. A few days."

"And nights," Nick added, still taking in the scene below.

"Quiet," Simon warned. "Nick and I passed a week here on the way to Italy. The Grand Tour."

Nick sat on the windowsill. "Remember Florence?"

"Florence?" Kate inquired deadpan. "Would that be the city or a chambermaid?"

"The city, darling," Simon said as he shoved Nick aside and closed the shutters. "The chambermaid was in Grenoble. And our tour was purely functional. Nick was showing me important magical objects and locations."

"Oh Jesus!" Nick guffawed. "Parma! I can't believe you're not still in prison."

Simon put an arm over his friend. "I really must insist you recall I have my powers back and am capable of killing you should you go on."

"Sure." Nick patted Simon's chest. "Kate, I applaud your father's choice of rooms here in Paris. There is little in life a man can't find at the Palais-Royal."

Kate arched a stern eyebrow at Nick. "Don't drag my father into your tales of debauchery. Unlike you and

Mr. Archer, my father surely chose this place for its strategic location in the city."

"Strategy." Simon nodded. "No doubt."

Nick rolled his eyes. "Simon, please tell me we'll have time for a few gambling houses."

"No. We're here on a mission. Our goal is to get in, scout the prison, and get out."

Nick watched the gold key dangling from Simon's hand. "I might need to borrow that bauble at some point. I didn't know it was so convenient."

"In due time." Simon reached into his pocket and pulled out a wallet full of francs. He distributed them around.

Kate waved her hand. "I have money."

"I know you do," Simon said. "This is yours. I took it from your safe. All right, everyone, remember, we are away from the relative protection of Hartley Hall and vulnerable to Gaios. I don't suspect he has any way of knowing we're here, but his resources are immense and we should be prepared for a strike. If you are separated from the group, make your way back here. This is the only location in the city where we can activate the portal. Who has been to Paris before?"

Kate, Nick, and Malcolm raised their hands.

Penny gave a sour look and crossed her arms. "I've never been anywhere."

Malcolm, having recovered his color, was checking a pistol. "Passed through on the way to Provence. Back in '23. Hunting werewolves."

Simon asked, "Do you speak French?"

"I did. I was going to settle near Avignon."

"Settle?" Penny looked at Malcolm with surprise. "Was there a woman involved?"

Malcolm holstered his pistol and buttoned his coat. Everyone waited for him to continue, which he did not.

Simon exchanged curious glances with Kate. Then her eyes darted toward his hand. He looked down too and noticed a section of the gold key was blinking. It wasn't giving off the same glow as it did when activating its magical portal. Rather, a small phrase of the inscribed runes blinked several times and went dark. Simon was puzzled; he had never seen that action before.

Penny noticed it too and pointed toward the still-shimmering portal back to Hartley Hall. "Flip back to the map."

Simon waved his hand in front of the hole in space with practiced skill and the shimmering view of Hartley Hall vanished to be replaced by a map of the world, replete with dots representing locations where the key would open its portal to allow the user to tread through time and space. He and Kate and Penny perused the world until Kate exclaimed.

"There. Batavia is back."

Indeed, one of the dots on Batavia on the island of Java, which had vanished along with all the others when the key had been drained by Ra, was now back in place. Over the last few months, the various sites had been popping back onto the map. This was the first time they had noticed a correlation between a portal's return, and some activity on the key itself.

Simon held the key up to his eyes and smiled. "That's fantastic! We've just seen the creation phrase in the inscription. Those runes control the creation of portals, in some fashion."

"And what does that do for us?" Penny asked with typical practicality.

He tapped Penny lovingly on the nose with the key. "It means, Miss Carter, that I may be able to create new portals. And we may be able to create new keys."

Penny and Kate exchanged excited glances.

Malcolm gargled with water and spat into a long-dead plant in the corner. "Could we handle one thing at a time for once? We're in Paris for a purpose."

"Marthsyl." Simon intoned the active phrase of the key's magic, the ancient Celtic word for miracle, and the portal spun into nothingness. He replaced the key in his waistcoat pocket with a chuckle. He bowed and extended his arm to the door. They all went out into the narrow corridor. They had come fashionably dressed, although Penny's twill and heavy rucksack made her appear a bit more the laborer. Malcolm also seemed out of place with his long wool greatcoat on a warm September day. They trooped down the stairs and out into the shadows of a leisurely afternoon. Simon pulled out an English-language guidebook and the company became just another group of tourists.

They hired a carriage and set off eastward through the dim warrens and grand boulevards. It rolled out of the crowded Rue Saint-Antoine into an open square where it creaked to a halt. Simon opened the door. Penny hopped out with a whispered curse of wonder.

"Is that a bleeding elephant?" she exclaimed.

In the center of the open plaza was a gigantic plaster elephant nearly a hundred feet high including the castle tower on its back. It stood on a small rise and was surrounded by a low wall.

"Are we there?" Penny looked around in confusion. "Where's the Bastille? Am I missing it? I thought it was big."

"It's gone," Kate replied. "It was pulled down early in the Revolution."

"They replaced it with a huge elephant?"

"Bonaparte," Kate said. "He intended it to be a colossal bronze elephant fountain, but this plaster model is the best they've managed so far."

"But wait." Penny shifted her heavy rucksack from one shoulder to another. "The Bastille was demolished? Aren't we here to find the cell where they kept Gaios?"

"We are." Simon brandished his guidebook again and led them through the river of carriages toward the huge elephant. They stopped at the low wall surrounding the plaster monument and Simon gestured as if lecturing from his book. "Pendragon's prisoners were bound in catacombs beneath the Bastille. We hope those cells still exist, and we're looking for a way down into them. We'll start with the elephant. It was intended to be a fountain, so I hope it was placed where they could access underground tunnels to the canals for water. If not, we'll expand our search for a passageway."

"If we find the cell, it will help us defeat Gaios?" Malcolm didn't look at the elephant but rather studied the area around them. Lights were appearing in the windows of surrounding buildings as long shadows crawled over the plaza. It was becoming a very pleasant late-summer evening in Paris, but Malcolm didn't seem to notice. He wasn't one to notice pleasant summer evenings ever.

"I hope so," Simon answered. "Pendragon inscribed the cell with spells to contain Gaios and his elemental powers. I hope there's information there I can use."

He hopped over the wall and approached the giant elephant. The beast towered over them like a multistory edifice. Large sections of its plaster skin peeled and puckered in disrepair.

"So we need to get inside this?" Malcolm asked.

Simon surveyed the ground beneath the colossus. Penny rummaged in her bag, and pulled out a small pistol with a tuning fork where the hammer should have been.

"Simon," she said, "I could use this."

Simon said, "I thought that gun was destroyed."

"I do make things, you know," she replied. "I made another."

"Excellent." Simon stood aside. "How do you intend to use it?"

Penny thumbed up the tuning fork. "At low power, it produces feedback that changes depending on the surface the sound strikes. Like an echo. I can find a passageway to the catacombs if there is one." With both arms extended, she aimed the pistol at the elephant's massive feet. She pulled the trigger and began to quiver slightly.

No sound came from the strange pistol, but from inside the elephant came an unnerving skittering. High-pitched squealing filled the air. A large piece of plaster from the elephant's front leg separated, pushed out by claws and wriggling snouts. Hundreds of red eyes appeared in an explosion of rats, an undulating carpet of greasy little bodies spreading out around the thick grey feet. The swarm passed by, streaming outward, causing the crowd around the elephant to shout with alarm and scatter.

Malcolm kicked out at a few grey brutes that swarmed over his feet and up his boots. "Jesus. Are we climbing into a great rat nest?"

"I hope that's all we find for a change." Penny pointed at the elephant's foot that the rats had abandoned. "There's a void of some sort under there."

Simon knelt beside the shattered front foot. He dug his fingers into the crumbling plaster and seized the framework of wood beneath and pulled. The backside of the elephant's leg tore free in a shower of dust and splinters. There was a clear hole in the ground inside the leg. He spat dust from his mouth and held up his hand. Penny tossed him a coil of rope she had pulled from her bag. Simon tied it off to a sturdy brace and tossed the end down into the hole. After a moment, he heard a faint thud. "Good. There's a bottom. Nick, you go first."

STONE ARCHES ROSE ABOVE THEM IN THE DARKness. Their footsteps mixed with the faint sounds of dripping water. The tunnel was built with stone, not carved from rock. Quavering lights from a small lantern carried by Malcolm in the lead, and a flame burning in Nick's hand at the rear of the group, slid along the rough grey walls.

The hallway turned to the right and Malcolm suddenly shouted, "Losh!" He brought his pistol up.

Simon and Kate were immediately at his side with sword cane, pistol, and crossbow at the ready. The yellow light played over a white bony face with jaws open. There were other skulls around it, stacked along the wall in a strange pattern. In the corridor going forward, as far as they could make out, the walls and ceiling were nothing but skulls and long bones crisscrossed. Malcolm snorted with embarrassment at crying out.

Simon used the tip of his sword to tap one of the frozen skeletal screams. "Like the catacombs south of the river. The art of the dead."

Malcolm led the way into the charnel tunnel. Black hollow eyes watched them all. Simon glanced back to check on Penny, but she was studying the surroundings as if for design tips.

Nick followed, holding a piece of bread over the flame in his hand, and grumbling, "We're in Paris, and I'm eating toast I made with my own hand. Sad."

"We can come back anytime, Nick. That's the miracle of the key. We have our lifetimes to dine in Paris. It can be like the old days again."

Nick suddenly took on a strange pensive look. He bit the bread and chewed sullenly.

Soon they encountered the first open room with its door torn off its hinges. Malcolm shined the lantern farther down the hall and reported several more open doorways before the corridor ended with a sealed room.

Simon borrowed a lantern and stepped inside the first room. It was barely fifteen feet square, certainly with no windows available so far below the streets of Paris. The walls were plain and bare. He took a thick stub of chalk from his pocket and began to draw on the floor. He scribed white runes in a circle, then knelt in the center. He placed his fingers against the stone. He spoke and the runes glowed green. The cell was suddenly full of strange markings, the walls, floor, and ceiling all crowded with runic etching usually invisible to the normal eye.

Kate gasped in wonder at the intricate handiwork. "Pendragon?"

"Yes," said Simon. "Gorgeous stuff. Incredibly powerful."

"Was this Gaios's cell?"

"No." Simon pointed to a string of runes on the ceiling. "If I'm reading this properly, this cell was prepared for our friend, Nephthys, the demon queen."

"Our late friend, Nephthys," Malcolm commented from the door.

"Just so." Simon smeared the chalk circle and the runes vanished. He then went to the other cells in the long hallway and repeated the ritual in each one. They glowed with hints of sorcerers and monsters they had encountered such as Gretta Aldfather and Ferghus O'Malley until all of the so-called Bastille Bastards were accounted for but one.

In the last open cell, Simon set about chalking. This

chamber was considerably larger, but no less dark. There were remnants of furniture constructed of excellent wood with traces of quality fabrics. Bits of porcelain and glass hinted of fine dishes and toiletries. When Pendragon's inscriptions flared to life, Simon exhaled in triumph. "This is it. Gaios was in this cell." He began to copy the complex runes into his notebook.

Kate said, "It's certainly nicer accommodations than the others."

"They were friends," Simon replied. "It says a great deal about Pendragon."

Nick muttered to himself as he strolled around the room, gazing at the runes. Then he pointed at the wall. "Have a look here."

Simon continued writing. "I saw it. Very similar to the phrases on the foundations of Hartley Hall. Obviously my father borrowed from Pendragon." He glanced at Kate. "Which gives me hope I can do the same thing and fashion magic to dampen Gaios's power."

Malcolm leaned against the doorjamb. "So you scribes can write spells to counter any other form of magic?"

"It's possible," Simon said. "But difficult."

"Then why don't the other magicians just kill all the scribes?"

Simon smiled. "They've tried. I am the last one." He glanced at Nick. "Which is why Ash wanted to cultivate me, I suppose."

"Or kill you?" Malcolm eyed Nick.

Nick froze, realizing everyone was staring at him. He turned with an annoyed glare. "If she'd wanted him dead, she wouldn't have had me waste my time with him. She would've told me to go to his home, smile in his face, and put a knife in his heart."

"Charming." Simon watched his friend in the weird light of the runes. Nick seemed pained more than insulted. Simon stood and crossed to the door, putting a hand on Nick's arm. "I've gotten all I can here. I do want to take a look in that last cell."

He went to the iron door at the end of the hall. He shined a lantern through the barred window. The beams danced around the room. It was clean, without the detritus of occupation or the wear of use, except for a corner where there was a low mound of something, a pile of objects smooth and irregular. Kate stood beside him, staring at the lump as well.

Then it moved.

A piece of the pile shifted with a dry clattering sound. Two dark holes turned toward the door. A skull. Another section of the mound moved and a recognizable skeletal hand slid alongside the jaw. And then another hand on the other side. With long arms, the hands lifted the skull from the pile and adjusted it atop a curved bumpy shaft—a spine. The hands pressed against the floor and lifted the rib cage. The head, now properly atop the neck, turned side to side to survey the area. One leg unfolded while the skeleton reached over and grabbed another leg, clicking it into its hip socket. The newly assembled skeleton clambered onto its knees with no more difficulty than someone rising groggily from bed. It reached behind itself to seize a long shaft of some sort. It used the pole like a staff and pushed itself up onto its bony feet with a creaking noise. Something bright reflected the lanternlight. It was a long curved blade on the skeleton's staff. The macabre figure leaned on a scythe and stared at the door.

Kate looked at Simon in surprise, and asked, "Who is that? An unknown prisoner?"

"I don't think so. The door is unlocked. He seems content to be in there. He's guarding the cell."

"From whom?"

"From anyone most likely." Simon studied the motionless skeleton. "We need to get inside."

Nick peered into the room. "Simon, mind, that isn't some random revenant. It's a lich. It has power. We have trouble enough without opening doors to let more of it out."

"Yes we do." Simon found the patient skeleton fascinating.

"Are you drunk from aether?" Nick queried.

Simon considered the possibility. He did feel a slight numbing of his fears and doubts. The magic intoxication could affect his judgment at times, but not now. All the prisoners of the Bastille were accounted for. All the prisoners they knew about, in any case. This cell made one too many. They could not leave without knowing who might have previously occupied this room.

Simon backed away from the door. "Kate, hit our friend there with treacle to hold him in place. Penny, can you try to knock him to pieces with your gun?"

Kate plunged a hand into the gathered velveteen at her hips, finding hidden pockets, and came out with a vial. She aimed the crossbow through the bars and fired. The creature seemed to move in slow motion as it brought the scythe around. Its place in the corner should have cramped its ability to swing the long-handled tool, but the scythe passed through the walls and floor as if they weren't there. The skeleton could have been swinging out in the middle of an open field. The lich swept the scythe up, pausing a split second to catch the vial on the flat of the blade, and followed through to toss the glass hard. The treacle smashed worthless on the far wall.

Before anyone could speak, the lich charged the door. Every motion of the skeleton was clear, creating an illusion of slowness, but Simon knew better. It was on them in an instant. Simon grabbed Kate and Penny and pulled them back. A blade penetrated the metal door like a large hooked claw and flowed smoothly down to the floor where it drew back inside the cell. A skeletal foot appeared and the lich stepped through the iron door as if it weren't there.

"Back!" Simon shouted and brought his stick sword to glittering life. Despite the wicked blue sheen, it seemed inadequate compared to the great blade of the lich.

Penny raised her pistol and fired. The hallway shuddered. Dust fell all around them. The lich was shoved back. Its head tilted and it swung the scythe to its side. The blade cut through the wall. The skeleton followed smoothly behind the stroke and disappeared from sight.

Nick was standing at the open door to Gaios's cell and let loose a ball of flame into the room. "It's in here!"

Simon reached the doorway in time to see the lich standing in a field of flame. It plunged the sickle into the floor and dropped from view. He turned back to the hall. "It's below us now."

"How could it be below—" Penny began when the scythe blade appeared at her feet like a shark fin slicing through the ocean. A skeletal hand reached up and seized her ankle. Penny's right foot was pulled into the floor and she started screaming in pain.

Kate and Simon grabbed her and pulled, but she was held fast as if her leg had been set into the masonry. Penny thrashed in agony, clutching at her trapped calf.

Simon caught a glimpse of steel in the wall behind Malcolm. He was about to call out, but the Scotsman was already turning and dropping into a crouch as bony fingers stretched out for him. The powerful Lancaster pistol roared, slamming four balls into the wall where the hand now disappeared. Malcolm drew his second pistol and bounded for the nearest doorway. Just as he reached it, he fell back and the scythe sliced past his head. The lich appeared, driving the sickle down just between Malcolm's legs.

Nick let loose another wash of fire with one hand,

nearly catching Malcolm in the blast. The lich now regarded Nick and spun gracefully, letting the shaft of its weapon slide through its hand, giving it nearly eight feet of range. The blade, again defying all logic, passed through the solid walls of the hallway and hissed in an arc level with Nick's throat.

Malcolm kicked up into the shaft of the scythe, knocking it just off line so that Nick's slow reaction still let the older man escape by inches. Malcolm screamed as if his leg had been shattered. The lich continued its motion, drawing the long wooden shaft closer, spinning it over its head to plunge the blade toward the writhing man on the floor.

The clang of metal on metal combined with a shower of blue sparks. Simon grunted with effort as his sword caught the scythe and turned it from Malcolm's unprotected chest. He recovered from his lunge, locking the blades tight, and leapt over Malcolm. He could see a bluish iciness seeping up the Scotsman's leg. Simon spun about to riposte, but the lich blocked it with the butt of the handle.

"Nick! Attend Malcolm!" Simon backed up the hall. The lich's scythe passed effortlessly through the walls of the corridor as the creature followed Simon with its empty eyes focused on the glowing sword.

Simon kept tapping the scythe to keep the feel of his opponent. The magic of his blade prevented it from being parted by the lich's preternatural weapon. Simon shifted his point only slightly to keep it ready to strike if he got the chance. He shuffled back, step by step, letting his fencing training take over. Unlike his opponent, Simon was constrained by the confines of the hallway.

The skeleton's skill with the scythe was impressive, even beautiful. It came on like a machine, spinning in a *danse macabre*. The lich jabbed, hoping to slip the curved blade past to hook Simon. He ducked and blocked, and quickly riposted with a short stroke that separated a rib from the breastbone. Simon came up on his toes, drew his sword back along his chest, and struck again for the skull. The lich ducked away, off balance. It swung wide, slicing through a wall and instantly vaulting out of the corridor.

Simon turned and ran, rounding the corner. Just ahead, he saw the dangling rope up to the elephant above. He heard a faint humming overhead and immediately ducked to the floor. The scythe blade plunged from the stone ceiling and whooshed past. The lich dropped before him.

Simon spun quickly and parried a blow that tore his coat. The lich struck again, pressing its advantage. Simon held it off for now, but the skeleton kept up the attack. It would never tire. Simon would eventually lose his aether and his stamina would drop just like his sword arm.

Kate rounded the corner behind the lich. The skeleton started to turn to her, but Simon made quick strikes to its chest. Before he could carry through to the neck, the lich whirled back to face him, blocking the sword. Simon was pushed off balance. He tried to recover, but his opponent drove forward.

Kate stopped just behind the lich, and stuck her fist inside its rib cage. She grimaced and squeezed. There was a crunch of broken glass. Kate pulled her hand out rapidly as an orange mist swirled inside the skeleton. The fog began to grow and harden. The lich paused when the expanding amber pressed against the inside of its ribs and spine. The bones started to bend and ribs snapped. The breastbone shattered. The spine stretched, fighting to hold itself together for a second before flying to pieces like a broken charm bracelet. The lich's skull clattered off the amber and dropped to the floor.

"That was lovely." Simon tapped the amber with his sword. "Very elegant."

"Thank you. I'm glad it worked because it was the last of my amber." She knelt and hesitantly touched the handle of the scythe. Nothing happened, so she grasped it. When she picked it up, the blade clanged off the wall. "I'll add this to our collection. Considering how many artifacts we've lost recently."

Simon whispered a bit of strength into his body and stomped his foot on the lich's skull, crushing it to bits. He went along with Kate back to the cells. Nick was coming to meet them. They turned the corner to see Malcolm kneeling beside Penny, whose foot was still embedded in the floor. She was pale and sweating. Malcolm whispered calmly to her.

Simon inspected the spot where her ankle disappeared into the floor. It appeared to be merely trapped rather than fused. Her leg was red and bloody, and it was possible bones were broken. He said, "Penny, I'm going to free you, but it may hurt."

The engineer gave him a satirical glare. "Oh may it?"

Simon smiled at her spirit. He placed two fingers on the floor near her leg. A tattoo flared and he sent powerful pulses into the stone. Penny grimaced and bit her lip. Simon pressed his fingers down harder, pushing vibrations deep into the floor. The young woman paled further, but she watched even so. The stone beneath Simon's fingers showed faint hairline cracks. Now he spoke a different word, strength filled him, and he drove his hand deep into the floor. He felt the rough stone shredding his skin, but he smashed even harder. The floor cracked and he wrenched a chunk of stone from around her ankle.

Malcolm took her calf and carefully worked her foot free from the clutching rock. Penny was breathing heavily with relief as Malcolm ran his hand over her ankle, like a groom checking the fetlock of a horse, and he said, "Seems sound enough."

"Thank God you won't have to put me down," Penny murmured through the pain.

Simon pointed at Malcolm's leg, which had been blue, and the Scotsman merely nodded that he was fine. Simon rose and pulled open the iron door of the lich's cell. "All right then. Let's have a look."

With a few strokes Simon chalked a circle on the floor of the cell. He spoke the spell alive and runes appeared all around him. Simon gasped against his will.

"Ash," he said. "This cell was for Ash."

Nick gave him a dubious look. "Pendragon never imprisoned Ash."

"I know." Simon slapped the floor. "He was obviously prepared to do it."

"And she found out," Kate added.

Simon grinned coldly. "That must be why she arranged for Gaios to escape. She had Pendragon killed, and she destroyed the Order of the Oak. She killed my father and broke yours, Malcolm, and hounded yours, Kate. All to save herself from the man she loved."

"All this carnage over unrequited love?" Penny raised her eyebrows in wonder. "Ash is a cold one."

"You have no idea," Nick muttered.

Chapter 14

SIMON CROUCHED IN THE CENTER OF THE RUNES designed to confine Gaios. They surrounded him, inscrutable and fascinating and beautiful. Pendragon was both a sorcerer and a craftsman. His artistry made Simon envious; the complexity of the phrasing was amazing. Pendragon used runes and marks from a variety of magical cultures, Celtic, Norse, Egyptian, even Persian, and he combined them in unexpected ways. It wasn't just the runes themselves but also their arrangement in space that gave them power. The cell was built to specifications that created sacred and powerful geometries. Simon felt an excited surge with every minute as he began to grasp the intricate premise and the complex execution of the inscription around him.

Simon heard a knock. His fists clenched in frustration. "I'm not to be disturbed."

"It's important," came Kate's voice.

Simon went to the door of his bedroom. Kate glanced inside where Simon had posted each rune on a sheet of paper tacked to the walls, floors, and ceiling.

"How import—" Simon began but stopped speaking when Kate held up the gold key. It was vibrating of its own accord. "That is unusual."

"It began a few minutes ago." Kate nodded to Penny, who stood behind her in work togs.

"I've never seen that before," Penny said.

Simon took the quivering key. It wasn't hot. It wasn't glowing. "Let's open it up and have a look."

They entered Sir Roland's private study. The rune on the wall that allowed the key to open a portal here was glowing slightly.

Simon held the key out and spoke the magic word. "Marthsyl." The rift opened, revealing the world map floating in the air, all as usual.

Penny stepped forward and pointed at one of the dots on the globe that was blinking. "That spot in India is new. Well, maybe not completely new. But it has just returned to the map in any case."

Simon reached out a finger to touch the dot, which was somewhere in northern India or Nepal.

A strange voice wafted into the room. "Hello? Is someone there?" Simon froze. Both Kate and Penny looked around but saw no one. They waited quietly.

"Is someone there?" The voice sounded as if it was coming through a long tunnel. It was weak and echoed. "Sir Roland, is that you?"

Kate's breath caught.

"Sir Roland?" came the faint words again. "The Stone. He's after the Stone, and he's close. I don't know how. You told me to contact you through the rune. Answer me, please."

Kate responded in a quavering voice, "Who is this?"

There was silence.

"Who is this?" she repeated. "Sir Roland isn't here. This is his daughter Katherine. Kate. Who are you?"

A long pause followed, and then, "What is your dog's name?"

Kate stiffened in confusion. "My dog?"

"What is your dog's name? Hurry, there isn't much power left."

"Aethelred."

They heard a soft exhalation of relief. "Where is your father, Miss Katherine? He isn't dead, is he? Gaios or Ash haven't caught up to him, have they?"

"No." Kate was firm. "He is gone. I have his key now. Who are you?"

"My name is Ishwar. I am your father's friend."

"Ishwar." She looked surprised. "Tell me about the Stone."

"The Stone of Scone. There is a man looking for it. No, not a man. A monster. He is scouring the temple precinct. Somehow he knows the Stone is here. He is killing the priests of the temple, but they don't know where it is." A whistling sound began to overwhelm the voice, pushing it into the background in crackling static. "We must move it."

"It's getting difficult to hear you, Shri Ishwar." Kate was practically shouting now.

A high-pitched hiss drowned out his reply. There was silence, and the dot near the Himalayas stopped blinking.

"Hello? Hello?" Kate called out. "Are you there?"

There was no answer. She reached out to touch the dot on the map.

Simon grasped her wrist. "Not yet, Kate. We don't know what's on the other side. It could be a ruse. You recognized the name Ishwar?" He closed the portal, fearful that someone could be listening in.

"Yes." Kate put a shaking hand to her forehead. "There was a magician named Ishwar whom my father met in India many years ago. He spoke very highly of the man in his journals. But what could he have to do with the Stone of Scone?" She went for the bellpull to summon Hogarth, but the manservant was already standing in the doorway. "Oh, Hogarth. Did you hear what happened?"

"I did, miss. I also know of Mr. Ishwar."

"Did you ever meet him? Did you recognize his voice?"

"I met him once many years ago. It was impossible for me to say if that was him speaking. I'm sorry, miss."

Kate went to Hogarth and stood close to him. "Would you trust this Ishwar?"

"I couldn't say, miss, but I'm sure your father would."

"If that was truly Ishwar." Simon began to twirl the empty chain on his waistcoat. "It could've been an agent of Gaios trying to draw us out using the slimmest bit of information, the name of a colleague of your father's."

Kate stared intensely at Hogarth. "Tell me, did my father steal the true Stone of Scone from Westminster?"

"I don't know, miss. Once I was given the duty of watching over you and Miss Imogen, he ceased to discuss his travels and plans with me. He felt it was safer for both of you if he kept elements of his life separate. That may also be why he gave the key to Mr. Archer's mother, knowing it would go to Mr. Archer, rather than to you, miss."

Kate turned back to Simon. "What if my father stole the Stone to keep it from Gaios? We know from the key map that he visited places Gaios has traveled over the last few decades. New Orleans. Batavia. And there are no journals from those expeditions, as if he made those journeys secretly." Kate began to walk along the shelves of her father's notebooks, studying the spines. "Hogarth, you're telling me the truth, aren't you? You haven't kept secrets from me about my father, even for my own good?"

"No, miss." Hogarth's stoic expression fell a little. "He told me nothing. My only duty was the welfare of you and your sister. I would very much regret having to report my failures to your father now."

"Failures?" Kate spun around in shock, almost angry. "How dare you think that? You have done more than any man could. Any failure relating to Imogen is mine. Do you understand me?"

"Yes, miss." Hogarth nodded slightly. There was no reading his emotions. It was impossible to tell if he was grateful for the words or unconvinced. But there was no more to be said about it.

Kate returned her attention to Simon and Penny. "I think my father stole the Stone of Scone and hid it, apparently in India. He must have discovered that Gaios needed it."

Simon looked dubious. "Why would he hide it there? He knew India was the home ground of Baroness Conrad."

"It does seem like a bold choice of a hiding spot, right in the enemy's backyard. Not atypical of my father."

"I like it," Penny said. "Why would the bad guys bother to look there?"

"So," Kate began, "we need to go to India, find Ishwar, and remove the Stone to a safer spot. I'll gather everyone. We should leave by tonight."

Simon held up his hand. "We need to consider this move carefully."

"Consider what? You heard Ishwar. There are people being killed in the search for the Stone. I'm tired of hiding in this dark house while Gaios moves with impunity."

"I'm not saying we aren't going. But I want to know more about what Gaios plans for the Stone."

"Why does that matter, Simon? We must act. Gaios has thrown wave after wave of attacks at us. He's mutilated my sister. He's destroyed my home. And we've done nothing in return!"

Simon ran his thumb over the key and re-placed it on the chain. He could sense that Kate was edging toward a ferocious anger. There was no point in disputing her. He chose his words carefully. "I agree with you, Kate. We have taken enormous damage. But we are marshaling our forces to strike back. It's imperative that we don't play into Gaios's hands by being instinctive in our reactions. I know you're eager to strike at him. I am too. However, we don't want to do something that could unleash power that Gaios could use to his advantage. If we don't know how the Stone will be used, we could easily stumble into a catastrophe."

"Fine." Kate took a deep breath that held little patience. "What do you suggest?"

"THIS SEEMS A DIRTY PLAY, SIMON." NICK ROLLED a small bottle between his fingers and glanced nervously at the steel door to the makeshift cell where Ferghus was held.

"I know." Simon rapped his fingers nervously against the wall.

"There's no choice." Kate paced outside the door. "We need information now."

Nick exhaled and continued to fidget with the vial.

Malcolm stepped closer and sneered. "What exactly is the problem, Barker? The man is a murderer many times over. He would've killed any of us, and almost did for Charlotte and Imogen. You're worried about *him*?"

Nick snorted in derision. "I don't expect any remorse from the one who nearly beat him to death."

"I wish I had finished it." Malcolm's voice was cold.

Nick glared at the Scotsman, but said, "Simon, Ferghus wasn't always the man you see. He couldn't control his power. He drank too much to hide from it. It drove him mad. That's something that could happen to any one of us."

Simon pursed his lips thoughtfully.

Nick gestured toward the cell door. "Now he hardly knows who or where he is. I don't relish the idea of being the last man to talk to him and lying to him on top of it."

"I appreciate that, Nick." Simon struggled to keep his tone even. He felt the fierce gaze of Kate on his back, and he understood her impatience. However, he sensed shame in Nick's voice that he'd never heard before. Simon's flexing hands betrayed his doubts, but he still knew which way they had to go. "It does you credit, but the man is an unrepentant villain. As Malcolm said, he's killed innocents and would again."

"Fine." Nick took a deep breath. "The Simon I knew a year ago wouldn't have countenanced this."

"Perhaps not. The Nick I knew wouldn't have been so hesitant, I think. This past year has done a lot to all of us. We are in a war for our survival and, like it or not, Ferghus is the enemy. We need to know what he knows. And we need it now. So I'm asking you to use the glamour spell to appear as Gaios and talk to him. Draw out whatever you can."

"I'll do it, but not as Gaios. There's only one man Ferghus would want to see." Nick popped the cork off the bottle and drank the elixir in a single swallow. As he wiped the back of his hand across his lips, he whispered a word and suddenly a new man stood in the hallway. He wore a long leather jerkin and knee boots from the seventeenth century. His hair was dark and fell in ringlets.

Simon's pulse jumped. He recognized the face from the background of a painting he had seen in the Medici Palace. "Pendragon."

"Yes." Nick's voice was now deep and authoritative, without its usual sneering petulance.

"Amazing. Is that how Pendragon sounded?"

"Close enough to fool that crazy bastard in there." Nick shook Pendragon's head sadly. "Damn me."

Simon pulled the bolt and swung the door open. He watched the uncanny figure walk into the room. Nick's step faltered. Despite the liberal use of carbolic cleansers and frequent changes of linen, the cell had the familiar scent of a death room. The once-vigorous fire elemental lay frail and weak on the bed. Covered by a sheet and simple blanket, his chest rose and fell with rapid breaths. His mouth gaped open, dry and cracked.

Nick made his way to the bedside. He steadied himself. A lamp stood on the table, glowing with the faint light of a single brownie. "Ferghus. Ferghus, wake up."

The elemental moved his mouth.

Nick bent over the yellowish face. "Ferghus! Open your eyes. Do you hear me? Open your eyes!" The Irishman's gasping mouth closed briefly and facial muscles ticked. Nick reached out and put his hand against the waxy cheek. "Ferghus! Open your bloody eyes!"

Crusty eyelids slitted. Ferghus stared at nothing. He snorted and choked, arching his back while desperately trying to draw breath. Then he took a wet gasp and settled back onto the mattress where he resumed his shallow breathing.

"Still with us?" Nick studied the quivering figure on the bed.

Ferghus actually shifted his watery gaze toward the man standing over him. After a second, his fishlike mouth curved into something like a painful smirk. He mouthed the word, "Byron."

Nick smoothed red hair from the elemental's forehead, which glistened with gel. "How do you feel?"

Ferghus worked his dry mouth, but couldn't make a

sound. Nick turned to a pitcher and poured water onto a cloth. He folded it and put the towel to the elemental's lips. Ferghus gratefully leaned forward into the moisture, closing his mouth around the wet cloth. Then he nodded slightly and turned his face toward Nick, who held the towel ready.

"Thanks," Ferghus whispered.

"You're welcome. I'm happy to see you again."

The Irishman closed his eyes briefly. "How did you find me? Where am I?"

"You're safe."

Ferghus struggled to pull his hand out from under the tangled bedclothes, fighting against the simple sheet as if it was a ponderous weight. Nick drew the sheet away so the Irishman could hold out his stiff hand. Nick hesitated, almost looked back at Simon, but then took the thin fingers with uncommon delicacy. Ferghus sighed and sank into his pillow.

"You're cold," Nick said. "Are you in pain?"

"Yes, but it's helping me focus. I've not been this clearheaded in centuries."

"You're sober," Nick chided softly.

Ferghus managed a weak grin. "The drink only lessened the pain, quieted the voices."

"I wish I could help you."

Ferghus tried to shrug.

Nick looked at the wall rather than the elemental. "I need to ask you something."

Ferghus didn't react; he simply waited.

Nick said, "Tell me about Gaios."

"He's sorry he killed you, Byron. He says it all the time."

"That's a comfort."

"He wants to hurt Ash."

"He's going to destroy Britain, isn't he?"

"Yes, he is. Because Ash loves it." Ferghus choked on

a strangled laugh. "She's not even English. She's German. She only loves England because you love it. But he's going to take it all."

Nick's posture changed to reveal more of himself. He lost the imperious Pendragon carriage, and slipped into his usual casual stance. "You think he can manage it?"

Ferghus breathed quietly for a moment and tried to lick his lips. Nick wiped them again with the wet cloth. The Irishman tried to swallow. His voice was still a hoarse whisper. "He's using the Stone of Scone. It's bound to Britain."

"I know, but even the Stone can't drop Britain into the sea."

Ferghus winced. "He's Gaios. Once he puts his gnarled old hands on the Stone, he's going to saturate it. He can open the way to the aether and seize all he wishes."

"How?"

"Lightning." Ferghus looked annoyed. "Lightning slits the barrier between our world and the aether. All elementals can do it, but lightning is stronger. I could've done it with fire, but he found a spark that would rip it wide open."

"A spark? A true lightning elemental?"

"Aye. Some mousy girl. Hardly has any sense. Dumb as a post. Always reading the Bible. Gaios says she'll be more powerful once he's trained her." The Irishman shook his head and let out a long breath. He let his cheek press into his pillow. "I don't care."

Nick leaned close to the elemental's face. He heard only faint breath. "Ferghus. Stay here."

"Thank you for coming, Byron." The Irishman squeezed Nick's hand but it was feeble like an old man. "I'm dying, ain't I?"

"Afraid so."

The Irishman shook his head slowly. "No less than I deserve. I'm sorry."

"Sorry for what?"

"Everything. I didn't want to hurt anyone. I tried. I know you had to put me away. An addle-minded man like me should've never been given so much power."

"Don't fret that."

"I didn't want to hurt anyone. Do you understand? I'm sorry." Ferghus could barely be heard now. "I'm sorry."

The lordly Pendragon vanished and Nick Barker slumped in his shabby coat, holding the dying man's hand. "I know, Ferghus. We're all sorry, but there's nothing we can do."

"Nick Barker?" The light in the Irishman's eyes was nearly faded.

"How are you, lad?"

Ferghus gave an exhausted smile. "Where's Byron?"

"He stepped away."

"It's cold." Ferghus looked up at Nick with grimacing effort. "Are you cold?"

"Freezing."

"I don't want to die cold. I need to be warm. Just one last time. Help a mate out."

"Right you are." Nick used the wet towel to gently wipe Ferghus's palm clean of the gel. A gentle flame rose from the center of Nick's hand.

Ferghus smiled and his weak fingers fumbled for the tiny flicker of fire. He drew it into the palm of his hand and sighed. Nick rose to his feet and backed away. Ferghus placed the ember in his mouth. Simon yelled from the door. He started toward the bed, but Nick held him back, shaking his head. Ferghus erupted into flame, his body lost in the blaze. This was no controlled elemental fire; it was a white-hot consuming rush of light and heat. Simon fell back, throwing his arms before his face.

After a moment, Nick stepped up to the flames and

took hold of Ferghus's charred hand. He drew the fire up onto his own arm and extinguished it. He stood, still holding the blackened smoking hand of Ferghus.

Kate jabbed a finger at him, livid. "What did you do? You murdered him!"

Nick ignored her, staring at the smoldering body.

"God damn it, Barker!" Malcolm towered over Nick. "We needed more than that! He could've told us where Gaios is."

"His choice," Nick muttered. The man dropped to his knees beside the bed, hanging his head in exhaustion. "He wanted to go. I only helped him."

"Easy, Malcolm." Simon stepped between Nick and the Scotsman as if protecting his old friend from the group's accusations. "I've got an idea what Gaios is about. I'm not sure what he meant about the lightning elemental, but even so, we can move forward."

"I know what he meant." Malcolm leaned against the wall. He looked stricken, as if he had just gotten unexpected tragic news. "I have something I need to tell you about a woman I met in London last year."

Chapter 15

IT WAS THE NIGHT AFTER FERGHUS'S DEATH AND Malcolm stared out the window of a carriage as it rumbled through London. It had been a difficult discussion with Simon about his encounter with Jane Somerset last year, and his decision to keep her a secret. It had been Jane's wish, and he had to honor it. In the end, Simon understood, and refused to accuse Malcolm of endangering either Jane or their own group. Simon didn't have to reprimand him because Malcolm knew well enough the peril he had unleashed by his silence. This was particularly true because they now had two pressing goals, and Simon was forced to split the group. While Kate, Nick, Hogarth, and Simon went through a portal to northern India in search of the Stone, Malcolm was tasked to find Jane Somerset.

The heavy stink of London crowding his nostrils always reminded him why he detested cities. Even the smell of the burnt Hartley Hall was preferable. Across from him, Charlotte fidgeted, shifting from side to side. Her hand rubbed furiously at her leg.

"Stop scratching," Malcolm told her.

"I can't! Everything itches!" She wore a petite green frock that boasted lace at the collar and sleeves.

"Because your skin is healing. But not if you keep scratching at it."

Imogen, who sat next to her, grabbed Charlotte's hand with boneless fingers. Sighing, Charlotte conceded, slumping back in her seat. Smoothing a ruffle on Imogen's black dress, she leaned against her friend.

Penny glanced away from the lanky Scotsman, trying to hide a chuckle and failing.

Malcolm afforded her a cantankerous glance. "What?"

She bit her lip to still the smile and failed again. "You remind me of my mum."

Malcolm slouched back in his seat and sighed. "I was aiming for something a bit more masculine than your mother."

"What do you mean?" Charlotte stopped fidgeting to regard them across the seat.

"I mean I'm yelling at you like I was your da," Malcolm muttered.

Charlotte's jaw opened and her eyes widened. She sat back, exchanging an elated grin at Imogen. They both beamed at Malcolm, their faces full of wonder and delight. He felt flushed and glanced away.

Penny propped a foot up on the coach's door frame. "So what's the story with this Jane woman?"

"Jane Somerset. I saved her from a cook."

Penny fought the muscles in her lips. "A cook?"

"Aye, a dead one." Malcolm practically growled at her. "An undead one."

Penny nodded, but then remarked candidly, "I'm not surprised."

"What does that mean?" Malcolm scowled at her, expecting her to make some sort of jest like Simon would.

"You risk your life for everyone. You like to play loner, but you're just a decent bloke with a great huge heart. So tell me about her."

Malcolm studied the grey city outside. He took a deep breath and shifted uncomfortably. "She's a God-fearing woman. Believes her elementalism is a curse. I should've protected her, even from herself. She needed help with her magic. I should've brought her to Hartley Hall. That would've solved everything. Now she's with Gaios and Lord knows what he's done to her." He had said more than he wished, exactly as he'd feared.

Penny leaned on her arm, watching him through the flicking bands of light from passing gas lamps. "So why didn't you?"

"She asked me to keep her secret. And I said I would."

The engineer shrugged with acceptance. "Oh. There you are then."

Malcolm shook his head, tamping down the anger at himself. "It's not so simple. It should be, but it isn't. I knew she needed a great deal of help even after she saved my life."

"Wait, she saved *your* life? I thought you said—"

"It was a bit of both."

Penny laughed. "When was the last time you saw her?"

Malcolm realized Penny harbored no blame for his actions with Jane. He valued her straightforward support. For Penny, everything was about solving the problem as it existed, not worrying about how it might have been a different problem. He rubbed the back of his neck. "I spoke with her the night before the row at St. Mary Woolnoth. A few weeks after that, I went by the soup kitchen and her home, but she wasn't there." Malcolm pulled a grey wool scarf from his coat pocket. "She made this and gave it to me the first time she saw me at her soup kitchen. Thought I was a bedraggled thing needing care."

Penny raised an eyebrow, allowing herself a winsome huff of laughter.

Malcolm folded the scarf and slipped it back in his pocket. "Her housekeeper said she had taken her sick father to a spa for treatment and wouldn't likely be back for a year or more. I checked on the soup kitchen a few times after. Never thought much of it because the kitchen kept running. If something had happened to Jane, I assumed it would close up."

"Do you think the housekeeper was lying?"

Malcolm looked grim. "That's what we're going to find out."

The carriage pulled up in a neighborhood that was in a state of decay that would be long and agonizing. Malcolm led the way to a door of a row house and knocked loudly on the brass plate. After several attempts, no one answered the summons. Malcolm's brow furrowed deeper. He stepped back and studied the house. It seemed normal enough. The windows were unbroken. Glancing down the quiet street, Malcolm pulled out a small set of slim tools and bent at the lock.

"What are you doing?" Charlotte leaned over him.

"We're housebreaking," Penny informed her.

"Oh!" The girl bounced excitedly on her toes. Imogen, with her veil now in place, turned to keep a lookout in case someone came strolling by.

It took less than a minute and they were inside. The interior was dark. Not a single room was lit. The floor was littered with refuse. Papers. Leaves. Dirt. It was as if the house had not been cleaned for months. There were also empty liquor bottles and open pails that had carried beer.

Charlotte sniffed the air and peered into the empty sitting room off the foyer. "Everything smells rotten."

Malcolm drew a line with his finger in the thick layer of dust on one of the tables. He turned toward the kitchen in the back of the home. The others trailed after him.

The kitchen was dead. No fire warmed the hearth, not even yesterday's banked coals. Cooking pots lay about with dried remnants of food. Insects crawled over the counters.

Penny picked up a spoon from the table. "It appears Miss Somerset isn't here, nor anyone else now."

"Someone's been living here." Malcolm sniffed a pot of moldy food. Some dishes appeared to have been used in the last few days.

"No sign of a fight." Imogen's deep voice observed from the other side of the room.

"Look around," Malcolm said. "We need to see if we can determine where she's been taken."

The girls complied and began rooting through the rooms for clues. Malcolm moved toward a pantry. It was unlocked and when he opened it, he gasped in surprise. The housekeeper sat there, her head bowed.

"Mrs. Cummings," Malcolm said quietly. Perhaps she had taken refuge inside the closet when she had heard intruders enter the house. Or maybe she was injured or worse.

The old woman lifted her head toward the voice and her eyes opened. She rose abruptly to her feet. She wore her service clothes and apron, but they were caked with dirt and old food as if the woman hadn't bathed or laundered for weeks.

"Do you remember me, Mrs. Cummings? I didn't mean to frighten you. I'm a friend of Miss Somerset's."

"She's not here!"

"I can see that, missus. Might you know where she's gone?"

The girls heard the commotion and came back into the kitchen. Imogen carried a tattered sheet of paper in her more human hand. A growl started low in Charlotte's chest.

Malcolm cast her a quick glance. "Charlotte, stop. The woman's frightened enough."

"Maybe she's not." Charlotte's voice was a low whisper. "She smells of oil and smoke."

It took a second before Malcolm understood what the girl meant, which was time enough for Mrs. Cummings to grab him up with her meaty fist. His feet came off the floor. He clutched at the hand around his throat while he pulled a pistol. Mrs. Cummings slapped the gun away with a powerful blow.

Charlotte was in midtransformation when Mrs. Cummings threw Malcolm at her. The two collided and careened over the kitchen table in a tumble of arms and legs.

Imogen yanked up her sleeve. She flexed her forearm and quills flew at the housekeeper. Each one struck the woman's chest with a faint pinging sound.

"She's half-machine!" Penny shouted.

"Dismantle her!" Malcolm clambered to his feet over the hairy limbs of Charlotte just as Penny fired a sonic blast from her pistol. The whine blossomed in his ears as everything around them started to shake. Dishes and bric-a-brac fell to the floor and shattered.

Smoke leaked from under Mrs. Cummings's dress and apron. Every movement of her limbs sounded like breaking twigs as she came out into the center of the kitchen floor. The housekeeper seized a table in desperation and tossed it like a bag of laundry at Penny. The nimble engineer ducked out into the hall just under the shattering oaken table, but the attack stopped the pulsations.

Imogen thrust another volley of quills. Mrs. Cummings held her right arm up to cover her face. One quill stuck in the housekeeper's bare hand.

Charlotte leapt over Malcolm onto Mrs. Cummings's

plump figure. Instead of being crushed to the floor, the housekeeper stood rooted in place. Charlotte's claws tore into the woman. The rips in the thick cloth of her tunic revealed shiny metal underneath. Mrs. Cummings scruffed Charlotte and dragged her off, shoving her to the ground. She lifted a foot to slam down on the wiggling werewolf, but a barrage from Malcolm's pistol pushed her backward.

Mrs. Cummings reached for the iron stove, but her fingers suddenly unclenched and her right hand hung from her wrist like it had been broken. Imogen's toxin was finally working. For a heavyset woman, Mrs. Cummings was spry. She leapt behind the stove and shoved it one-handed at Malcolm. It tore from the walls with a geyser of black coal dust and rushed toward him like a rampaging wagon. He backed away, but Charlotte streaked across the kitchen and carried him through the door into the hall. The iron stove smashed into the doorway behind them.

Penny took advantage of the distraction and powered up her wee pistol once more. Mrs. Cummings turned, glaring at the engineer. Penny aimed as best she could as the pistol moved with a mind of its own. The discharge swept through the room and shoved Penny back five feet, tumbling her on top of Imogen. Black smoke poured from the housekeeper's chest. Her movements were chaotic and jerky.

"Get down! She's going to blow apart!" Penny tried to herd Imogen over the upturned stove and out the door.

Caught up in the fever of battle, Imogen shook her off and turned to snap off more quills. One struck the woman's cheek, sticking to her skin like a stray whisker. The girl grinned in triumph. Malcolm leapt back into the kitchen, tackling Imogen to the floor just as Mrs. Cummings exploded. Metal and flesh hit everywhere, coating the town house with black oil and bloody smears.

"Losh!" Charlotte exclaimed from the hall in a near-perfect imitation of Malcolm.

Penny popped up. She looked for the Scotsman and a flash of relief washed over her when she saw he and Imogen were all right. Then a crooked grimace took its place. "Your friend won't like how we redecorated."

Malcolm assisted Imogen to her feet. The girl hung her head apologetically at him. At least she knew she had done something foolish.

Penny plucked a piece of Mrs. Cummings from the floor. To Malcolm's relief, it was metallic. The piece twisted and turned in her hands as she examined every wire and nook and gear. "This is the Baroness's work. Same as we came across with Dr. White." She tossed it to the side. "She's really starting to annoy me."

"She won't much longer."

Penny toed another metal chunk of housekeeper. "She's actually quite brilliant."

"So are you."

"I know, but . . ."

"You're much younger, and you're already a genius."

"Genius?" Penny puffed with pride, but the brief interlude didn't last as she remembered their purpose and the implication of the debris on the floor. "I guess this proves your friend is with Gaios."

Malcolm gritted his teeth. Gaios had already had the infernal housekeeper in place, watching Jane last year, and Malcolm had realized nothing. A steady ache of shame built in his chest; he feared that he had unwittingly left Jane to be swept up by evil.

"I found this before. I saw several of them." Imogen held up the ragged sheet of paper she had been holding. Malcolm took it from her.

Charlotte's snout towered over him. "That's not something a lady has in the house. Even I know that."

She was right. It was a broadsheet for a bawdy tavern at the waterfront called the Hanged Mermaid. A bare-breasted mermaid was posing, offering sailors more than just a free drink.

Charlotte reverted to her human shape. Penny didn't think twice but reached into her rucksack and pulled out a cloak for the nearly naked girl. They had several changes of clothes for her in the carriage; it was a necessity with the young werewolf.

"We're heading for the waterfront." Malcolm shoved the paper into his pocket.

Charlotte started bouncing up and down. "Are we going to find some pirates now?"

"Pirates?" Malcolm sucked in a calming breath. "You two will stay in the coach."

Immediately Charlotte's smile faded. Her arms crossed dejectedly.

Imogen leaned over. "At least we're going with them."

Charlotte brightened and leapt into the carriage. "Aye, matey!"

The coach driver leaned over with the practiced calm of a long-standing Anstruther retainer. "I heard noises inside, sir. Is all well?"

"Quarrel with the help. Take us to Limehouse."

MALCOLM AND PENNY EXITED THE CARRIAGE onto a fog-bound Limehouse street across from the Hanged Mermaid. The waterfront smelled of haddock and brine. He signaled the two girls to wait. Imogen nodded, leaning back in the seat while Charlotte peeked through the window shade at the press of strange people shuffling past.

Penny glanced behind them at the coach. "She's not going to stay there. You know that."

"She will if she knows what's best."

Penny patted his arm. "You just keep thinking that."

Malcolm marched into the tavern, already focused on things besides the minding of children. Penny came in behind him but sidled off to the side to watch his flank. She really was quite good at gauging a situation to her best advantage. He never felt ill at ease with her at his back.

Unwashed faces turned toward him suspiciously, their porters and meals forgotten for a moment. Most went back to their lives, but a few continued to stare at Malcolm's dark form. They marked him as a stranger.

He ordered a pint and leaned against the bar, filling a narrow space between cramped shoulders. He debated how to broach the subject of a missing woman and a maniacal demigod, but decided just to listen. Conversations picked up again, creating a low buzz. He sipped his warm beer and tried to listen in on various dialogues. Unfortunately, the whispers were too soft or the discussion too benign.

Malcolm glanced behind him to check on Penny. To his surprise, she sat at a table with a bunch of fellows, grinning broadly. They leaned close, eager to listen to her. They all burst out into laughter. Malcolm scowled. It shouldn't bother him, but it did. She was in her element. Despite her brilliance, she was one of the working class and they recognized their kin. He took his pint and headed over to her. The men around her quieted at his approach.

"Nothing here for you, mate," snarled one of them who looked older than his father.

"There you'd be wrong," was Malcolm's dark reply, his eyes darting toward Penny.

Her head tilted with exasperation and her mouth quirked. "Stand easy, lads. He's with me."

Disappointment swept through the small contingent and they all sat back. She waved a jaunty farewell and slipped her arm through Malcolm's, leading him back toward the bar.

He asked, "Why didn't you tell me you'd been here before?"

"Because I haven't."

"They seemed awful friendly toward you," he muttered.

"It's because I don't glower."

"What are you implying?"

"That you glower." Penny laughed.

He changed his expression even though he knew it was too late. "It's gotten me what I needed before."

"Maybe, but there's no need of it here. Those blokes are happy enough to talk. Besides that, I'm a woman, not some dark Scottish ghost off the moors. Far less threatening."

"What did you find out?"

"There's a new island."

"What do you mean?"

"A new island. It just appeared a few months ago. Off the coast of Allhallows. None of the sailors or rivermen remember it being there before."

"Bloody hell. Only one person I know can make an island." Malcolm spotted a man with a dark tattoo on his neck seated near the front of the bar. A frown emerged when he thought another eager bloke was eyeing Penny. Then he realized the man was watching him. When the man noticed Malcolm's attention, he turned back to his drink.

Penny swigged down the last of her beer. "What do we do now?"

"We go check it out."

"Without the others?"

"They're in India. No idea when they'll be back."

"Just us two against Gaios? Four, if you count the girls. I'm not sure I like those odds."

"I don't plan to fight Gaios. Just find Jane and get her away."

"That's a poor bet."

"If we don't find her, we head back and wait for Simon."

"Sure this isn't your guilt talking?"

"We're running out of time." That was all he said. There was no point in explaining or discussing. They had one choice.

The tattooed man rose and slipped out the front. Malcolm stood and pulled Penny with him.

"Where we going?" she asked.

"That man was a bit too interested."

"What man?"

"He's already out the door. Tall man with a tattoo on his neck." They stepped out to the fog-shrouded street. People bustled eerily around them.

"I don't see him."

"There." Malcolm pointed out the fellow shoving into the crowd.

Across the street, Charlotte leaned halfway out of the coach window and waved. Malcolm glared at her, indicating that she should stay out of sight. She made a face and retreated inside, almost.

Penny had eyes on their quarry and Malcolm raced to catch up to her as she weaved quickly through the throngs of people. The tattooed man led them toward the docks where two other men joined him. They spoke with brief agitation before continuing on.

"You know," Penny pointed out, "he could have just disliked your choice of beer. People are peculiar in this part of London."

Malcolm grunted. "He didn't look at us until we started talking about this island of yours. That's enough for me."

Penny shrugged. "Any lead is a good lead."

Malcolm pulled her behind some crates at the wharf as the trio of men paused in front of a ramp. A sixty-foot steam launch was moored below them. On either side were affixed massive paddle wheels. Malcolm brought his spyglass up. He spotted about fifteen men on board. Crates were being loaded in the hold. "That's the same boat I saw at Westminster that spirited the Baroness and Ferghus away."

Penny took the glass and stiffened in concentration. "I bet she does ten knots on the Thames. Woe to anyone she passes. They're about to cast off."

"Blast it all." Malcolm got ready to move.

"What about the girls?"

"They're safer where they are. The driver will take them home in the carriage."

Penny glanced over her shoulder and grinned broadly. "Then again maybe not. They're right behind you."

Malcolm spun about and, sure enough, Imogen and Charlotte were slinking toward them in their affluent attire, causing one or two rivermen to regard them curiously. He stalked back and pulled them down to the crates. "I told you to stay in the coach."

"That was hours ago," Charlotte pointed out. "Are those pirates? They look like pirates."

Penny shoved Charlotte's head down below the line of crates. "Yes. We're going to board that vessel."

Charlotte's voice rose an octave. "We're going to plunder her!"

Malcolm rolled his eyes. "What books have you been reading?"

"They're pulling up the gangplank." Penny whisked

the bone-and-steel fan into her hand. Charlotte cooed over how lovely it was.

Green smoke billowed from a singular stovepipe. Two crewmen were using long gaffs to push off. Malcolm raced down the jetty and leapt across the widening gap, legs tight together and lifted to clear the rail of the boat. His black coat flew out behind him. He landed between the crewmen, crashing a fist into the face of one and slamming the butt of his Lancaster into the other. They both went down. Malcolm grabbed one of the poles and hooked the wharf as Charlotte vaulted aboard. A group of sailors paused in surprise when they saw a girl coming at them. They grinned with mad assured glee, until she began to change in front of them under the awning of the wheelhouse. They drew back in horror at the bone-cracking transformation.

Penny helped the awkward Imogen cross the gap, then she turned into the melee, whipping up her fan in almost coy defense. The first man to reach for her received an electric shock with a single tap. He dropped in a wild flail. Penny spun to the next man, striking a glancing blow across his back with the bladed fins of the dainty fan. He dropped as well. When the next sailor came at her with a short axe raised, she bent under the blow like an exotic dancer and thrust out her arm. The fan collapsed with the momentum and its end tapped against the man's chest with a crack of voltage. He stiffened and flew backward. A crewman thrust at her with a long knife; she straightened, snapping open the fan again, holding it in front of her. The fan caught the blade and closed around it. With a twist of her wrist she sent another electrical charge out along the steel fins to course down the blade and envelop the sailor.

Imogen pulled up her sleeve and the filaments on her arm quivered. With a single flex of a muscle, three needles flew in a wide arc toward three men rushing at Malcolm. Each quill found a mark. The men bore Malcolm to the deck with weapons flashing, but suddenly their raised arms shook. Their eyes held terror as palsied muscles betrayed them. Malcolm slammed his fists into their unprotected chins and laid out all three men on the deck.

Charlotte was in full form now and towered over four cowering men. Her deafening roar sent them scattering. She grabbed one pirate and hurled the screaming man at the backs of those fleeing, bowling them over the rail and into the water. Malcolm swore he heard her laugh.

He launched himself up a ladder to the wheelhouse. No doubt the girls could handle a few remaining roughnecks. He heard more bodies make a splash over the side as proof. Warily, he lifted his head over the last step and the whine of a pistol ball careened near his ear.

Malcolm's Lancaster boomed over the lip of the stairs, forcing the captain to leap for cover. Malcolm sprang up and kicked into the wheelhouse.

The captain, a square-faced man with dark sharp eyes, twisted and aimed a second pistol. He didn't have time to fire. The roof above him exploded and a hairy hand reached in. Long clawed fingers encaged the man's head, lifting him off the deck. Malcolm knocked the pistol from the man's hand. He grinned up at Charlotte, who clung to the rocking roof, peering in through the hole she had made. The captain gasped and struggled as Charlotte's grip tightened, sharp claws digging into the soft tissue of his neck.

Malcolm blocked his kicking legs. "Stop squirming or she'll rip your bloody head clean off. You've lost."

The man went limp. He gurgled something unintelligible. Charlotte released him and he dropped to the wooden deck. Malcolm laid the cold steel of the Lancaster against the back of the captain's skull. "You're taking us to Gaios's new island. Don't bother pretending you don't understand. Yes?"

Trembling, the captain stared up at Charlotte. "Yes."

Chapter 16

THE PADDLES CHUNKED IN THE MUDDY WATER as the steamer slipped out of the long mouth of the Thames into the sea. Allhallows lay hazy off to starboard. A crowded parade of ships came and went around them, some on short sail slipping in for London Town and others letting canvas out making for the North Sea or the Channel. The steamer veered south of the most crowded section of the route. It wasn't a surprise to Malcolm that Gaios wanted to remain undisturbed. What was surprising was that more people hadn't seen the island. A new landmass of any size off the coast was both a curiosity and a hazard. Or perhaps it had been visited, and those that had dared never returned.

After steaming for an hour, the captain signaled to slow. From out of the dark waters jutted a cruel stone. Then more around it, each of them capable of tearing a ship apart with but a gentle tap. The slowly revolving paddles were just keeping headway as the boat steamed into the forest of dragon's teeth.

Malcolm nudged his pistol barrel against the man's spine. "If we go down, you won't live to die a watery death."

The captain continued to watch nervously ahead. "I've no mind to die for the likes of him."

At the bow, Penny stood guard over the mate who peered into the hazy sea and signaled directions back to the helm. The motions were practiced from many passages through these hazards, but hardly routine. The mate kept a long pole handy to shove off from rocks that drew too close. Perspiration covered his face as the huge obsidian knives inched past the rail with the sound of water lapping on the glassy black stones.

After a long silent journey, the deadly stones dropped astern and a small island loomed ahead. Malcolm estimated it was five miles across. There was a narrow strip of stony black shore, then the entire island was lush and green. Even more peculiar, it appeared to be covered in tropical jungle. The air was remarkably warm and dense with moisture. Malcolm removed his heavy coat and laid it aside. He eyed the landscape for sentries as the steamer churned toward a wooden dock. When the boat came alongside the jetty, the mate tied off the spring line with one wary eye on Penny. Once the boat was made fast, Malcolm sent the captain and the mate below with Penny to be secured with the other survivors.

Penny and the girls returned on deck. Charlotte was up on her toes in her excitement, peering into the dark foliage, probably seeing far more than Malcolm could. Imogen stood beside her, quiet and seemingly serene. The quills on her bare arm whipped back and forth in the wind. Her pale, featureless face waited patiently.

Malcolm laid a hand on Charlotte's shoulder. She looked up at him, full of eagerness. But her face fell before he could say, "Charlotte, I need you and Imogen to stay with the boat."

"But the pirates are all tied up. They won't be going anywhere." Her voice held only frustration. "Please let me come with you! I'll be good. I swear. I'll only do what you tell me to do!"

"I know you will. That's why I'm leaving this in your hands." He knelt beside her. "This boat is our only way home. Do you understand? Without it, we will be trapped here with Gaios. I am leaving it in both your hands." He took in Imogen with his stern gaze.

Imogen straightened, realizing what he was asking was no small matter. "You can count on us."

Charlotte huffed a resigned sigh and nodded. "You just better come back for us."

Malcolm rose to his feet and motioned to Penny. They left the boat with the eyes of the two girls following them as they crossed the stony shore into the foreboding thicket. The sky darkened when they entered. Everything smelled of dank earth and rotting vegetation. Cut off from the sea breeze, the air warmed quickly and soon both of them were perspiring.

"Holy God." Penny swept a hand over her damp brow. "Did we cross the Equator?"

Malcolm knelt and put his hand down on the ground. "It feels hot. How is that even possible?"

"Here's how."

Penny found herself at the edge of a small fissure deep into the crust of the island. Red lava glowed in the dark below.

"A bloody volcano." Malcolm came up next to her.

"Cor." Penny was silent a moment, but then admitted, "I'm glad Simon has his powers back."

"I'm not sure even he could stop a volcano if Gaios chooses to make London the new Pompeii."

"Simon will try though."

"Yes, he will."

They silently moved into the steamy jungle. Even though the going was rougher, they stayed off the main path. A few minutes later the jungle opened up improbably onto English farmland. There were vast acres of crops. And what crops. Wheat heads the size of American maize. Vegetables were enormous and perfectly shaped, with hardly a blemish. They hung heavy on their stalks, ready to be picked. The air blew clean and moist.

Beyond the verdant fields, they saw a building. It held a glimmer of pomp, luxury, and ostentation in its structure. It was grand, with numerous bow windows to allow generous light of day. The front was a tad showy, even palatial, with unneeded Corinthian columns. It exuded the strange confidence of the normal here on this abnormal island.

Penny seized one of the bursting heads of grain and whistled in admiration. "I don't get it. Does he want to kill us or feed us?"

"I don't care which. Let's keep going." Malcolm hurried along a path between high stalks of corn and glistening apple trees.

The stalks far ahead rustled like dry bones and there was a strange grunting. Malcolm motioned Penny quickly to the left, keeping whatever it was upwind from them. Down a long narrow row, a hulking shape of flesh and metal appeared. A gorilla thrust its broad frame into view, walking heavy on its steel knuckles. Its large head swept the area. When it turned toward them, they could see that its jaws and ragged teeth were made of dark iron, like a cruel hunter's trap. A guttural snort sounded as it paused, its nostrils flaring wide. The breeze swept the smell of oil and animal musk toward them. The gorilla moved on, with the whir of grinding gears and rapidly shifting pistons. Sunlight glinted off the metal lining its spine.

When they finally emerged from the field, Penny spat. "That woman is sick. What she does to those poor creatures isn't right. That's not what the Maddy Boys were about. They would be horrified at what she's done here."

"Write a letter to the dean later." Malcolm crossed the manicured lawn at the rear of the expansive building; the first door they tried was unlocked.

"Trusting fellow," Penny commented dryly. "Or maybe it really is a spa. Looks like one. Bit off the beaten track though."

Malcolm and Penny found themselves in something of a coffee room, empty but complete with orderly chairs and tables, all clean and set. The interior was dim and comforting. The hearth was unlit though that might have been due to the warm air of the island rather than disuse. They cautiously moved to the door and went into the vacant hallway. The radiant sitting rooms of the main floor were empty so they climbed upstairs to where they assumed any patients were located.

Crouching on the top step, Penny spied a man in a white coat. They watched him walk to the end of the hall and enter a room. They padded quickly down the corridor, noting numerous private rooms lining both sides. All were empty. They crept to the last room where voices spoke softly. When footsteps came toward the door, Malcolm and Penny darted out of sight.

The man in the white coat walked past and as soon as he went downstairs, they peeked into the last room. Jane's father lay in a clean bed, partially covered with a stark white sheet. At their entrance, he turned his head to regard them.

His brow creased in confusion, but then recognition lit his face. "Captain Perry!"

Malcolm smiled gently at the elderly man, recalling that the addled Mr. Somerset had once confused him with Jane's fiancé, who had died while in service to the navy. "Mr. Somerset, I'm Malcolm MacFarlane."

"MacFarlane?" Panic started to settle in Mr. Somerset's eyes. Then it passed like a sudden storm. "Oh yes, the man who enjoys poetry. Jane's acquaintance from church."

"Well, that's right, sir. You have remarkable recall."

Penny raised a bemused eyebrow at Malcolm but remained quiet. She pushed the door nearly shut and stayed there as a lookout.

Mr. Somerset regarded Malcolm in a beseeching manner. "Have you seen Jane?"

Malcolm's eyes narrowed. "She's not here with you? On the island?"

"Island?" The old man seemed more disoriented than before. Though for someone in his condition, anyplace other than his home would be befuddling. "She comes to see me every day even though she is very busy here."

"She is all right?"

Mr. Somerset attempted to rise from his bed. "Has something happened to her?"

"No, Mr. Somerset," Malcolm hurriedly assured the confused man. "I want to see her. Is she about?"

"She should be at prayer." Mr. Somerset leaned forward so he could see out the window next to his bed. He gestured toward a simple rectangular stone building just off the side of the manor house. It was about twenty feet square with a single door and no windows. "In the chapel. She prays a great deal. For me, I know. She worries so."

The old man's flash of clarity about his daughter touched Malcolm. He looked into the troubled eyes, which were struggling against vacancy. "She cares for you, sir."

"She should pray for herself, Captain Perry."

Malcolm felt compelled to pat the man's gnarled hand. Then he glanced at Penny. "Can we get down from here?"

She brightened and pulled a coil of rope from her

backpack. "Simple. Only two floors. We could shimmy down a pipe if need be."

"I'll use the rope."

"Are we taking him with us?" Penny indicated Mr. Somerset, who had closed his eyes and appeared to be dozing.

"Let's find Jane first."

Penny flung open the window and tied off the rope to an overhang outside. Without further pretense, she slid over the sill and scampered down as if she did such things every day.

Shaking his head in amazement, Malcolm turned back to Mr. Somerset. "I'll find Jane and come back."

Mr. Somerset opened his eyes wearily and nodded, trusting Malcolm at his word. He didn't bat an eye at their odd behavior. "Close the window after you leave, if you would please, Captain Perry. It's a bit drafty otherwise."

"Of course, sir." Malcolm followed after Penny.

The grounds surrounding the house were adequately tended, with green grass higher than proper and numerous marble benches. They could have been strolling the institutional landscape of any health spa south of London. They made their way to the chapel and cautiously pushed open the door. The inside had a familiar Presbyterian plainness except that at the far end was a large ornate altar that didn't belong to any denomination. A woman knelt in prayer before it. If she heard them enter, she did not give any sign.

Malcolm hesitated a moment, not sure why. Seeing the small form kneeling in supplication, he again fought back shame and guilt for not protecting her. There was no telling what she had endured at the hands of Gaios. He took a step forward and called softly, "Miss Somerset."

The woman didn't react at first and he wondered if

she had heard him. He called out again and finally she rose to her feet and took several breaths as if recovering from exertion. When she turned, she uttered a gasp of astonishment. "Mr. MacFarlane!"

Malcolm nodded with awkward formality. Relief flooded him that she appeared well. She looked tired, her eyes a trifle dark behind her glasses. Her porcelain skin was dotted with beads of perspiration although it wasn't hot inside the chapel. Still dressed the same, modest to the point of prudish, complete with a white bonnet tied over her honey hair. She was as thin and drawn as ever but seemed stronger and strangely vigorous rather than frail as she had before.

"Why are you here?" Jane's mouth was round with surprise, particularly when she stared at the heavy guns he wore. Then her eyes strayed up to the grey scarf looped around his neck, the very scarf she had given him, and her pleased smile assured Malcolm he had reached her in time. "*How* are you here? I didn't think visitors were encouraged yet."

"I'm here for you."

Jane pressed a hand to her breast. "Oh, Mr. MacFarlane, you astound me." She glanced at Penny with a quizzical expression.

Malcolm waved hurriedly back at Penny. "That's my partner, Miss Carter."

"Miss Carter. A pleasure." Jane nodded a polite greeting to the engineer, who was heading for the altar, then turned a confused but eager face back to Malcolm. Her petite mouth lifted into a genuine smile. "I can't believe you came all this way for me, with Miss Carter. How did you know? You must have spoken with Mrs. Cummings."

"Yes. She wasn't quite herself."

The slump of Jane's shoulders was penitent. "I fear

my sudden departure may have upset her. She was quite beside herself."

Penny snorted from behind the altar. "Well, she is now."

Malcolm took Jane's hands in a strong grip. "We don't have time to waste. I've come to rescue you."

The petite woman started. "Rescue? I miss your meaning."

"You're a prisoner."

Jane gave a confounded turn of her head as if trying to diagnose some mental failing in him. "Mr. MacFarlane, are you well?"

"Yes, I'm bloody well fine. I just want to know why you are here."

She chided him with raised eyebrows. "Now, you are being overly forceful, sir. I would ask you to remember you are in God's house."

"God's house?" Malcolm huffed with disdain. "Jane, you have no idea what you are in the middle of. I hope."

"Well, despite your lack of confidence, I am fully aware." Her tone was disapproving. "Wasn't it you who told me that I should value my . . ." Jane glanced suspiciously toward the altar where Penny had disappeared and was busy making the grunts and toolish bangings of fascinated investigation. She leaned closer to Malcolm and whispered, ". . . my abilities. That is what I am doing here, along with Gaios."

"Gaios." Malcolm stiffened, squeezing her hands hard. "So you do know him as Gaios? I beg you to tell me you are not a willing member of his circle."

"I am indeed, sir." Jane pulled from his grip and turned away briskly out of insult. "Who are you to come here and speak to me so? You know nothing of Gaios and his dreams. He has done miracles." She spun back, full of fire. "Miracles with the land. Miracles with my father. Miracles with me. And he will bring those miracles to everyone soon."

"I don't doubt that." Malcolm knew Jane didn't truly grasp what Gaios represented. He couldn't conceive that the timid and righteous women he had met last year while she served meals to the London poor could have been twisted into a conscious tool by Gaios. Clearly she was deluded. "What miracles has he wrought?"

"If you must know, Mr. MacFarlane, we're doing God's work here. He has encouraged me to use my . . ." Again she glanced at the altar and continued quietly, ". . . my abilities. He believes I have the power to enrich the land, to make it more fertile. You perhaps saw the cropland outside? That is the results of our work. At his direction, I seed the land with my . . . abilities. And the bountiful results are self-evident. God's hand is in this. We will feed the hungry, here in Britain and beyond. God will see that no one need go hungry. And I am blessed that Gaios found me and has allowed me to play a small part in that great event." Her gaze cast out toward the fields as if she could see them through the stone walls of the chapel.

"I'll admit, those crops are impressive, but this island is volcanic. The earth is very rich. And I suspect Gaios can enhance the fertility of the soil with his own abilities."

Jane straightened in surprise. "Gaios has no abilities, if I take your meaning, aside from being a man of great vision and godliness."

Malcolm laughed, as did Penny from behind the altar. The Scotsman exhaled. "Jane, you've been hoodwinked. Gaios is a fiend of the highest order."

"How dare you, sir. You don't know—"

"I know, Jane! Trust me, I know. Gaios is an elemental, such as you are, but he is of the earth. He is likely the least godly man you could meet on this planet. He intends to use his magic to destroy Britain and kill everyone who lives here. Do you understand me? He will kill everyone. And he will use you to do it."

Jane stared silently at him as if he had just tried to convince her they were on the Moon.

Penny rose into view with a spanner in her hand. "Oh, just grab her and let's go."

Malcolm held up a cautionary hand. "No. I don't intend to just grab her. I've seen what she can do."

"Well"—Penny tapped the altar with her tool—"maybe if Miss Somerset saw this, she might wonder about her benefactor."

Malcolm moved past Jane around the altar to Penny's side. "What is it?"

"This altar is a machine. The Baroness's work."

"What does it do?"

"Not exactly sure. Look here." Penny gestured to where she had removed a panel. Inside was a complex array of pipes, valves, gears, and a glowing crystal the size of a cat's head.

"What happens here, Jane?" Malcolm asked.

Jane peered almost unwillingly into the open panel. She seemed confused by the internal workings of the altar. "What do you mean? I come here to pray. This is the first place of worship that has made me feel like I'm worthy of my gift. I feel better when I'm here. What is all that?" She pointed at the machinery.

Penny shook her head as she crawled over the altar, tapping and peering closely at every facet. She eyed Jane. "All you do here is pray?"

"Yes, Miss Carter." Jane tilted her head in confusion at the engineer.

"Spectacular," the engineer murmured, dropping back behind the altar again. "Everything that multiple-armed freak does is spectacular. It would take a year to understand and replicate this." Penny growled with effort for a moment. Her arms were buried deep inside the altar. She clanged tools and swore. With a great tug, she pulled a piece of metal and the crystal from the guts of the holy machine. She held it up like a treasure hunter, eyes wide in disbelief. "I think this is an aether siphon of some sort."

"Aether?" Jane scoffed. "What foolishness are you talking?"

Malcolm leaned on the altar and said to Penny with alarm, "Gaios is siphoning aether from her?"

"Other way around, I think." Penny sat back and rubbed her chin with the spanner. "I'd bet he's drawing aether. And putting it in her."

Malcolm and Penny slowly turned to look at Jane. She stared back defiantly though it was clear she had no clue what they were talking about.

Malcolm towered over her, seeking to overawe her with his size and presence. "Jane, you must come with us now." He took hold of her arm. They were wasting valuable time. Someone was bound to discover them. Every passing moment he left Charlotte and Imogen alone made his gut twist more.

Jane pulled away. "My father is here."

"Yes, I know. We'll get him."

"Gaios is helping him."

"No, he is not."

"This is a spa. Gaios has a treatment that will improve my father's condition."

"There are no other patients here," Penny told Jane as she secured the heart of the altar in her bag. "Don't you find that odd?"

"His treatments are experimental. It requires solitude. However, if it works, we can use it to help many afflicted. It is one of his many areas of research. As I said, he intends to transform the world in all ways."

The light in the chapel dimmed as someone entered.

Malcolm spun about, yanking his Lancasters. The tall broad frame of Gaios was silhouetted in the doorway. Malcolm's stomach fell.

"Gaios!" Jane called out with relief. "These are my friends. They came to see me because they are worried about me."

"I see." The fiery gaze of Gaios instantly took the measure of the situation. "There is no need for them to fear . . . for you."

Chapter 17

MALCOLM THOUGHT HE FELT THE GROUND quiver under his feet. He had never been this close to Gaios before. There was something inhuman in the elemental's eyes. He could understand why Jane had mistaken it for zealotry. Gaios seemed to fill the chapel and diminish the others by his mere presence. The white hair and beard gave him the patina of an Old Testament prophet.

Gaios spoke with a voice that resonated throughout the building. "Did they interrupt your prayer?"

"No," Jane replied quickly. "I was finished for today."

"And you feel well?"

"I feel marvelous, as I always do after prayer."

Malcolm eyed the layout of the chapel, making overly hopeful contingency plans. He wondered if he could pull a gun and fire before Gaios could react. "Why don't you tell Jane what you're truly doing to her?"

The elemental scowled angrily. The chapel shivered. Jane looked alarmed. His eyes flicked to her and the tremors ceased. He made an effort to relax his features.

Jane showed no fear of the great magician, which was both disconcerting and comforting. However, she acted embarrassed, as if from harsh words spoken at a polite dinner. "Please don't be angry, Gaios. Mr. MacFarlane is a friend of mine from London. He was concerned for me and my father, not knowing where we had gone."

Gaios nodded and came across the floor. Malcolm purposefully refused to move as he approached, forcing the white-haired demigod to step around him.

Gaios took Jane's hand. "You do understand that our work must remain secret for now? No one should know until we are ready to share it with the world."

"Yes, I know." Jane sighed with self-reproach. "I'm sorry. I'm sure Mr. MacFarlane won't say anything."

Malcolm glanced at Penny, who clutched her rucksack. She seemed on the verge of doing something rash, so Malcolm smiled and winked as if this was a chat with the vicar after services.

Gaios continued to stare at Malcolm, but said to Jane, "They disturbed your father in his room. I managed to calm him, but he was quite unsettled by the incident."

Jane spun to Malcolm with hurt surprise.

Malcolm retorted, "He told us where you were. He was calm when we left. He still thinks I'm Captain Perry."

Jane softened and smiled. "Bless his heart. Father liked you very much despite his misapprehension."

Malcolm noted the growing rage in Gaios's eyes, which the elemental struggled to contain in front of the sensitive Miss Somerset. The ancient magician had constructed a complex ruse and needed for her to continue to believe in it. So Malcolm pushed a bit more. "Jane, I'd like you and your father to come with me."

Jane gasped with pain as Gaios inadvertently crushed her hand. He bowed his head apologetically and patted her fingers. "She will, of course, go nowhere with you."

Jane looked as if she was about to upbraid Gaios for

speaking for her, but she bit back the impolite words. "Mr. MacFarlane, I cannot leave. Our work is not yet done. You can clearly see I am in no danger. Whatever ideas you had are obviously incorrect."

"Obviously." Gaios smiled. "I will have one of my boats take you back to London."

Malcolm could see that Jane had no intention of leaving. There seemed no way to break her faith short of goading Gaios into killing. That seemed a senseless ploy although Malcolm could see from the old elemental's annoyed features, barely frozen to cover his burning rage, that it wouldn't take much effort. The Scotsman signaled to Penny and they started slowly toward the door. Gaios followed a few steps behind.

Jane called out quietly, "I do thank you, Mr. MacFarlane. I am grateful for your concern."

Malcolm paused in the doorway to look at the winsome figure standing in front of the altar. Then the fierce countenance of Gaios blocked his view. The Scotsman said, loudly enough for Jane to hear, "If you harm her, I will kill you."

"Threats in a house of God. Shame." Gaios shook his head to show how sorry he was that Jane's friends had revealed themselves as faithless boors. Jane came up behind Gaios, following them to the door. Gaios leaned toward Malcolm, eyes narrowing into blast furnaces, and he whispered, "Archer has killed you both."

Malcolm looked into the demigod's gaze with a quiet calm before turning away. He walked past a field of corn toward the forest's edge. The spot between his shoulders twitched as he felt Gaios's powerful stare following him. He knew Jane was watching them too. Penny's steps beside him were frantic and quick. His mind raced to work out their next move as he tried to slow Penny's pace. Just inside the tree line only fifty yards away, he could see a hunched shape angling toward the spot where their path would enter the jungle.

Malcolm eyed the dark thing. "I'm betting that beast won't come out of the forest where Jane might see."

"But we have to go through the forest to get back to the boat."

"True."

"What are we going to do?" Penny saw signs of the skulking monster and slowed.

"No idea."

"That's not very comforting."

"It wasn't meant to be."

"Word of advice. Try to be more comforting in dire situations. Simon makes jokes."

"Simon thinks the world is funny but he's wrong." Malcolm noted a white smoke plume drifting onto the green lawn ahead and off to the right.

"I'd feel better if you did. A little wit would go a long way."

Malcolm suddenly grabbed Penny's hand. Her head lifted in surprise until he pulled her abruptly toward the smoke.

"What is that?" she asked.

"Another lava pit hopefully."

"How is that a good idea?"

"There's something that separates us from the apes. We have an edge. Brain over brawn."

"I know there's a joke in there somewhere but I'm too terrified to think of it."

As always, Malcolm took comfort in Penny's spunk. "Your brains and my brawn can overcome most anything. I couldn't ask for a better cohort strolling into hell."

Immediately he regretted saying the truth out loud. The expression on Penny's face told him that she remembered his statement on that winter night outside the Mansfield estate. He had meant it then and he meant it now.

The air thickened in their throats and a wash of heat made their skin prickle. They saw a vast crevice that stretched from the edge of the lawn toward the coast, burning a raw scar through the jungle. The ravine spread quickly to fifty yards or more. Both sides of its jagged rim were covered with smoking black pumice. They passed the end of the crevice and darted into the trees, putting the steaming canyon between them and the gorilla.

Malcolm and Penny ran along the side of the glowing canyon. To their relief, the gorilla rumbled to a halt at the opposite edge. It slammed a metal fist against the earth in anger. Rocks cascaded down fifty feet into the river of bubbling magma.

Penny pulled the collar of her leather jacket across her mouth. Malcolm drew up the grey scarf around his mouth and nose to keep the acrid air from his lungs. Neither was adequate protection. The hot sand and rocks seared the soles of their shoes. Malcolm had his bearings and moved along the side of the ravine toward the sea, which was nearly a mile away. Penny stumbled and Malcolm caught her quickly before her hand touched the burning ground. She nodded gratefully, but he could see that the heat and fumes were taking their toll. She handed him a vial of Kate's fire-retardant gel and they coated any bare skin.

A thunderous roar shook the air. The trees on the far side of the ravine crashed together. The mechanical gorilla burst from the jungle and galloped with startling speed across the black soil. Malcolm saw that it was angling toward a spot where the canyon narrowed. It pounded to the edge and launched itself into the smoky air. The beast sailed over the lava and crashed barely ten yards ahead of Malcolm and Penny. The earth started to crumble under it, but the gorilla sank its massive hands into the soil and fought onto firm ground.

The mass of furious muscle turned immediately and charged them. Long metal canines bared as the ape bellowed. Malcolm raised a pistol and let loose a barrage. Four shots slammed into the chest of the gorilla, drawing blood. The thing was so enraged it scarcely felt them. Stumbling under a swing of its massive arm, Malcolm lost his grip on one of his pistols.

He dove aside as the huge shape roared onto them. Penny tried to do the same, but she lost her balance and her foot slipped off the edge of the ravine. With a shout, she tumbled over. Her hands, wet from the protective gel, slapped out. She desperately hooked her elbow, which was protected by the sleeve of her leather jacket, around a rock and hung with her feet dangling over the distant lava.

"Malcolm!" she shouted. The rest was drowned out by her coughing against the fumes leeching from below.

Malcolm jumped up to run to Penny's aid. He heard the ape snorting and wheeling for another attack. He drew his second pistol and fired three shots as it rampaged forward. A steel-plated arm swung at him, but Malcolm ducked. He swayed back over the soft, uneven ground. Furious, the gorilla beat the earth with its metal fists, sending shards of stones in all directions in its desperation to hit Malcolm. Every blow drove the hunter closer to the edge of the ravine. Malcolm sidestepped a powerful swipe and rolled forward as the great beast roared its frustration, throwing its arms up. Malcolm came up right in front of the ape just as the great forearms descended. He slammed his pistol barrel into the bottom of its chin and pulled the trigger. The ball punched up through the jaw and ricocheted a few times inside the metal skullplate until it came back out through the gorilla's eye.

The behemoth stood perplexed a moment before it finally toppled toward Malcolm. He tried to get out from under it, but failed and as the ape collapsed halfway off the side of the ravine, the massive weight of the creature drove him to the searing ground. His legs were trapped under the hairy pile. He struggled to get up. The beast began to slide over the cliff. Malcolm felt himself going with it. He saw that his leather gun belt was caught on a broken metal rod protruding from the gorilla's chest. He fought to unfasten the holster, but it was pulled too tight against the buckle. Dropping his pistol, he reached out to stop his slide but there was nothing to grab onto. Malcolm drew his dagger and started sawing through the leather strap. He was still cutting even as the giant ape dragged him over the edge.

The Scotsman slipped free of the broken harness, but it was too late. He plummeted behind the dead brute. Suddenly he felt himself jerk to a stop as the scarf around his throat tightened. He swung out over the magma, twisting in the scorching air enough to see Penny clutching the end of his wool scarf. She cried out in pain as she took his full weight and fought to keep the scarf from slipping through her grip.

He slammed against the ravine wall. Ignoring the searing pain, he fought for a handhold, a foothold, anything before he pulled Penny off her perch or strangled to death.

"Hold on!" he croaked.

"Hurry!" She slipped down with a jolt, but refused to let go of the scarf.

Malcolm dug in and found a solid ledge for his foot.

His dragging weight eased off her. He dared to use one hand to loosen the wool noose from around his neck. A knot had somehow formed, which prevented it from tightening fully. He wound the end of the scarf around his hand.

"I'm all right!" Malcolm called. It wasn't the truth. The heat and the fumes were overwhelming. A cough crawled its way up out of his throat. They had to get out or they would die. He started climbing, using her as his anchor until he was next to her. Penny's face was flushed and her eyes tearing.

Malcolm took her around the waist and pushed her back up top. She rolled over the edge onto solid ground. The scarf still connected them and she hauled on it until he crawled up and collapsed next to her on the steaming black dirt. She wrapped her arms around him and held him tightly.

"Oh God," she whispered.

He stiffened at her sudden embrace, but he could feel her trembling. His arms awkwardly enveloped her, his hand rubbing her back. Her forehead rested in his shoulder. It fit perfectly. He shoved himself to his feet with unexpected reluctance. "We have to keep moving."

Penny nodded and let herself be hoisted up, standing on shaking legs. She pulled some vials from her satchel and handed him one. Kate's *elixir vitae*. He took a deep swig and threw away the empty vial. Penny did the same. Then he looked around and gathered up his wayward pistols, gingerly holding them in his burnt hands. The pain was already receding, but it wouldn't stay away for long.

Penny grabbed her rucksack. "That's a good scarf. Lucky it didn't snap your neck."

Malcolm grunted in agreement and touched the grey length of wool with gratitude. Then he had an irrational thought. "I'm glad the Lancasters didn't fall in or you would have been furious with me."

She gave a hiccuping laugh. "Damn right."

They leaned on each other as they staggered away from the boiling ravine and found a new trail toward the coast. They emerged from the forest onto the rocky beach. A clean sea breeze hit their faces and they breathed the wonderful air so deeply, they both started coughing again. Malcolm took his bearings. He started along the beach toward the dock where they had left Charlotte and Imogen. It couldn't have been more than a half a mile away.

They had gone five hundred feet when they felt it. A tremor. Penny's face fell with dismay as the ground shook. The rocky terrain was precarious, but only when the ground beneath them actually shifted did they stumble. Gaios surely realized his pet had failed to kill them and was taking the matter into his own hands. The earth beneath them shuddered again. Everything started to quake and rumble. Trees cracked and fell at the jungle's edge. The ocean water flinched with a frothy slap against the shore. Malcolm pulled Penny upright.

They ran faster now, risking a broken limb on the slippery rocks. Finally Malcolm recognized the area ahead of them. This was where they had landed. But when they rounded a rocky outcrop, the dock was empty. The boat was gone.

Penny let loose a hoarse shout. "No!"

Malcolm exhaled heavily, fear gripping his chest. Did the crew somehow overpower the girls? Or some other of Gaios's sentry creatures happened onto them? Either way, he should never have left them.

An ear-rending crack split the earth. The ground shifted unnaturally under their feet and they struggled to keep their balance. A huge fissure opened high on the shore and ripped its jagged way along the edge of the forest, creating a domino crash of trees. Gaios was going to tear off a piece of his island to smash them.

Behind them, a high-pitched shout pierced the low rumbling. "Mr. Malcolm! Miss Penny!"

The paddle steamer came chugging around the shoreline. Charlotte leaned over the bow, waving frantically. Imogen stood in the wheelhouse. The boat rocked in the rough water, but Imogen angled awkwardly for the dock. Penny and Malcolm ran out onto the twisting jetty. Charlotte lifted a coil of line, but Malcolm motioned her aside.

"Jump for it!" he roared at Penny, hoping she heard him, as the boat rolled toward them, smacking into the pilings. They both leapt as wooden planks cracked. They cleared the rail and spilled onto the deck in a heap.

"What's happening?" Charlotte's eyes widened as she stared at the fracturing island.

"Get us out of here!" Malcolm waved his arm at Imogen. "Head for open water." As she frantically wrestled the wheel over, he shouted to Penny, "Get to the engine and scrape whatever you can out of her."

Penny ran to the stern and pulled open a hatch. She grabbed tools from her bag, peering through the access way at the churning machinery of the motor. She whistled and shook her head at another example of the Baroness's design prowess. Then she grinned with excitement and leapt into the hatch.

Malcolm joined Imogen in the wheelhouse. "Do you know how to handle this thing?"

"Father took us sailing." Her mechanical eye jutted out to focus far beyond the bow.

"This isn't a pleasure skiff."

She cast a baleful glare at him. "I'm an Anstruther. We don't use pleasure skiffs."

Malcolm grinned at her spirit. "Then take us out, love."

Crack after resounding crack echoed from the island until it became a single roar, almost like an artillery barrage. The fissure widened. Enormous piles of dirt and rocks cascaded in with a hissing sound. The shoreline behind them started to roll. The roar filled their ears. A huge expanse of rock lifted in a spray of water, almost seeming to rise from the ocean, before it crashed back down in a vast plume of spray. A wave of rolling water came at them, growing larger with each second.

Ahead of the steamer rose the jagged spears of rock that surrounded the island. Malcolm stood by the wheel and helped Imogen steer toward the barrier of dragon's teeth. Charlotte perched at the bow, trying to shout directions, but the roar of the earth and sea made it impossible to hear her.

Imogen pointed as the waterline dropped away ahead, exposing more of the deadly shoals. "We'll be crushed!"

The massive wave caught up and lifted the boat. They tipped forward, eliciting a scream from Imogen as they almost pitched on their prow. The sluggish paddle wheels groaned at the amount of fast-moving water rushing through them. They were heading helplessly for the massive rocks.

The engine revved suddenly loud and furious. The stovepipe above belched a huge green cloud. The paddle wheels spun faster with a frantic whine at Penny's command, digging hard into the water.

The crest of the wave rushed past them and they rolled back, prow in the air. The flood filled in the shoals, but the boat was still caught in the tumult of surging water. The force of it was trying to shove the vessel over. Malcolm heaved back on the wheel, his hands next to Imogen's tentacle fingers. Her grip was solid but it needed both their strength to keep the wheel from spinning wild.

Charlotte clung to the bow, sodden and desperate, now

in full werewolf form. Only her inhuman strength kept her on board the boat as it flung itself about in the chaos. She pointed frantically to the left and Imogen spun the wheel as a craggy spire of rock jutted out from under the water. They missed it by inches. The water was deep now, but jagged teeth still loomed close. One terrible stone bent over at nearly a sixty-degree angle. Half of the stovepipe sheared off with a horrendous groan. Charlotte barely dodged the dark iron that slid across the deck and crashed over the starboard side, taking out the rail before it fell into the torrent. She waded through cascading waves, her claws digging deep into the wooden deck. A loud howl erupted from her throat, her arm gesturing wildly to the left again. A long deadly spear of stone reared up in their path. Malcolm and Imogen tried to steer away, but too much force of water was pushing them. The stern swung wide. They were going to hit.

Malcolm's ears rang. Imogen's human hand went to her head as the whine built in intensity. It was Penny's sonic weapon. The jagged stone abruptly shattered to bits as the sound wave hammered it. The boat swept over the spot where it had been.

Suddenly they were in open water. Imogen shouted in triumph and Charlotte answered it with a howl that pierced the steady roar of the sea. Penny staggered up the ladder to the wheelhouse, drenched and weary, wearing a smirk of victory. Even Malcolm felt the elation of survival in his chest. He took a step toward Penny, but Imogen jumped in and hugged him in her jubilation.

Charlotte bounded onto the upper deck and grabbed up Penny, jumping up and down. "We did it! We did it!" Laughter swelled out over the boat as it settled over the gradually calming water.

Malcolm sobered. They had to get back to London. He took the wheel and steered toward home. They had accomplished little and his disappointment must have been plain on his face. Penny extracted herself from Charlotte and came over to him. The two girls went belowdecks to check on the prisoners and the damage.

"We'll find a way to help your friend," Penny told Malcolm.

"She doesn't want our help." He bitterly shook her head. "She's his."

"No. She just doesn't know him yet." Penny wrung out her hair. "Trust me. Even I could see that your friend isn't the evil type. Gaios preyed on her most obvious desire. Helping her father. Anyone might fall for that. She'll tumble to the truth."

"Then she'll be in even more danger." Malcolm gave a final glance at the rapidly diminishing view of the island. He hoped the rest had fared better in India.

Chapter 18

THE COLD TORE THOUGH SIMON'S THICK FUR-lined coat. Overwhelmed by the colors of white and grey, he feared the key had malfunctioned. He turned his head to orient himself and sensed Kate beside him.

She exhaled in frosty amazement and immediately reached up to fasten her collar. "Good God! How is it this cold?"

"This is horrible. People can't live in these places." Nick's incredulous voice came from behind. He had steadfastly refused to dress for the trip and he looked ludicrous now standing in wintry Nepal in his usual rough London tweeds.

They all stood on a craggy trail. A huge mountain behind them jutted up into the clouds. Stark grey rocks protruded from the white ground broken only by the occasional yellowed scrub or frozen ice floe that had once been a powerful cascading waterfall. Columns of bleak sun stabbed through the cloud cover. Their narrow trail led along the side of the mountain up to a hazy plateau.

Hogarth was the last from the portal. He wore an

outfit similar to Simon's, remnants of an old arctic expedition by Sir Roland. He surveyed the surroundings without reaction, hefting a heavy rucksack and his large mace. They all leaned into the bitter wind. Simon anchored his hood with a heavy-mittened hand and closed the portal. He spotted a small glimmer from the familiar compass-shaped rune on a rough stone column standing only a few feet away.

Nick's hand glowed red as he attempted to keep warm. He drank water from a tin canteen, or at least it should have been water. "No Ishwar to meet us, I see."

"We can't wait out here for long." Simon felt his cheeks numbing against the cold. It was difficult to breathe at this altitude. "But wandering off into the snow might not be wise."

He went to the stone column where the portal rune was etched. He noticed a whitish coloring below the rune and pulled on the tangling dead roots. They fell away easily as if they had been torn free previously and simply replaced. An arrow had been chipped into the surface of the column along with another simplistic carving of the word *El*. It appeared to have been done recently because it was not weathered to the color of the rest of the stone, and Simon's glove brought away a fine trace of dust when he touched it. The arrow pointed up the barely passable trail. "Seems to be a message here."

Kate joined him to study the mark. Her wild auburn hair tried to escape from a fur hat that fit snug over her ears. "El. It means *god* in Hebrew."

"And?" Simon blinked stinging windblown ice from his eyes.

"And Ishwar is a modern version of the Sanskrit word for *god*. This was carved here by Ishwar, sending us up that trail."

"That's a reach." Nick snorted derisively. "You want to walk into that stark hell based on a few chips on a stone?"

Kate cast him a scathing stare. "Perhaps you prefer to sit here pointlessly, then go home?"

"Easy." Simon's voice was harsher than he intended.

"How do we know this Ishwar is still alive?" Nick buttoned his thin coat as high as he could, not quite as daunted by the cold as the others. "How do we know he even exists?"

"We don't." Simon wore thick leggings, probably sealskin, stuffed into fur-topped boots. Drawing his stick sword from the back of his rucksack, he shifted the bag, which carried simple food and medical material. "We're going to move."

He started up the trail. Kate followed in heavy pants and boots, showing no discomfort. She wore her bandolier over her coat.

The path was rarely used. Large fallen boulders threatened to block the way in spots, and scrub grass broke through the coating of dry snow that continued to swirl. The wind gusted so violently at times it stopped them in their tracks for fear of being blown off course. They climbed, legs growing weary, breath rasping. Hogarth took the lead because he alone had experience in this sort of endeavor, having traveled distant continents with Sir Roland for many years. He forged ahead with his compass, making note of their movements and keeping them from straying off the path into a crevasse even when their trail vanished under heavy snow. Simon welcomed Hogarth's reconnoitering expertise because, despite their magical key, if they were unable to find their way back to the rune where they had arrived, there might be no escape short of walking off the mountain.

Simon could dress the part, but he knew that he was no explorer and was out of his element here. He could lead them through Paris because at least in a city there were streets and proper destinations, and ready food and water. In general, his most audacious expedition consisted of venturing from Soho to Kensington without a specific café destination in mind. The rest of his team was no more at home in the Himalayas. Kate was the daughter of a famous explorer, but she had never accompanied her father on his great journeys. And while Simon didn't know everything about Nick's past, nothing in the man's tavern-loving nature hinted at being a mountaineer.

Simon caught a slight glint in the light. The white snow and pale stone ahead of them hid filaments hanging in midair like a spider's web. He yelled, "Trap!"

Hogarth looked down suddenly at the feel of something on his legs. A gentle click came from beneath his feet. Kate grabbed the back of his coat and yanked with all of her might. He fell backward with a shout as three small circular blades curved up out of the snow and slashed across the path.

Simon rushed forward, helping Hogarth to his feet. The manservant gaped at the bright blades as they slowly spun to a stop on thin flexible stalks. The top one would have taken his head, the middle his waist, and the last his knees.

Kate cautiously slid her foot under the snow and touched the edge of a metallic plate. Now that she was aware of its existence, she saw short translucent posts only a few inches high on either side of the plate. The triggering thread had been strung between them. The trio of saws had been encased somehow in the metal plate and sprang into deadly action when the thread was broken. She grimaced. It was a hunter's trap of some sort.

It was beyond just being an efficient killing machine; it was gruesome. Any one blade would have been enough to kill. Three was just cruel.

"Someone doesn't want us around," Nick observed dryly.

Hogarth brushed snow from his clothes. "Thank you, Miss Kate."

Kate smiled at him. "I'll not be the one to bring back such sad news to Imogen and Charlotte. I didn't see the blasted thing, even so close." She glanced back at Simon.

The magician touched a long thread. "If the light hadn't hit it just right as I turned, I wouldn't have either. Sophisticated little death trap."

They continued on, much more wary of what lay before them. Simon and Nick walked slowly ahead of the compass-wielding Hogarth. Simon waved his walking stick and used it to prod the snow. Nick sent bursts of flame out to intercept any other hidden triggers. They encountered none, but it was nerve-wracking.

Finally, Simon struggled over a lip of stone to find himself at the edge of a plateau where a crumbled wall stood. He peered through a jagged gap in the masonry. Kate came up beside him and gasped. Stretching out before them was an incredible city of temples. Some of the structures were rubble, while others retained their grand beauty. It appeared to be a ghost city.

Simon cautiously passed through the wrecked wall. Their footfalls crunched over the icy ground. They saw endless grey stone structures along grand avenues and huddled over narrow alleys. The walls and façades were peopled with countless carved figures, crowded bas-reliefs of dancing deities and fantastical creatures. Thick snowdrifts clutched columns and slouched over domes and high spiked minarets. Scattered around the complex were numerous pools, temple tanks, some with water, some ice, some empty.

As they slowly rounded the corner of a collapsed shrine, they came to the edge of a courtyard. It was littered with dead bodies. Half a dozen men, monks by their bright red and yellow robes, lay in horrific positions. Each had been killed in some grisly way. One impaled by several metal spears. Another one lay in pieces, dismembered by the same saw trap that almost killed Hogarth. Coiling steel tendrils crushed yet another monk's twisted body.

In the chilling silence, they heard voices. One sounded strong and threatening, and the other was broken with cries of pain. They seemed to be coming from farther ahead along the central avenue they had been skirting. Hunching low, they crept up, keeping hidden in the shadows of the scattered ruins. Simon settied behind a broken staircase to a pagoda and pulled a telescope from his pack.

Through the blowing snow, about a hundred yards away, he saw a great temple with several towers layered like stepped minarets, and festooned with sacred carvings and spires reaching up to rival the mountainsides in the background. Those towers sat atop a monumental palace of dark stone with a fine long veranda. A long suite of steps led down from the terrace to a great rectangular temple tank.

A man, or what had once been a man, stood in the center of the veranda. His attention was directed at something lying at his feet, obscured by a bonfire. The man's face was badly scarred and his eyes were covered, or perhaps replaced, by gogglelike protuberances. Atop his head, he wore a multicolored turban of the sort often adopted by military officers of the East India Company. Long blond hair tied in a queue draped down his back. He sported the blue tunic of the Honorable Company fastened tight as if for inspection despite the fact that it was stained and its gold piping was torn. Beyond the frayed cuffs of the tunic, his hands were unnatural; they appeared to be composed of four metal claws. Below his waist, the wide trousers couldn't conceal his increasingly strange nature. He stood tall upon wide metallic pads that appeared to be his feet rather than shoes or boots. His legs bent backward at the knees and moved in an unusual way that revealed them to be metal. He held a massive bow, far too large for a normal person to wield. Strapped onto his back was a quiver full of arrows the size of javelins.

Several small shapes hopped about him. Monkeys. They appeared to be normal little simians except their eyes were replaced with jutting cones, like small telescopes. No doubt minions of the Baroness. Simon handed the spyglass to Kate.

"My God, it's Emmett Walker," she breathed with shock. "At least I think it is."

Simon glanced at her. "Your father's old hunting companion?"

"We've believed him dead all these years. At least my father said he was dead."

"He looks spry enough," Nick noted.

"Though hardly whole," was Simon's response. "It appears he fell afoul of the Baroness."

Simon took a telescope provided by Hogarth and studied the area around the distant temple. He spotted an odd pile and, tightening the focus, saw more bodies all wrapped in torn red cloth. There were at least twenty dead monks in the heap, and perhaps more. "Not shy about killing."

Kate leaned her elbows on a broken stone tablet and peered out. She made a variety of angry and disgusted noises as she scanned the scene. "Wait, there's someone with him. Tied to a column on the terrace."

The bound man was Indian, tall and thin with a long white beard. His head slumped against his chest. He wore a simple white cloth and shivered in the cold. There were scars and welts on his body and he was covered in dried blood.

Walker approached the prisoner, dragging something in his steel grip. The burden was another monk, still alive but barely so. Simon and the others couldn't hear what was being said, but the intention was clear. Walker shook the monk like a rag doll, furiously growling down at the bound man. Then through the thin air, Simon heard a sharp voice ring clear.

"The Stone! Where is it?"

The bound man shook his head. Walker tightened his grip on the monk's neck. The holy man thrashed. At first Simon thought he was trying to get free, but then the monk pulled a kris knife from his robe and thrust the wavy blade triumphantly into Walker's chest. Oil and green fluid spewed forth. Walker jerked, and for a moment, Simon thought the monk's desperate gamble had been successful. Then Walker crushed the monk's neck in his hand. When he tossed the dead man aside, the body went one way and the head went another. The bound man slumped.

"Damn me! Let's go." Simon rose to his feet, getting ready to move forward to save Walker's prisoner.

"Miss Anstruther!" a voice hissed from behind them. "Do not move." On the far side of a small covered platform, an elderly Indian man crouched. His bright blue eyes shone with alarm. He was tall and thin with a long white beard. He wore nothing more than a simple thin white dhoti, which seemed incredible in the frigid air.

Simon spun on the old man, sparking a tattoo to call forth his strength.

The man who had beckoned to Kate raised a cautioning hand, and whispered, "You are a few feet from one of the hunter's traps. Come toward me. You're fortunate not to have been killed on your way across the city."

Kate twisted her head to look at the old man, face clouded in confusion. "That man there tied to the column, are you his twin brother?"

"No. I am the man you see bound there. He is Ishwar. As am I." The old man gestured for them to follow. "Hurry! This way. One of the hunter's spies may see us."

Kate looked to Hogarth for confirmation. The manservant studied the elderly man, and said cautiously, "It has been many years, but he certainly resembles the Shri Ishwar I remember."

She raised her crossbow to the stranger. "What are you playing at?"

The old man came out from behind his protection and scurried toward them. His voice was hushed. "I'm afraid the hunter captured me yesterday, just after I contacted you. He knows me; knows I am connected to Sir Roland. So he believes I know where the Stone is hidden. He has been torturing me quite mercilessly. But it is becoming difficult to be elsewhere. If you don't steal the Stone away very soon, knowing myself quite well, I may falter and tell him where it is."

Nick snarled, "What the hell is that crazy old fakir talking about? This lunatic is the Ishwar we came to find?"

The elderly man glowered at Nick, then turned back to Kate. "If you care to observe, Miss Anstruther, I will explain." He quivered and grew very still. His wrinkled skin darkened like soil. The contours of muscles and joints grew rough and indistinct. The man transformed into a lifeless, vaguely man-shaped pile of mud.

"Holy Mother," Kate exclaimed.

"Is it a golem?" Simon stared at the muck that used to be Ishwar without touching it.

"No, I think it's vivimancy," Nick said, impressed. "Looks like he's mastered vitalism. I was wrong. He's no crazy old fakir."

Kate tore her stunned gaze from the glistening mound of mud and raised the spyglass. The figure tied to the distant stone column had his head slumped against his chest. As Kate watched, he lifted his face. He nodded toward her in desperation. It was clearly Ishwar. She turned back to watch the mud on the ground re-form into the shape of the elderly magician.

Ishwar blinked his shining eyes at Kate as if waking from a pleasant nap. "There isn't much time. You must seize the Stone and take it away."

"Where is it?" Kate asked.

"I will take you." Ishwar motioned them to follow and walked toward a small temple behind him.

Kate exchanged a glance with Simon. They didn't hesitate and strode after Ishwar. Nick grumbled, obviously ill at ease with the whole situation.

As Ishwar led them inside, Simon looked at the stonework around them. "Is it in here?"

"No." Ishwar took the arm of a carved god on the wall and pulled it. A portion of the floor pivoted down to reveal a dark tunnel into the ground. "This route will save us from being unfortunately skewered."

"Wait a damn second." Nick fixed Simon with a look of incredulity. "Are you just going to trust this man?"

Simon started into the tunnel. "It's either him or the metal man and his death traps outside."

Kate followed, then Hogarth. Ishwar waited until finally Nick growled and also dropped into the dark tunnel. Ishwar came after and worked some counterweight to return the cover stone to its place.

In the darkness ahead, Simon paused to make a show of removing a stone from his boot. In fact, he quickly drew the gold key from his coat pocket, keeping it hidden from Ishwar with crafty sleight of hand, and dropped it into his right boot.

Ishwar smiled approvingly at the fire that burst from Nick's hand to light the darkness. "Good trick. The light is unnecessary. Go forward. There is only forward now."

"I'll keep it if you don't mind." Nick let Ishwar pass in front of him so he was bringing up the rear and could keep an eye on the wizened man.

Simon stamped his boot back on. "Kate, what more can you tell us about this Walker chap?"

"He traveled with my father occasionally, as I mentioned. Died in India on my father's last expedition there. Or so I thought. He had been an infrequent hunting companion of my father. When I was a little girl, he would come out to Hartley Hall at times for shooting parties, like many people did."

"And what did you think of him?"

"He was a brute. He treated animals harshly. I saw him beat horses. Once Aethelstan, Aethelred's mother, bit him and Walker went to shoot her."

"Did he?"

"No. I stopped him long enough for Father to come and smooth things over." Kate grinned with righteous anger. "He deserved to be bitten, and worse."

Ishwar said, "You brought your father's key, yes?" When no one replied, the old man smiled. "Do you not trust me, Miss Anstruther?"

Kate looked back. "Shri Ishwar, do you know where my father is?"

"No, Miss Anstruther. I haven't heard from him in the years since he hid the Stone here. You have not either?"

"No." Kate shook her head. "Why not simply destroy the Stone?"

"No!" Ishwar leaned forward with a look of distress. "No, Miss Anstruther. Your father knew the karma from such an atrocity. The Stone is a great relic and more important than our lives."

"More important than your life maybe," Nick muttered.

Ishwar didn't even glance at the sour man. "Hide it far away. If Gaios finds it again, then hide it again. As many times as necessary."

Kate shook her head in confusion. "Why would he hide it here so close to Baroness Conrad's home? He knew she was in league with Gaios."

"He believed he had killed the Baroness years ago in revenge for her slaughter of his expedition. He was wrong."

"My father battled with the Baroness?"

"Yes, Miss Anstruther. He came here many years ago trying to find more information about Gaios's plans. She trapped his expedition and killed most of them."

Kate exhaled heavily. "Damn it, he never told me."

"Your father believed she was dead. And he believed the intrinsic power of this temple would help hide the Stone from the potential gaze of an earth elemental, even one as powerful as Gaios. He was wrong again. But even the great Gaios must have his limits. He obviously cannot tell the hunter the exact location of the Stone, or it would be on its way to England now. He only knows that it is somewhere here in this vast temple city. That is why Walker tortured the poor monks who reside here, but they did not know."

"But you know?"

"I do. I helped your father put it here three years ago. And I have watched it ever since."

Simon noticed Kate pulling her coat tighter. He knew her chills were not completely from the cold. The memories of her father were near and she was unnerved by them. "How did you contact us in England, Shri Ishwar? Do you have a key of your own?"

"I have this." Ishwar hopped, showing a small silver chain around his bare ankle. Dangling from the chain was a metal trinket shaped like the compass or sunrise rune from the key. "Your father made these speaking charms and gave me one. It is drained of aether now and useless. Fortunately, I reached you, Miss Anstruther, and you came. And you will keep the Stone safe with your life, as I have done."

As they continued, the tunnel grew narrow so they had to drop to their hands and knees, and crawl, pushing their packs ahead of them. The oppressive sense of surrounding earth began to trouble Simon, but he refused to show it. The dirt of the tunnel scraped both shoulders and the top of his head. He could not turn or look back. He only knew that Kate was there by her breath, and he could hear the sounds of the others crawling behind. The pale light of the tunnel grew even smaller ahead so he had to drop to his chest and wriggle through an opening barely wide enough for a human shape.

The other side opened into a broader chamber that allowed him to stand. He stooped to pull Kate out and she took a deep breath of relief. Hogarth struggled from the tunnel as if it were giving birth to an elephant.

Ishwar sidled to the front of the group. He fumbled his fingers along the wall and a small rectangular section swung open. One by one, they followed him onto a tiled floor. They found themselves next to a statue of a cross-legged Shiva holding a trident in one hand.

"We are in the northwest corner of the great temple where Walker has me prisoner," announced Ishwar.

"That can't be wise." Simon regarded the old man.

"Unfortunately, the Stone rests in this very temple. Did I neglect to say this to you?"

Simon laughed.

Kate rolled her eyes in exasperation. "You find that funny?"

He shook his head with great solemnity. "Not funny in the traditional sense, no."

Ishwar pointed. "The Stone is in that direction. I am being held at the east terrace."

Ishwar silently led the way forward across the vast chamber. Diffused moonlight filtering through the exterior lattice walls created long silvery shadows. They passed cautiously through the voluptuous interior thick with statues. Many sculptures wore frightening faces and did not appear to be any of the Hindu deities Simon knew.

At the far side of the crowded deity room, they came to an open archway. Simon and Ishwar peered through the arch, looking into a grand entry hall. Fifty feet away was a row of widely spaced columns separating the hall from the east terrace with its bonfire crackling. The true Ishwar was tied to one of the pillars. He sat on the frigid stone floor, head down, apparently unconscious. There was no sign of Walker at the moment.

Kneeling beside Simon, Ishwar put a hesitant hand up as if gesturing to his own distant form. "I may not live much longer."

Simon said, "Aren't you a vivimancer of some sort?

You have the power of life. Why can't you heal yourself?"

"I have, which is why I am still alive at all. I cannot now spare the power to heal and keep myself"—he touched his chest—"up and about. I can only imbue life to one form at a time."

"The sooner we get the Stone, the sooner we can rescue you," Nick hissed. "So where is it?"

Ishwar started from the edge of the archway and moved along the wall of the deity room, counting stones across, then up. He touched a mottled grey stone, which was the proper size of the relic they sought.

Simon reached up. It felt like any other cold rock. "You're sure?"

"This is the location. From the arch, nine stones across and six up. Nine for Katherine. Six for Imogen."

Kate put a hand over her mouth to stifle an uncharacteristic sob. Her eyes suddenly glistened.

Simon understood her emotional reaction to Sir Roland using his daughters' names as a guide to hide this relic from Gaios. It was like overhearing an unexpected word of praise from her father. "Odd that something this powerful seems so normal."

"This one is normal. That isn't the Stone of Scone."

"What?"

Ishwar looked embarrassed. "Your Stone is at this spot, but it is on the other side of this wall."

"In the entry hall? In full view of the enemy." Simon leaned heavily against the wall with an exhale of defeat. He quickly recovered; it was untoward for him to show any weakness or frustration in front of the others. "How thick is this wall? Can we get to the Stone from this side?"

"It is very thick. Many layers of stone. Even if you had the power to tear through it, the hunter would hear you first, or perhaps the wall would collapse. Your Stone is facing out on the far side. You have but to loosen it and go."

"Oh, is that all?" Simon pinched the bridge of his nose and smiled. "Fine. There's no point in waiting. Walker isn't around so let's get you and the Stone, and be off."

Chapter 19

THEY WENT THROUGH THE ARCHWAY FROM THE deity room into the entry hall. Frigid wind blew through the row of columns open to the outside. Simon counted off along the interior wall until he put his hand on the proper stone. It too felt like a normal rock and it looked exactly like every stone on the wall. But Ishwar nodded with a slight smile. Simon ran his fingers over the rough surface of the Stone of Scone, trapped here so far from home in the wall of a temple in the foothills of the Himalayas.

Kate moved to the front of the entry hall and knelt by the slumped form of the real Ishwar. Nick crouched behind a neighboring column, staring out onto the snowy terrace and city beyond. He swore.

"Those damned monkeys are everywhere out there. Can you get the Stone back through the tunnel?"

Simon shook his head. "I don't think so. There were spots where it was far too narrow. We barely squeezed through."

"If we try to stroll out of here," Nick said, "Walker will be on us. And he seems unpleasant. Plus, this city is riddled with death traps."

Simon pressed his foot against the floor. "I have an

idea. I believe I can create a new portal with the key. Here. And we can simply drop the Stone back to London."

Kate looked up. "You can do that?"

"I'm not sure, but our discovery of the creation phrase put me on the right path."

She nodded in agreement. "Try it. What's the worst that can happen?"

Simon pursed his lips sourly at her. "You should never tempt fate, my dear." He pulled his sword and sparked it to life, holding it out to Kate. She sheathed her own sword and took his, mindful not to touch the blade. Simon looked at the wall carefully. He pressed his right foot onto the floor. "Daros Marthsyl."

"What are you saying? *Door* in ancient Celtic?"

"Yes. I can feel something starting to happen. I don't know if it will work, or how long it will take."

"Where is the key?" Kate asked.

"In my boot. Monkey, darling."

"Monkey darling what?" Kate caught a glimpse of one of the little hairy figures hanging from the beams overhead. "Jesus!"

A fireball streaked at the dangling beast, but it squealed and swung up out of sight. Nick slapped his hand against the column. "Damn it! We're in for it now."

"Simon," Kate began, but as she turned back to him, she saw he was frozen with his eyes closed. He was in a deep trance. Tendrils of aether were rising from the ground around his foot. The power of the key had locked him in place. She spun back, glowing sword in hand. "Everyone get ready. We have to hold this ground."

Seconds later a shout came from outside. "Who is up there? There are no more monks so you must be new arrivals." Walker came striding up the steps onto the veranda. He was framed by the thickening snow blowing in the wind. He held his massive bow with a javelin-sized arrow already notched, but it was pointing at the ground. A monkey crouched on Walker's steel arm, eating fruit, no doubt a reward for its spying prowess. The hunter stared between the columns at the group inside the entry hall. He grinned with delight. "Katie Anstruther! Is that you? The Baroness said you were looking for the Stone too."

Kate froze. She and Nick peered out at the huge mechanical man on the edge of the terrace.

"I was hoping you would come," Walker continued. "Do I look different to you now, Katie?" He flexed one of his steel arms with a mechanical whine. "I don't think I had these little appendages when we last met, did I? No, I couldn't have because I acquired them thanks to your father. He left me for dead, Katie. If Baroness Conrad hadn't saved me, well, I'd be as dead as this fellow." Walker kicked the decapitated body of the monk. His gogglelike eyes glowed red. "Speak up, Katie! Nothing to say about your murdering father? Do all you Anstruthers stick together? Oh, and how is your sister, Imogen?"

Kate gripped Nick's arm so tightly she was in danger of tearing it off.

The hunter came closer with thudding steps. "Did my old friend, Colonel Hibbert, enjoy her? I'm sure he did." He grinned.

Walker raised his bow. Only then did he see the second Ishwar standing behind Kate, and he hesitated in surprise. He looked toward his prisoner, still tied to the column, and back up at the other Ishwar in confusion.

Kate popped the treacle out of her crossbow and took some grim pleasure in seizing a different load. She fired between a column. A potion smashed against Walker's chest. The drenching chemical solution transformed into a bilious green cloud. He gagged on the toxic fumes and ducked back, swinging the bow wide.

Kate shouted orders. "Ishwar, free yourself! Hogarth, Nick, on Walker!"

Hogarth leapt between the columns onto the terrace and leveled his mace into the hunter's chest. Walker gasped and staggered back toward the steps. His evil glare went to Hogarth. When the mace swung for another blow, a metal claw met it. The heavy weapon bounced off as if it had struck a mountain. Walker reached out and grabbed Hogarth.

"I remember you bowing and scraping at Hartley Hall," Walked snarled at the burly servant. "I dislike being manhandled by stableboys."

A pistol cracked and Kate stood with her arm straight and smoking weapon extended. The ball ricocheted off the plate beneath the hunter's chest. Walker shouted in surprise and dropped Hogarth down the steps.

Kate threw a vial of treacle at Walker's feet. The black ooze spread over his metal treads, locking him in place. The hunter glared down at the mess and started to raise one of his feet. It hung in the treacle for a second before tearing free. It appeared that he had actually sloughed off a thin layer of steel from his feet to escape. The metal looked to be knitting itself over, reinforcing the areas where he had lost coverage.

Walker stepped free of the treacle, none the worse for it. The hunter raised his bow and took the nock of the huge arrow into his claw. He aimed at Kate and drew back the string. The arrow began to glow.

"I'd hoped for better from you than trying to stop me with a little putty," Walker growled. "Well, you're not your father then, are you, Katie? He may've been a bastard, but he got a job done."

Nick stepped in front of her.

Walker narrowed his eyes. "Your heroism won't save her."

"I don't do heroism, mate." Nick raised his hands again and closed his eyes. He gritted his teeth and suppressed a scream. His fingers twisted into a fist. An arc of lightning crackled out and enveloped Walker in a sheen of blue. The hunter shrieked, but it was silent under the snapping of electricity. Walker convulsed, bending at the waist. The javelin arrow blackened and fell from his fingers. Smoke rose from around his torso and he took two steps back. His metal feet hit the edge of the terrace and he dropped hard, cracking the stones. Walker rolled back down the steps with a thundering sound, then crashed to a wheezing halt of powerless machinery.

Nick gasped for breath and fell against a pillar. Kate reached for him, but he waved her off. His hands were red and blistered.

Kate said quietly, "I didn't know you could summon lightning."

"I don't do it often." Nick tried to sound tough, but he wasn't successful. "Now I remember why."

Hogarth staggered back up the steps to the veranda, sparing an impressed glance at Nick, and went to where Ishwar was still struggling to untie the cords around his true self. Hogarth pulled a small dagger from his boot and cut the ropes. The real Ishwar flopped onto the floor and groaned. Their Ishwar suddenly froze in place and began to transform into loamy soil. Hogarth and Kate helped the newly conscious vivimancer into a sitting position. She looked at the collapsing mound of mud with some regret.

Nick pushed himself to his feet with a groan and started unsteadily toward the edge of the terrace, muttering something to himself. Kate turned to warn him to be careful, when his body jerked as if hit by a powerful blow and he flew back to slam into one of the columns. He hung there, shaking uncontrollably, his feet dangling above the paving stones. A glowing javelin protruded from his chest, pinning him to the stone pillar like an insect in a collection.

"Nick!" Kate shouted and started toward him.

A steady stream of blood ran from Nick's body and stained the snowdrift red. His eyes were open and he struggled to breathe. His jaw hung slack and red liquid dribbled from his lips. Hogarth joined Kate and put his strong hand on the now cold javelin. Behind them, they heard the whirring of Walker's machinery and thudding footfalls coming up the steps. Kate motioned for Hogarth to free Nick as she turned to look out over the snowy terrace. She brandished her weapons, listening to the grinding sound of metal limbs drawing nearer.

Ishwar leaned weakly between columns. "I will see to your friend."

Hogarth slowly pulled the long steel lance from Nick's chest, eliciting a pathetic grunt of pain from the wounded man. He caught the bloody figure in his powerful arms and set Nick down next to Ishwar, who was struggling to his knees.

"Katie!" Walker's voice rang out. He was still out of sight and the sounds of his movement had ceased. "Come out, Katie! I can come up and get you, but make it easy on yourself. I'm going to kill you and cut off your head so I can show it to your father one day, just before I dismember him."

Kate stayed quiet, watching Ishwar place his swollen bloody hands on Nick's slack face. The vivimancer closed his eyes and began to chant quietly.

From inside the entry hall, a sudden blinding light shot up from the floor beneath Simon's boot and knocked him onto his back. The key's runic symbol glowed from the flagstone and the air began to shimmer a few feet above it. The usual circle of disruption swirled into being. This time, however, it was horizontal, like a pool of weirdness a few inches thick hanging above the ground. The world map appeared and a new dot flickered to life nearly on top of the spot already located in Nepal.

From the floor, Simon laughed in triumph and turned expectantly to find the others. When he took in the frightful faces on the far side of the columns, and saw the blood-drenched form of Nick, he scrambled toward them frantically. "Good God. What happened?"

A shadow rose up at the edge of the terrace with a sudden roar of machinery. Walker appeared again and charged at Kate. She had been looking at Nick, and was surprised by the sudden appearance of Simon who rushed past her, shouting an ancient word in a fury. Walker was fast and a metal fist swept out. Simon barely had time to get his hands up before a great weight crashed against him like a battering ram. Before he could recover, a steel hand clamped his neck.

Simon grabbed the metal fingers in a grip to rival the hunter's. His other hand struck at Walker's unprotected head, tearing at the inhuman eyes. The hunter howled and flung his head back, but his grip only loosened slightly. Sparks flared in Simon's vision as more and more oxygen was denied him.

Kate appeared and thrust Simon's glowing sword into Walker's side. It slipped through the metal easily. She spun with a ragged cry, dragging the blade out Walker's back, hoping to rip through his spine. The big man reeled backward and kicked out at Kate, forcing her to leap away.

Simon slammed his palm into the elbow of the arm that held him, inward and down, forcing him closer. He crashed his forehead into the hunter's face. Blood spurted as Walker's lips and nose split. He roared. The hold lessened and Simon sucked in a lungful of air. He took Walker's arm and twisted it around, forcing the steel ball and joint at the shoulder to creak with unexpected strain. A whine built up as the gears tried to compensate.

Walker's eyes widened as he realized Simon was much more than human. The hunter released his hold because his arm was partially torn from its socket. Simon leaned back, yanking Walker off balance. Slowly rotating into a spin like a hammer thrower, he pulled the stumbling hunter along. The mechanical man couldn't keep up, hopping and finally lifting off the ground. Simon let go and hurled the huge man away. Stones and ice broke away as the mechanized man slid along the terrace. The metal body collided with several columns, which cracked at their bases and toppled in a ground-shaking crash.

Steel hands pressed against the ground and Walker gained his feet, rotating his shoulder and loosening the laboring pistons and joints. To Simon's stunned surprise, Walker's machinery shifted and moved like a living thing as the dangling arm was pulled back into its socket. The metal was repairing itself.

Kate fired two vials at once and they crashed against Walker's chest in a cloud of green smoke. Acid began to eat away at the steel, but as fast as it was destroyed, new sections ratcheted into its place.

Simon grabbed one of the broken columns. It was thick and pitted and cold under his hands. His fingers dug deep into the cracks. He swung it at Walker, who put out his arms to catch it. The force of the blow struck the hunter square in the chest and sent him airborne. He flew off the terrace, crashed once on the steps with an explosion of stone, bounced, and rolled uncontrollably through the dirt over the lip of a temple tank where he landed with a high plume of water.

Simon was already in motion, racing for the cistern. He would have preferred Nick's assistance, but there was no time. If Nick was even still alive. Shoving the image of his friend's bleeding body from his mind, Simon vaulted down the steps and slid onto his knees in front of the temple tank. Its expanse would call for ample quantities of aether and Simon beckoned all he could.

Walker was already striding along the bottom of the cistern beneath ten feet of water. Simon scrabbled in his pocket and found the stump of chalk he usually carried. He had no idea how long that mechanical horror could hold his breath, but Simon intended to find out. He scribed a simple rune on one corner of the tank. Walker looked up through the churning water and actually grinned at Simon.

Freezing water was one of the first spells any scribe practiced. Simon had barely placed his hand on the rune and spoken a word when ice began to crystallize faster than nature allowed. The fracturing crystals groaned and creaked as a thin layer of ice spread across the surface of the tank. Walker still moved unencumbered at the bottom, but the ice was reproducing wildly thanks to the aether urging it on. The crystals extended deeper, growing larger as they went. Simon watched as Walker's movements became slower and slower in the thickening water. The hunter abruptly stopped in midstep, trapped in the embrace of the ice.

Breathing heavily, Simon shoved himself to his feet and ran back up to the terrace. Ishwar still worked over Nick's motionless body. The pool of blood around them was wide. Ishwar rocked up and down. He dug two fingers into Nick's mouth and grasped the jaw of the dying man. A rush of aether burst from Ishwar and traveled into Nick.

Nick gagged and tried to sit up. He pushed the strange fingers from his mouth. He glanced around in confusion. Simon gasped out in relief and turned grateful eyes on Ishwar. The old man nodded wearily.

"The Stone . . ." he urged.

"We're ready to go." Simon helped Nick to his feet.

The group returned to the entry hall and approached the new portal swirling above the floor. Then the sound of shattering ice came from outside.

Kate took a heavy breath. "Jesus. He doesn't stop, does he?"

With more pounding steps, Walker soon appeared at the edge of the veranda. His eyes were fierce. Rivulets of blood and slush poured off him. Any damage had been repaired as if it had never been. He stomped across the terrace and kicked one of the columns, smashing the stone pillar into pieces. Huge chunks of stone flew into the entry hall, tumbling past Simon and his group.

The hunter glared at Simon, clutching one remaining javelin. "I see now who is the most powerful. Why didn't I kill you first?"

"Because you're ridiculously stupid." Simon started toward the metal man. "And we've had just about enough of you. Kate, my sword."

She tossed the glowing blade, which Simon caught out of the air. Then she dropped her crossbow and drew her sword and pistol. She sprinted toward Walker while Simon and Hogarth ran at him from different directions. The hunter raised the javelin and let it fly at Kate. She caught the deadly missile with her sword, barely deflecting it away.

Kate raised the gun and fired. The ball penetrated flesh at the hunter's hip and the man grunted. He turned toward her, towering over the woman. He leveled a decapitating blow at her. Kate ducked and plunged her blade up under his massive metal arm. It cut into flesh, but quickly struck steel and turned aside.

With a roar, Walker's arm came down and caught Kate before she could escape. He crushed her against his chest and laughed. "You're still an insufferable little wretch. All of you Anstruthers think you're nobility, but you're no better than me."

"God forbid." Kate gasped for air. She dropped her pistol and scrabbled at the bandolier with thick-gloved fingers.

Hogarth leapt onto Walker's back and wrenched his powerful arm around the hunter's neck. Simon hacked at the hunter's leg with his glowing blue sword, slicing through struts and cables, causing the mechanical man to lurch.

"Damn you! You always did have large dogs around." Walker twisted violently and Hogarth's legs collided with Simon. The hunter smashed backward into a column, crushing the manservant but unable to dislodge him. He came forward, legs grinding, and drove back again. The column cracked and Hogarth grunted in pain, but kept his tight lock around Walker's neck.

Simon latched onto the metal wrist holding Kate. He could feel her struggling under Walker's grasp. A tattoo flared, and with intense effort, he dragged the steel arm out, giving Kate an inch of space to breathe.

"Too late, Archer!" Walker shrieked. "She's not leaving my embrace alive."

Kate's hand plunged under Walker's tattered regimental tunic. She quickly drew it back out and smashed her open palm against a small lump under the wool cloth. Glass shattered. Walker hesitated, unsure of what he felt. Then he screamed.

"Hogarth!" Kate shouted. "Get off!"

As the manservant abandoned his grip on the hunter, Simon wrenched the steel arm back and sliced through the wrist with his sword. The clawed hand fell to the temple floor with a heavy clang. Kate pushed free from Walker, and she and Simon ran away from the thrashing hunter as blue fire blossomed from him.

Walker stumbled forward, cursing and flailing at his

burning chest. Kate's Greek fire ate into steel and flesh alike, burning faster than the machinery could repair itself. Walker looked up in agonizing horror and dropped heavily to his knees.

"Nothing clever to say?" Kate glared viciously at him. "I'll give my sister your regards. You may give our regards to Colonel Hibbert in hell."

Simon watched Walker's massive frame collapse to the floor. The crackling sound of the eldritch fire accented the melting of failing gears. Walker's scream dissolved into a gurgling silence as the flames licked up at the last bit of remaining flesh. In the midst of the burning morass, Simon saw a small crystal, glowing green with aether. But then Kate's fire caught it as well and the crystal broke into colorless shards.

Simon walked with Kate, putting a hand against her stiff back. She looked at him with eyes that were cold and distant. Simon's breath locked in his chest. Though he had told the king they weren't assassins for the Crown, their hands were bloodied. And worse, it wasn't his hands alone. The purest of them were now tainted. There were no words of consolation he could offer. He let her alone and returned to the wall where the Stone of Scone resided.

Chapter 20

THE SOUND OF THE WIND SWIRLING IN THE smashed foyer could be heard throughout Hartley Hall. It was a breezy evening with a hint of autumn chilling the house. Certainly it was far warmer than the frozen landscape of Nepal where they had left the grateful Ishwar after he refused their kind offer to return with them. Kate sat staring out at the light of the setting sun through the trees. She preferred the Blue Parlor to the library now because some of the landscape in the rear of the house had survived. The vestiges of the old gardens calmed her. She was also warmed by the sound of Imogen's soft breathing. Her sister sat on the sofa next to her with her head on Kate's shoulder. She had drifted off to sleep almost an hour ago. Her little hedgehog curled on her lap, making drowsy snorting sounds. Kate knew she should send Imogen off to bed—tomorrow would be a grueling day—but she couldn't bear to wake her.

Her thoughts strayed to the last blood test she had run on Imogen. She had incorporated elements of the active substance that Penny had discovered in the key. Kate was convinced there had been a transformation in Imogen's inhuman blood; it seemed to have changed color to a deeper red. She knew she was on the right path to grasping the biological mechanism of Imogen's alteration. She was gaining on Dr. White's knowledge of advanced alchemy. Soon, she would catch him and undo his vile work.

Charlotte lay on the floor near the popping coal grate. She hummed happily and drew pictures. Lying beside her was Aethelred, his warm brown eyes watched Charlotte furiously sketching. The girl needed little sleep. Her fire burned hot at all times. Kate watched the small hand grasping a thick pencil; that hand would soon turn huge and violent and deal out death. It was still an incomprehensible thing.

Kate shoved those thoughts from her head. "What are you drawing, dear? Is it a cow?"

Charlotte looked at Kate with indignation. "A cow? No!" She held up the large sheet, tugging it free from under the dog's chin. It was the back of a strip of wallpaper from one of the house's wrecked walls. "It's Mr. Malcolm!"

"Oh?" Kate squinted at the dark shape. "Oh. Yes, of course. I see it clearly. Is that his . . . *arm*?"

"It's his gun." Charlotte raised her pencil toward the window like the barrel of a pistol. "Boom! Boom!"

"Shh, dear." Kate glanced stiffly at her sister, who hadn't moved. "Imogen is sleeping."

Charlotte clamped a hand over her mouth, and mumbled, "Sorry."

Kate smiled and consulted the clock on the mantel. "It's time for your wulfsyl." She made a mental note to test the latest batch precipitating in the laboratory.

The girl huffed. "Can I wait for few more minutes?" Wulfsyl was usually the sign it was time for bed.

Kate knew it was best to preserve routine, particularly during chaotic times, but again, she wanted to sit in the quiet parlor with her two girls for a while longer. "Very well. Just a few minutes."

"Thank you. Who should I draw now?"

"*Whom* should I draw now? Why don't you draw yourself?"

Charlotte pursed her lips in doubt. "No. I'm not good at hair."

"All right. What about Imogen?"

"She doesn't like it."

Kate tilted her head in confusion. "What do you mean?"

"I drew her once last winter, but she got mad and tore it up."

"Was it a mean drawing?"

"No!" Charlotte covered her mouth again. "No. It was nice. It looked like her, and she didn't like it."

Kate felt a sharp pang in her chest at the thought of Imogen confronting a drawing of her mutated appearance. She reached up and laid a gentle hand on her sister's cheek. Imogen stirred restlessly, then settled back against Kate with a sigh.

Charlotte rolled back onto her paper and brandished her pencil. "I'll draw you and Mr. Simon."

"All right. That sounds nice."

Charlotte started scribbling. "Miss Kate, are you going to marry Mr. Simon?"

"I don't know, dear." Kate chuckled as she stroked Imogen's misshapen hand. "Do you think I should?"

"I think you should. He's funny."

"Yes, he is funny. But he hasn't asked me to marry him."

"He will."

"Well, I'll make that decision when he does."

Charlotte bolted up with sudden alarm. Her face was stricken. "You won't say no, will you?"

"Calm yourself, dear. Are you that worried about it?"

Charlotte's lower lip protruded and began to quiver. "If you say no, he might leave. And then what happens to all of us? Where will Mr. Malcolm live?"

Kate tried to lean forward without disturbing Imogen. "Relax, Charlotte. No one is leaving. All of us will live here at Hartley Hall for as long as we wish. You, me, Mr. Simon, and Mr. Malcolm."

"And Miss Penny?"

"Yes. Her too."

"And Imogen!"

"Of course. This is our house. We'll all be together."

Charlotte let out a great breath and fell back against the wolfhound. "Oh good!"

The door creaked open and Penny appeared. She glanced in but hesitated to enter, as if she was concerned about interrupting a family moment of which she was no part. Kate caught the engineer's eye and motioned her inside. Penny carried the steel-and-crystal heart of the altar from Gaios's island.

"Penny," Kate said with mild disapproval, "are you still working with that thing? You should take a moment at least to relax."

"This is relaxing." Penny waved at Charlotte and pointed at the picture. "Nice one of Malcolm."

Kate rolled her eyes, and asked, "Were you looking for Simon? I believe he's in the library."

"No." Penny seemed a bit awkward and unsure of being with Kate and the girls, which was unusual for the woman who was at ease barging in anywhere. "Well, eventually. I want to tell him about this device." She stood rooted to the rug.

"Sit and talk with us, if you're not in a hurry." Kate nodded toward an armchair beside the sofa. "We're just discussing art."

"And marriage!" Charlotte added gleefully.

"Oh." Penny hopped into the chair and threw one leg

up over the arm. She began to toss the altar heart up and down in one hand. "Those are two topics that are mysteries to me."

Charlotte looked over at Penny. "Miss Kate is going to marry Mr. Simon."

"That's nice," Penny droned calmly, regarding the device as it sparkled in the firelight. Then the words sank in and she froze. "What? When?"

"No, no." Kate held up her hand and laughed. "We were talking about the possibilities of the future."

"Oh." Penny laughed too and nodded knowingly. "Well, a woman could do far worse, Kate. A man who's funny, smart, handsome, and strong."

"And bullheaded and contrary."

"He loves you like a hawk loves a clear sky. Have you ever seen him look at you?"

Kate felt herself blush. "I have indeed. Like a duelist over crossed blades sometimes."

"Exactly. I knew Simon for years in London, although he was Mr. Archer to me then. He was constantly in my shop. I can see he respects you more than any man. I think he's a little afraid of you."

"That doesn't sound good."

"Oh, it's very good. You want a man to be a little afraid, or they take you for granted." Penny stared again at the device, as if lost in her own thoughts. "Some women live their whole lives without a man looking at them like that."

Charlotte giggled and started a little singsong, kicking her feet while she drew her picture. "Miss Kate and Mr. Simon."

Kate was warmed by Penny's matter-of-fact words. They flooded her with memories of the night with Simon, as well as their many conversations and glances and touches. She realized how often he put a gentle hand on her shoulder as he passed, how he simply looked at her when she spoke, nodding and listening with interest to her thoughts.

Charlotte laid her head down on the paper. "I'm going to marry Mr. Malcolm."

Penny exhaled and shook her head, muttering, "That's just great."

Kate stared at Penny, and the two women locked eyes. They began to laugh.

Footsteps sounded behind them as Simon, Malcolm, and Nick entered the room. They each carried glasses of whiskey, obviously coming from some sort of boy's chitchat. Malcolm was muttering. "How are we going to keep a tutor? She does read quite well though, but she seems drawn to lurid adventure stories. But she'll need a tutor, and not just for music and art. I want her to learn mathematics and the sciences and geography."

Simon said, "Well, Malcolm, I suspect we could manage something even without engaging a tutor. I'm rather learned in many areas."

Malcolm rubbed at his temples. "I don't want Charlotte to know about those areas."

Charlotte bounded to her feet and rushed the group, eager to show them her art. Simon took the paper from her. "What a lovely sketch of Kate. You captured her arched eyebrow perfectly. And how handsome I look in such a big . . . hat?"

"That's your hair," Charlotte told him.

"Of course it is." He exchanged a bemused look with Kate as he settled on the arm of the sofa next to her. He studied the runes he had inked onto the palm of his left hand. It was brighter and much more complex than the temporary runes he had drawn on the backs of everyone's hands for communication. "Damn, this inscription itches like hell."

"So," Nick said, plopping down into an overstuffed chair and propping his feet atop a strange square table covered with a white tablecloth. "You're so powerful now you'll beat Gaios with one hand?"

"Yes." Simon smiled. "And my other tied behind my back."

"If we've got him on the run, why do you look worried?" Malcolm groused as he leaned against the wall near the fire.

"Do I? I thought I looked confident and assured." Simon showed the runes on his palm. "If I've properly deciphered the Bastille containment spell. And properly inscribed the creation phrase on my hand."

"And if you can get close enough to Gaios to touch the runes to him," Kate pointed out.

"Well, yes, that too. If so, I should be able to cut him off from the aether."

"So we expect him to come here?" Penny asked.

"That's my plan. We're choosing the battleground. We've cleared out as many of the tenants from the estate as we could. And he'll be here, sooner or later."

Nick tapped his whiskey against the strange table and lifted the corner of the tablecloth to reveal the Stone of Scone resting on the floor of the Blue Parlor. "We've got what he wants."

"Yes indeed. Only I've managed to alter it a bit so it won't be exactly what he hoped." Simon rose and moved to the sideboard, pouring a measure of whiskey into the glasses gathered there.

Nick asked, "Did you tell your master we had succeeded?"

Simon ignored the jabbing tone. "I wrote to King William that we had recovered the Stone but warned him that the danger had not passed. I instructed them to hold the militia and home guard in preparation for possible attacks on the city. Mrs. North—or Ash—sent back His Majesty's gratitude and also let us know that the king refused to leave the people of London despite the peril of Gaios. However, they are taking the princess Victoria away to safety."

"Thank God the princess will be safe," Nick muttered as he raised his glass to be refilled to the rim. "To the millions of poor who cannot flee the city, too bad on you."

"The millions of poor have us, Nick." Simon turned to encompass all within the small battered room with the tray in hand, distributing glasses all around, except for Charlotte, who pouted. "We won't fail them."

Imogen stirred against Kate's side and stretched out her arms. She opened her milky human eye and gave her strange rictus smile up at Kate. "Is it late?"

"Yes," Kate rubbed her sister's hand. "You should go to bed."

"Not yet." Imogen sat up, careful to shift the hedgehog into a better position, and accepted a small dram of whiskey from the tray.

Simon lifted his glass. "Ladies and gentlemen, join me, please."

Malcolm stepped from the warm fire and took Charlotte's hand. Nick rose from the chair with an inebriated groan. The women followed suit until all their glasses touched in the firelight.

Simon looked each of them in the eye. "There are no people in this world that I love and respect more than all of you. Nick, you trained me in more ways than you know. When I came to London looking for a path, you put me on it and kept me true to it."

Nick started to interrupt, but Simon knew he was going to qualify it with a guilty admission of his goal of attaining Simon for Ash.

Simon made a silencing sound and gave his friend a confident smile. "Don't. I owe you much. More than I can repay. And Malcolm, you have come into this group in a way that you thought was unnatural for you. You never wanted to be a part of a team of any sort, but you are now the heart of this one. Your honesty steered us when we were lost. Your uncluttered reason has kept us focused. Kate loves you. Penny loves you. The girls love you. Without you, there is no family here."

Malcolm's cheeks actually colored and Penny grinned, her eyes darting to the ground.

Simon turned to the young engineer. "And to you Penny. You are an absolute genius. You give us that extra edge, which enables us to stand toe-to-toe with madmen and gods alike." Her face lifted to his with gratitude shining in her smile.

"To Imogen and Charlotte, who bring joy into this house and teach us what is worth fighting for." He paused a moment, his gaze sweeping over. "And Kate."

The depth of adoration and tenderness in his eyes brought warmth spreading out from Kate's chest.

"Kate," he repeated softly. "Your unflagging thirst for knowledge and truth propels us always forward to a place where anything is possible." His free hand brushed against hers, twining their fingers. He raised his glass, preparing to finish the toast.

Kate drew in a deep breath, her heart lifting higher. "And to you, dear Simon. In whose fearless footsteps we follow. In darkness from which all of humanity would flee, you remain stalwart."

Simon's face shone in the firelight. His glass pushed toward the others. "I wish us all success and long life. I expect that we shall all gather here again, well and healthy. I thank you."

The multitude of glasses clinked and they all drank.

"What about Mr. Hogarth?" Charlotte asked. "He's our protector."

"And to Hogarth," Simon agreed.

"Charlotte and I are relieving Hogarth on the roof."

Imogen reached for the bottle of whiskey. "We'll tell him."

"No, ma'am, you are not." Kate looked from Imogen to Charlotte as she pulled the bottle from her sister's hand. "You're both getting some sleep."

"We can't. It's our turn." Imogen was firm but polite. Charlotte bounded over to her, trailing her drawing from her hand, and leaned against Imogen. "You should get some sleep, Kate. You look tired."

Kate put on her stern face. "I won't be disobeyed, Imogen. I want you to go to bed."

Imogen shook her head and said in her strange calm voice, "Malcolm will take over from us in a few hours, and we'll sleep then."

Kate could sense stubbornness in her sister that reminded her of the old willful Imogen. Except that it wasn't selfishness; she was trying to help. In truth, Kate was too exhausted to fight this battle, which she probably shouldn't.

"Very well." Kate rubbed her face and stifled a yawn. "Off you go then, but please be careful on the roof. There are holes everywhere and weak spots that can't be seen."

"I know." Imogen took Charlotte's hand. She inclined her head to regard Kate. "Sleep."

Kate laughed. "I would love to, but I have several hours of work in the laboratory ahead of me. I'm cooking up a little amber. And there's another series of your blood to finish tonight." Kate continued to talk, but more to herself. "I'm beginning to understand the structural changes I'm seeing. I need a much better microscope. I'll send for a new catalog from Germany." She tapped her forehead as a reminder. "I'll do that tomorrow. Oh no, not tomorrow; I have plans. The next day then."

"Kate." Imogen laid her long boneless fingers against her sister's face. "Stop, please."

"Stop what? What am I doing?"

Imogen stared into Kate's eyes with the one white human orb. "Stop trying to bring me back."

Kate flushed with panic. It seemed they had come so far, but now Imogen was returning to her old morose futile self. Her sister had surrendered again to hopelessness after all the time Kate had labored to reassure her and to show her that she would never rest until Imogen was restored to normal. Kate clenched her fists. Her gaze flew over her sister's face in despair.

"Imogen, please, you can't give up," Kate whispered in a ragged voice.

"I'm not giving up," Imogen replied softly. "But you are killing yourself. Stop."

"I can't!" Kate closed her eyes and pressed Imogen's hand against her face. She felt the inhuman touch of the tendril fingers. "I won't."

"Kate. Look at me."

Kate opened her eyes and gazed on her sister. Her rubbery skin was so white, it was almost blue. Her once-full lips were slits across her face. The delightful nose that once graced her beautiful features was nothing more than two holes. However, when she came this near, Kate could see the remnants of the old Imogen in her face. The line of the chin. The curve of the cheek. The slight tilt of her head. These were vestiges of the original woman that had not, and could not, be changed.

"You don't have to bring me back." Imogen kissed Kate on the cheek. "I'm here."

It had been years since Imogen had kissed her in more than a perfunctory or begrudging way. She felt a warmth and kindness that had been gone since they were little girls. Kate threw her arms around Imogen. She kissed her sister and embraced her tightly, feeling strength in Imogen that she had either not seen or denied since they had brought her back from Bedlam on that dreadful night last year. Kate felt her sister's fingers wiping tears from her cheeks and she pressed her face into the touch.

Imogen gently pulled away from Kate and took Charlotte's hand again. The two started for the door.

Kate covered her mouth to stifle her crying as she watched them through new eyes. After they left the room, Kate called out, "Charlotte! Take your wulfsyl before you go on the roof!"

"Aw!" came the distressed reply and the girls' footfalls disappeared down the hall.

Chapter 21

IT WAS A CLOUDLESS NIGHT OF STARS. MALCOLM picked his way carefully across the rooftop, testing shingles and the exposed rafters before settling his weight on them. At the edge of the roof sat Imogen and Charlotte.

Charlotte waved enthusiastically as if Malcolm had been away for months rather than just a few hours. It was that eagerness that made Charlotte such a sweet child. It's what kept the monster in her at bay. He doubted that Kate's wulfsyl alone would have been enough. The two girls rose to their feet. Imogen was a study of calm reserve, while Charlotte saluted him.

"Nothing to report!" she declared. "No sign of anyone except a few deer." Her arm dropped, then she impulsively hugged him.

Malcolm allowed himself the luxury of returning the girl's embrace. After a moment, she reluctantly released him and brought her head up from the warmth of his wool coat. She regarded the long rifle across his back, but the smile didn't leave her face.

"When that crazy old man shows up here, we'll be ready," Charlotte assured him.

Malcolm wondered if she truly understood what was

happening. Their world was on the brink of annihilation, and she behaved like it was a day at the beach. It was that sort of recklessness that made him worry for her safety. She could be strong and quick, but she didn't understand the ruthless complexity of the world. One day she would.

That was a day he never wanted to face.

Charlotte regarded her friend behind her. "Mr. Simon's ever so clever. He'll make sure Gaios won't hurt anyone." She rocked back on her heels in obvious devotion.

Malcolm's heart filled once more with dismay. "Gaios isn't just some doddering warlock, Charlotte. He's very dangerous."

Charlotte's bright blue eyes rose to meet his. Those iridescent orbs seemed old beyond years. "I know that. Even Gretta spoke of him only in whispers."

That communicated leagues of Gaios's mythical weight. Gretta Aldfather was a centuries-old lycanthrope and Charlotte's past brutal mentor, a furious legend in her own right.

Imogen pressed close to Charlotte. "We both know what he's capable of, Malcolm. But we'll stand together."

He nodded, his throat tight. Simon was right. There would be no sending them away even if it was for the best. When he spoke, it was deeper than usual. "Go down and get something to eat. Then off to bed with you both. We need you fresh and ready when the time comes."

Charlotte offered a smile that would melt solid ice and scampered off like an acrobat. Imogen moved slowly and carefully. He stared after them when Charlotte darted back to him. She tugged him down by his lapels, then stood on her tiptoes and planted a kiss on his cheek with an enthusiastic, "Good night!" She ran off again, grabbing Imogen's hand and helping her along the tricky slope to the ladder sticking up though a gap in the roof.

Drawing a hand across his cheek, Malcolm settled himself in their little nest of warm blankets and plush pillows, amused at their desire for simple comforts even for this small task. He wouldn't be surprised if there was a picnic basket about somewhere to go along with it. He was tempted to look when his stomach growled. Utilizing Penny's miraculous long-range scope on the rifle, he made a quick scan of the surrounding area. It appeared serene and still, despite the ravaged grounds. It remained that way for almost two hours.

The sun was beginning to filter over the distant hillocks when the earth shook. Malcolm grabbed hold of the roof's trembling edge and lifted the rifle. Gaios came riding atop a chunk of earth the size of a farmer's cottage, pulled by what Malcolm could only call dog-like golems. The creatures drew the chariot faster than a fleet coach, leaving a deep, rough furrow behind. Gaios was dressed in a long white garment with a crimson mantle over one shoulder similar to the toga of an ancient Roman nobleman. His long white hair flowed in the wind like Zeus descending to Earth. Cowering next to him were Jane and her father.

Malcolm sounded the alarm by slapping the back of his hands together. The temporary tattoos flared, as they would on everyone's hands below, warning them of an incoming enemy. Malcolm lifted the rifle and took aim at Gaios. When the target rumbled into range, he squeezed the trigger. The shell was on target, but with a flick of his wrist, Gaios brought up a section of his stony chariot and deflected the shot.

Malcolm heard footsteps as Simon came up quickly behind and crouched at his side. "We're out of time, Simon. I hope we're ready."

"We are," was all Simon said.

"He isn't alone." Malcolm's voice held an edge. "Jane Somerset and her father are with him."

"His lightning elemental?"

"They are *innocents* in this. She won't hurt anyone." Malcolm paused before growling, "And I won't hurt her."

"I'm not asking you to." Regret touched Simon's eyes. "But she may not be given that choice."

Malcolm knew he was right.

"Let's see what our guest wants," Simon said, turning to head back down. "Penny's on her way to take this position. And that poor woman down there will need to see a familiar face."

Malcolm set down the rifle in case Penny wanted to use it, and he followed Simon. By the time they stepped out through the wrecked front of Hartley Hall, everyone had taken up their prearranged positions around the mansion, arsenals at the ready. The two girls had barely slept, but still they both looked spry, their enhanced natures keeping them going far beyond any normal human.

The land and air trembled. Gaios's chariot tore through the grounds as the massive stone monsters dragged it closer. They roared some fifty yards from the portico and stopped in a cloud of dirt and crumbling rock. The beasts collapsed into dust so Gaios could stare down unhindered, his face a mask of rage. Mr. Somerset was held in a prison of hardened dirt that came up to his chest. He looked like a man caught in a nightmare. Jane was on the other side of the earth elemental, on her knees, encased in stone as well. Her pleading eyes were on her father.

Malcolm saw pure red. Jane had believed in the goodness of Gaios. Guilt stabbed him, knowing he could have stopped this before it began.

"Archer!" Gaios's voice boomed down from his mount.

"I know you have the Stone. I feel it. Give it to me or this man dies. Now."

"Please don't hurt my father!" beseeched Jane, struggling to move. "Take me instead!"

Simon's attention never wavered from Gaios. "We've danced this waltz already if I remember."

"He will die and you will be the cause!" shouted Gaios. The ground shook violently and everyone struggled to stay on their feet. Mr. Somerset screamed in pain with the stone prison twisting around him. "And when he is dead, I will reach out my hand and kill anyone within my power. And I will keep killing until you bring me the Stone. How much blood do you want on your conscience, Archer?"

All eyes turned to Simon. He paused for a second before his breath left in a defeated rush. "All right. I'll bring the Stone."

"If you cross me," Gaios warned.

"You will release those two in return for the Stone."

"Don't dictate terms to me! Bring it!"

Nick stood at the door and he took Simon's arm. He leaned close. "Are you thinking? If you give it to him, he'll kill millions. Including us."

Malcolm rushed back to them, his fists clenched. "Shut up, Barker! Would you condemn those two up there? They have nothing to do with this."

Nick didn't flinch at Malcolm's bluster. "Hardly. She's the key to Gaios's scheme. And better those two die than everyone else."

The ground heaved violently and the loose stones around Gaios rose slowly into the air, lifted with the man's mounting rage. "His life is measured in seconds, Archer!"

"No," cried Jane to Gaios. "I beg you."

"I'll bring the Stone, Gaios." Simon turned back to the door. "Stand aside, Nick."

Nick hesitated. Then with a curse, he stepped aside. "Simon, you're too good for the bad business we're in."

Malcolm cast Nick a scathing glare as Simon swept into the house, but Nick didn't even look at him. Malcolm strode down from the portico and shouted up at Jane. "Don't worry. You and your father will be fine." He then glared at Gaios. "If you dare hurt them, I swear to you, I will kill you."

Gaios's gaze didn't shift. He had greater things in his vision. Malcolm was not even a bothersome insect beneath the demigod's foot.

When Simon appeared in the doorway, he held the bone of contention in his arms. Nick watched him pass, hauling the heavy Stone down the steps of the portico. Gaios stared eagerly as Simon walked away from the safety of the house. The huge block of stone that served as Gaios's chariot split open into a staircase in the front and the elemental walked down.

Simon stopped a few yards away. "Free your prisoners."

Without removing his attention from the Stone of Scone, the demigod waved a hand and the earth prisons around Jane and Mr. Somerset crumbled. Jane caught her father. The elderly man was so overwhelmed he could barely speak and what did pass his lips was unintelligible. Jane spoke soothingly to him as she led him to the edge of the high stone platform and they came slowly down the steps. Gaios reached out an arm and prevented them from passing.

"Let them go," Simon demanded.

"When I am done with them. Don't vex me. You are outside your safe house now." Gaios pointed to the ground at his feet and gave Simon a stern glare. Simon stepped forward and set the Stone down. He then took a step back where he stood waiting.

"Miss Somerset," Gaios commanded, "come here."

She flinched at Gaios's hard tone. She left her father leaning against the rock, apparently unaware of anything. She obeyed with her back straight despite her fear.

"Bring your lightning to bear on the Stone. Seed it as I taught you to do to the earth."

"You lied about everything." The muscles in Jane's clenched jaw twitched.

"I didn't lie about your power. If they knew, they would fear you."

"You should as well." Her eyes sparked with an unearthly light.

Gaios smiled at her as if she were an angry infant and glanced menacingly back at her father.

"Stop!" The light faded from Jane's eyes and she put out her hands. "I'll do it! Please don't hurt him."

Simon took a step forward, but Gaios looked up and the ground shook with a warning rumble.

Jane lifted her hands over the Stone. Her red-rimmed eyes searched for Malcolm. Anguish was written on her face. Her lips moved as if she was praying. Tendrils of light coiled around her hands as she held them out. Small at first, the electricity began to build, growing brighter and larger. It crawled from her hand onto the Stone in cascading arcs. Even Gaios stepped back, with an arm thrown up against the lightning bolts that roared around her. Daylight faded into night as dark clouds billowed to engulf the sky above them. A rumble of thunder sounded. The Stone glowed unnaturally as lightning spread over its craggy surface.

Jane slumped. The electricity faded from her hands. She staggered back as the rush of energy left her. Reaching out for her father, she lifted her head at Gaios. "I've done as you asked. Please let us go."

Gaios studied the Stone closely with a wild grin on

his face. "Your father may go. You stay until I am finished here."

Hogarth ran up to help. The manservant gently relieved Jane of the burden of her father. Jane's expression was filled with disgrace and regret. Tears fell from her eyes in silent sorrow. Hogarth whispered comforting words to her as he hefted the frail man into his arms and started for the house.

Gaios dropped to his knees next to the Stone. He held his hands over the grey surface as if warming them over a fire. He laughed. "Thank you, Archer. Finally the world will be set right. It is time for Ash to pay."

He slapped his palms against the Stone and there was an explosion. The grey lump of rock and the elemental clutching it disappeared in a flash of white. Great arcs of lightning flared into the sky and ground. All the power that Jane had sent into the Stone now roared out. Simon had runed it to resist enhancement. He felt blistering heat and a tremendous force blasting him back. But his aether-driven strength rooted him to the spot near the Stone. He saw the figure of Jane cast away in the eruption. She had an almost comical look of surprise on her face, but the lightning could cause her no pain.

Gaios screamed and tried to keep his grip on the Stone. The incredible power surging out finally ripped him free as well and hurled him back against the jagged surface of his huge rock chariot and he lay smoldering in the dirt. The burning ozone cracked into the atmosphere and left the ground around the Stone scorched and dry.

Now was his chance. Simon leapt for Gaios. The elemental moved slightly, stunned and barely conscious. Simon raised his left hand to press the powerful rune against the old man's bare face. His arm jerked to the side with horrible force. He caught a glimpse of a monstrous face, a combination of beast and stone leaking red magma from its crevices. Massive jaws clamped around his forearm. It was one of the doglike stone golems that had pulled Gaios's chariot. It had appeared out of the ground in an instant to protect its master. The creature shook Simon wildly, threatening to tear his arm from the socket. With a guttural growl, it tossed its jagged head and sent Simon sailing toward the house.

Simon hit the dirt and rolled, holding his singed arm close to his body. He came up on his feet and whirled to face back in the direction of Gaios. The two monstrous dogs stood beside their fallen master. Their huge heads were held low and massive shoulders bunched some ten feet above the ground. Burning stone drizzled from their mouths.

Malcolm raced out for Jane, who was moaning where she had been thrown many yards from the Stone. He lifted the dazed woman to her feet, helping her back toward the house. One of the dogs turned its head toward him and started into a rumbling lope. Malcolm scooped Jane up and kept running, but the beast came on fast.

A large shape sped past Malcolm in the opposite direction and Charlotte bounded into the air, lunging at the charging monster. The werewolf landed on its snout, knocking the stone head down, causing it to stumble. Malcolm vaulted up onto the portico with Jane in his arms.

Charlotte cried out in pain and leapt into the air from the monster's head. She trailed smoke and her fur showed red singe lines from the lava secretions. She fell heavily and rolled in the dirt to smother the flames.

The huge dog turned toward her with steam boiling from its nostrils. It opened its mouth to reveal that instead of teeth, both the upper and lower surfaces were covered in long jagged stalactites and stalagmites. Charlotte struggled up awkwardly onto her feet despite the agonizing burns.

A high arcing object spiraled in from the sky with a long smoke trail behind it. The beast glanced up at it, then its head exploded. Penny whooped in excitement from the roof of Hartley Hall and loaded another canister into her blunderbuss. The decapitated stone dog spewed streams of magma from its throat. Charlotte yelped in fear and scrambled away from the moving fountain of lava, which wandered in a circle.

When the first dog had gone for Malcolm and Jane, the second had immediately lunged for Simon. Before the scribe could react, a small object whizzed past his ear and black treacle blossomed at the monster dog's feet. It halted, trying to pull free. Kate appeared at Simon's side, watching the immobile beast with some pride. Then the monster began to regurgitate magma from its mouth onto the ground around it.

Nick raised his hands and immediately the great hound began to sizzle. Steam poured off the monster and it shook its head, looking around for the source of the disturbance. It ripped a huge stone paw from the burning treacle. Nick grunted and redoubled his efforts. Soon a slight sheen of ice began to appear over the creature. It started to boil in a frothy black-and-yellow amalgam. Cooling black bubbles formed on its back. Still Nick fought on and the ice on the steaming monster grew thicker. The bright lava glowed under the thick frosty layer, deteriorating the ice from every angle. Brittle fractures crackled across the stone. Magma oozed from the fissures and dripped down the dog's sides.

Simon ran forward. The monstrous golem turned slowly to face him, creaking like bronze. Simon shouted an ancient word and slammed himself against the head. He strained, glowing green with the aether of his tattoos. The muscles of his arms were bulging cords. The beast fought, struggling to free itself again. Simon arched his back and wrenched the igneous head in the opposite direction. Rock ruptured with a groaning crack and the monster split open. Lava gushed out. Simon ran to escape the spreading pool of magma, which Nick fought to cool quickly.

Then, over the remnant of the canine golem, Simon saw Gaios rise to his feet. The elemental's eyes were clear now and filled with hate. The earth trembled.

"Everyone back!" Simon yelled. There was no chance at Gaios now. The only tactic was retreat and survive. Simon moved back slowly, holding the elemental's attention. He then felt Kate at his side. He snapped at her, "Aren't you part of *everyone*?"

"No."

Gaios bellowed at Simon, "What did you do?" The ground heaved violently with his rage. Dead trees began to roll with the undulating earth.

Simon faced the wrathful demigod. "Just a little magic trick. I rendered the stone inert."

The ground rushed toward them in a wave. Simon and Kate were flung into the air like insects off a twig. The thunderous wave of earth crashed near Hartley Hall and the once-grand estate shook. Another section of the roof collapsed and what was left of an upper wall toppled. Fissures appeared in the ground near Simon and Kate, separating them from the house.

Malcolm stepped out onto the wrecked portico. "Jump!"

Simon didn't see anyplace to jump as the crack widened into a crevasse. Suddenly the air turned an ocher color in front of him. It solidified into a chunk of amber that provided solid footing over the widening crack. Simon grabbed Kate and leapt the distance to the rock.

Gaios waved his hand toward them and the scrap of land shifted again, the amber careening with it. As they were being dragged farther away from safety, Simon whispered strength into his limbs, then lifted Kate and tossed her toward the house. She fell on the edge of the growing canyon where Malcolm seized her and pulled her up. From the roof above, Penny fired her cannon. The explosive shell impacted in front of the demigod on a wall of rock he hastily raised. It delayed Gaios long enough for Simon to make a frantic leap. His feet hit the rim of the crevasse and he found multiple hands ready to drag him forward.

"Inside!" Simon shouted.

Kate tried to stay upright on the undulating steps. She practically crawled into the house with Simon and Malcolm following after.

The house shuddered and shifted. Malcolm's stomach turned as if the great house were suddenly lifted and dropped, then lifted again. The sounds of glass shattering and wood breaking came from all around them. He heard Jane's fearful cries. Even Charlotte and Imogen screamed. An internal gas line ruptured and a geyser of flame roared from the wall. Nick shoved clear of Jane and her father, and flung out his arms. The flames veered toward him. He directed the deadly fire out through the roof.

The violent tremors stopped. Hartley Hall still stood, even if it was in a worse shambles. Simon rose from the cracked floor and ran for a jagged gap in the front wall. The ground outside was gone. The house stood on a pinnacle of sorts, and it was surrounded by a canyon some half a mile wide. Gaios had torn the earth away from the house, leaving it on a new mountain.

On the far edge of the new deep moat, Gaios lowered his arms, panting heavily at the futile exertion against the warded house. He stood atop his stone chariot again and the earth around him moved like boiling liquid. The two doglike rock creatures rose anew out of it, weeping hot magma.

"You haven't stopped me! I'll destroy this land acre

by acre if need be. Starting with its heart!" With a wave of his hands, the snarling beasts turned and dragged the stone chariot through the ruined grounds on a straight course for London.

Simon spun around to face the others. "We must stop him. Gather what you can. We leave for London as soon as possible."

"London is huge. He could be anywhere in the city!" growled Malcolm.

Jane rose to her feet, staring at Malcolm with tear-stricken eyes. "I know where we can find him."

Chapter 22

THEY RAN UP OUT OF THE CELLARS AT SOMERSET House where the portal was located in London and into the grand courtyard. They had allowed only enough time to collect and reload weapons before slipping into the portal hardly twenty minutes after Gaios had vanished from the front of Hartley Hall. Nothing seemed amiss on the street outside the gateway arch. Traffic streamed along the Strand as normal. A few heads turned to peer at the strangely disheveled group, particularly given the fact that the women were dressed in inappropriate buccaneer leathers and carried heavy weapons and strange contraptions. Simon noted a passing unit of the militia on the street.

Malcolm supported Jane by the elbow because the woman was still shaky from her first passage through the portal. "What's our first move?"

Just as they exited under the classical front, they felt a shaking beneath their feet. They all stopped dead. Jane clutched Malcolm's arm. Her face was frozen, trying to hide the dread she felt. She was unsuccessful, but probably no less than any of them.

A deep rumbling sound rose from the earth. Windows shattered all around. Church bells began to ring out in raucous disharmony as steeples across London swayed in the tumult.

People in the courtyard stumbled like drunkards and many hit the ground. Some managed to reach out for anything solid in an attempt to hold themselves up. Seconds passed that seemed like minutes. The quaking intensified and the surprised people who hung on to cracking stone balustrades or clutched the trembling bricks started to show fear.

The rolling of the ground lessened. A blessed stability returned. Those who had just been thrown about gaped in shock or grasped loved ones. They started rising from the cracked uneven ground hesitantly, as if not trusting their feet. The air was filled with shouts and crying and the sound of horses. The militia attempted to calm and gather people out of the buildings.

Simon stopped to set a pram right on its wheels. He inspected the squalling baby quickly as Kate helped the mother to her feet. Simon handed the child, who was more surprised than hurt, to the woman and continued weaving through stragglers.

They started off on foot eastward along the Strand. The traffic was nearly at a standstill, with many cries of alarm, but little cursing or aggression, as if the earthquake had shocked the impatience out of citizens. Crowds streamed out of shops and offices, gathering in clutches to discuss the event. Broken glass and shattered bricks littered the walkways. Those unlucky enough to be struck were tended by others. The bells of St. Mary's and St. Clement's were still clanging as they passed. The venerable old arch of the Temple Bar was intact, but the congestion was extreme. It took anxious minutes for them to navigate their way through the melee.

They made better time on wide Fleet Street when the ground began to shake again. Screams erupted all around. The vibrations were violent and wracking. The coaches swayed and horses reared in terror. Chunks of stone cornices cracked from rooftops and smashed to the ground on both sides of the street. Figures fled in random directions, unsure of how to find safety.

"These poor people!" Jane alternated gripping Malcolm's arm and reaching out to the frightened crowd.

Simon couldn't help but run to a man who knelt on the sidewalk with blood running down his face. The man pointed toward a pile of rubble, so Simon shoved aside the heavy wreckage to find a woman trapped beneath. She was alive and the bloody man embraced her. Simon called for a nearby lad to come to their assistance, which he did with no hesitation.

He stared around him at the staggering crowds, distraught and frightened. Men and women and children lay injured and crying. People shouted for help. Simon wanted to go to each of them.

Kate took his arm. "Come on, Simon. I know what you want. I want it too. But we can help best by stopping Gaios. Others can assist these people. Only we can stop him."

They were just reaching the environs of St. Paul's when a huge explosion roared from the south. They all turned, as did everyone in the vicinity, and felt heat on their faces. A massive red-and-black fireball rose over the Thames.

"The gasworks," said Penny.

Several members of the militia spurred their horses toward the south, for all the good they could do. At least they were trying.

Kate watched the smoke rising in the distance. "Where the hell is Ash? Isn't there something she can do with all her power?"

Simon shook his head. "She's gone. There is no way under heaven that she is still in London. We're on our own." He took her hand. "As always."

London east of St. Paul's was a vision of Hell. People fled in mass confusion and panic as buildings collapsed. Fires raged everywhere as gas lines burst. Ashes drifted in the air like a snowy day in December.

As Simon and his team rounded onto Walbrook Street, where Jane had indicated Gaios would be, they came upon an incredible massive structure of glistening black obsidian. It was long and rectangular, with columns lining the sides. It was a classical Roman temple, but on a gargantuan scale. The long peaked roof dwarfed St. Paul's dome in the distance. The huge edifice steamed as if the black stone was newly formed, and the earth around it was wet and warm, the loamy scent of it filling the air.

"Well, this is new," Nick commented.

Kate stared up with awe on her face. "Gaios created his own temple."

"Just in time to have his new Vesuvius destroy it." Simon was grim.

"If he's in there, how do we get him?" Malcolm demanded.

Simon pointed to a huge ebony door set in the front of the structure, large enough to allow several carriages to ride inside. To their surprise it opened. A wave of insufferable heat hit them. They could feel it even through the fire-retardant gel slathered on their skin.

"That doesn't smell of a trap," mumbled Malcolm, but still he led them to the door of the temple of Gaios.

The interior was a single vast gallery. They passed along the nave, which was divided from raised aisles by sleeper-walls, each of which carried glistening columns. The constellations of the night sky crawled across the ceiling as if they were journeying across the heavens.

As they moved inside, it was clear the temple was still forming and reshaping around them. Walls and floors shifted before their eyes with hypnotic effect. Stalagmites rose in groups and fused into single broad columns. The interior was illuminated not by torches or candles but by a river of lava glowing between the cracks in the floor. At the distant end of the temple, a cascade of magma passed under a raised platform and disappeared into a black cave hewn from solid rock. From its depths could be heard the crackling and shifting of the earth.

Simon couldn't help but recall a line from Shakespeare. "Devouring Time, blunt thou the lion's paws, and make the earth devour her own sweet brood."

"Please tell me we're not going down into the pit," Nick said, but despite his hesitation, his hands were already aflame.

"Of course we are." Simon inclined his head and they continued forward. He noticed that Imogen paused with a look of fear at the dim cavern, falling to the rear of the group.

The shadows of the dark hole behind the dais shifted. From out of the subterranean depths stepped Baroness Conrad. Her torso was encased by a steel-lined corset and chain mail. An elaborate mechanical helmet with goggles that glowed like enormous inhuman red eyes covered her head and face. One goggle eye had the audacity to have crosshairs over it. The helmet covered her facial expressions, but her walk was a nearly bawdy strut, grotesque in its execution.

"How fortunate," the Baroness's voice projected from her helmet, "that you've come. Now we won't have to seek you out to ensure you've been extinguished. I look forward to remaking you in the future." She nodded toward Simon. "Particularly you."

At her side was another of her silverbacked apes. She had a hand on its hip. This beast was no less massive in size than the previous gorillas, but now it was entirely covered in armor with a coppery sheen that gave it the look of a horrific bronze statue. Thin seams in the plate showed that it was still mostly flesh and blood underneath. Like its mistress, smoke and steam wafted out of numerous orifices as machined parts moved and shifted. The Baroness had learned, and adjusted her arsenal because of it. She boldly approached with her arm raised, preparing to make some further pronouncement of villainy.

Simon cast a sharp glance over at Malcolm. "Take her."

Malcolm nodded. His Lancasters rose and the barrels spun furiously, spitting bullet after bullet at the Baroness, interrupting her speech. Penny's blunderbuss flipped to her shoulder and the startled Baroness barely avoided the canister by ducking behind one of the columns.

The team split smoothly with Simon striding for the cavern with Kate, Nick, and Charlotte while Malcolm drew Penny, Imogen, Hogarth, and the stunned Jane with him. The ape roared in defiance and leapt at Malcolm. Jane covered her ears in shock. It landed in front of him, its iron knuckles slammed into the floor hard enough to crack the black surface. Hogarth attacked and his hammer of steel slammed into the silverback. Weird threads sliced the air and struck the metal ape but did no damage. It took Malcolm a moment to realize they were poison filaments from Imogen. She slipped around to get a better angle, her quills quivering straight up on her bare arm. Hogarth moved to stand beside her and the ape pounded the floor.

Penny started across the temple, following the Baroness. Malcolm trusted that Hogarth and Imogen could handle the ape and he ran to support Penny. Just then, two odd-shaped metal stars suddenly bounced on the floor around Malcolm. He grabbed Penny and ran for cover behind one of the tall pillars. He covered the engineer, but after a moment of silence he looked back. The metal stars had failed to go off.

"Ha! They're duds!" exulted Penny.

Malcolm shook his head at her exclamation.

Penny hefted her stovepipe blunderbuss and took aim on the column the Baroness hid behind. A shot shattered it. The structure rumbled and bits of ash drifted down from above.

"You're going to bring the roof down on us!" Malcolm shouted. "An engineer should know better!"

Penny's angry countenance when she turned to him spoke volumes. Her fury wasn't directed at him. His gut wanted to tell her to blast the Baroness to kingdom come no matter the risk, but thankfully, Penny flipped the weapon across her back.

A ratcheting noise sounded and one of the Baroness's mechanical arms transformed into a new contraption. Instead of a hand, three gun barrels with twice the bore of Malcolm's quad Lancasters trained on them. The Baroness laid down a murderous swathe of gunfire and chunks of stone flew up into the air.

When the barrage ended, Malcolm spun out of cover and returned one of his own. Penny stepped out with him. In her hand, she held the wee sonic pistol. Penny was a walking means of annihilation in her own right, but most of her weapons were as harmful to her as to her enemies.

She darted as close to the Baroness as she dared with bullets flying and unleashed a sonic wave aimed not directly at the pillar obscuring the Baroness, but near it. The noise and pressure built until Penny collapsed to the floor on her hands and knees with blood dripping from her nose and ears. Malcolm could only spare her a glance as the Baroness fled from her refuge, holding her head. He shot at her fleeting shape. Her rapid-fire gun arm lifted even though she wasn't looking at him. Malcolm dove to the floor. She tossed two more of the star-shaped objects, forcing Malcolm to roll farther away. Strangely, these failed as well.

On the other side of the temple, the ape ran at Hogarth. The muscled man performed an uppercut with his hammer, clapping the steel jaw of the ape shut with a clang. When a huge metal forearm lifted, Imogen closed the distance and flung quills out. The steel-plated chest deflected them all.

Jane screamed as a thick fist slammed into the pillar beside her. Her arms rose in front of her. A bolt of lightning cracked in the confined space. It struck the ape's head and skittered over the metal armor, making its yellowish brown color glow a bright copper. The bolt discharged into the wall. A roll of thunder echoed in the chamber. The gorilla stood as if stunned.

Imogen dragged the terrified Jane away. Her mechanical eye rotated over to Hogarth. "I only need to hit something flesh and I can slow it down."

"Yes, miss." The manservant breathed heavily and roared at the beast again, careening his hammer off its armored pauldron. He pounded the same spot over and over in a maddening onslaught. The sound clanged like a team of men driving pilings. The ape's steel shoulder plate began to bend and a tuft of fur popped out. Imogen stepped up. Her bare arm snapped out and a volley of quills embedded in the monster's flesh.

The ape weaved on its feet. It raised a fist to crush Hogarth, but then the silverback stiffened and fell over in a great tumult that sounded like an armory collapsing.

Meanwhile, Malcolm scrambled for Penny, who had regained her senses. The back of her hand smeared the blood across her face. She got to her feet and held out a pair of dice. "Cover your eyes," she cautioned as she brought her goggles down. She tossed the dice. A bright light filled the front of the temple.

Penny didn't wait. She was running toward the Baroness even before the flash faded. But the Baroness wore her own goggles. Thin protective membranes now lifted from the lens on her eyes. Penny's steel-and-bone fan flicked open.

Just as the Baroness trained her gun on Penny, Malcolm steadied his Lancaster and shot the woman. The shell hit her high and wide, sparking off the armor. It didn't strike flesh, but it did jerk the Baroness aside. Penny darted past the Baroness and her fan sliced cables and tubes running to her mechanized-gun arm. Black and green chemicals spewed, and the arm dropped limp.

Malcolm could have shouted his delight at Penny's brashness even if it was foolhardy. The petite engineer quickly maneuvered behind the stunned Baroness. The villain still had three working arms, and one smacked Penny aside before she could raise her fan once more. Malcolm targeted for a head shot, but the Baroness scurried away like an insect. Malcolm's bullets raked after her as he raced forward to cover Penny.

"Next time warn me when you're going to do something so daft." Malcolm pulled her behind another column.

"That's one arm down." Penny rubbed an aching knee. "Now you think you can bloody well shoot her?"

"I bloody well would if I could get past the bloody armor." He reloaded his pistols.

Penny peered around the column. "Oh look. The Baroness had time to barricade herself behind another pillar."

"Shut it," Malcolm groused, leaning out and peppering the area. He pulled back as the Baroness returned fire with a brace of pistols. Stone dust coated them. After the barrage ended, two more of the spiked devices fell nearby. Penny stared at them, and her head twisted to take in the pattern of the others that had encircled them. One of them sparked. Her eyes widened.

"Get out!" She shoved Malcolm hard.

He fell backward outside the ring of stars, and rolled to his feet. In horror, he watched as sparks careened around the devices, creating a large lightning dome with Penny in the center. He stepped forward to help her.

"Don't touch it!" Penny shouted.

The dome started shrinking around her. Malcolm yelled, "Get out of there!"

"Working on it!" Falling to her knees, Penny shrugged off her rucksack. She pulled out a short copper spike with a green glass ball on top. Jamming the end into a crack in the floor, she scuttled away. She crouched, making her body lower than the top of the staff. The ends of her blond hair began to rise up away from her head.

Malcolm shifted his gaze back and forth from Penny to the Baroness, waiting for an attack. Amazingly, she seemed content to watch Penny attempt to free herself.

Crisscrossing bolts of electricity bled from the lightning dome and into the orb at the top of the spike. The green glass glowed with fel fire. Suddenly the lightning discharged straight up into the air with a loud crack. The cage dissipated and Penny was free. She snatched up her satchel and the copper spike and staggered toward Malcolm.

He caught her and was stunned to see the tips of her hair burning. He brushed a hand over them, snuffing the embers. "Bloody hell! Why weren't you fried like a chicken in a tempest?"

Penny held up the spike. "Grounded the damn thing. Once I knew that the Baroness had worked with a lightning elemental, I tossed this in my pack."

Malcolm only wanted to know one thing. "How many other bloody toys does she have?"

Penny arched an eyebrow at him. "Not sure. She's good. Damnably good."

He scowled. Engineers. He loved them and cursed them at the same time. "We need to end this fight now."

"She's powered by an aether engine. If I can disable it, she'll just be like any typical four-armed freak." Penny pulled large pliers from her bag.

"I'll distract her," Malcolm whispered. "Keep her talking till I get in position."

"Shouldn't be hard."

Penny slapped him hard on the shoulder in a manly sort of way, which earned her a look though she didn't notice. Her attention was already focused on the target.

"So, Baroness," Penny shouted into the temple, "I've enjoyed seeing some of your little gadgets. But I guess you didn't have time to prepare any real weapons, huh?"

The Baroness called out, "Your derivative technology is impressive, Miss Carter. Professor Watkins indicated you were an excellent mimic."

Penny's face twisted in spite to hear her mentor's name so casually spoken by that fiend. "Funny. He never mentioned *you* to me. I guess your research didn't leave much of an impression at Cambridge."

"It's difficult for idiots to understand the level on which I work. The laborer turning the same bolt day after day can hardly grasp the vision of the engineer who designed the machine. Some people are never truly qualified to face their greatest challenge. For example, the time I just spent delaying you has allowed my mechanicals to repair themselves." The disabled machine-gun arm lifted as if it were brand-new.

"Repair?" Penny grumbled. "How damned smart is she?"

Malcolm dove from behind a distant column, rolling to his feet. He ran, guns blazing. He tried for a head shot. There was little enough target with the Baroness's blasted helmet, but it would get her attention. The first shot knocked her head to the side, and the second and third brought the whistling whine of escaping steam. Malcolm smirked. *Dodge that, you four-armed blighter.*

One of the Baroness's mechanized arms rotated ninety degrees behind her seemingly of its volition. Something rattled and clicked, and it vomited a long snakelike appendage from its forearm. Her metal fingers grasped the cable and whipped it toward Malcolm.

He realized too late he was within striking range. The whip wrapped around his chest, pinning his arms against his torso. He tried to raise his Lancasters toward her, but a current of energy surged through the metal whip, locking his muscles and even clamping his jaw shut. The robot arm yanked and he toppled over like a dead tree. The whip began to retract, dragging him closer to the Baroness. He lost his grip on the pistols. He couldn't move his head and his only view was the stars etched on the volcanic ceiling. He heard Baroness Conrad yelling something to Penny. He feared he had stumbled into a stupid trap, and he prayed Penny wouldn't do something foolish to rescue him.

A strange shape moved into Malcolm's line of sight. To his shock, he realized it was Imogen. Her skin showed a milky white against the dark stone. She had torn her dress short so it wouldn't encumber her legs. Her shoes were off and her wide-splayed toes and fingers clutched the rippled surface of the ceiling. She scuttled over the Baroness and dropped like a spider on top of her.

Startled, the Baroness reared back, unsure what had attacked her. Penny burst from cover and raced forward. Hogarth ran up to free Malcolm, but the moment the manservant's hands touched the coils, he too locked rigid. Malcolm could do nothing.

Jane appeared and grabbed Hogarth. The current

crawled over her as well, but had no effect. She pulled the big man away, breaking his grip. As soon as Hogarth's hands were released, he gasped and fell backward. The manservant lumbered to his feet, shaking off the effects like a big bear, and rounded on the Baroness. He braced his feet and locked one of her arms in a wrestling hold. Jane touched the whip and a visible bolt of light sped back up the snake into the mechanical arm, ending in an explosive shower of sparks. Malcolm could move once again although he was stiff like an old man as he tried to lurch to his feet.

Imogen was still hanging on to the Baroness's head, dodging wild blows from mechanical arms. Her quills pinged off armor, but she spotted bare skin through a seam at the back of the Baroness's neck. She jammed her forearm against the gap in the armor and stabbed several quills into flesh.

Penny had positioned herself behind the villain's back, nearly lost in the cloud of steam escaping from the damaged armor. She jammed her pliers into the circuitry built into the Baroness's back, her hands moving quickly and deliberately. She knew exactly what she was after. Even though the Baroness's work was intricate in construction, it was also clear in design and function.

Malcolm pulled his long blade from his coat as he staggered up to the Baroness. He jammed the blade between armor plates on her side and shoved it in as hard as he could, twisting it back and forth to widen the gap. It didn't go in nearly far enough to kill, but he took great pleasure in the scream of pain. The Baroness grabbed his arms. Her metal fingers dug deep into his all-too-tender flesh. She started pulling him apart. His scream matched her own.

There was another loud snap and a harsh tearing sound of metal against metal. Penny fell back with a glowing piece of metal in her pliers. The Baroness shuddered. Her remaining limbs flailed as she lost control of them with a cry of fear and despair. She thrashed with unrestrained mechanical power and her armor threw off a massive electrical pulse that blasted her attackers aside. The Baroness screamed with pain as her own mechanical body revolted against her. She ran toward the open door, slamming against the jamb, losing her helmet. With eyes clear, the Baroness fled.

"She's getting away," Penny shouted, already legging it after the escaping Baroness.

"What did you do to her?" Malcolm asked breathlessly as he retrieved his pistols. The fight had taken more out of him than he cared to admit.

"She had a little siphon crystal like the altar and that goon from India. So I took it; she won't be repairing herself. And I made some dirty adjustments to her aether motor."

They ran out of the stifling temple into the hurricane of heat that was London. They both stopped in their tracks. The city around them was ablaze. Smoke obscured much of the familiar cityscape, which was jagged and broken. Streams of lava slid along paving stones, burning swathes in the earth. Dead bodies littered the ground. The temple itself was stable, but when they reeled dumbstruck off the steps, they felt the ground shaking. Gaios was ripping the city to pieces.

Penny managed to overcome her shock and climbed on a pile of bricks. "There!"

They were off and running again. The Baroness could be seen just ahead of them, racing south. Her metal limbs hung useless.

"She's heading for the river! If she has a boat there, we'll lose her." Malcolm sprinted, forcing his legs to pump harder despite the pain spiking through them. He pulled ahead of Penny, but the rubble in the streets and the chaos of injured and terrified people hampered him. "I thought you took out her infernal engine."

"I didn't have time to shut it down completely. It must be powering her heart too, or Imogen's quills would've stopped her."

The Baroness raced into the ruins of a house. Malcolm leapt over the remains of the stoop and ducked inside after her. There was a hole in the back wall. As the Baroness ran toward it she slammed her shoulder into the bricks. The wall started to collapse behind her. Malcolm spun and blocked the charging Penny just in time. He turned her aside, covering her as the cascade of bricks crashed to the ground. The rubble scattered across the carcass of the town house, raising a cloud of dust. Malcolm dragged Penny after him, fighting against the heat and thick air.

By the time they scrambled over the bricks, the Baroness had gained considerable distance, weaving through narrow lanes. Both Malcolm and Penny were laboring for breath, but neither would relent. Between buildings, the Thames came into view. She was going to reach the river before they could stop her. Malcolm could see green smoke boiling from a docked boat, similar to the one they had hijacked to Gaios's island.

Without breaking stride, the Baroness weaved around overturned wagons and vaulted the many bodies that littered the broken street. She reached the steps down to the river where her boat waited with its funnel steaming and ready. A quick hop onto the deck and she would be away. The Baroness glanced back with an obnoxious grin. She would have a waved a jaunty hand if her arms had worked.

"No," Penny moaned, coming to a halt in the center of the street.

Malcolm ran a few steps more and stopped too. His fingers trembled with exhaustion as he tried to jam thick cartridges into the chambers of one of his pistols. Penny had something in her hand and she threw it hard. He realized it was one of her clockwork messenger birds. It buzzed through the air and struck the Baroness in the back of the head hard like a cricket ball. With no way to catch herself, she fell forward in a hard tumble on the stone steps to the edge of the water.

Several men scrambled from the boat and laid hands on her. They heaved the Baroness to her feet, where she cursed and bodily shoved them away. They all shrank back.

Malcolm braced himself with his feet apart. He grasped the wrist of his gun hand to steady his aim. The Baroness stepped to the edge of the jetty. The heavy paddle wheels of the steamer churned the water. She smiled at him, licking blood from her lips. Then Malcolm's bullet put a red streak across her unprotected temple.

Her eyes went wide. She was slammed off the dock. She hit the bow of the steamer and hung there for a split second. Her arms flew helplessly around her. She bounced off the rail and splashed into the river. Her head bobbed up once and she screamed. Then a heavy plank of the paddle wheel swept down and smashed her beneath the water. Her metal form rose again briefly before another paddle crashed onto her and dragged her under the dark river.

Malcolm and Penny reached the edge of the jetty. The steamboat was roaring away into the river with its crew hardly sparing a look back at their lost mistress. Malcolm kept his pistol trained on the boat in case they attempted an attack, but the crew had nothing in mind but escape.

Penny stared down at the foaming water slapping heavily against the dock.

Malcolm returned his pistol to its holster. "It's over. With that iron body she's on the bottom of the Thames, where she'll stay. She's an anchor now." His hand reached over to grab Penny's and she turned to him. She let out a hard breath and nodded.

They both turned around and saw Jane stricken. She leaned on the side of a demolished building, a ruin of bricks, staring at the dead lying around her. A trembling hand clutched her glasses as if trying to decide whether to drag them off her face so she could see no more. Malcolm turned her to look at him.

"Jane."

Now she covered her ears, trying to block out the sound of the dying city. Her tear-streaked face was inconsolable. "I did this. This is all my fault."

"That's a load of shite. This is about that madman. This is his doing, his revenge for an age-old crime. You were nothing but a pawn."

She searched his face for redemption. "But I did what he asked."

"To save the life of your father. I would have done the same for anyone here."

She took in the devastation around her, her voice but a shadow. "How can one man do all of this?"

"Because he believes he can do as he pleases. We believe otherwise. One can do good or ill. He chose poorly. What about you?"

Something changed in Jane's eyes as she looked up at him. The fear and despair faded to be replaced with purpose. "What do I have to do?"

Chapter 23

AFTER LEAVING MALCOLM TO HANDLE THE BARoness, Kate and the others followed Simon down the steep slope into the stygian blackness. The cave walls around them were alive and shifting constantly. They had to move quickly to stay ahead of it as the very floor tried to drag them back to the main temple above. In the distance a deep red glow beckoned.

It was hard to tell how long they struggled through the madhouse of a tunnel, but eventually the ground settled into a permanent state. They rushed forward until finally they turned a corner and stared into a vast cavern. Fifty feet ahead of them, the black volcanic soil ended abruptly in a massive lava pool, bubbling like a witch's cauldron, which dominated the huge center of the chamber. Magma exploded from the pool in orange geysers, bursting in evanescent arches of liquid rock morphing from orange to black in midair as they cooled. The lake seemed to breathe, expanding and contracting, rising and falling, its surface level changing several feet in a matter of minutes, spectacular and terrifying at once. Black plates, cut by jagged cracks of orange, floated atop the magma. They shifted and rolled like a child's puzzle with the pieces skewed.

An island rose in the center of the burning pool. It was nearly one hundred feet across and Gaios knelt with his arms buried in the ground as the earth heaved and bucked at his command. The waves of blistering heat made the air shimmer.

Simon slipped off his coat and flung it aside. He loosened the collar of his white shirt and rolled up the sleeves. His chest glowed as the runic tattoos flared.

Kate pulled several vials from her bandolier and handed them out. She stared pointedly at Simon. "Put on more of this before you do something stupid."

"You mean *in case*." Simon uncorked it with his thumb and poured a generous amount in his hand.

"I mean *before*." Kate made sure they all slathered the heavy lotion over their exposed skin.

"Gaios is in a trance," Nick pointed out, allowing the gel to be placed only on his face and neck. "He's drawing power from the Earth."

"Then he's vulnerable. Be ready." Simon was in motion. He raced to the edge of the lava and bounded onto the tilting stone platforms, hopscotching across the lake. He didn't see the column of rock that rose and slammed into his midsection, shoving him up against the roof of the cave forty feet above.

"You seek to harm me in my own temple?" Gaios turned slowly around, his hands coming loose from the volcanic soil. "Is there no end to you fools? There is nothing you can do against me. Why won't you learn?"

Simon shouted in pain as the pressure threatened to crush him. Gasping out a spell, a tattoo flared again and his skin solidified into stone, holding back the column. Below him, Nick's hands coated with ice. Steam rose as the cold vapors evaporated in the heat, encircling him in mist. Nick flung bolts at Gaios, but a curtain of magma lifted and the ice lances merely evaporated. Charlotte tried to fight through a rain of stones. Kate vaulted from rock floe to rock floe until she was near enough to shoot a vial and throw several more with her other hand. Gaios raised a maelstrom of swirling stones that smashed them all, save one, which broke against the demigod's calf. He screamed as acid ate at his still-very-human flesh.

Kate leapt the final gap across the molten pool to the shore of Gaios's island, her pistol flashing from its holster. They had to keep the elemental's attention on them and give Simon a chance to free himself. Nick swung his arms out and a wave of lava rose straight up out of the back of the pool and flopped toward Gaios. The demigod saw it at the last moment and held up a hand, solidifying it into solid black stone.

Kate launched another vial. A cloud of amber swirled around Gaios and solidified on his chest and head. She let loose a cry of triumph.

Kate saw something hurtling toward her as Gaios yanked Simon off the ceiling and threw him at her. Simon's stone spell made his form something Gaios could manipulate. Simon couldn't even cry out to warn Kate. He was going to crush her.

She tried to jump clear but Simon veered with her. He screamed with tremendous effort as his body suddenly shifted, the hardened shell around him cracking and flying out behind him. He collided with Kate as flesh and bone. Her vision went brilliant white. The hard impact sent them tumbling toward the edge of the lava pool. She lay beneath him as he thrust his arms and legs out spread-eagle to halt their momentum. Kate stirred under Simon's desperate hand and her eyes blinked open. They had skidded to a stop inches from the edge. The heat from the lava seared their exposed skin even through the gel. They came to their feet.

Gaios's amber prison abruptly shattered, sending shards

of it everywhere. Simon covered Kate and a few of the slivers struck them, but none were debilitating. Simon spun back to face Gaios. The elemental straightened, brushing the remainder of the amber from his robes with annoyance. His eyes grew dark and seemed to roll into his head. His fingers stretched taut.

"Come, children," he pronounced. "I want you to see the end."

Simon and Kate started desperately for Gaios again, but their knees buckled under them. The singular sound of their footsteps in the rough soil was quickly shattered by a splitting noise like giant trees cracking open and the ground was wracked by a tremor. Simon crashed into the dirt. Kate tumbled next to him. The earth roared and a huge wave of force washed over them. The roof of the chamber exploded outward. Columns toppled and smashed into pieces. Huge chunks of flaming marble blasted into the sky. Flames spewed forth from the rent ground. The vulnerable humans were thrown about like leaves. They reached for one another, trying to help, trying to support. Chunks of black stone rained down around them.

Then the sky broke open. The blackness split into a grey haze. A burning stench rolled over them in a wave of smoke. The quaking earth wrenched to a stop. The stone walls around them had disappeared and they saw the smashed remnants of the black basalt temple and beyond that, the crumbling bricks and stones of London. Gaios had brought the floor of his chamber to the surface, destroying much of his temple in the process.

Kate pushed herself up on shaking arms. Simon was fighting his way back to his feet as well. She looked around and saw Nick and Charlotte nearby, recovering their wits quickly. The earth shook under her, rattling through her aching bones. Her eyes quickly found Gaios.

A hot wind blew the demigod's hair and robes. Smoke

from burning London swept past him. Gaios laughed wildly. He raised his arms like a symphony conductor calling down the triumphant finale. The ground around him began to crack and magma seeped up to the surface.

Kate and Simon jumped to their feet. Searing ooze rolled toward them. They ran as more geysers of lava erupted everywhere. Terrible heat roared over them. They pounded over the quaking ground, cracks and crevasses opening all around. Nick came at them from one side and Charlotte loped from the other. They all hurtled onto a huge mound of bricks and stones that had once been a building. A sputtering trail of magma lapped at the base. With arms grasping those who faltered, they climbed above the red pools. Their safe harbor was going to be short-lived, Kate feared, because she could feel it shifting beneath their feet.

Over the sounds of destruction and Gaios's hoarse laughter, stones clattered down the far side of the mound. Kate looked over the crest to see Malcolm and Penny climbing toward them. The hunter carried her rucksack and blunderbuss as Penny labored up the hill. She was smeared with blood and ash. Malcolm assisted Jane, and Hogarth came after Imogen over the rough terrain. Kate ran down and took hold of her sister. A quick examination assured Kate she was fine.

"He's killing the city," Malcolm shouted over the roaring wind that whipped his black hair in streams around his head.

Penny dropped to her knees. At first, Kate thought she was too exhausted to stand. Indeed she might have been, but she was working carefully on something. A device of metal and crystal sat in her lap. It was the heart of the altar from Gaios's island. She had a panel off the back and a small tool inside it. She made frantic adjustments despite the rocking stones on which she sat.

A wave of lava broke from the ground at the foot of their refuge and swept up toward them. Nick shoved in front of the rest and raised a wall of ice, screaming with effort as he did so in the blasting heat. The globs of magma struck the white shield and sizzled it away, but Nick kept it thick until the lava slid back down the stone slope.

Gaios laughed harder from the distance. A huge plume of magma exploded behind him, silhouetting him black against the red.

Nick slumped onto his knees. "I can't hold it off next time."

"Won't be a next time." Penny stood with the strange device. It glittered in the weak sunlight. "I need a power source and I can knock Gaios on his ass. For a second."

Simon didn't question her. "Nick, you're up."

The older magician groaned but started to his feet.

Jane stepped forward, staring at the device with shame and anger. "I'll do it."

"No, Miss Somerset. You're—"

"Mr. Archer, please!" she demanded. The once-mousy woman stood with hair astray and face coated with grime. She ceased clutching her torn disheveled clothes. There was an extraordinary force of will behind her eyes. She glanced over at Malcolm, who nodded to her with approval.

The mound of stones shook. Heavy rocks and chunks of concrete rolled down.

Simon started toward the bottom of their crumbling mountain. "Everyone spread out and distract Gaios when Penny gives us the chance. Don't get too close. Charlotte, stay back in reserve. Don't charge him!" The werewolf growled with annoyance, but trailed Simon dutifully.

Penny held the device in her outstretched arms until she could see the inverted image of Gaios in the crystal.

Jane came next to her. There was a sudden calmness to the lightning elemental though her face held nothing but sheer determination. A roar built as the smoldering soul of the woman gave birth to a ribbon of electricity. It broke from her hands and cracked from her fingers to strike the device.

Penny gritted her teeth, losing sensation in her arms and hands. She didn't feel as if she was being struck by the lightning although her teeth chattered from the feedback of so much power only inches from her. Her hands tried to shake, but she forced them to stay steady.

When the heart of the altar could hold no more of Jane's power, it bucked in Penny's hands. A weird disruption spread from the crystal. It seemed to tear open the air as it stretched across the ruined square. The disturbance slithered around Gaios, coating him in an unseen sheath, as his face twisted in alarm. He was torn free from the earth and suspended in space, buffeted as if caught in a brutal gale. Green swirls of aether streamed out of him from his eyes and mouth. The demigod collapsed to the ground in a rain of rocks. He fell limply to his hands and knees. The magma lake ceased roiling. London stopped shaking.

Simon led the charge off the mound of stones and across the lava-drenched battlefield toward the black basalt remnant of the temple.

The elemental struggled to his feet, wide-eyed, waving a hand. A rock rose up from the ground, wobbling and slow, to block a volley of Imogen's quills. An ice lance impaled Gaios in the shoulder, spinning him back. Malcolm rolled to his belly and rested Penny's blunderbuss on a rock. He fired off a shell. The stunned elemental lifted his hands, calling forth a stone shield. Its flimsy surface shattered from the impact, sending shrapnel flying back into the demigod. Kate lobbed three vials of treacle at Gaios, pinning him in place. Imogen fired more quills at him while a bolt of lightning struck the elemental square in the chest. Gaios screamed and hunched over the pain, his limbs going limp in the wake of Imogen's toxins.

Under the cover of the barrage, Simon appeared before Gaios now, the runes on his body flaring through the smoke of the lightning. He reached out for the trapped elemental. "Your time is up."

Then the world around them went mad as Gaios lost control of his power. The earth rumbled and bucked. Everyone was thrown to the ground. Geysers of flame spewed from cracks ripped in the crust. Choking ash and dust filled the air.

Even Gaios was no longer immune to the upheaval. He was thrown into the air and fell back limp. Like an old man who suddenly found his body betraying him, he labored to rise. He looked frightened as he tried to bring his earth under control, but nothing happened. He raised his fists with soil sifting out from between his fingers.

"Gaios!" Simon shouted. "Stop!"

Gaios turned to the scribe, who was reaching out toward him. The elemental began to shake. Magma splashed high, like whitecaps in a storm. Streams of black and red lava swirled through the air and converged on Gaios. He stood with arms upraised as the searing river of boiling rock poured over him.

There was no chance for Simon to touch the elemental now. Fire rained down everywhere. Even Simon's stone form would not save him from this. Kate rushed toward him, shouting for him to run. Globs of lava fell all around him.

The air seemed suddenly frigid. Magma spouts froze black. The open square transformed into a weird gallery of stalagmites of solid basalt, glittering in the half-light. It was a forest of large black spikes sticking out of the earth. The strange formations were thicker and more numerous closer to the center of the square where a great single pillar of stone stood with Gaios buried inside. From within that rock, a primal scream ripped out with a voice that came from deep inside the earth.

The surrounding obsidian pillars shattered in an instant. The air filled with a terrifying mix of huge stones rocketing amidst a black razor dust. It was like being trapped inside a storm, with thunder clouds roaring and lightning cracking overhead. The air was thick and difficult to breathe.

Kate shouted, still too far from Simon. She watched with relief as he turned his body to nearly impervious rock, his only hope of surviving so close to the center of the maelstrom. Kate saw the rest of the team spread out to her right, scrambling to protect themselves. She agonized that she was too far away to help.

Kate saw that Jane had come down from the hill of wreckage. Penny crouched near her, pulling Hogarth close. At the same time, Hogarth had his broad arms wrapped about Charlotte's furry form. Spears of light arced from Jane's fingers, filling the air around her, smashing the large projectiles to bits, then dancing through the deadly shards, ripping them from the air. Her protective lightning spread to cover those at her feet.

Nearest Kate by several yards, Malcolm reached out and pulled Imogen close to him. Nick swore in pain, fighting through the sharp haze to reach the Scotsman and the woman. He hunkered low and raised a rudimentary ice shield that covered their front and flanks. Heavy stones smashed into it and razor shards quickly started tearing it away. Nick continued to reinforce the ice with more and more frost in a struggle to keep them safe.

All this occurred in seconds, leaving Kate to stand

alone amidst the gale that would flay her alive. Her hands flew to her bandolier. She threw vials out onto the ground all around her, creating walls of amber.

She watched in dismay as great chunks of obsidian collided with the amber, smashing it, while smaller shards gouged out pieces. Her safety would be short-lived and her protective fortress would soon be rendered to dust. Kate threw more amber vials in hopes of reinforcing it. Glistening ocher bloomed hard around her in the hellish air, only to be cracked and shattered yet again.

Kate's hands fumbled at her bandolier, but she touched only empty loops. Her actions stilled. Across the way she saw Imogen struggling against Malcolm's grip, trying to get to her. Agony ripped through Kate's heart. She had no way to comfort her sister.

Her green eyes sought out Simon. Despite his stone form, she sensed the panic and desperation in him. She straightened calmly, a sad smile on her lips. She feared that Simon was prepared to drop his spell and run to her, even though he had to know he wouldn't reach her before he was struck down too. His mind wouldn't win that argument. She shook her head as the last remnant of her amber shelter shattered in the storm. She stumbled, her clothes and hair flying. Smaller rocks cut her face and arms like razors. A chunk of obsidian clipped her side, knocking her down to her knees.

A pale shape appeared next to Kate. The strange vision of white and black was Imogen, her mourning dress shredded by the razor dust, exposing her pale flesh. She threw herself on Kate, shoving her to the ground and burying her sister beneath her. Kate yelled, angry at Imogen's foolhardiness. But Imogen was stronger; so much stronger. Kate cried out as bright red blood poured down Imogen's face above her. Heavier stones struck the young woman, knocking her head aside. Still, she shoved

Kate down and settled atop her. Kate struggled to drag Imogen closer, fighting to protect her young sister. Detritus tumbled over Imogen. She was slammed down again, her pale body jerking like a doll. Her white skin was visible briefly until more shards crashed down.

Kate's world went dark, everything lost in a tempest of obsidian. She tasted iron as she tried to swallow against the grit. The full weight of her sister pressed against her. She took some calming solace in the touch of Imogen's cool cheek against hers. Kate tried to move but she was pinned; rough stones and rocks pressed into her legs and arms. There was no sound beyond the roaring in her ears and Kate fought panic in the pitch-black and the suffocating air.

Knowing the terror of the dark must be tenfold for Imogen, Kate twisted her hands in the tight space, clawing at the sharp rocks around her, trying to gain some wiggle room. She shoved with her very limited leverage, but they were wedged in tight. With shallow pants, Kate struggled to whisper soothing words in her sister's ear. "It's all right, Imogen. They'll find us. No need to fear. We're together."

Finally above her, she sensed movement and heard the scrabbling of claws and furious digging. A huge chunk of masonry was lifted and tossed aside. A stream of thin daylight shone in. The hazy sky greeted Kate's blurred vision, but then it was blocked as the great werewolf crouched, peering down.

"Hello?" Charlotte growled.

Relieved, Kate couldn't draw enough breath to answer her. She tried weakly to rouse her sister to no avail. Kate now heard Simon's desperate voice. More rubble was shoved away and she drew in a deeper breath. Craggy stones and basalt soil sloughed off Imogen as Charlotte pulled the limp form up into her powerful arms.

"Kate!" Simon shouted, his hands bloody from digging through the razor-sharp dirt.

Her eyes were wide with shock and her limbs trembled as she reached for him. Simon lifted her carefully out of the debris, holding her tight, checking her for serious injury. Kate shoved his hands away, her head turned to her sister. Dark dust coated Imogen's fair skin. Charlotte settled Imogen's form into the dirt and crouched over her as Kate reached out. Imogen's white skin was slathered with blood. She had numerous gashes on her face and chest. One pale arm was crooked and her head was turned farther past her shoulder than it should have been.

"Oh God, please. Oh God!" Kate shouted, her voice hoarse against the drifting ash and raw emotion. She put a hand on her sister's arm. She felt a terrible lack of response although she tried to ignore it. Imogen's muscles were slack. There was no resistance. Kate touched Imogen's dust-caked cheek and the girl's head jostled lifelessly. Kate gasped and her trembling worsened.

Charlotte's massive head turned and her yellow eyes grew round and frightened. "Miss Kate?"

Kate sensed the fear and aching need coming from Charlotte so she reached out and took the beast's clawed hand. There was nothing she could say to the monstrous face before her that looked for all the world like a scared little girl.

Malcolm fell to his knees next to Imogen and put his gentle hands on her face. He inspected her carefully, checking her eyes and sliding a finger along her neck, seeking a pulse. After a second, his head dropped and he let his hand caress the poor girl's arm. His great frame shook silently.

Kate watched Simon desperately for the barest hint of hope that he might tell her something other than what she knew.

He couldn't manage to raise his voice above a despairing whisper. "I'm sorry, Kate. I'm so sorry."

"Nick!" Kate cried, her chest tight with rising dread. "Help her! Do something!"

Nick appeared stunned by the sight. He shook his head in horror, looking at Simon as if in apology. "I can't help her. I don't have that power anymore."

Kate slid away from Charlotte. Frantic, she wiped away the blood on Imogen's face, but it was everywhere. There was no response to her ministrations, not a moan or even eye movement beneath her blood-crusted lids. She pushed her face against her sister's cool skin. All she could do was whisper in Imogen's ear, "No no no no no."

She barely felt Simon's steadying hand upon her back. A strange peacefulness descended on London, but Kate noticed none of it. Her world had shattered.

Chapter 24

SOUNDS OF GRIEF PIERCED THE NIGHT. SMOKE billowed from fires that burned in the city all around them. Kate's sobs filled the still air, cutting deep into Simon's heart as he stared down at the pale figure in the black dirt. Charlotte hunched near him with her mouth frozen open. Malcolm drew the werewolf against him silently. Her long arms wrapped around his waist and she buried her head inside his coat. Penny had her hands on her head, disbelieving. Jane seemed disturbed to be witnessing such grief, but unable to offer comfort. Even the stoic Hogarth's granite face cracked, his guilt over the loss of his charge all too evident.

Behind them a great column of basalt still stood in the center of the raised platform, presumably with Gaios encased inside. Simon stared hard at it. All this anguish because of one man's vendetta over an old crime. The waste. The ruin of it all. So pointless.

Above them, the world darkened suddenly and the ground offered a distant rumble. From the center of the demolished temple, the thick black pillar began to move. Liquid bubbled on its surface and the black turned red and transformed into a large blob of slithering lava. It rolled and glistened for a moment before it collapsed as if popped with a needle. It revealed a figure standing on the jagged ruins of the marble temple floor amidst receding magma. He was black and shining bright. He appeared to be made of flat slabs of obsidian. Then the black glass folded away from the figure's head.

Gaios took a deep breath like a diver emerging from the sea. His eyes focused on his surroundings and he scowled. The obsidian instantly reshaped itself from simple protective planks into a beautiful armor reminiscent of a Roman praetor. He wore a carved black cuirass and a skirt of stone strips protecting his thighs. His arms were sheathed in bracers and his lower legs were covered by greaves, all likewise made of obsidian.

"Everyone, back on your feet," Simon ordered.

Charlotte pulled away from Malcolm and dropped onto all fours, charging like an attack dog. She loped over the wreckage and launched herself across the moat of lava surrounding the marble platform where Gaios stood. Her speed took the elemental by surprise and he actually flinched as the huge savage thing hurtled at him. Charlotte slammed into the black-armored figure, knocking him back only a step. He managed to bring up his sheathed hand and jam it against her hairy throat, holding the snapping jaws away from his head.

Suddenly a jagged shaft of obsidian shot out the back of Charlotte's neck. She stiffened. Her eyes rolled up and her claws scrabbled off Gaios's impervious chest. The elemental lowered his arm and the werewolf slid off the long stone spike that extended from his fist. She collapsed in a heap at his feet and began to shrink back into the shape of a helpless, quivering little girl. Blood dripped from the sharp stone as it flowed back up to become the gauntlet over Gaios's hand.

Malcolm screamed his throat raw and pulled his pistols. He ran toward the crumbled temple. The Lancasters boomed.

"Malcolm, no!" Simon shouted. He grabbed Kate as she started toward Gaios with the blood of her sister painted on her hands. "Don't go near him!"

Kate turned on Simon, fury welling in her face like an oncoming storm. But with tremendous effort she held on to the last vestiges of her sanity. She took a step back to his side, her hand reaching for her pistol.

"We have to work together!" he said. "Or we have no chance."

Malcolm's heavy shells smashed cracks in the black obsidian cuirass. Gaios was slammed onto his back. Malcolm threw both empty pistols aside as he ran and drew his dagger. He jumped over the magma, his long black coat fluttering behind him, and landed hard at the feet of the elemental. Without pause, Malcolm raised the knife over his head and let out a Gaelic war cry.

Two columns of stone rose on either side of him. When they smashed together, Malcolm was not between them. He had flipped backward, his feet landing just inches short of the bubbling lava.

Gaios rose on obsidian tendrils that pushed him up to his feet, then retracted into his armor. He glared down at Malcolm, but suddenly a slim javelin flew toward him. It was a shaft glowing blue, Simon's sword. The blade sank into Gaios's shoulder as if he wore no armor. Before he could react, his head was covered in ice. A large shape moved alongside Malcolm and Hogarth drew back his war maul. The mace collided with Gaios and sent black stone flying in glittering shards. The elemental went to one knee.

"Take Charlotte!" Simon shouted at Malcolm as Hogarth swung another colossal blow against Gaios, sending him spinning.

Malcolm gathered the limp form of Charlotte in his arms. Blood seeped from a horrid gash in her neck, but she was breathing. He carried her back to where Simon and Kate waited.

Jane ran up to them. She leaned over Charlotte when he set her down and began to wrap a bandage torn from her own dress around the girl's throat. Simon pulled Malcolm away from her. Kate loaded her crossbow, her face harsh like Medusa, her gaze never leaving the armored demigod.

The ground where Hogarth stood was upended and he tumbled away from Gaios. Carried by the weight of his mace, he slid down the marble slab and crashed to the ground some twenty yards from the elemental. A sudden blast of lava boiled up through the paving stones and enveloped his legs. Hogarth screamed.

Penny struggled toward Hogarth even though her steps were weak and labored. She grabbed his arm and started to pull. Hogarth's weight nearly dragged her into the lava. She dug her boot heels against some wreckage and hooked her elbow under his arm. The exhausted engineer pulled the large man out of the burning pool. He collapsed onto the ground in a gasping catatonic lump, his legs black, withered, and steaming. The engineer started to stand.

"Penny!" Simon shouted, climbing back to his feet. "Get back!"

Gaios turned toward her even as he ripped Simon's sword from his body. Stones flew off the ground and shot at Penny with high-pitched whistles. She raised her arms over her head, but the rocks pounded her with sick thudding sounds. Penny collapsed to the ground, unable to protect herself from being crushed to a pulp. Fortunately the barrage ceased when Nick hit Gaios with a shaft of ice, distracting the furious elemental.

Through a shower of blackened rocks and bits of pumice, Malcolm ran to Penny's side. He inspected her unconscious figure and seemed relieved. He rummaged through her rucksack and pulled out her small sound pistol. With a quick hand on her bruised bloody face, he turned back to Gaios. Ashes were falling everywhere now, dark and dense.

Gaios threw the sword aside and it sank into a pool of magma. He was breathing hard and his brow furrowed. Gaios looked at the remaining five, his eyes wild. "Tell me where the coward Ash is now!"

They were failing, their plans gone to ruin. Even though Gaios apparently could no longer extend his wrath across London, he still had a fearful power here in the wreckage of his temple. Simon needed to get close to Gaios in order to do any good. The group spread out to surround the elemental. Nick and the surprisingly focused Jane went off for the far side of the platform where Gaios stood. Malcolm moved in the opposite direction. Kate pulled her last two cartridges. She loaded her single-shot pistol and clamped the last metallic cartridge between her teeth.

The white-haired elemental dropped to one knee and slapped his hands onto the ground. A black stone visor lowered over the front of his helmet, completely obscuring his face.

Nick unleashed a furious attack on Gaios. Immediately the black armor was coated with a sheen of ice. And then a lightning storm erupted from Nick's fingertips along with a scream of pain. The slender streaks of electricity felt their way around the black figure. Gaios staggered. Nick fell and the electricity crackled to a halt, his hands burnt.

Jane stood nearby with one hand raised. A stroke of lightning arced from the heavens and struck Gaios with a splitting crack. She shouted and called another jagged spear to smash Gaios flat on his back. Blinding bolts crashed onto him until her hands were lit with fire.

Suddenly, the earth sundered beneath both her and Nick, a cauldron of magma below them. Nick fell, barely catching the edge with clawlike hands. Jane managed to grab him but didn't have the strength to haul him up. They clung there, hanging over hell's mouth.

Kate ran forward and fired her last vial of black treacle at the fallen elemental. It shattered onto his chest and sticky ooze poured down the sides of his cuirass onto the ground beneath. Malcolm charged Gaios, dropping next to him and placing the muzzle of Penny's small pistol against the obsidian helmet. He pulled the trigger. He didn't know how to regulate the weapon, and it bucked violently. Malcolm's arm shook and he grasped his wrist to hold it steady. The obsidian began to crack.

Kate slammed her pistol against the black helmet. It shattered and revealed Gaios's tortured face beneath. His mouth stretched wide in pain as the sound waves pounded into his head. She leveled her pistol and fired, but the shell was deflected by the disruption from Penny's gun.

Kate spat the last cartridge into her hand. "Shut it off, Malcolm!"

The Scotsman released the trigger and slumped onto his elbows. Blood flowed from his ears along his jawline.

Simon appeared beside Kate and reached out for Gaios's unprotected head with his left hand. His palm held the inscribed rune. The power of it tingled along his arm. He felt an odd tightness in his chest. He stretched his hand to place it on the bearded face, but suddenly he couldn't move.

Looking down, Simon saw strange black rods sticking into his ribs. Sharp pain cut through him and he had trouble drawing breath. He heard Kate scream and saw numerous pencil-thin shafts of obsidian encaging her head. They were dug in like claws, leaking bright red blood. It was difficult to understand what he was seeing. Even grimacing with agony, Kate twisted her pistol and took the shot. The shell cracked the black armor of Gaios's stomach.

Simon and Kate were shoved away from Gaios. Malcolm was lifted into the air by black spikes stuck into his arms and hands. All three of them were impaled on thin spines of obsidian that emerged from the ground around Gaios like shining onyx tendrils.

Gaios rose to his feet, lifted by the earth itself. He stood in the center of the three who were crucified on his obsidian lances. His body was hunched. His black armor was shattered and dangled in pieces from his battered frame.

Simon gritted his teeth, trying to remain conscious. He clutched at the bloody stone shaft buried in his chest and summoned the aether. He attempted to break it, but could feel the stone replenishing itself under his hands, growing continually stronger so that it would always be too powerful to shatter.

Gaios struggled to straighten his back. "Stop fighting, Archer. You've lost. London is mine. You were strong, but now you'll die." He gestured and another stone spike drove into Simon's body.

Simon screamed.

"Tell me who Ash is pretending to be now, and at least I'll stop the pain." Blood from his nose trickled through Gaios's white beard. "She could have helped you but she ran and left you all to die."

Simon fought to breathe. His legs were numb. He could hear his heartbeat roaring in his ears. Tears rolled down his cheeks. He reached out feebly, and whispered, "Kate."

"Tell me who Ash is!"

"Oh God, Kate. I must hold her . . . before . . . please . . . please . . ."

"You're pathetic, Archer. You're no Pendragon. He never begged, even when I killed him. I was wrong to fear you."

"Just once . . . then I'll tell you . . . Ash's . . ."

The elemental raised his weary head to Simon. With a mere glance, the stone claws clutching Kate's scalp opened and she fell to the ground. She lay gasping for air. Gaios reached down and pulled her up. "Anstruther, go to him. Keep him alive long enough so he can tell me what I need."

Kate weakly tried to pull her arm from the elemental's grasp. She nearly toppled as Gaios dragged her toward the impaled Simon.

Rivers of red streamed down Kate's horror-stricken face. She could barely stand. Her clothes were torn. Simon smiled down at her and reached out.

"Kate," he said. "Take my hand, please."

He felt her stiff cold fingers slip against his. He pursed his lips and whispered a secret word. Aether surged down his arm into her hand. He saw Kate jerk with alarm and a bright glow shot from above her heart. Her green eyes streamed aether and glittered bright with the same power that flowed through Simon.

Gaios turned his head to Kate. She returned his gaze with a fierce grin. Her hand came up and it glowed from a green rune that appeared on her palm. The elemental shouted and started to back away, but Kate grasped his face between her searing fingers. A blast of aether tore from her hand.

Gaios shook free, but a rune was emblazoned across his features. He roared in anger and extended his hands, fingers like claws. But nothing happened. The obsidian tendrils holding Simon crumbled and he dropped hard to the ground. On Kate's other side, Malcolm fell too. In the distance, Jane dragged Nick back to solid ground, each collapsing against the other.

Kate grabbed Gaios as the old elemental tumbled backward. He tried to shove her away, but his strength had fled with his magic. He seemed to grow older and more wizened. Kate knocked his hands aside and slammed her fist into his face. He stumbled back. She struck him again and Gaios fell to one knee. Kate herself couldn't stay on her feet and fell onto her hands and knees, gasping for breath. The elemental scrabbled weakly across the dirt and seized a jagged shard of obsidian. He rose onto one knee and lifted the blade to plunge it into her unprotected back.

A hand grabbed Gaios's wrist and an arm clasped the old man's unprotected throat. Simon tightened his forearm on Gaios's neck until the elemental began to choke, his tongue lolling from his mouth, eyes rolling up in his head. Gaios tried to raise his feeble hand and stab Simon with the stone blade. The razor black stone jabbed into Simon's leg.

"No . . . more." Simon shut his eyes against the blossom of new pain. He gritted his teeth and drew a final burst of runic strength into his wracked form. His arm cracked through the remnants of the obsidian armor and crushed against Gaios's throat. The elemental gagged, but he still raised the knife to strike again. Simon tightened with all his might, nearly blacking out. Gaios's arm faltered at its apex and the old man stopped moving. He slumped. Simon kept up his death grip on the elemental's throat for another minute, until darkness swallowed his vision. Finally, they both collapsed unmoving into the dust.

Kate crawled to Simon. She struggled to unbend his arm from around Gaios's neck and roll the elemental's lifeless body aside. Simon was still breathing. He looked up at her with a tired, grateful expression. She should have had nothing left, but she still lifted him into her arms. Then she saw his red wounds and pulled him against her breast.

After a moment, she shifted him back slightly and looked down. “You are going to live, aren’t you?”

“If you are, I will.” Simon put his head on her lap.

Chapter 25

IT WAS A MONTH AFTER THE TERRIBLE DISASTER that became known, rather prosaically, as the Great London Earthquake. The city was just beginning to get its feet under it and move forward again. Bodies had been gathered and largely buried or disposed of. The number of dead was lower than might have been expected given the fires and collapsed buildings in crowded tenement blocks. Rubble was being cleared. The wreckage along the riverfront was being carted away. Most main streets were open to traffic and business had begun to revive. Goods could move freely and shops were struggling back to life to supplement the always thriving street vendors, provided the teamsters and lightermen and shopkeepers were still alive. The worst of the damage had struck the heart of the City eastward, with relatively less structural failure and loss of life west into Westminster and Kensington, or north to suburbs such as Islington, or south beyond the Thames.

It was a chilly day in early October when King William requested Grace North join him to make a tour of damaged buildings and dislocated people. The pair rode in a carriage viewing one of the remaining open fissures near Cannon Street. Grace seemed so overcome by her emotions that she couldn't bear to emerge from her carriage. So beloved was she that the crowd was soon comforting her, assuring her that they were well and would muddle through. *God bless you, ma'am,* they called after her as the coach rolled away with her covering her stricken face with a handkerchief.

In the northern part of the city, the tour moved on to inspect a prison that had been commandeered as temporary housing for refugees from shattered parishes to the south. They met the governor of the prison, now turned into a hotelier, who showed them the crowded courtyard and first-floor cells. Cooking fires were everywhere. Laundry was strung across the grounds. There was much bowing and curtsying from the surprised residents.

At the end of a hallway, King William extended his hand toward a short set of steps and the door at the bottom. "This room hosts a ward of injured children, orphans now. I should like to visit them. There is little we could do better on this day than raise the spirits of suffering children, don't you agree?"

"I do, Your Majesty." Grace nodded pleasantly and they started down the steps.

The king looked back at the governor. "Sir, I would like to come upon these children alone, with Mrs. North. It would be a terrific treat for them if their king wandered in unannounced. Would you stay where you are?"

The governor looked confused but bowed and remained planted at the top of the steps. King William opened the heavy door himself and allowed Grace to enter first. She covered her nose with a handkerchief to fight the dank stench. The king paused to mop his brow before they proceeded along a narrow corridor lit only by a dim flickering light at the end.

They entered a large room with several other doors

opening off it. With only a single gas jet on the wall, it was still quite dark. Through one of the open doors, Grace saw the back of a woman, with her head bandaged, bent over the form of a young girl. However, King William indicated another open door on their right and he went to it. He stepped aside and Grace went in without a thought.

The door slammed shut and a bright green glow flashed.

Grace North stood frozen. The walls pulsed with runes brought to life with the shutting of the door and the joining inscriptions around the perimeter of the room. She turned back to the door and grasped the handle, pulling violently on it. It was locked.

"What is this?" Grace hissed like a caged cat.

The king drifted back into the shadows where he intersected with a new shape who was barely visible. The two figures exchanged a few whispered words. The king moved quickly to depart the prison suite while the second form detached itself from the darkness and limped forward into the light of the gas jet, leaning heavily on a cane.

"Welcome back to London, Ash." Simon Archer's voice quivered with restrained emotion. "By the way, you are my prisoner."

Ash's eyes were wide with fury and she jabbed a hand toward him. She glared in anger and squeezed her fingers into a fist. Simon scoffed at her attempt to curse him. He shook his head. After a moment of effort, Ash realized her magic was gone, and anger turned to fear.

"What have you done?" she cried.

"I have trapped you. Byron Pendragon had prepared a cell for you in the Bastille, which I suspect you knew. Well, I have re-created that cell here. And you will stay here until you die."

"We had a deal, Archer!" Ash screamed. "You traitorous bastard! We had a deal!"

"Deal? I don't recall a deal. My people stopped Gaios from destroying Britain. Meanwhile, you abandoned the people you love so dear. For all your crimes, your life belongs to me now."

From the open cell on the far side, Kate and Charlotte emerged. They wore shabby clothes that had allowed them to pass for displaced wretches in the dim light. Kate's mouth was a grim line, watching the captured necromancer. Charlotte hid behind her, still more fearful than normal since Imogen's death.

Kate put a comforting arm around the child. "Don't worry, dear. She can't hurt you."

Malcolm and Penny entered slowly through the main door where they had hidden outside in case the scheme went wrong. Malcolm noted the sight of Ash behind bars with a sigh of relief. Penny leaned heavily on a crutch yet laughed cheerfully. Deep bruises still covered her face. She slapped the Scotsman on the arm with satisfaction. Malcolm winced. She winced too.

Ash pressed against the door. "You must be insane. I am Grace North. I'm the wife of the prime minister of England. How long before everyone in this country starts to ask where I am? Did you even think about that? When the people find out what you've done, they will tear you apart." She pointed at Kate. "Even your damned name won't protect you. They'll string you up in the streets! All of you! Even your dog!"

Kate pulled Charlotte close. Malcolm raised his bandaged hands with a snarl and stepped forward, looking for a fight. Penny tugged him back.

Simon grew uncannily quiet. "We prepared ample evidence to show that Grace North, tiring of her dull husband, has run off with a minor German count with a reputation as a lady's man. Unfortunately, the pleasure yacht carrying the two of them toward some lovers' rendezvous on the sunny Mediterranean will be found off Majorca, or at least parts of it will be found. Grace North will be lost at sea. The terrible scandal will, no doubt, be covered up with stories protecting your reputation and that of the prime minister. I regret the honorable Mr. North's discomfort, but there is no answer for it. You are a tumor and must be cut out. There will be scarring. But when it is done, the nation and the world will be better for it."

"How dare you!" Ash spat. "You worthless scribe. You miserable little piece of filth! Who are you to do this to me?"

"I'm Simon Archer. Son of Catherine Archer, whom I believe you know." He stopped talking, not trusting his voice to stay firm. He felt Kate press closer to him. His fists clenched, straightening from the cane and taking several deep breaths. "And I am the heir to Pendragon because I am the son of Edward Cavendish."

Ash froze with her mouth open. She regarded Simon closely as if looking for physical signs of his father in him. Then she smiled with cold understanding.

Simon struggled to keep his emotions under the cover of his stern features. He feared he would crush Kate's hand in his fingers. She didn't react to the pressure.

"I underestimated you, Archer. Damn me but I did." Ash slid her fingers gently up and down the bars in the small window. She grinned with a manic fervor that seemed out of place on Grace North's face. "I never thought you to be this sort of man. I thought you truly were a dilettante at heart. A gadfly who only cared for what magic could do for you. I never believed you had the ambition and the steel to become the *eminence grise* behind the throne. I'm impressed. However did you enchant the king to play the betrayer?"

Simon hesitated for a second and Ash narrowed her

eyes with suspicion. "That wasn't the king who came with me, was it? Of course it wasn't. It was someone under an illusion. The true king doesn't know what you're doing here, does he? How long do you think you can keep this from him?"

Kate's eyes flicked with concern toward Simon. He gave her a calm smile, as if no secrets mattered now that Ash was contained. By locking the necromancer away, all could be free. Secrets he had been carrying for years now seemed to hold no danger for him. Even here in this dank prison cellar, there was a cleanliness to the air that was invigorating to him.

"I'll tell His Majesty once I've prepared him," Simon said. "Eventually, he'll be ready to believe that the lovely Grace North was indeed the vile Ash. And His Majesty will be grateful that I already have you under lock and key. You're done, Ash. We've won."

"I see." Ash chuckled politely as if she were stuck in a brief conversation at a dinner party she'd rather not be attending but knew would end soon enough. All the panic, all the dismay, was gone from her assured gaze. Her voice was quiet and simple. "You have no chance against me, Archer. I've bested centuries of challengers. I finished off Pendragon when he rejected me. And now I've rid myself of Gaios when he dared come against me. Do you truly believe *you* stand a chance? I'll get out of this place eventually; and then I will visit such horrors on you and your companions that you will wish to God I did not exist."

Simon's ferocity over Ash was spent. Despite what Ash had done to his mother with necromancy, the fact that his mother had been stronger and was now at peace thanks to Nick put that atrocity into the distant past. Simon felt that the terrible chaos created by the murder of Pendragon and the collapse of the Order of the Oak was soothed now. Of the three great demigods who founded that venerable old magic guild, two were dead and the last was here under Simon's control. The torch had passed. He faced a future of immense toil to rebuild the useful aspects of the old Order. For now, Simon just felt tired. He turned away with Kate and Charlotte. "Your threats are meaningless, Ash. You have nothing left."

"I have the man who killed your father."

Simon froze in his steps but didn't look back. Kate's hand tightened around his and he could sense her gaze boring into him, waiting for him to react. He exchanged a wondering glance with Malcolm. The Scotsman was tense, also eager for Simon's response.

"No." The pain of Simon's wounds flared again. He started to limp toward the door.

"Would you like me to tell you?" Ash asked with a pleasant lilt. "You can have your revenge. That will make everything right, won't it?"

Kate whispered into Simon's ear, "Don't listen to her. Walk away now."

Simon ushered everyone out into the corridor and started to push the heavy door closed. "You'll never get out, Ash. You'll grow old and eventually you will die. As you should."

"Nick Barker," came the voice of the necromancer.

A jolt surged through Simon and he felt dizzy for a second. He peered through the narrow space and met Ash's eyes to find she was staring intently at him. He took a breath and went to shove the door shut.

"Nick Barker murdered your father."

Simon stopped, leaving a few inches of open space into the cells.

Ash called out, "I know Barker is with your little group. I know you saved him that night at St. Giles. He was

King William today, wasn't he? He used that damned glamour spell of his."

That was true. Nick had pretended to be the king to lure Ash to the prison, and he had slipped out, they hoped, before she could see through the disguise.

"I don't believe you," Simon said, but the claim wasn't convincing.

"Ask him." Ash stared into the narrow gap between the door and the jamb. "I ordered another man to do the job, but he failed. A miserable drunk."

Malcolm turned away. He leaned on the wall with his head bowed.

"When I told Barker to kill Cavendish, he didn't ask why. He didn't care. He just did it. Barker smiled in his face and murdered your father."

Kate tried to pull Simon away from the door and shut it, but he kept it open against her.

"It's true," Ash said. "Ask Barker. If you can find him. He knows now that you have me, that I might find out who your father is, and that I might tell you the name of the killer to bargain my way out of prison. Or just because I know."

Simon stood silently, shaking his head.

Ash attempted to catch Simon's gaze again. "Archer? Where's that miraculous key you carry?"

Simon's hand went to his waistcoat pocket in reflex. He felt the gold chain and ran his fingers down to the end to find it empty. He pulled the chain out and the fob hung alone. Simon knew he'd had it earlier. He knew it. He spun to Kate on the desperate chance that she had the key, as it sometimes changed hands. She shook her head.

Ash's laughter was melodious. "I don't know how your key works exactly, but if Barker does, you'll never see him again."

Simon closed the door. He felt numb. "I have to go to Gaunt Lane, Kate. That's the closest portal."

Kate touched his arm. "Nick is your friend. If he . . . why would he come back? Why would he stay with you all these years?"

Simon turned to find Malcolm standing in front of him. "You can't believe Ash, Simon. She's trying to have her revenge. Don't go down a path from which you can never return."

"I must go to Gaunt Lane." He stepped past them, increasing his stride down the corridor, whispering a rune to life. He vaulted up the steps, ignoring the searing pain in his chest, and sprinted across the crowded courtyard toward their waiting carriage. He didn't see the bloodstain that was spreading across his white shirt. His pounding steps couldn't outpace the beating of his heart or drown the sounds of Ash's laughter.

THE HOUSE AT GAUNT LANE WAS SILENT. SIMON quietly closed the front door behind him. Nick had never been an unobtrusive man, and in their years together, he could always be heard bustling about. There was nothing.

He stepped past the sitting room on the right and something caught his attention. In the center of the room was a swirling portal. Simon had established a new link here a week ago and now it had been activated. In the quivering oval, he saw the shuttered window in the room in the Palais-Royal.

Simon walked into the sitting room, looking into the rippling view of distant Paris. If Nick had stolen the key, as Ash said, and used it to open the portal, he was gone now. Simon could follow, but the odds of finding one man in that teeming city were very thin. And, if

Nick was trying to lose himself, he would likely open a second portal from Paris and vanish into that.

Perhaps there was another reason that Simon wasn't seeing. Just because Nick had worked for Ash, just because he had secretly watched Simon for her, just because Nick lied about it all, didn't mean Ash was telling the truth now. Malcolm warned him, wisely, not to trust her. Ash lied out of habit and with a long-game agenda that few could penetrate. Perhaps Simon just couldn't fathom the perverse leverage Ash was trying to exert on him and his team.

Simon lifted a hand to the portal and brushed the softness of the otherworldly surface. The evidence that shimmered in front of him was inconclusive. He muttered, "Nick. Did you want me to follow? Why didn't you close the portal behind you?"

"Because," came a voice from the corner, "I didn't leave."

Simon spun to see Nick lounging in his usual spot on the tattered sofa. The older magician looked exhausted. His eyes were ringed with dark circles. There was a whiskey bottle and empty glass on the table next to him. Nick lifted one hand off his chest and tossed an object across the room.

Simon caught the gold key out of the air. He slowly looked up from the glittering device in the palm of his hand to his friend. Nick couldn't meet his gaze and threw his forearm over his eyes. Simon waited for the explanation, however twisted, however disappointing, that would strike Ash's lie into the dust.

"Why did you take it?" Simon asked.

Nick glanced from under his arm with a look of curious annoyance. His confusion dissipated when he realized Simon was still searching for excuses. He took a deep breath. "Ash told you, didn't she? You wouldn't be here looking like that, asking me stupid questions otherwise."

Simon stared at Nick but saw someone different. Not the man who helped him, who advised him, who toasted innumerable drinks with him and carried him home after nights that went on a bit too long.

"Tell me, Nick." Simon could barely make himself heard.

Nick sat up. He let his hand rest on the neck of the bottle but then released it. "You already know. Why drag it out?"

Simon took a step toward him. He couldn't feel the floor under his feet. He seemed to be floating in another world. "You tell me."

"Simon, I'm not going to fight you. I'm tired. Do what you want to me. I don't care."

"Tell me, Nick." Simon lost all sense of place in a haze of confused rage. "*You* tell me!"

Nick looked up. "I did it."

"Did what?"

"For God's sake, Simon." He glanced away. "I killed your father."

"Why?" A coldness slipped through Simon's body. What little vigor his spell had given faded. He was losing touch with the room, with his thoughts.

Nick laughed and shook his head. "Ash told me to do it."

"That's all? You didn't hate him? Some past wrong he did you? Some old grudge to settle?"

"I'd never seen him until that night." Nick started to shift, but Simon leaned forward slightly as a warning so he settled back. "There was a war in the Order of the Oak. I was on Ash's side then."

"Why did you come to me when you knew I was his son?"

"I had no idea at first," Nick retorted angrily. "I didn't know you were Edward Cavendish's son until last year. You told me when you were drunk."

"And you didn't tell Ash?"

"No, of course not. By then, I knew I wasn't going to let her have you."

"Even though she would kill you for failing?"

"I didn't want you to be like me." Nick rolled glistening eyes at the memory. "Just kill me and be done with it."

Simon stared at his old friend for a long time in motionless silence.

Finally, Nick rubbed a hand over his face and looked up, almost in anger. "Don't play your games with me. Either kill me or stand there while I walk through that portal." He struggled to his feet and faced Simon.

"No, you're not running away this time."

"I'm not going to rot in that new Bastille of yours." Nick jabbed a finger at him. "I swear to you, I'm not."

"Don't you dare fight me."

Nick sneered and started toward the portal when an arm rose in front of his chest like an iron bar. The two men stood nearly nose to nose. Simon stared, dark emotions locked under the surface. Nick sighed and quickly raised his hand, trailing flame. Simon ducked as the fire surged past him.

A powerful fist drove into Nick's jaw and sent the man sailing across the room. He crashed into a desk, overturning it in a noisy pile. Nick surged quickly to his feet with fire flying from his waving hands.

Simon was struck by a bolt of flame. He didn't cry out but spun around, his coat afire. Ignoring it, he clapped his hands together in front of him and sent out a powerful concussion. The force blasted Nick off his feet. The room shook and books flew from the shelves.

Simon didn't move closer. He stood in the middle of the room and slammed his hands together again. The windows blew out. The flames were snuffed. The floor started to buckle. The walls cracked. Another wave rolled out and shoved Nick back as if an elephant had kicked him.

Simon slammed his hands once more. Nick was crushed into a large mahogany bookcase, cracking the sturdy shelves. Another blast buried Nick into the plaster.

And again Simon struck. The ceiling showered down across the smashed floor. Nick was crushed deep through the wall like an insect pressed under a pane of glass.

Then again.

And again.

In the swirling clouds of dust, the sitting room was gone. The wooden framing was visible under the shattered walls, much of it cracked and splintered, along with the bricks of the outer wall. Simon shoved a heavy beam aside and pushed through the jagged hole in the wall into the disheveled pantry. With both hands, he tossed wreckage until he found what he sought.

Nick was limp. His face was bloody. His clothes were torn and the flesh underneath was blue and swollen as if he had been crushed for hours in the unforgiving gears of a heavy machine. Red liquid bubbled from his lips.

"Is this what you wanted, old man?" Simon pulled him up. Nick's limbs dangled like deadweight. Simon turned and dragged his friend over the wreckage back into the ruins of the sitting room. The portal stood shimmering in the dust. He shook his old friend. Nick's bruised eyelids slowly slit open. His mouth gaped, confused and disoriented.

Simon felt blood dripping warm across his belly. Wariness gripped him. All the seething rage he had held for so long turned to regret. "My father helped make this key. He was a man who could have done things no one could've imagined. But he's not here."

Nick was speaking, or trying to. He struggled to keep his head up. With a hard shove, Simon propelled Nick into the portal. The surface puckered and drew him in, then Nick appeared sprawling in the Parisian chamber. He blinked in shock and stared back at Simon. He shook his head as if wishing, even begging, that this would go a different way.

Simon heard a sound, and turned away to see Kate and Malcolm in the tumbled doorway of the sitting room. Charlotte and Penny stood behind them. They all had faces as if they had been watching a dangerous acrobatic act, and only now realized someone wasn't going to step off the high wire and plunge to his death in front of their eyes.

Simon knelt because of a stab in his chest. He met Kate's gaze, trying not to show pain. He couldn't think of anything proper to say. She dropped in front of him, checking him, then glancing over at the portal and Nick.

"The bastard really did kill your father?" Malcolm reached for his pistol. "I can take him if you wish."

"No. Leave him." Simon shook his head. The Scotsman withdrew his hand from his holster with a confused look. Simon held up the key without turning back to the portal. "Marthsyl."

Nick Barker vanished.

Simon dropped the key to the floor. He leaned the top of his head against Kate's forehead.

Kate took his drained face in one of her hands; the other tentatively touched the bloodstain on his chest.

"I couldn't kill him."

Kate's cool fingers slipped over the back of his neck. "Of course not."

"Was it wise to let him go?" Malcolm asked, hovering over the pair. "One day you'll want to go after him."

"Nick once told me to stay on the path I'm on. If I wander off, I'll never find my way back." That memory hurt, and he wondered if those words of guidance had been nothing more than a cruel diversion to hide a monstrous act. Still, Simon clung to them as if they were truth.

Epilogue

AUTUMN SUNLIGHT STREAMED INTO EVERY CORner of Hartley Hall. There was little to block the rays with the gaps in the walls and roof. Repairs were under way most everywhere in the house. But the Blue Parlor was left alone for now to provide a refuge. Kate looked out over the open terrace that had been repaired. It now stretched fifty yards from the house to a wide timber bridge built to span the canyon surrounding the house.

Kate turned from the altered southern grounds. Everyone stood somber and alone, hardly speaking. The house had become much quieter over the last few weeks. Charlotte lay on the floor with Aethelred, her arm draped over his form, his large head pressed against her cheek, his thick fur soaking up the remainder of her tears. Simon sat on the sofa, staring into a past that threatened to consume him. Malcolm stood like a dark wraith with Penny silently nearby.

The room felt cold and empty. Kate couldn't control the terrifying premonition that everyone was drifting away. The moorings to one another were fraying. Lives had been irrevocably changed. Everything felt different.

That dreadful sense was much stronger now. They had all just returned from the cemetery where Imogen was buried in a family plot alongside their mother and the servants who had given their lives in defense of the estate. This had been the first visit to the grave since the burial service, and it was so much worse for everyone. The reality that poor Imogen was gone and lying under the earth was undeniable now, and no longer obscured by the hectic events of a funeral. They knew now there was no magic that would bring her back to them. There were no miracles to be had. Kate's heart felt like it had stopped beating even though it rhythmically thudded beneath her breast. She was numb and disconnected. She hadn't been able to conjure any interest in working in her laboratory, which always brought her peace during troubled times. The reminders of her failure were thick there.

Imogen had gone through so much. She had transformed from a rebellious younger sister to a frightening monster to a stalwart protector. Despite the darkness that had enveloped her, she had bravely stepped out into the light. Imogen had embraced a new life no matter what trauma it threw at her.

Tears of pride welled in Kate's eyes. By her actions Imogen had changed all of them, from the cheerfully lonely Simon, to the wild Charlotte, to the brooding Malcolm, and even to Kate herself. Sometimes it was the journey that made the impact rather than the end. Her sister had shown them the way, and, by God, Kate would follow in her example.

She brushed her eyes with her sleeve and strode inside. She went over to Simon and curled up next to him. His arm did not instinctively curve around her shoulders. Charlotte looked up at her with red-rimmed eyes and Kate extended her arm toward the child, inviting her onto her lap. Charlotte immediately came over, laying her head against Kate's chest.

"I miss her," was her sob.

"Of course you do. We all do. We always will. Family must never be forgotten."

"Family?" Charlotte's haunted gaze darted fearfully to Malcolm, as if expecting him at any second to pick up a bag and walk into the fog.

Kate held the child close. "Yes. You are as much a sister to her as I am. As you are to me. And for that reason, she would want you to have this." From her sweater pocket, Kate produced the little hedgehog. Charlotte's tears fell harder, but she snatched up the little creature and placed her cheek against its prickly quills. Kate kissed the top of Charlotte's head.

Simon's arm now slipped around Kate and his hand gave her a gentle squeeze. It kindled her hope that he was listening. Taking a deep breath, she regarded those in the room. "I am adding a new wing to Hartley Hall. Everyone has a home here. A place to call his or her own."

Malcolm began, "I don't think that's—"

Kate cut him off. "Don't you dare. We haven't gone through all of this to scatter now. The original Order shattered because they were petty and self-absorbed, more consumed with abusing the power given to them. Even Pendragon."

When Simon raised a cynical brow, Kate scowled at him. "Pendragon was perhaps the worst. He doubted the people he had once loved, people he should have considered family. Instead he chose to believe those who were callous and manipulative. That was his downfall. Order reigns when it is built on trust and love, not the lust for power and glory."

Simon shook his head and glanced away. "I loved Nick and look what that wrought."

Charlotte looked up from Kate's lap. "I don't understand what happened to him. Was Mr. Nick a bad man?

He was grouchy, but he seemed to like us. Most of us. Wasn't he your friend, Mr. Simon? Why did he go away?"

"He was my friend, Charlotte." Simon took the girl's hand. He ran his thumb over her soft palm as if marveling that her hands were still so clean. "He wasn't bad. He just couldn't stay."

"Oh." The girl sighed. "He was teaching me to play cards."

"Cards?" Kate asked with bemused annoyance.

Charlotte looked worried. "He told me not to tell. That I shouldn't be gambling at my age."

Malcolm gave the girl a hard look. "Did he teach you how to cheat?"

"A little."

The Scotsman shook his head angrily. "Glad he's gone."

"Charlotte." Penny snorted an uncontrolled laugh, "Mr. Malcolm doesn't believe in cheating."

"Oh, I can teach you!" Charlotte exclaimed.

Malcolm grunted. Penny edged a bit closer to him as the dark shroud around him faded.

Kate eyed Malcolm across the room. "Some things will always stay the same, like dour Scotsmen. Some of those traits define us. Some are more tolerable than others. Some even comforting." Her eyes glowed with a fire that matched her tone. "This family will stay together. For Imogen's sake. For her memory. Without her, we would never have found one another. This group formed because of her."

Charlotte looked up at Kate, suddenly her countenance a bit brighter. "That's right! You found me because you were looking for Imogen."

Kate smiled at the young girl. She felt Simon take her hand and she looked back at him. "Imogen brought us together as well," she told him, her voice breaking ever so slightly.

The deep creases in Simon's face finally relaxed. "You're right. Of course."

Penny let out a long relieved breath and went to a table where she pulled a sketchbook out of her satchel. "Since we're all staying, it wouldn't hurt to show you the new project I've been working on." She opened the portfolio and handed everyone a piece of paper. The sketches on them showed decorated keys, each with a unique crest on the bow, distinctive in its design and linked to the individual holding it. A pair of crossed pistols for Malcolm. A pentagram for Charlotte. And, for Kate, an open book with one page inscribed with a stylized initial *I* to represent Imogen.

"Penny, they're beautiful," Kate replied, staring at the sketch with a wistful smile on her lips.

Penny toed the fringe on the rug. "They're just my ideas of what suited everyone."

Charlotte clutched the drawing tightly with both hands. She squirmed so much the little hedgehog crawled across her and settled in Kate's stationary lap. "You mean I get one too?" The child's bouncing made the entire settee shake.

Her infectious joy was so welcome that Kate didn't even reprimand her.

Penny took a final drawing from the case and extended her arm toward a small figure sitting in the corner. Jane seemed to glance up in surprise from her knitting but didn't react otherwise. Penny walked over and pressed the paper into the woman's hand.

Jane stared at the sketch. "But I didn't think to stay. I was only tarrying while—"

"You're here, Jane," Kate interrupted. "You will stay as long as you like, which I hope will be a long while.

Your father is actually quite at home here. He seems to think he is supervising the construction."

"I'm sorry, Miss Anstruther," Jane replied. "I'll tell him again to stay away."

"Not at all." Simon laughed. "He's doing a marvelous job. And some of his unusual suggestions lend extra character to the house."

"God bless you all." Jane smiled gratefully, glancing from Simon to Penny to Malcolm. She immediately returned to knitting. "I shall have to make each of you something."

Malcolm patted the grey scarf Jane had given him months before. It hung from his coat pocket, as it usually did. "I'll take a case of these damn things. Saved my life before, and that's not bad for a bloody scarf."

"Language, please, Mr. MacFarlane," Jane murmured.

Malcolm nodded contritely. "Sorry."

Simon chuckled as he kissed Kate's hand with unspoken praise and gratitude. He came to his feet and faced the small congregation. "Penny, you are, as always, the marvel of our age."

The engineer shrugged and waved a cavalier hand. "We can start on the keys whenever you're ready. It will take all three of us."

"They will be the miracle of our combined powers, an example of how we work together, never against one another." He lifted the gold key. "For Imogen."

Everyone came to their feet, following his lead. "For Imogen," they echoed.

Kate's eyes shone bright and her throat tightened. She had never felt so proud of her sister.

A knock sounded on the door and Hogarth entered. He stood on gleaming metal struts, rudimentary steel legs powered by tiny motors of Penny's ingenious design. He bowed awkwardly, still learning to maneuver with the strange devices. He straightened with a wink at Penny, who grinned broadly at his progress.

"I'll forge up a nicer set than these in no time." She pulled a screwdriver from her pocket and knelt beside him to make an adjustment on the knee. Penny's face lit with possibilities as she eyed the metal. "Now that I have you up and about, I should be able to modify these plans for Charles. I can't wait to see his face when I tell him he can throw away that chair of his."

Kate said, "Your mother would be proud, Penny. I want to be there when Charles takes his first steps."

"You will." Penny kept her faced turned toward her work but dragged her sleeve across her sniffling nose. Then she tapped the leg with her screwdriver. "So, Hogarth, you want to be able to jump across the Thames?"

Hogarth looked uncomfortable to have the engineer working on his legs in front of others. "Merely leaping a trout stream should suffice, miss."

Kate regarded Simon. "You mentioned a private little stream in Scotland once. Does it have trout?"

The corners of Simon's mouth lifted. "I believe it does."

"I think then we are in need of visiting it."

Charlotte immediately began jumping up and down, and squealed, "A holiday!"

Simon leaned toward Kate. "I thought of it as our own private spot."

Kate's eyes danced with mischievous delight. "Of course, dear, but family comes first."

Hogarth cleared his throat with a calm professional demeanor. "Miss Kate, a messenger from the king. It appears a demon has been summoned near Cardiff and is menacing the Welsh countryside. What should I tell him? That you are in Scotland, fishing?"

Kate came over to stand beside Simon, her hand reaching for his. In her other hand she held her bandolier full of alchemical vials.

Simon looked down at her beaming confident face, then at the determined expressions of the others. Penny shouldered her rucksack. Malcolm slipped his pistols into their holsters as Charlotte grabbed his greatcoat.

"Tell His Majesty we are bound for Wales," Simon announced with a telltale smile.